THE STEAM WALKER

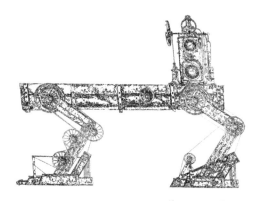

TODD J. MCCAFFREY

A Foxxe Frey Book

Books by The Winner Twins and Todd McCaffrey

Nonfiction:

The Write Path: World Building

Books by McCaffrey-Winner

Twin Soul Series:

Winter Wyvern

Cloud Conqueror

Frozen Sky

Wyvern's Fate

Wyvern's Wrath

Ophidian's Oath

Snow Serpent

Iron Air

Ophidian's Honor

To see the full list, scan the QR Code below!

DEDICATION

For the faculty and staff, past, present, and future of the

College of Technology, Bolton Street,

Dublin, Ireland

CONTENTS

Chapter One

It was a dark and grey day, cold with the first of what promised to be a bitter spring, just a fortnight after the New Year. It was the 14th day of January, in the year of Our Lord 1745.

"Bessie," I nudged the girl in bed beside me. "Bessie, get up! The cock didn't crow!"

Bessie mumbled and tried to move away from me. I shoved her. "Bessie, get up now! Father will be wanting his tea."

Behind me Jamie rumbled in his sleep and I elbowed him in the ribs.

I pushed Bessie out of the bed, following her into the cold morning air, my breath misting as I said, "You get the fires and the candles, I'll see to the forge."

"But —" Bessie protested, even as she pulled on her dress and apron.

"Go!" There was no time for subterfuge, father would be waking soon and if there wasn't something warm in front of him and a hot forge afterwards, there'd be sore backsides for certain.

Bessie ducked her head in submission and took off down the narrow staircase to the kitchen to start the fire and put on the kettle.

In the distance I could hear the horses in the far fields neighing and whinnying to each other. Belatedly one of the dratted cocks crowed with a desultory, almost abashed noise.

"Foul rooster!" I muttered to myself as I turned to the back door and rushed across the yard to the forge, thinking that that particular bird was soon for the pot. Probably, I thought, it'd turn out gamey.

I was delighted to see a burst of flame in front of me.

"We just put the coals on now Bess —" a young boy's voice piped up only to cut short as the child was elbowed into silence by another hissing, "That's not Bessie!"

"No, it isn't," I said, "now get going." I moved away from the voices even as the urchins scattered and closer to the forge. Looking at it, I decided that they'd done a good job getting the fire going again. I glanced at the pile of coal I'd left for feed and saw that they'd been good — they hadn't pilfered any or used it up during the night.

"That was a girl!" a boy's voice hissed loudly under the archway as the urchins scarpered. That remark was answered by muffled guffaws from the others.

My secret was safe, I could tell. Not that anyone would ever listen to a homeless orphan nor would any orphan be foolish enough to speak where the wrong ears might hear. Still — it wouldn't be out of place reminding Bessie that her "boyfriends" — I always said it to see her blush — had best keep their mouths shut if they wanted to stay warm this winter.

And it looked to be a bitter, cold winter. Maybe every bit as bad as the year before, when I'd found little Bessie, cold, feverish and near death's door, shivering and tucked as close as she could get to the warmth of our forge.

It had taken more work on father than on the child to get him to agree to take her on as a chambermaid.

"Taking on airs, are we?" he'd taunted. "Hoping to be a great lady, our Danni coal-face?"

I'd let him rant and tease as much as he wanted just to be certain that he agreed to keep her.

"She's to pull her weight," he'd said finally. "No shirking her duties —" he'd wagged a finger at me warningly "— or taking *airs* —" he'd said that to see me blush again "— she's to work hard, like she was a proper Scotswoman and not one of those English toffs."

"Yes, father," I'd said. "I'll beat her daily, if it'll help."

He scowled at me. My father had sworn nearly every day to beat either me or Jamie — and while he'd done it more than once it'd never been without more than good reason.

"Just don't go making her bottom as red as your hair or we'll get no work out of her at all," he'd said finally, teasing me once more for my hair. His was black, just like Jamie's — blast them both.

So we kept Bessie. And I did beat her, hard when she wouldn't let me cut her hair to rid her of the lice, and again when she'd refused her first bath — "I'll die, miss, I'll die in the cold!"

She didn't die in the cold, her hair was growing back — as was mine, casualty to the same foul lice — and she kept my front warm as Jamie kept my back from freezing. I *did* have airs; I hoped to set her up as a proper maid, in a big house with a good mistress and stern master and a life without freezing at night or crying from an empty belly in the day.

It was all part of my plans for the future.

I suppose it was fitting justice that none of them turned out right. What gall has a fourteen year-old girl, red-haired and Scottish, to think that she can plan her future in the Year of Our Lord, 1745?

#

"She's a wicked one, you can tell from the hair!" they'd say when they thought I didn't hear. Often as not, though, another would mutter in my defense:

"Ach, it's no more than most have, and the lass has no mother, not since her wee brother came into the world!"

"She has no breeding, her father's a smith, what more can you expect?"

"She'll end up in someone's bed before too long!"

"Her? She's too scrawny! No, it's the poorhouse for her, you can be certain of that. Her father's not long for this world and then it'll be all over. She's no proper respect for the Lord, so I've been told."

The old wags and witches of the Grassmarket had been discussing my fate since I was ten and taken on by Mr. Pugh.

"And he's mad, just mad to have her in his shop!"

"Aye, but he's the best watchmaker in all Edinburgh, that's got to count for something."

"If he weren't you could be certain the Deacon would be saying something."

After that pronouncement there was a lengthy silence. It wasn't all that long ago that a lad just eighteen had been hanged for heresy simply on an idle jest that he'd prefer the fires of Hell to the cold of Edinburgh. People still talked of it, shaking their heads.

#

This day, I'd taken precautions against their mutterings. And so now, instead they said: "Oh, look! It's young master Jamie!"

I hurried on, pulling my hat tightly over my head, striding boldly in trousers that Jamie had just outgrown.

"Jamie, how are you this morning?" someone called after me. I lowered my head, raised an arm in a wave, and hurried on, looking as busy as any apprentice.

I was bound for the university and no one knew about it. Edinburgh University wasn't so much a place as a group of buildings with students of various talents and degrees of sobriety. Some were the second sons of lairds destined either for the clergy or the military; some were bright lads of rich shopkeepers.

I was neither but today I did my best to look the part. I had a satchel over one shoulder with a sketchpad and some nice charcoals, freshly made — a sideline I'd convinced father to take on two years back when I'd needed the materials myself. It didn't make us much money but it set us apart from other smiths in the town and our clientele improved, much to the disgust of MacAllister, the nearest smith and father's greatest rival.

Hamish MacAllister was a devil of a man, all agreed. He worked hard, fought hard, and drank hard. There was nothing enjoyable about him. He did his work, got paid and that was that. He hated my father with a passion, spat at Jamie's shadow and gazed at me with lidded eyes when he thought I couldn't see. Just the thought of him made me shiver. Still, he had a good livery, apprentices and all — and was considered by many to be a man of property, more so than my father. His was the first smithy on the way into town; he got a lot of work from those leading in a horse with a thrown shoe.

While our forge was nestled in the shadows of Edinburgh Castle, his was two miles further west in an area that was more outlier than town proper. Two miles is only half an hour on foot for a lazy person and nothing at all on horse, so he and his apprentices were seen a lot in the town, particularly in the bawdier taverns on the nights.

The distance between MacAllister's forge and Edinburgh University was measured less in miles than in learning. I'd heard from Mr. Pugh that they had just got one of the Newcomen Steam Engines and I was going to draw it.

Mr. Pugh knew and let me; father did not and would have forbidden me had he known. I could imagine him saying, "You've enough foolish notions in your head, girl, without adding anymore!"

Mr. Pugh was English, a watchmaker by way of the Germanys or perhaps Holland — his story seemed to change every month. He was old now and didn't have the hands for the delicate brass castings sometimes needed to replace worn cogs and gears. So he convinced my father to loan me to him — how, I'll never quite know.

If you've ever made a mold, ever etched the light teeth of gears into fine sand, if you've ever watched the molten brass or bronze puddle and set into a shape of your own forming, then you understand the magic of casting. I was enraptured the very first time.

From then on, father had added precision casting to his offerings and Walker forge had profited nicely, building tackle, gearings, and other iron castings for the fort and the ships in the harbor at Leith even though we weren't the nearest smithy by half a dozen.

But the casting of the pieces, the gears, the tackle, all were a special secret to the family. Because however hard father and Jamie tried, they never quite had the same feel for metal as I did.

Father and Jamie could shoe a horse, make swords, cut nails all in half the time I could — but neither could make a better casting, could build a mold, or complete a pour.

"It's almost as if you've got a Faerie gift there, Danni," Jamie had said one day as he'd watched me pour our largest iron casting.

"Faeries can't use iron!"

"Then some other gift, from a darker master," Jamie had said heavily. I'd looked over at him and saw the seriousness in his eyes. He'd looked away, in shame or fear — I don't know, but still he said, "A girl's not supposed to know such things."

But this girl did, and now she was taking herself, dressed as her brother without either his or her father's knowledge, off to the University to draw the steam engine there. I felt neither ruled by Faerie nor a darker master but rather drawn by the impulse to see more, learn more, know more. I couldn't see how that was a terrible thing.

#

"Steam engine? Oh, do you mean that thing they've got at the docks?" the porter said when I asked him. "It's on its way to the mines, I'm told." He gave me a wink as he added, "I hear that some beer was involved in stopping it for a bit."

"The docks, you say?" I asked, starting off again.

"Ye'd best hurry, if you want to see it!" the porter cried after me.

It was only a half an hour to the docks of Leith, and I was pretty certain that the beer would last that long. As I walked, I thought about how it must work.

The principle of its action dates back to the Magdeburg hemispheres developed in the last century and, even earlier, to the aeolipile described by Hero of Alexandria. The Magdeburg hemispheres were built by Herr Guericke to demonstrate the power of his vacuum pump. The two copper halves were sealed with grease and the pump sucked out the air so well that not even thirty horses could separate them. I'd seen a demonstration at the university and wondered how such strength could be used.

The Englishman Thomas Newcomen adapted steam to produce the steam engine I was going to draw. The steam engine worked by allowing hot steam into a cylinder which pushed a free moving piston upwards. Then cold water was introduced to the cylinder, cooling the steam and causing it to condense. The condensed steam produced a vacuum which caused the air above the piston to push it back down. After that, the cold water and the condensed steam were drained off and the cycle repeated with more live steam. A trained boy, called a plugman, operated the plugs which turned to allow the steam, water, and condensate to enter or leave the cylinder as required. I'd heard it said that a good plugman could get the engine to make twenty cycles a minute but I wasn't sure I believed it.

The engine was set up so that the piston was connected to a lever and the far side of the lever was connected to a pump as the Newcomen engine was usually used to pump water from coal mines.

I imagined that the up and down motion could be used for other things and, as I trotted on the way to the port, I idly considered some possibilities.

I remembered how, at fair over the summer, my brother had been entranced by a man on stilts. I thought the whole motion rather ungainly but I agreed that being that much taller could provide an advantage.

"It makes you half a giant!" Jamie had exclaimed resentfully. "Why you could walk up to the walls of the castle and over them in one stride!"

Well, really, that was impossible but I could see his point. Later I fashioned a pair of low stilts for him and he spent many hours tramping about our yard. I even managed to coax Bessie into them but she lost her footing and landed rather hard on the ground and we could get her to try them no more.

But with a steam engine, wouldn't it be possible to lift stilts? I wondered idly. I built this image in my head. Naturally two stilts wouldn't be enough — four would be needed like the legs of a large steam horse.

A steam horse! The notion stopped me in my tracks. Someone knocked into me and cursed me for stupidity. I numbly apologized even as the idea burst full-blown in my head.

A steam horse. What could it do? Well, to hear tell about the Newcomen engine, it could run nigh on forever, given enough coal. It would never rest.

Make it big enough — and suddenly I recalled the ancient Trojan Horse — and you could scale castle walls.

Make it a wagon, instead or rather a wagon on stilts and you could mount guns and musketeers and it would be unstoppable, being taller than any cavalryman and more powerful.

Suddenly, I had to see that engine!

I started forward again and quickly broke from my steady walk into a long, slow trot.

#

"A steam horse?" Jamie said to me when I showed him my sketches. I had spent all my spare hours from January to August working on the idea — now I was finally ready to show them. He rolled his eyes skyward. "Danni, you're mad! You're more of a loon than any loon has a right to be!"

"It wouldn't be a steam horse," I said, "it'd be more like a wagon on stilts."

"A wagon on stilts? And what would be the purpose of that?"

"It could go for as long as it had steam," I told him. "It would be up high and it could carry heavy loads."

"So? A wagon does all that already."

"But a wagon doesn't walk on its own," I told him temptingly. "And a wagon on stilts would be able to climb over things that a wheeled cart couldn't."

"Aye," Jamie allowed, scratching his face the way our father sometimes did when he was thoughtful, "there's that."

Bessie, who was working on our dinner in the kitchen gave a small, despairing sigh. I winked at Jamie, nodding my head toward Bessie's outburst. His eyes gleamed and he continued in full brogue, "Ach aye, sister, ye ken the way of things mechanical quite nicely!"

"Tut!" we heard Bessie splutter from the kitchen. She'd been born English and it had taken her the better part of a year to ken to our ways. She still spoke a bit different but there were many people in Edinburgh who spoke no better. I recall, just shortly after we'd rid her of lice, nits — and most of her hair — she'd exploded on me. "Why don't you speak English?"

"I am," I had said, feeling sore at her abuse. "Do you not ken what I'm saying?"

"What do you mean, 'ken'?" Bessie had shot back. "And why do you see 'ye' instead of you? And what does 'nae' mean?"

"Och —" I said, shaking my head and putting up with another splutter from the blond-haired girl "— that's just the way we speak here in Scotland, Bessie."

"But I don't know what it *means!*" Bessie said with tears in her voice. "And I don't want to get it wrong and have you — have you —" and she broke down completely. I pulled her against me and patted her.

"We say 'nae' when we mean 'no' or 'not'," I told her in a soft voice. "We say 'och' when we are surprised or sorry. We say 'aye' when we mean 'yes' or sometimes 'yes' very strongly."

Bessie had sniffed and wiped her nose as she absorbed the words, nodding slightly to show that she understood.

"We say 'ye' because we've been saying that instead of 'you' ever since I can remember," I had added. I smiled down at her. "And I have to think that you, being far older than the baby I was when I learned how to speak, won't have any trouble learning our language."

"Your father won't send me away because I'm English, will he?" She had then asked. I realized, then, that *that* had been the real reason for her outburst.

"Once I take you in, you're mine," I had told her, wrapping her tightly in my arms. That seemed to settle her and — aside from the occasional snort or 'tut' from the kitchen — we heard no more on the matter.

Ignoring Bessie's latest 'tut', I pulled my sketches out of my sack and laid them in front of Jaimie.

"Look, here's the steam engine," I said. I showed him the drawing, explained the workings and let him ponder on them. I could see his face grow thoughtful — Jamie hadn't my love of metal but he was just as quick in seeing how things moved as I was and I could see his excitement grow as he imagined how the engine moved.

"It's not very efficient," Jamie said and I grinned at him.

"Aye, it's not," I agreed. "Nothing a Scotsman couldn't fix."

"If ye had the right Scotsman," he muttered doubtfully. I smiled at him and he groaned. "Not you!"

I pulled out my next sketch and just laid it under his eyes. I didn't say anything, letting him follow the logic himself. I held my breath because Jamie was very clever and if anyone could find fault, it'd be he.

He pointed at the one plug that was left in my drawing. "This starts it and stops it?"

I nodded. He smiled. "Very nice," he allowed. "Efficient."

I said nothing but inside, I beamed.

Then Jamie shook his head. "So, it's nice but what of it, Danni?"

I pulled out the next sketch and Jamie grunted in surprise. He picked it up and poured over it, followed the motions with his finger and went back and forth several times.

"Aye," he said finally, "it'd work." A moment later he passed the sketch back to me. "Pity."

"What?"

"Well, sister, for what purpose do you think father would spend so much on something no one's ever seen, let alone tried?" Jamie demanded irritably. I could tell that the sketch intrigued him and he was furious with me to taunt him so — he knew just as well as I that father couldn't afford to build something for no purpose.

Of course, I'd thought of that already. I'd had a long time to think on the walk back from the port. And I had an answer.

"What if it were on a wager?" I said, raising my eyebrows challengingly. "What if MacAllister were on the other side?"

Jamie was silent for a long while, his expression growing more cheerful as he considered the notion. Finally he swotted my hair, saying, "Aye, it's not for nought that you've that hair, red Danni!"

I didn't know then how right he was.

#

"A steam horse?" my father spluttered the next week as he staggered home from the local pub. "Can you imagine a steam horse?"

"What, father?" I asked, all innocence. I had been hoping to hear him say this — had been hoping to hear it over all the tavern talk of 'the King Over the Water' — James Edward Stuart — and the exploits of his dashing son, Prince Charles. The one that everyone called "Bonnie Prince Charlie"; the one who'd landed in the north of Scotland, raised the banner of rebellion and had brought the Highland clans together under his standard. Who, even now, was reputed to have his eyes set on Edinburgh and then, later, to restore his father to the combined throne of England, Scotland, Ireland and Wales — displacing the current German King, George II.

Everyone knew that the Scottish King, James VI, had become James I, King of England back when the English Queen Elizabeth had died. And we all learned early on how his grandson, Charles II, had been deposed and replaced. His family had escaped and his son, James Edward Stuart, sought the restoration of his monarchy. Indeed, he'd led a rebellion in 1715 that had been crushed by the English King. Now *his* son, Charles Edward Stuart, was fighting to put his father back in his 'rightful' place. 'Rightful' as some had thought it.

I'd nearly despaired of ever hearing a peep about my steam horse. In the end, I cooked up a plan.

#

My plan had taken no time to put into practice. Fortunately, Samuel Cattan had been more than willing to play his part. Poor Sam was one of MacAllister's apprentices and a more miserable young man you couldn't imagine. Och, he was a handsome lad in his own right but he was sore used by MacAllister — as were they all.

So it was no problem at all on my part to plant the notion with Samuel. It was easier still because I was one of the few girls Samuel Cattan ever saw and for some reason he liked the look of me.

Samuel posed the question late one night when the master was in his cups. As MacAllister was often in his cups, there was nothing particular strange in that. The trouble was to get him to remember in the morning and for that Sam had to take a beating — for MacAllister never liked being told what he'd said the night before, nor challenged on his word.

"A steam horse?" MacAllister's below could be heard as he stormed up to our forge late the next morning. "Walker, have ye ever heard the like?"

"Pardon?" my father asked, his eyes narrowing as he spotted the forlorn look on Samuel Cattan's face.

"This — this —" MacAllister smacked the back of Samuel's head "— excrescence had the nerve to suggest that I'd said I could make a steam horse last night!"

"And could ye?" my father asked, scratching his chin thoughtfully. "Ye'd use that Newcomen engine, then?"

"What?" MacAllister said, brought up short in his tirade. "Ye think I'd try something that mad?"

"Well, no," my father said. "I ken that ye'd not, Hamish. And I don't doubt the wisdom in it, either. 'Twould be a fierce expense and for what reward?"

"Expense?" Hamish said, brows waggling. "Are you trying to say I've not the money for such a venture, Daniel?"

I got my name, Danielle, from father's, if you're wondering.

"I wouldn't be one to know your finances, Hamish," my father said easily enough, "but I could certainly understand your reluctance to engage in such a frivolous adventure."

"Yeah," Hamish said, turning to look at his apprentice. "'Twould be mad, it would."

"Perhaps not mad," my father said now, having thought on the notion for a bit just as I'd guessed he would. "You're talking about a steam-powered wagon, are ye?"

"Something like that," Hamish said slowly, his lips turning down into a frown as he once more faced my father.

"It'd go longer than a horse," my father said. "I expect they could use it down at the docks, maybe even in the mines."

"At the docks?" Hamish's eyes started to gleam.

"But I don't know if it'd be worth it," my father said. "You know how they are down there, slow to try something new." He shook his head firmly. "No, you're best off without it, Hamish. It'd be too much to try."

"Are you saying I couldn't do it?" Hamish said, his eyes starting to smoulder with anger. "And would you like to put some money on that, Mr. Walker?"

"I don't think I would," father said. "Either way, it would be money for no purpose and I'd not like to take it off you."

"Take it?" Hamish boomed. "And what, Daniel Walker, makes you think ye'd take that money?"

"I said I wouldn't bet you Hamish, so the question is moot," father said.

"Ye're afraid, aren't you Walker?" Hamish said, bringing up a thick finger and pointing it in father's direction. "Ye're scared that I'll make it before ye and reap all the profits." He shook his head. "Don't think I can't see what ye're thinking, laddie!"

"Hamish —"

"Ten guineas!" Hamish said. "Ten guineas says that my steam horse will move before yours!"

Father's eyes suddenly gleamed. "My Walker over yours, is it Hamish?"

"Aye, 'Walker'," Hamish said, extending a hand. "And no money if ye've nought before the year's end."

My father nodded slowly, extending his hand in return. "Hamish MacAllister, ye've a bet."

#

"Father, I've got an idea," I said later that night as we sat at dinner. My sack with my sketches was close to hand.

"And why, Danielle Walker, am I not surprised?" my father said in reply. He gestured toward my sack. "Pass it over and I'll have a look."

Jamie shot me a quick look, half-warning, half-encouragement but I paid him no mind as I passed my father the first drawing.

"That's the engine, is it?" father said as he poured over the drawing. "Jamie, bring the light to the table, I can hardly see."

Jamie brought the lamp over and father sat it beside him, leaning forward to pour over my sketch. After a moment he leaned back and looked at me. "You were at the docks?"

How did he know?

My father smiled at my look. "You're too skilled, Danni," he said, pointing to a spot at the top of the drawing. "You sketched in the skyline."

"Yes, I went to see the engine," I told him.

He looked at me for a long moment. "I've seen Samuel Cattan looking at you, lass," he said. "The way that boy looks at ye, he'd do a lot for a smile."

Jamie squirmed nervously in his chair. Father glanced his way, then back to me.

"Would I be right in guessing that Hamish was encouraged to this wager?" My father said, gesturing for the next drawing.

Turning red, I passed it to him. He placed it over the first and bent down to look at it. He scanned it only a moment, then said to Jamie, "And this would work?"

"I think so," Jamie said, surprised that he'd been asked his opinion.

"And the last, then lass," father said, stretching a hand for me to pass him my last sketch. I smiled as I did and he smiled back but his look faded when he'd stretched the paper out over the other two sketches and examined it. He was silent for a long while. Finally he looked me in the eye and said, "And whatever has Hamish MacAllister done that you to want to short him of ten guineas?"

"He looks at her funny, father," Jamie spoke up. Father glanced his way and he added, "I don't like it when he looks at her."

My father sat back in his seat. Finally he said lightly, "Jamie, do you honestly think that our Danni would ever allow herself to be charmed by Hamish MacAllister?"

Jamie shook his head. "But —"

"Well," my father cut across him, "I know that our Danni won't ever have a man she doesn't want." He smiled wanly as he added, "I doubt there's a man in all Scotland who could put his will against hers." He shook his head and leaned forward again, peering at my drawing. "And how, Danielle Walker, are we to build one of these engines?"

"I've got the plans, father," I told him.

"And so you'd steal some other's work and claim as your own?" he asked, his dark brows drawing together thunderously.

"Och, no, father!" Jamie said, rushing to my defense. "She's got a better design than that stinkin' old Englishman's!"

"Well enough, then lass," my father said to me. "But how are we going to afford all this? We haven't got ten guineas to lose, as you well know, you doing the books and all."

"Ah, I have a plan for that," I told him.

My father, bless him, looked heavenward for strength. "And am I going to be sorry to ask about it?"

I smiled at him.

#

A fortnight later, my work was done.

"What in the name of the Maker is that?" one of the little urchins asked me early that dark morning when I first prepared to fire up the beast.

"What, have you no seen a hammer afore?" a girl's voice called from near the first voice. A lost Scots girl, from her way of speaking.

"The hammer I've seen," the urchin allowed, "it's all that it's connected to that fashes me."

"Help me lay the fire," I said to the two them. I could sense their wariness. "Help me lay the fire and you'll have a bite to eat before you leave and a place to sleep this evening."

I near died when I saw the two skeletons that made their way out of the gloom, silhouetted by the last embers of our forge. If I'd known what sort of state they were in, I would have offered breakfast first — be damned the expense.

"There's a barrow over there and you know where the coal is," I said, passing the shovel to the girl. The boy reached for it but I snatched it away from him. "The barrow'll be heavy enough for you when she's filled it. Or you can take turns."

The boy grunted and the girl grabbed the shovel, giving him a triumphant look. The barrow squeaked across the yard and soon I could hear the coal being shoveled in.

"More of your strays?" my father's voice spoke in my ear, so startling that I jumped. He laughed. "Don't make the mistake of feeding them out of our hearth and home."

"I won't," I promised. "But it's our Christian duty."

"First it's my duty to keep you fed, child, after that we'll talk about others," father said. I could hear him disappear back into the darkness as the two children scuttled back, the boy and girl each on a handle and straining mightily.

"Now go take the shovel and bring me some live embers from the forge," I told the boy. He wiped the sweat off his brow and trudged back. The red glow of hot coals lit his way back.

I instructed him on how to lay the coals in the bottom of the boiler, then how to lay fresh coals on top. I checked to make sure that the grate was open and that there was a good draw of air.

"So the boiler's going to make steam, soon," I told them, explaining not so much for their ears as for mine — and perhaps God's. Didn't He look out for fools?

"The steam will push up the piston inside that cylinder and the lever will make the other side go down," I said. "And then the plugs will turn and the cylinder will be cooled. When that happens, the outside air will push the piston back down, dragging the lever on the far side up. The cylinder will be emptied and then fresh steam admitted, repeating the cycle."

"Yes, missy," the boy said, feeling compelled to say something. He nudged the girl beside him and she piped up, "Very keen, miss."

"Run to the kitchen, the back door and tell Bessie that I said you're to be given something hot, oats if we've got it," I said to them. As they scampered off, I called, "And don't try to scam her, she's sharper than your bones!"

On the far end of the lever, I attached one of old hammers and placed it over my old anvil.

The first thing an apprentice ever makes is a decent anvil and my first wasn't that bad at all, even father admitted it.

Slowly the water boiled. It seemed forever, the sun was brightening the day, and then I heard motion. The piston was going up. I could see slack on the chain at the far side of the lever. I knew from my set up how much slack I should see before the valves would be switched and the lever start to rise.

Almost... almost... now! I started to breathe even as the sound of cool water gurgled around the walls of the cylinder. The Newcomen design had the water go in the cylinder but I figured I could just as easily let the water wash the outside of the cylinder — and I was right. The piston started back down, dragging against the lever on one side and raising it on the other. I stood transfixed watching my steam engine really work until —

Bang! I jumped and shrieked only to realize that the sound was the hammer hitting the anvil. It worked! By all that was Holy, it worked!

Bang! Again. And not long after, *Bang!*

"Danni, what's that racket? What are you making?" my father called from the rear window over the kitchen.

"I think I'll make a sword," I called back, going to the forge and pulling a long strip of iron out. It wasn't really proper, not even heated, but it would serve.

"You can't make swords!" Jamie cried.

"Come and see for yourself, then!" I said, racing back to the hammer and anvil just in time to thrust the metal in as the hammer fell.

Clang! It wasn't much, it wasn't all that strong but a moment later, *Clang!* And then *Clang! Clang! Clang!*

"No one can move a hammer that fast!" Jamie cried, running out to stand beside me. His jaw dropped as he followed the hammer back to the lever and then to the cylinder and the boiler.

"Put some more coal in," I told him, nodding toward the shovel even as the hammer clanged once more on the metal rod which, for all its flaws was even now beginning to change shape.

"Hang on a moment and we'll give it a real try," my father said coming up beside me and moving off toward the forge. "How high does your hammer go?"

"Half a foot," I said, "but I could make it higher."

"Half a foot will do," my father said. Presently the clanging came faster.

"How fast will it go, Danni?" Jamie asked, leaning on his shovel. I scowled at him and gestured for him to get back to work.

"I don't quite know," I told him honestly. "I think perhaps twenty, maybe even thirty times a minute."

"That's twice as fast as a man with a hammer," my father said, returning with a glowing hot strip of metal that he held in tongs. I moved my practice piece away as he moved in to the falling hammer in time to have it strike sparks on his workpiece.

"Danni, how do you stop it?" Jamie asked minutes later as father stood back with a well-forged sword at the end of his tongs.

"Feed it no coal and it'll slow down and stop for lack of steam," I told him. "Or you can turn that plug from the boiler to the cylinder and that'll stop it right away."

"And if you turn it back?" my father called over his shoulder as he quenched the wrought sword in water.

"Then, if you've the heat and enough steam, it'll start straight back up," I told him. I grabbed the tongs I'd had earlier and moved forward, cautious of the flames from the coal fire, leaned in and turned the plug.

In mid-stroke the engine stopped.

"You can't do it for too long without quenching the fire," I said, "or the steam will build up too much for the boiler."

"And then what?" Jamie asked, eyeing the steaming boiler nervously.

"I guess it'd blow up and spray everything with live steam," I said.

"So ye've got to be careful," my father said, returning to eye the boiler carefully. He nodded to me for the tongs and I passed them to him. With a deft twist, he had turned the plug so the steam once again moved to fill the cylinder. He cocked his head at me as he asked, "And what else, instead of the hammer?"

"A chisel or tool to cut," I said.

"We could make nails!"

"With the right tool we might be able to make them in one go," father said, eyeing the falling hammer judiciously. He moved over and grabbed me around the shoulders. "Good job, Danni, good job!"

"But," Jamie said slowly, even as he nodded in agreement, "at even thirty rounds a minute, that's an awfully slow step, Danni."

"Ah," I said, smiling at him. "This is only the practice piece." I pointed to my old anvil and then gestured toward the much larger anvil in the distance — my finished piece, the one father and Jamie used for the best forgings.

"But Danni," my father began, "we've no money for another —"

"Walker!" a voice bellowed from the distance. "By the name of all that's Holy, what's that racket?"

Hamish MacAllister trotted in to view with an alarmed Samuel Cattan in tow and skidded to a stop as the hammer fell once more — *Clang!*

"What in the Devil's name is that?" he said, eyes going round.

"Danni..." my father said warningly as he leaned over me.

"There's our money, father."

CHAPTER TWO

HAMISH MACALLISTER GAVE ME A JAUNDICED LOOK AS HIS APPRENTICES FINISHED loading up the last of the steam engine into his heavy cart the next week.

"And I'm to have the drawings as well, aren't I?" Hamish called down to my father from his seat.

Without expression, my father passed him up the rolled up drawings. "All there, Hamish, as agreed."

Hamish looked past him to me. "Ye realize, don't ye lass, that no one will believe your word against mine?"

I nodded silently, glowering. Hamish didn't like girls who spoke and this once, I didn't want to anger him.

Hamish threw down a heavy purse and my father caught it.

"There! Forty guineas, as promised," Hamish said, nodding to Samuel who flicked the horses into motion. As they passed under our gate, Hamish let out a huge laugh. "Och, and Walker, don't ye forget our wager!"

I gave father a quick nudge in reminder and he called back, "Hamish, let's double the wager but change the bet!"

"What?" Hamish MacAllister roared, his cart suddenly pulled to a halt. "Twenty guineas?"

"Twenty guineas for the first to walk the length of the Grass Market, turn around and come back," my father called just as I'd coached him. He looked down at me and shook his head warningly, saying, for my ears only, "Ye'd best be right in this, lassie."

"The copper's on the docks, father," I told him. "And the best oak I've ever seen is just in from the colonies."

Hamish roared back a laugh. "Aye, twenty guineas it is, then!" We heard the horses start to move again as Hamish called back, "And Daniel, ye've heard that Bonnie Prince Charlie has landed. He'll be needing fresh swords, no doubt. I want to thank ye for delivering them into my hands!"

#

"Try it again, you're moving too fast," I called out, looking out at our work yard.

"She keeps stumbling, Danni," Jamie complained from his position in the lead of our hasty contraption.

"I am not!" Bessie cried, even as she stumbled once more. I couldn't quite blame her, to keep them even she had to have the higher stilts and the girl was not nearly as keen on the project as my brother.

"Ooof!" Jamie said as the motion pitched him down to the ground, the light timber frame falling to one side. Bessie let go her end, doddered a few steps and fell — hard — on her knees. I put my drawing aside and raced over to her, helping her out of her stilts and making soothing noises.

"Don't make me try that again, miss, please don't!" Bessie cried. Her hands fussed with the over-sized trousers I'd made her wear. "I don't like these pants, miss, I'm not like you! A nice dress, even a sack, that would do me just fine."

"It's all right, Bessie, I've enough to go on with," I assured her. I helped her to her feet and guided her toward the kitchen. "Go, get changed and get the dinner set, we'll be along soon enough."

With a troubled look toward Jamie, she set off on her way to the kitchen, tugging the awkward trousers with both hands and eager to get back into her dress.

"It's not strange the way she takes on," Jamie said from behind me as he slid out of his stilts. "It's you, sister, that's the changeling." A moment later, he kicked the four bits of wood that I'd tacked together to make a platform and muttered to me, "Are ye sure ye've got it, Danni?"

I nodded, still staring at the kitchen, not trusting my voice nor the look of my face. Trousers made more sense than dresses. I could never understand why a girl didn't freeze to death with the draught — although the Highlanders had no better with their kilts.

"I've got to get back to the boiler anyway," I told him, finally allowing myself to look at him. "How are you coming with the cylinder?"

"It's not that hard," Jamie allowed. "But how are we going to know —"

"That they'll take the pressure?" I asked. "Well, we'll have to test them, won't we?"

"And I suppose you've figured you'll manage that?"

"Och aye," I said, slipping into the broader brogue of the Highlands.

Jamie raised his eyebrows at me. "Ye're not worried about that Prince are ye?"

"They say there's nothing between him and us," I replied. The news that Prince Charles had landed in Scotland and was heading towards Edinburgh had come swiftly to our town, it being the current object of his attentions.

"I don't see how we'd come to harm," Jamie said.

"Let's get back to work," I told him. "Our job is to beat Hamish."

Neither my brother nor my father were fools. They knew full well the sort of risks I was suggesting but they trusted me. The first steam engine had proved well enough and now they were willing to try my new thinking. If I was right, I'd have an engine that was four times more powerful and easily four times faster than the steam engine MacAllister now had.

Better, it would be so different from his that no one could challenge our rights to it.

I was betting on our ability to make something so strong it could handle five times the weight of air that normally pressed down on us. So my new steam engine wouldn't use the weight of air to press down on a vacuum — it would use the power of its greater steam pressure to push *up* against the air. And down again, with the same pressure.

But first we needed to build a boiler that could handle more than five atmospheres of pressure. And then a cylinder and piston with their own special valves built so that once the piston had pushed fully up, the valves would reverse, let the steam out of the filled cylinder while admitting steam to the top *above* the piston and force it back down. The cycle would reverse, letting the steam out of the top and admitting it from the bottom to push the piston back up. It would be double-acting and even more automatic than my first design.

"It's bloody genius!" Jamie had exclaimed when I first showed the sketches.

"What are the dangers?" my father had asked shrewdly.

"If we can't build vessels to take the pressure, then it won't work," I admitted. "But in that case, we can fall back to something like the old design — only using the double-action to our advantage."

"Wouldn't Hamish have a claim, then?" Jamie asked, turning his eyes to father.

"It's hard to say," father replied with a shrug. He smiled at me. "One thing's for certain — they don't make any smarter than our Danni for these things."

The trouble with the boiler, more than anything was the openings. Keeping them from bursting would be the hardest. The same was true for the seals on the cylinder, both from the sides where the steam would enter and leave and also from the top where the piston lever would emerge.

Fortunately, I was very good at casting and so I made all the valves and casings myself, careful to ensure that they were built to withstand twice the pressure we'd designed for.

"What if the pressure gets too great?" my father had asked as he looked over the drawings.

"It won't," I said, pointing to a small tube coming out of the top of the boiler tank, separate from the output tube. "We're going to put a small metal cap on that weighed so that it will fall off at more than five atmospheres."

"And the steam will escape, dropping the pressure," Jamie said, eagerly following my logic.

"Aye, that works," father allowed approvingly. "And what about your cylinder, then?"

"Well, if the pressure going in can never exceed five atmospheres, then we needn't worry about measuring it," I told him.

"Unless one of your valve sticks or the piston gets cater-cornered," father objected.

"The piston is big enough it won't get stuck, father," Jamie said, pointing to the drawing. He looked to me for the answer to the second question.

I shook my head. "If the valves get stuck, the piston will stop and there'll be no more movement."

"Right," father said, nodding slowly as he considered my words. "I think that should work, then."

#

The boiler and engine weren't my biggest worries. Nor was the platform, as we'd just taken a wagon bed and started from that. It was the legs and the whole mechanism of walking that caused me the most thought.

I've shod and helped shoe enough horses to know that their legs are a marvel of muscle, sinew, and bone. At a walk, a horse moves the near foreleg first, then the rear hind, far foreleg and, finally, the near hind. The cycle then repeats.

Turning was another issue. I decided to have each "foot" be able to rotate free of the leg. That way when we wanted to turn, we could move three legs while keeping the fourth in place. Going backwards just required reversing the normal order of things.

I gathered some old bits of wood and tried putting them together for a quick model of a leg but it was no good — until Jamie took pity on me and lent a hand. As much as metal bends for me, wood melts in his hands.

"Danni," he said to me later that day as I put his model leg through its paces, "this might really work."

From skeptical Jamie that was marvelous to hear.

"Aye, but it'd be easier if we just let the legs slide forward under their own weight," I said as I examined the model. Jamie sighed and grabbed the model back.

"You'd need to put in a stop or the legs would just slide right off," he said, frowning as he considered how to work that into his model. "And how'd that work? You lift the leg off the ground, it slides forward and —"

"Then you —" I stopped, completely at a loss for words. How was that going to work? "Horses do it!"

"Horses have knees and tendons and muscle," Jamie said.

"We don't have time for such things," I groused, kicking a rock and watching it fly away with no satisfaction.

"Maybe you've got the wrong animal, Danni," Jamie said after a moment. "A spider might work better."

"A spider?" I cried. "Eight legs, are you mad, Jamie?"

"Not the legs, the motion," he said. "Like a rowboat."

"A rowboat?" I cried. Since when was a rowboat at all like a spider? Jamie dropped his model and made the motion of the rowers in the Leith. My expression changed completely. "So it wouldn't walk, it'd scuttle."

"Yes," Jamie said.

"It'd lift a leg, swivel it forward, put it down," I said, bringing the image to my mind. "And the same with — och, but Jamie that motion can't clear any ground!"

"What?"

"How would it climb a hill or go over a wall?"

"A wall? Climb?" Jamie repeated in exasperation. "Girl, isn't it enough that the blessed thing *moves?*"

"No point in doing it if it can't be done right," I told him. "No, we pivot at the shoulder, we slide the leg forward and then —" I sighed. "— we've got to lock it so that it can bear weight as we move on it."

"But the wood will give a bit as it takes the weight, Danni," Jamie objected.

"What?" I said, my eyes going wide. "What did you say?"

"The wood," he said, "it'll give as it takes the weight, you know that."

Stupid, stupid, stupid! I thought to myself, my eyes flashing. I was too used to unbending metal; I'd forgotten I was building with wood.

"Ach, that's *it* Jamie! We let the wood do the work!"

"It might not be enough," he told me, "but you could work in some springs —"

"Springs, ach, Jamie, I'm an idiot!" I cried, jumping up and rushing indoors for my paper and charcoal. Jamie followed me and sat by quietly while I started drawing. He muttered a few suggestions which I incorporated with quick nods and, twenty minutes later we had it. "And it'll ride much smoother and we can adjust the tension of the springs for rough or easy going —"

"And you could alter the angle of the wagon itself," Jamie observed.

"Aye, we could at that," I allowed. I punched him lightly on the shoulder. "I'm very lucky to have a brother as clever as you."

"Tell me that after we beat MacAllister," Jamie said glumly.

"Ach, Jamie, that's no problem," I assured him. "MacAllister's engine is a poor second to ours and I can't imagine he's got nearly as decent a design as ours."

"He'll want to steal it, likely as not," Jamie agreed. I nodded solemnly and then I choked on a fresh idea and Jamie gave me the look he always gave when I was thinking something particularly mischievous. Cautiously, he said, "What's gotten into that head of yours, sister?"

"Well, brother," I said my voice all sweetness and light with my eyes gleaming, "if MacAllister wants to steal our plans, I think we should be sure he succeeds."

I waved a hand to our discarded "spider" sketches.

"Oh, Danni, that's cruel, that is!" Jamie said even as his eyes took on the same mischievous gleam as mine.

CHAPTER THREE

"I TOLD HIM I'D NOT DO IT AND HE THREATENED TO WHIP ME," SAMUEL TOLD US AT OUR forge two days later as he relayed how his master, Hamish MacAllister, had ordered him to steal our plans. Officially he was on his way to the port to pick up some supplies but he was long-legged and knew he'd be able to chat with us for a bit, finish his errand, and still get back before MacAllister would get suspicious.

"And did he?" Jamie asked.

"No," Samuel said, smiling at me, "because just about then Weasel came running in with the plans himself." He glanced from me to Jamie and back. "So, that was no surprise to you, about the Weasel?"

"Well, it doesn't take a smart man to ken what MacAllister would want," Jamie said.

"By which I'd guess that the Weasel got bad plans," Samuel said with the faintest of frowns on his face. There was no love lost between him and the Weasel — for no one bothered to call Jock Adams anything else — from face to form he was one giant weasel, excepting perhaps that weasels weren't as given to spots as he. And, generally, they were better company. No, what bothered Samuel was the thought that bad plans would put MacAllister in a whipping rage — something he got often enough that more than one apprentice had taken to their heels rather than stick to their oath of service.

"Nay," I said, punching him lightly on the shoulder, "have you not told me enough of your gracious master?"

"He got good plans?" Samuel yelped in surprise. His face colored as he continued, "But Danni, that's not fair either. You shouldn't be worried about my backside so much that your father will lose the wager!"

"Oh, I'd not worry on that score," Jamie put in dourly. "Our Danni's not *that* sort."

I punched him, hard. Instead of crying out, Jamie merely commenced to rubbing the sore spot and looking at Samuel as though I'd proved his point.

"The plans will work, if he doesn't make a bollocks of it," I told Samuel. Then I pointed toward the archway that led out to the street. "You'd best be going, if you want to get to those errands."

Samuel nodded and strode off. In the archway, he turned back and waved.

"Danni, don't you know he'd rather be staying?" Jamie asked me teasingly.

"Get back to work," I growled. "You've got plenty of it, slacking off the way you've been."

Jamie shot me a knowing look but went back to the forge. "Have you got those test plugs for me?"

"Don't tell me you're ready to test the boiler?" I cried in surprise. Sure, I'd been the one to shape the boiler halves and set the piping but I'd left it to Jamie to finish rigging the boiler in its frame, build the gasket and bolt the two halves together.

"Almost."

"Well, when you're ready you let me know," I warned him sternly. "In the meantime, I've enough work of me own."

"Master Pugh will be looking for you," Jamie said by way of agreement. I nodded and rushed out under the archway, following Samuel's footsteps.

But where Samuel continued through the Grass Market and on to the Cow Market and hence down to Leith port, I stopped at the first shop in the Grass Market.

Bells rang when I entered and old Mr. Pugh came bustling out, glasses resting on his brow. "Oh, it's you!"

"Sorry I'm late, Mr. Pugh," I told him breathlessly. I looked around the shop and sniffed. The smell of hot metal came from the workshop in the back. "Are we ready to pour?"

"Lead's all ready," Mr. Pugh said, turning to lead the way back. "But I'm surprised you're all so charged up."

I gave him an inquiring look.

"Didn't I just see your fine young Samuel trot on by, looking late for an appointment?" Mr. Pugh asked me with an impish smile. The old man didn't miss much.

"He's not *mine*," I corrected. "But, yes, Samuel Cattan was chatting with us on his way through."

"Bit out of the way," Mr. Pugh observed tartly. "Enough that he was on the trot for his real errand."

I said nothing, allowing the old man to delight in his teasing. He grunted and then we were in the workshop and he waved a hand toward a set of molds.

"Not much to look at," he said.

"Just plugs for the engine, Mr. Pugh," I told him.

"Why so many?" Mr. Pugh asked. We were going to cast five this morning and when they'd set, they'd be my safety plugs. "And your numbers are strange, Danni. Why 'four', 'five', 'seven', 'eight' and 'ten'?"

"They're marked for the pressure," I told him.

"Pressure, is it?" Mr. Pugh said, looking toward the molds and the hot lead. "Well, they're ready for pouring just as you asked." He gave me an odd look. "Seems strange to be casting in lead."

"It's heaviest, so it makes for the smallest plugs," I told him, carefully donning my gloves and the large goggles that I always used before pouring.

"You could take a nasty burn and still live, as long as it wasn't in your eyes," Mr. Pugh had explained when I'd first started making molds, over two years ago.

I pulled on a smock and tied it, not too poorly with my gloved hands and then went to the fire, taking the tongs and the dish of molten lead.

"It doesn't have to be a perfect pour," I said as I lifted the dish with tongs.

"It does if it's to come out of *my* shop," Mr. Pugh corrected me with a bark. I ducked my head in acknowledgement but I wasn't as afraid of his tone as I would have been had it come from someone like Hamish MacAllister — Mr. Pugh's bark was always worse than his bite. "But ye haven't convinced me yet that it should."

I smiled and moved over to the molds, carefully pouring each, topping it off before moving on to the next.

Lead is a strange metal — it melts easily, forms easily and weighs more than iron or copper. Mixed with silver it makes pewter. It's often found in places where something might be beaten to shape, such as the touch-plug on most cannon.

All in all, it's a friendly metal and I knew that the pours were all up to Mr. Pugh's exacting standards even before I put the empty dish back in its place.

Mr. Pugh had kept a watchful eye on my work and it was only when I was done that he turned back to his own bench, satisfied.

"Jamie's finishing the fixings for the new boiler," I told him. "These plugs will let us test it properly."

"Pressure," Mr. Pugh reminded me.

"Aye, the plugs are weighted for the pressure the boiler will take," I told him. "'Four' for four atmospheres and so on up to ten atmospheres."

"I'm sure that means something to you, lass but I'm only a simple clockmaker," Mr. Pugh replied.

I snorted at him. There was nothing "simple" about Mr. Everett Pugh; that I'd learned years back. He was a bit like my father — he felt that a good description showed a good grasp of the topic. We'd started that way when we'd first met and he'd started teaching me about gears and gearing and continued through to casting, molding, finishing — the whole lot of a clockmaker.

"You've the eye for it," Mr. Pugh had said to me after my first year with him. "If you weren't a girl, you'd be a good clockmaker." He smiled when he saw me start to go red. "As it is, if you got yourself the right man, you could be a good clockmaker and he could be a good shopkeeper."

That idea didn't ease me.

"What about Boadicea and her chariot?" I asked. "Or Queen Elizabeth or Queen Mary?"

"Which Mary?" Mr. Pugh had countered. "Bloody or silly?" He shook his head and sighed. "Lass, it'll take a lot more good Queen Besses to wipe the stain of her Mary cousins from men's minds."

I couldn't argue that but the look he gave me got me to wondering. "Was there ever a Mrs. Pugh, if you don't mind me asking?"

"I don't," Mr. Pugh had said softly, his eyes going wistful. He nodded. "Yes, there was." He smiled at some distant memory. "A long time back."

I didn't ask what had happened to her. Women die so easily — from the ague, from a beating, from childbirth, from nursing, from a fall, as well as just from all the things that can just as easily carry away a man. Mr. Pugh had come here from the continent and before he'd grown up in England — his accent alone made that clear. No one asked him about his past and he offered nothing in return.

"We didn't need it for the first boiler as that only made steam to regular pressure," I told him. Mr. Pugh knew a bit about pressure, being well-read and also using it for some of the more difficult castings. "With this new one, we're going to work at five times the atmosphere."

"What's that in feet of water?" Mr. Pugh asked. It wasn't as odd a question as it sounded — we were near enough to Leith port that we knew of sailors — half of Mr. Pugh's trade came that way and so we understood about pressure at depth. Besides, the work of Lord Boyle from Ireland was available in the University library — Mr. Pugh had brought it to my attention a year or more before when I'd been arguing with him about pressure.

"An atmosphere is thirty-two feet, so that would work out to the pressure of a column of one hundred and sixty feet of water," I told him, the numbers working through my head quickly.

Mr. Pugh whistled. "And why the ten atmospheres?"

"The five is what we're aiming for," I told him. "But I figure that if we test the boiler at ten, then we'll have some safety."

"So this boiler is like those Magdeburg hemispheres of Herr Guericke's only in reverse," Mr. Pugh said thoughtfully.

"Well, except that the hemispheres only had one atmosphere working on them, the boiler will have five trying to burst it," I said.

"Which is why we cast it so thick," Mr. Pugh guessed. "But that thick, it'll take longer to heat."

"It will but once heated, it'll keep it well enough," I said.

"If you want to keep a horse warm on a cold day, you put on a blanket," Mr. Pugh observed.

"Are you saying that we should make a blanket for the boiler?" I cried in surprise. "Wouldn't it catch fire?"

"Keep it from the flames," Mr. Pugh suggested. He shrugged. "It's worth thinking on, isn't it?"

I'd known Mr. Pugh long enough to know that he wasn't wrong. It was worth thinking on. What could take that sort of heat and be easily formed, I wondered?

"Soapstone!" I cried. "We could use soapstone!"

Soapstone was ancient, the Vikings used it for cookware and we often used it for molds because it was easy to carve and handled most heat easily.

Mr. Pugh smiled at me and I knew that he'd already had that thought — he was just, as usual, letting me find it for myself. "I suppose you could at that."

"It'd take more soapstone than we have to hand," I said.

"And I'm not likely to sell it for some fool venture," he warned me.

"Well then, we'll wait until we've won our wager," I said.

"So, you've explained your five and ten," Mr. Pugh said, coming back to our original topic, "but what about the others?"

"The four's in case the boiler doesn't seem up to five," I told him. "Seven and eight are just in case."

"So you test to ten to be sure the boiler's sound," Mr. Pugh observed, "then run it at half that." He nodded. "That seems wise." Then he made a face. "But you think twice, Danielle Walker, before you ever fit the seven or eight plug."

"I will, Mr. Pugh, be certain I will," I told him. I knew that Mr. Boyle in his tests had built pressure vessels to handle many atmospheres but to my knowledge no one had thought to build a pressure boiler. And if the Magdeburg hemispheres, with the force of one atmosphere keeping them together were so powerful that thirty horses couldn't part them, I couldn't imagine what an explosion of five atmospheres of steam would be like.

I'd been burnt enough from mistakes in castings, I'd been scalded once, too — I had no desire to find out what five atmospheres of steam would do to a person.

"These plugs are awfully small, Danni," Mr. Pugh said as he broke open the first mold and inspected it.

"They sit into a hole a sixteenth of an inch in diameter," I told him.

"And the pressure will push them out if it's great enough," Mr. Pugh said approvingly.

"That's the hope," I said, smiling at him.

#

"Arrgh!" I cried late that night as I crumpled up the latest set of drawings. No matter how I tried, I just *couldn't* seem to figure out how to work the legs.

Jamie looked up, unsurprised, from the paper he was reading by the fire.

"I can't get the legs to work," I told him sourly.

"So are you giving up?" Bessie asked from her place by the fire where she was scooping out the ashes.

"Nae, Danni never gives up," Jamie told her. "Especially not with our father over at the pub bragging about his forthcoming contraption."

"Well the boiler and the engine work just fine," I snarled at him. "How was I to know the bleeding *legs* would be so awkward?"

"And doesn't our father always tell us to beware the easy things?" Jamie said, raising an eyebrow. "But, Danni, if ye can't figure it, there's no worries — not only have we got twenty guineas to find for MacAllister but by now our father will have wagered easily another forty around the town." He nodded at me. "So, no worries, Danni lass, we'll do fine in the poor house."

I scowled at him, reached to the floor and pulled up the crumpled paper. Carefully I smoothed it out once more and looked at it. It was the fourth try I'd had at the legs. How hard can they be, after all? A fool horse has four and no trouble moving them. For that matter, so does the lowly ass!

"It's not my place," Bessie spoke up glaring over at Jamie, "but if it were I'd say it's not fair of ye, Master Jamie, to be playing your sister like a puppet."

Jamie turned bright red and opened his mouth to tell little Bessie off but my cry of joy startled the pair of them.

"Oh, that's it!" I cried. I beamed at the young stray I'd taken in. "Ach, Bessie, you've the way of it!"

"Miss?" Bessie said, bending her head back to the floor and her sweeping of the ashes, hoping to avoid a beating or a tongue-lashing.

"Puppets!" I said. Jamie's brow furrowed, so I explained, "Jamie, there's a puppet-maker at the end of High Street."

"Aye," Jamie agreed slowly.

"I'll get him to help!"

#

"Och, there's nought to it miss," Mr. Gillie said as he showed me the movements. "I've to do this all the time at the theatre, particularly when doing Jack and the Beanstalk."

"Oh, Mr. Gillie, you don't know how much trouble you've saved me!" I told him relievedly as I sketched the various connections and movements of his hastily built up cart.

"I might at that, given that the whole town knows about your father's bet," Mr. Gillie said, smiling down as he watched me sketch. "You know, if you'd like, I could probably build ye a miniature —"

"I'm afraid I don't have the money, sir," I told him sadly, looking up from my sketching.

"And do ye not think that there won't be some who'd pay good money to see the story told on the small stage?" Mr. Gillie said, waggling his bushy eyebrows as he waved to his small stage in the back of his shop.

I hadn't thought of that and it showed on my face.

Mr. Gillie smiled. "If you'll let me keep it when you're done with it, I'll make you a model for free!"

"Ah, that'd be marvelous," I said, my tone depressed. "But we've no time to waste!"

"I could have it for you tomorrow morning," Mr. Gillie promised. He made a face. "I suppose it's too much to hope that you could make one of those engines of yours small enough to fit."

I shook my head. "No, I only wish. At that size, it'd weigh practically nothing."

"Ach, it was only a thought," Mr. Gillie said, waving the notion away. He started walking me toward his door. "Come back tomorrow at noon."

#

Father was furious when I got back later that day.

"Ye're not to go out without someone from now on, Danni!" He shouted at me, making me quake in my shoes. He grabbed my shoulders with both his hands and squeezed. "If Hamish MacAllister has his way, you'll be put away."

"Put away?"

"As a witch," my father told me.

"What?" Jamie cried from where he'd stood torn between intervening on my behalf and pitching in on father's.

"He's saying that your full of ideas that only one from the dark world could have and ye're a bad influence on things," father said. He let me go and stepped back, the fire in his eyes dimming. "He's even said that when Bonnie Prince Charlie comes, he'll have ye burned."

"What?" I cried.

"Hadn't ye heard?" Father said. "Or were ye all too busy with this foolishness?"

Well, everyone had heard that Bonnie Prince Charlie had landed in the Highlands and had raised a force in rebellion against the English King George II in favor of his father, James. Talk in town was mixed but he was far away and I couldn't imagine what he'd mean to me.

"They say he's coming to Edinburgh," father said, catching my interest. "And they say he and his father want to push their Catholic ways." He raised his eyes to mine. "And if your brains weren't full of mush, ye'd recall that Bloody Mary was all too happy to burn witches."

"I'm not a witch!"

"Ye've red hair," father said, "and there are some who say you act unwomnly."

Jamie snorted and I glared at him. "Well, you can't deny that, Danni!"

"I've little time for foolish things like needlework," I admitted, trying to find my pride.

"That's part of it," father agreed. "But MacAllister's worried about this bet and I wouldn't put anything past him."

"But surely everyone knows that Danni —" Jamie began.

"Ach, they all 'know' that Danni's working on this steam horse of ours but they all *say* that it's mine," father cut across him. "So if she were to disappear or be held as a heretic, it'd be up to me to finish."

"We're nearly done, father," I told him, lifting the rolled sketches off the table. "Mr. Gillie showed me how to handle the legs. All we've got to do is cut the lumber, cap the spares, run up the cables and —"

"That's all?" Father cried. "Why not ask for gold to rain from Heaven, child? Have ye any idea how long that'll take?"

"If we get some help from the shipwrights, less than four days," I told him.

"What?" He was startled by my number. "Which shipwrights?"

"MacArdle, Henry, and Stoops," I told him. "I showed them the plans and they say they can have it built in three days."

"So why did you say four?"

"Because on the fourth day, we mount the boiler and the engine," I told him.

"Four days?" He asked me, catching my eyes. When I nodded he blew out a sigh of relief. "That's good because Hamish says his'll be ready in five." His expression changed once more. "And how much will your 'friends' be wanting for all this work?"

"I've arranged the work on exchange," I told him.

"Exchange for what?"

"Well, they've thought of a few ways they could use the engine," I told him. "I allowed as how if they'd help, I could build them an engine for a mere forty guineas."

"Forty guineas!" Jamie said.

"And they'd pay that?"

"They've some notion to hook it up to power a ship," I said with a shrug. He gave me a stern look and I sighed. "Well, all right, if you must know, I might have suggested the paddle idea to them but it seemed simple enough and they were taken with the notion."

"Forty guineas!" Jamie repeated. He turned to our father. "Even if we lose with Hamish, we'd break even!"

"And you can bet that if the engine works as planned, there'll be demand for more," father agreed. He pursed his lips for a moment, then nodded. "Very well, we'll go with your friends." He shook a finger at me. "But I mean what I say, from now on, take someone with you."

"I'll take Bessie," I said.

"No, she's too small," father said with a shake of his head.

"I'll find someone."

"Maybe you should stay here," father said with a frown. "Your nautical friends don't need you and the yard's safe enough."

"What if I find someone?"

"Someone Hamish and his men can't handle?" Father asked doubtfully. "No, they'd pay a lot now to have you out of their way."

#

"Father's right, you know," Jamie said as we got ready for bed. He must have seen my mulish look. He saw the way I flushed and laughed. "Ah, Danni, you're as open as a book to me!"

"I know a way," Bessie spoke up from where she sat on the stool. I was brushing her hair; I'd insisted on it after we'd gotten rid of the lice — I was *not* going to have that sort of vermin back again — and while she'd resisted at first, she'd grown to like it. I suppose it wasn't proper, like the noblewomen would have said but it was the way I wanted it. Better a clean maid than a dirty me, I thought.

"How?" I said, pulling on her hair in my irritation. She winced in pain. "Sorry."

"It's just that... well, you know, there are the ones who sleep by the forge," Bessie said.

"We ought to know, you were one," Jamie said.

"Well, there's enough of them to keep an eye on you," Bessie said.

"Hamish MacAllister would skewer them sure as look at them," Jamie said dismissively.

"Only if he saw them," Bessie said slyly, turning her head out of my grasp to look Jamie in the eyes. "All they have to do is keep an eye on our miss, and let us know."

"It'd be too late then," Jamie said. "They'd be thinking of hauling her straight off."

"Well then, they could interfere," Bessie said.

"Why would they want to help?"

"If you'd let them stay at the forge over the winter, miss, that'd save a lot of them," Bessie allowed.

"Is there one of them you're sweet on, little Bessie?" Jamie asked tauntingly.

"Jamie!" I said, turning around and swatting at him with the brush. I turned back again just as quickly and said to Bessie, "It's a brilliant idea. Now sit straight, I've got to finish your hair."

Bessie was a long time turning around so when she did, I leaned forward and whispered in her ear, "He's just a silly boy!"

Bessie sniffed at that. I could tell that, to her at least, Jamie was the biggest and best boy in her whole world.

CHAPTER FOUR

"Danni! Danni! Danni, wake up!" Jamie's voice was loud and right in my ear.

"Go 'way, Jamie!"

"Danni, get up now! There're soldiers, lots of them!" Bessie said. "Your father says to wear your dress."

Drat! I flumped in the bed and dragged my eyes open. Jamie was on one side, Bessie on the other, glaring at him and holding my best dress in her hands.

"James Walker, ye know better than to be present when a lady's dressing!" Bessie said like she was a lady's proper maid. Jamie started to answer, thought better of it and left. "Quick, ye've got to get this on!"

"Soldiers?" I mumbled as I allowed her to force me into the dress and lace me up.

"Aye, so many of them!" Bessie said. "First there were the English but they ran and then there was the Scottish." Her voice dropped to a whisper of awe. "They say that Bonnie Prince Charlie himself is here!"

"Oh, that's nice," I mumbled. "But we've got to get to work, I can't wear a dress today."

I was so tired because the night before we'd managed to mount both the boiler and the engine on the platform. All that was needed now was the rigging of the gear and we'd be ready.

It had been a tough several days, mostly without sleep and one particularly nervous day as we tested the boiler to ten atmospheres. Jamie insisted on being the one to do the test, even though I swore it was my job.

"And what sort of chances would ye have if ye were scalded by a burst?" Jamie had demanded.

"No worse than you!"

"Ach, but I'm not looking for a husband, am I?" Jamie had demanded. "It's my job, Danni, and I know how to handle it."

Father agreed and together, we'd worked out the best way to approach it. We had Jamie dressed in an oilskin and arranged for him to rush behind a stout wall as the boiler reached full pressure. Of course, we'd tested it at one atmosphere and slowly at all the other pressures up to the final full ten atmospheres.

I'd nearly cried with relief when I heard the plug blow and heard Jamie's shout of triumph. "We did it, Danni, we did it!"

Hooking up the engine after had been time-consuming, tiring work but nothing as worrying as the boiler test.

Our shipwrights had been most impressed with the results, particularly when I gave them a low-pressure demonstration of the full engine.

"That's only four atmospheres," I told them. "We'll run it at five when we've got it hooked to the legs."

"Well, missy, the sooner the better," Mr. MacArdle said.

"Aye," Mr. Henry agreed, looking oddly at the engine and boiler. To me he said, "But lass, why not run it hotter?"

"For safety, Mr. Henry," I told him. "We don't know how the boiler will behave over long periods of time."

"The best way is to just try," Mr. Henry said to me.

"Have you ever been scalded, Mr. Henry?" Jamie said, moving over and pulling up his sleeve to reveal a nasty red scar. "That's what a regular boiler can do."

"That's not so bad," Mr. Henry said, eyeing the scar critically.

"The steam in our boiler is five times worse, Mr. Henry," I told him. "And that's only at five atmospheres."

Mr. Henry grunted at that and we turned to our proper task of assembling the walker.

#

I wore my dress all that day and the next but once they told me that the soldiers had left for the south of the city, I was back in trousers. Nothing had been done in the past two days and I didn't want MacAllister to beat us.

The walker was all set up, the boiler and engine were set in their place at the back. At the front we'd have to rig some ballast to counterweight them.

"In future, that'll be cargo, of course," Mr. Henry had predicted sagely.

Our supply of coal was set in a bin to the side of the boiler.

From the engine snaked several large cables.

"Are they strong enough?" I'd asked when the shipwrights had first brought them.

"Strong enough?" Mr. MacArdle had laughed. "Lass, why with any one of them cables you could lift a ship of war!"

"Not quite what I had in mind, Mr. MacArdle, but I suppose they'll do."

"If anything's going to break, miss, it won't be the cables," Mr. Henry assured me. "Of course," he said, glancing around the tall platform at the cables, "first something's got to work, hasn't it?"

"We've still the rigging to complete," I reminded him.

"Aye, and it's an amazement in itself," Mr. Stoops said.

"Wouldn't it work in a ship?" I asked, gesturing to my sketches and the cables.

"Lass, have ye ever heard of a ship that walked?" Mr. Stoops replied. He knew I hadn't; no one had. "So how can ye be sure all this will work?"

"We'll learn in the trying, Mr. Stoops," I told him, pointing toward a cable. "That one goes to the near foreleg."

"The what?"

"Port forrard beam, Stoopie, the lass means the port forrard beam," Mr. Henry told him, glancing down at me and nodding with a wink.

"And why didn't she say so, then?"

"Ach, she's only a wee lass, Stoopie, she's no knowledge of the sea, has she?"

"Probably just as well, she'd be taming the very waves next," Mr. Stoops said, dragging the cable to the near foreleg.

"This is a walking horse, Mr. Stoops," I said to him, "it's best to think of it that way." I pointed to the near foreleg and named it, then the far foreleg, the near hind leg and, finally, the far hind leg.

"What a daft set o' names!" Mr. Stoops allowed, even as he followed my instructions on the setting of the cable.

Mr. Gillie had worked it out a treat: we had cables to raise the calf beam and the thigh beam, cables to lower both, and cables to move the whole leg. That was easy enough, the trick was in building the gearing that moved the whole leg and all four legs in the right order. Worse, we had to gear the whole to allow us to reverse and to turn, to raise the front or the rear of the platform.

Mr. Pugh and I spent a lot of time casting the gears, Mr. Gillie threw up his hands after figuring out the easiest parts of the walk; Mr. Pugh, Jamie, and I figured out the rest.

When started, the engine would first drive nothing. It would take throwing a lever to get it engaged and then, as the steam rose, it would start moving forward faster and faster. Neither Jamie nor I were quite sure how fast so I'd decided we'd start with only four atmospheres — the greater the pressure the greater the power and speed of the engine.

To stop all that was needed was to throw the lever again. Turning was a slower affair — we'd rigged a tiller which would alter the rate at which the legs moved, slower to the left when the tiller pointed left, slower to the right when the tiller pointed right. For reverse, we had to throw a different lever which reversed the order of the legs and their movement.

Of course, all that was in theory.

If I was right, when she was moving, the walker would only need a stoker for the boiler and a gearman for the motion.

"And this will beat MacAllister's Scuttler, will it?" My father had asked late last night as we finished the last of the rigging.

"It should do, it's got four times more power," I told him.

MacAllister's apprentices had been whipped raw in his fury to get his walker done first — they'd just tested theirs the day before.

"Ye've got two days, Walker!" A drunken MacAllister had declared triumphantly that evening when he'd visited, eyeing our walker intently — clearly disturbed that it looked nothing at all like his quickly-named Scuttler.

I was glad that the Scuttler worked, it proved most of my fears baseless, but it was just as ugly and ungainly as I'd first thought it might be. It worked by wobbling from leg to leg and I was pretty sure it could neither turn nor reverse — something that Mr. MacAllister clearly hadn't considered when he'd reiterated the terms of the wager — "The first one to walk from the far side of the Grass Market to the end and back."

It was clear he hadn't thought of how his Scuttler was going to turn around or reverse its way.

#

"I've got to do this, father!" I cried the next morning as he grabbed at me as I clambered up the side of the walker.

"Let Jamie do it, you stay down here."

"It takes two, father and we're the lightest," I told him. I saw his look and explained, "We don't know how slow or fast the walker will be."

"And we can jump and roll," Jamie said from his position high above on the walker platform. He gestured to ropes that were draped around the sides. "Or clamber down the safety lines."

"Bessie —"

"Bessie knows nothing of gears or steam," I told him, not bothering to add that Bessie, wise lass, was no doubt trembling in the darkest part of the root cellar against just such an occasion.

Father sighed, and with a boost, lifted me up to the platform.

"Remember, everything can be repaired except your bones and your skull," he called up to me.

"We'll remember," I promised, nudging Jamie and rushing to my place by the gears. "We're going with four atmospheres."

"Good," father said, moving off to stand by the three shipwrights. Mr. Pugh came through the arches at that moment, with Mr. Gillie in tow. "Are we too late?"

"Just building steam now," father called to him, gesturing for them to join their group.

In a voice that carried only to my ears, Jamie said, "This had better work."

"I know, I know," I said, looking at the boiler and gesturing for him to shovel in more coal. I shouldn't have worried, the pressure rose and rose. Mr. Pugh had figured out a simple way to measure the pressure, based on my idea with the weights and we'd switched from my rather poor idea to his so that I could now see that the boiler was over three atmospheres and steadily rising.

"I'm turning on the engine," I called out loud, putting on the thick insulated gloves and moving to turn the large valve that separated the boiler from the engine.

I jumped as the engine started and then began turning, faster and faster, the rod going back and forth, back and forth.

With a silent prayer, I called out, "I'm engaging the legs."

I slid the lever that connected the engine to the leg cables and the running gear and then I jumped over to the tiller.

If we were wrong, if the cables snapped —

— a creaking noise startled me and, out of the corner of my eye, I saw Jamie jump —

— and then the platform lurched.

"It's going to fall!" My father cried. "Jump!"

"No," I shouted back, "It's working!"

The next leg moved and the platform leveled. And then another leg and another and —

"You're going to crash!" Mr. Pugh shouted.

— we were headed to the archway and we were going to get jammed.

I pushed hard on the tiller and slowly, very slowly, we turned. It wasn't enough.

I jumped back to the power lever and kicked it so that the legs were free of the engine.

With a lurch we stopped.

"Whew!" Jamie called. "That was close!"

"Now what are you going to do?" Mr. Stoops called, looking at our precarious position. "You're too close to the entrance and you're not lined up."

"Ach, that's easy," I said, kicking the lever over, "we're going to back up!"

In truth, I held my breath as the platform slowly started moving again and only let it out in a silent curse as I realized that I'd left us turning the wrong way. I raced back to the tiller, pushed it over and slowly we backed up, turning to line up with the archway.

"You need to go slower!" Mr. Henry called from below.

"Yes," I said, glancing around at the boiler and the engine. I hadn't thought of that, I'd been too worried about going at all. And then — I grabbed the thick gloves and turned the valve halfway between the engine and the boiler.

"Danni, are ye daft?" Jamie called, eyes wide but we slowed down. "Och, you're daft all right."

I smiled at him, kicked the lever over again and the walker started to move forward at about half the earlier speed. I could still work the tiller, so I lined us up with the archway.

"Danni, no!" Father called as soon as he saw what I'd planned.

"But we've got to know if she can do it!" I called.

"No, you've done your part, Danni, it's time to hand it over to me and the others," father said. "Now stop the engine and let us get up."

Jamie cocked his head at me to say that father had the right of it. I couldn't argue, so instead, I kicked the power lever away and called down, "Come on up!"

\#

"Now, I want to take it slow, Danni," father said. "Can we do that?"

"I'll turn the steam back down," I said, moving to get the gloves.

"No, let me," father said. When I gave him a hurt look, he explained, "I need to know how to do this so there'll be no doubt who's in charge."

"Remember MacAllister," Jamie muttered at my back.

I passed the gloves to my father. He turned the valve connecting the boiler and the engine, closing it further.

"Now, you push the lever over to engage the legs," I told him.

"Aye," father said. He wagged a finger at me. "I think I ken this well enough, lass. Ye need only tell me when I'm going wrong."

Father turned the walker turned the archway and lined it up perfectly. Slowly, the beast lurched and creaked into and through the archway and out on the main path that curved around our premises.

"We could go faster now," I said to my father.

"Ach, no, child!" Father said to me, shaking his head. "And put the fear of losing into MacAllister?" He went back and turned down the steam some more so that in a few moments we were barely crawling along.

"Jamie, you'd best leave off on the shoveling," I said, "the pressure will get too high." At this slow pace, we weren't using steam as fast as the boiler was making it.

"Just a nice pleasant stroll over to MacAllister's and back," my father said to me. He glanced around at the view spread before him. "I must say, lass, ye've done us proud!"

A grin split my face, I couldn't help it. The walker was ambling along with slow, steady movements. We were perched atop it, nearly eight feet off the ground and moving with all the ease of a person on stilts.

"This'll make a fortune!" Mr. Stoops declared proudly.

"What are ye going to do with your engine, then?" father asked the sailors.

The three exchanged glances before Hoop replied, "Well, if we can walk on land, can we not *paddle* on the sea?"

"I suppose you could at that," father allowed with a thoughtful look.

#

"Hoy, Hamish, are ye ready?" Father called as the walker crawled up the path to MacAllister's forge.

A group of boys and dogs had followed us and the crowd grew bigger as the apprentices and maids from Hamish's premises came away from their work, following father's challenge.

Hamish MacAllister came away from his forge to stand with both his hands on his hips, staring up with a dirty look at my father perched high atop the walker.

"What's that ye've got there, Walker?" Hamish shouted back.

"It's our Walker, Hamish, and I'm here to set down the challenge," he waved a hand toward the other machine in the distance. "Is yours ready or do ye need more time?"

Hamish's eyes narrowed angrily. "Ach, it's ready all right. Name the time and the place, and be sure to have your money to hand."

"Tomorrow night," father called back. "The stakes and the bet as before — first to go lengthwise down the Grass Market and back."

Hamish snorted. "I'll see ye tomorrow night, then."

"A pleasure, Hamish, 'twill be a pleasure," my father called. He engaged the power once more and the walker started forward, causing the gathered crowd to spring back. "Ach! I forgot, this beast is a poor turner!"

Moving to the steam valve, father turned it nearly full closed before beginning to very slowly turn the walker around.

On the ground, Hamish MacAllister nearly beamed with delight.

"Good luck, Walker!" He moved back to his forge, shaking his head and saying loud enough to be heard, "Ye'll need it."

"And luck to you, too!" Father called back as he got the walker pointed back the way it came. In a voice which Hamish couldn't hear, he added, "And *ye'll* need it!"

#

"Why did you say tomorrow night, father?" I asked when we'd returned to our home. "Why not tonight?"

"Ach, lass, ye know a lot about steam but nothing about bets," father said, shaking his head. "With another days' betting, we'll be sure to double our winnings."

"He's right, Danni," Jamie agreed. "When word gets out how slow our walker moved, everyone will be betting double against us."

"And what's so good about that?"

"We'll make twice as much money, ye ninny," Jamie told me, shaking his head. He glanced at his father. "She knows nothing about betting."

"Well, that's fair enough, most know nothing of steam," father allowed. He glanced up at the sky then turned to me. "I'll have my dinner now, I'll be heading into town soon."

I looked at him in surprise. Jamie explained, "He's going to the pub to take bets."

"Oh," I said with a shake of my head, turning to the kitchen. With a grin, I said to Jamie, "So it's up to you to empty the ashes, refill the boiler, and clean up."

Jamie groaned. Father laughed.

CHAPTER FIVE

AFTER DINNER, I BUSIED MYSELF WITH CLEANING UP THE KITCHEN AND GETTING BESSIE sorted before I went to the study — there were some things I wanted to think about and I was either going to read or draw — maybe both.

Jamie scowled when he found me bent over our large table, busy with new drawings. "And what of the Walker?" he demanded.

"What about it?"

"Well, father's in the pub getting bets, what's to stop Hamish from sending someone *here* to make sure he loses?"

I glanced up from my work, horrified.

"Didn't think of that, did you?" he said, sounding pleased to catch me out. He shook his head. "Ach, you're good with dead things but not so good with what's alive, are ye?"

"So what do we do?" I said, ignoring his taunt. "We could stand guard, I suppose?"

"And do what in the morning?" When I gave him a puzzled look, he explained, "What'll we do for sleep, then?"

"Oh." I sat back in my chair. "Well maybe you could keep watch."

"All *night?*"

"I could help," Bessie's voice piped up from the hallway.

I bristled, ready to tell her her place — she was supposed to be *help*, after all — but Jamie stopped me with an upraised hand.

"And what would ye do, little Bessie, if one of MacAllister's apprentices tried to sabotage our Walker?"

"He wouldn't get that far," Bessie said, walking to the doorway and peeking in. "I'd scream my head off the moment I saw him —"

"And how would *that* help?" Jamie demanded.

"Actually," I said thoughtfully, "it'd probably be enough, especially if we slept in the kitchen, ready to help."

Jamie mulled that over for a second and nodded.

"But one's not enough," I continued, eyeing Bessie suspiciously. "And you weren't thinking of doing it by yourself, were you?"

Bessie's eyes went wide and she shook her head anxiously, "Miss, I —"

"Oh, stop it!" I told her. Jamie looked between the two of us, his mouth wide open in his confusion. "Ach, Jamie, ye say I know nothing of living things but ye might want to recall who it was found Bessie, and where."

Light dawned in Jamie's eyes and he turned to our maid. "There's other Brits up here?"

"Just orphans, mostly," Bessie said. "And they're Scots, mostly." She made a face. "They found the forge, same as I did and I didn't have the heart to send them away, particularly now as it's so cold."

"You haven't been feeding them have you?" I asked.

Bessie made a face at me and shook her head wildly. "You'd send me away if I did that."

"They could have the scraps," I relented. "We're not rich, you know."

"We'll be a lot richer tomorrow," Jamie said, rubbing his hands together in anticipation.

"But not so rich as we can feed every orphan in Edinburgh," I snapped.

"No," Jamie shook his head, "I suppose not."

I thought for a moment and then said to Bessie, "How many are there?"

"I don't rightly know, miss," Bessie said, biting her lower lip. "They mostly scatter when I get near."

"Guess."

"Three? Four?"

"It's getting awfully cold these nights," Jamie said, looking at me.

"Father didn't eat all his plate," I said to Bessie. "Can you divide what's left into quarters?"

"I could, miss," Bessie allowed.

"Okay, so here's what we'll do," I said and I laid out the plan for the Walker Guard.

\#

Jamie had banked the furnace properly as well as tending to the Walker, so there was a dim red glow and a wall of warmth as I walked up to it after dark.

I saw no one but I knew they were out there, just as I'd known Bessie was hiding when I'd first found her.

"I've some food, if ye'll deal with me," I called out into the darkness.

I heard a rustling then a hiss and no more. I moved over to the Walker and patted one of its huge legs loudly.

"Ye've seen our Walker, haven't ye?" I said, turning as I spoke so my voice carried into all the dark corners of our courtyard. "If we're lucky, we'll win when we race against MacAllister." Another rustle. "If we're not, we'll lose a lot of money and we'll have to cut back, be more careful with our coal, work harder."

The silence was thoughtful.

"If we win, we won't have to worry so much," I said, moving back toward the forge. "All we need is a set of watchful eyes and a voice to shout alarm."

From behind me there was a rustle. I turned and a small, grubby boy moved into view.

"If we do that, can we eat?" the boy said, his big eyes looking up at me mournfully.

"Nah," I said, my heart near to breaking at this wee one — mustn't have been more than six — with his ribs poking through the threadbare sack of cloth that covered him. "Ye eat first, but not so much that it sends you to sleep."

The boy made a face.

"And then we send you something in the morning, something warm —"

"Warm?" a girl's voice called of the darkness, from behind me. "Really? Promise?"

"Aye," I said, solemnly crossing myself. "Ye'll be helping us win and we'd be pretty sorry not to be thankful for that."

"I could stab at 'em with a poker," a boy's voice called out.

"Just shout, we'll come running," I replied. I turned around, looking toward the girl's voice. "Is that it, then, just the three of ye?"

"And me," a fourth voice spoke up, "please let me!" A small blond shape bonded into view and came to a rest next to small boy. It was a little girl, near twin to our Bessie, save years younger.

"No food until you all come out, I see you and I get your names and your word," I said, even as I knew that if they balked, I'd end up leaving the food regardless.

Father always said I was too soft.

There was a rustle and two more shapes joined the boy and the girl.

"I'm Mapes," the eldest boy said. "If you feed us, I swear, we'll keep guard."

"You can only swear for yourself," the new girl said. She had red hair like me but all matted and greasy. It took an effort not to back away from her — I was sure I could see lice moving at the crown of her head. Probably all of these orphans had lice — and fleas — and it was doubtful if they'd make it to another year.

"I'm Meara," the girl said in a strange accent. She must have noticed my reaction because she added, "I'm Irish."

"I'm Mary," the littlest girl said. And she nodded toward the boy. "This is Billy."

"I can talk!" Little Billy protested.

I looked them all over, then said, "Do you swear to keep guard?"

"Yes," four voices said distinctly.

I laid the tray that I'd been carrying over on my old anvil. "Then eat this, and we'll talk about watches."

"Littlest first, eldest later," Mapes said. "That's the way we always do it."

"The little ones fall asleep," Meara explained to me, moving to the tray and glancing at it with wide, hungry eyes.

"Makes sense," I said. I realized that they were a gang in their own right and saw how awkwardly they looked at me. I turned back to the kitchen. "I'm going inside, to the kitchen."

They all looked at me.

"We'll be there tonight, so you've only to shout loud enough to wake us," I said.

"Okay," Mapes said, turning to the tray and batting at Billy's hand as the little boy tried to snatch a bite.

I walked away slowly, listening to them talk amongst each other, hearing little Billy wheedle for a bigger piece, little Mary shush him and Mapes and Meara speak like ancient parents to their young.

Back in the kitchen, I turned to Jamie and said fiercely, "We'd better win tomorrow."

"First, we need to *get* to tomorrow."

\#

Father came rumbling in near midnight, a wide grin on his face and walking with an unsteady gait.

"We're all set!" he told us as Jamie and I hustled him up into his bed while Bessie pulled out the warming pan and set a pitcher of fresh water on his nightstand. He smiled blearily at us at his door, saying, "I'll see you in the morning!"

I was glad he didn't think to ask why we were awake or what our plans were because I wasn't sure he'd approve.

"Youngest first," I said to Bessie as we made ourselves as comfortable as we could at the small table in the kitchen. "Wake me at two."

Of course, I didn't get much sleep, opening an eye every once in a while to be certain that Bessie was still awake. Once, I think I saw Jamie's eyes gleam as he checked on her, too. She yawned once or twice but no more.

When the clock chimed two, I opened my eyes. Bessie was looking straight at me.

"I'm going to check on them," I said, moving toward the back door.

"It's wee Mary on guard, miss," Bessie said. "And you've no worries with her, I spotted her ten minutes back."

"She looks a lot like you," I said.

"Ach, she's just English, we all look much the same," Bessie said with a wave of her hand. She yawned which set me off.

"Get yourself to bed, Bessie, you've done enough for the night," I told her.

"If you please, Miss, I'd be cold up in that bed all by myself," she said, moving over to lean against Jamie. "And I'd be too slow to help if needed."

She closed her eyes, resting her head against Jamie's shoulder. I shook my head. She was too young to be really sweet on anyone but she fancied herself sweet on him — and he took her attentions with a mixture of awe and pride.

I turned to the back yard once more and stood up to look out the window. A cold breeze washed over me and I shivered. I spotted a small figure in the distance and saw it raise hands to rub over the heat of the forge — little Mary was awake.

Back at the table, I rested my head on my outstretched arm for a while, then looked over at Jamie and Bessie. Jamie might not be quite asleep but Bessie was snoring softly, completely relaxed against the warmth of his side.

I thought of little Mary shivering outside and rose from the table, pulling on my cloak and quietly heading out the door.

I mustn't have been as quiet as I'd thought for Mary's head popped around in my direction the moment I'd opened the door. I moved quickly to the forge, nodding to her and whispering, "Are ye warm enough?"

"Y-yes, miss," Mary said, her small body shivering uncontrollably.

I shucked off my cloak and draped it around her shoulders. How I'd get it clean of fleas, I couldn't imagine but at the moment I didn't care.

A moment later she stopped shivering, and looked up at me with wide eyes. "I'm too warm now, I'll fall asleep."

"Warm up a bit and give it back to me after," I said. I thought about the others. "In fact, take it off when you're warm enough and pass it on to the next on watch."

Solemnly she told me, "I will, Miss."

I smiled at her and walked briskly back to the kitchen, pausing over the stove long enough to warm myself up. When I went back to the window moments later, I saw that Mary had taken off the cloak. I couldn't spot where she'd put it and then I realized that she'd probably used it to cover the others.

I watched her for a bit surreptitiously then sat back at the kitchen table. A moment later, I lay my head on my arm again.

I was sure I hadn't fallen asleep but suddenly I was alarmed by loud cries from the yard, "Walker! Walker!"

I was out the door in an instant, followed just as quickly by Jamie and Bessie.

"Who goes there?" Jamie bellowed as loudly and deeply as he could, as he raced to block the archway entrance to the yard.

Bessie and I tore over to the Walker. When I got there, I raced around it and then clambered up, looking for any sign of tampering or mischief.

"They ran off, miss," Mapes' voice called up to me. "Little Mary scared them with her cry."

Jamie joined us, saying, "I saw three in the distance, they were running down the road back to town."

I turned to the orphans and smiled at them, "Thank you."

"Just keeping our word, miss," Mapes said stoically.

"Bessie, can you heat us a pot of tea?" I said, turning to her. "I think we can use the warmth."

"Aye, miss," Bessie said, sounding a bit surly.

"Mugs for seven!" I called after her and she turned back, a smile beaming on her face, before she ran off to the kitchen.

"We don't need that, miss," Meara said.

"Maybe you don't, but it'll help keep you awake," I told her. Jamie glanced over my way with an expression that showed that *he* knew that wasn't my reason. I gave him a half-shrug.

"They came through the archway?" I said, turning to little Mary.

"I think so," Mary said. "I heard a noise that way, and then I saw a flash of light — maybe a belt buckle —"

"Or a sword," Jamie interrupted. I glared at him. I didn't want these kids to run off in fear of their lives. Jamie glared back and motioned with his head toward Mapes. The oldest orphan stood straighter, eyes gleaming as though the thought of a battle thrilled him.

Maybe Jamie wasn't so wrong to have them thinking they were guarding against great peril.

To me, Jamie added, "Think, Danni! How would they wreck the Walker?"

I frowned at that and moved quickly to the Walker again, going over every part that I could see in the dim night. No cables were cut or even frayed and there was no sign of fire or other mischief.

"They didn't get near it," I said when I came back to the group. I smiled down at little Mary. "Our Mary put the fear of God into them!"

Mary smiled back up shyly at me and I began to think that perhaps if things went well, we'd need *two* maids in the Walker house.

My brother knew me too well, spotting the look and snorting at me. To Mapes he said, "Have ye ever thought of making swords?"

Mapes shook his head in surprise but turned back to the forge with a very thoughtful look.

"Could I, too?" little Billy asked.

"Only when you're bigger, titch," Meara told him, ruffling his matted hair with a hand and turning to me. She moved close enough to speak to me alone, saying quietly, "I can take care of myself, miss."

I said nothing to that and was glad when a noise from the house turned out to be Bessie trudging to us with a well-laden tray.

The tea was warm and I nodded to Meara, saying, "Would you pour?"

The red-head gave me a look, then nodded, pouring smaller portions for the two little ones and a good dollop for Mapes. She poured the largest amounts for Jamie and me and only slightly less for Bessie.

I shook my head at the mug she handed toward me, "That's too much, I'll be up all night."

The other sniggered as they figured my meaning but Meara went nearly as red as her hair.

"Please," I said to her, "you drink it, you'll need it."

Meara and I locked eyes for a moment and I began to realize why people were so intimidated by red-heads. Then she smiled at me and passed me the mug she'd poured for herself, taking the one I'd rejected and carefully pouring out just enough to make the two equal.

"I'll probably be up all night," she said to me, "but not at the jakes."

I figured that, just like Bessie, the orphans used one of the stalls for their jakes. For a moment I mentally reviewed our housewares to see if we had a spare chamber pot but dismissed the idea as impractical. I'd been caught out on long walks often enough that I knew how to relieve myself in the wild and I don't think these orphans would think twice about it themselves.

I waited until the tea was all finished and then yawned hugely.

"Mary, go off with Billy and get some sleep," Meara said. As the two little ones moved out of earshot, she said to me, "There was a cloak —"

"It's mine," I told her.

"Mary didn't take it then?"

I shook my head. "You're welcome to it, to keep off the cold."

"It must be nice to have clothes to throw away," Meara said in a flash of bitterness.

"I don't," I told her, "I expect it back in the morning." I looked her up and down. "But you're about Bessie's size and she's going to get new clothes if we win tomorrow."

Bessie gasped at the news.

"I don't need —"

"Meara, shut yer gob," Mapes said, shaking his head. To me he said, "What she means to say is thank you, miss."

Beside me, Jamie stifled a laugh. I glared at him but Bessie smiled at the two of us.

I glanced at Mapes and frowned. "You're more my size than Jamie's —"

"I won't wear no dress!" Mapes cried throwing up his hands.

"Mapes, shut yer gob," Meara told him, waving a hand at me. "When have ye ever seen the lass in a dress?"

"But still —"

"It's getting cold, Mapes," I said, cutting him off. "Winter will be on us soon and what you're wearing won't last. There's no saying that I'll have anything your size, anyway."

Mapes relaxed just slightly. "It's just that you Scots are all for them silly dresses."

"That's the Highlanders," Jamie said, pointing down to his sturdy trousers.

"I saw them marching through with yer Prince," Mapes said. He shook his head solemnly. "I'll not dress like a girl."

"Don't ever say that to a Highlander," Jamie warned him. "Although as a Sassenach, they're sooner to split yer head than talk to you."

"Well, they're gone, they went south," Mapes said. He seemed happier as he added, "They couldn't get the castle, though."

I was more worried about the race tomorrow than the soldiers. They'd rushed through, hard on the heels of the English dragoons who'd fled for their lives and, finding the castle guarded, had gone on south and out of my thinking.

"Come on," I said to Jamie and Bessie, grabbing up the tea tray, "let's go."

"We'll shout again, if we hear anything," Meara called as we left.

"Miss," Bessie said, moving to get the tray from me, "that's my job."

"I'll not argue," I said, still holding the tray. Bessie made a noise but Jamie merely chuckled. "Leave her be, little Bessie, ye know she's practicing to be a maid."

In the kitchen once more, I made no protest as Jamie decided it was his turn on watch.

"Wake me if that bloody cock doesn't crow," I grumbled, lying my head against the pillow Bessie had brought down earlier and pulling her tight against my free side.

"I will."

#

"We'll not race until nightfall," father told Bessie when I rushed her upstairs at first light with a pot of tea and a slice of toast, "so tell that mistress of yours to leave me be."

Bessie curtsied and carried the tray back downstairs, relaying father's words to me when I saw her and started to berate her.

"I *told* you he'd call when he was ready," Jamie said with a satisfied smirk on his face.

A sound from the front door distracted us and I sent Bessie off to answer it. She came rushing back, all excited.

"There's men at the door!" she hissed at me. "They've got horses that want shoeing."

"Ach, that's easy enough," Jamie said, "send them through the archway and I'll meet them."

"I'll come with you," I said, moving to follow.

"Ye will not!" Jamie cried, turning back to block my path, his eyes flashing. "Ye'll stay inside. They're strangers Danni, and you know how people go on about you being a *girl*."

With a growl, I let him go, glancing through the kitchen window to watch.

There were three men, all mounted, all soldiers. Jamie nodded to them and they gave him alarmed looks — like they weren't too happy with a mere boy working on their horses. He pointed out the way to MacAllister's but apparently they'd already been there and liked not their reception.

They dismounted and I called to Bessie, "Bessie, go out there and see if they'd like some water."

"I could bring them the tea," she said, pointing at the pot that she'd brought down, still full, from father's room.

"Aye, may as well."

I helped her get ready, made sure she looked the part and held the door for her as she struggled outside with the tray.

"They could be up to no good, so keep your eyes open," I said as she left. Bessie nodded curtly. I bet her eyes flashed, too, with anger at my needless prodding but I could only see her back.

The soldiers looked around as she approached. Jamie waved to her and glanced quickly back to the kitchen, hiding a grin as he spotted me in the window. The soldiers — they were obviously officers — took the tea gladly and nodded with thanks, then said something to Jamie who spoke to Bessie who came rushing back to the kitchen.

"They say he's not fast enough," Bessie said as soon as she saw me. "You're to come out and help."

I was out the door before she'd finished but she caught my arm and pulled me back.

"Not with your hair like that!" she cried, rushing to the front hallway and grabbing a hat. She slapped it on my head, pushed my red hair under it and then turned me back to the door. "There! Don't flick your head too much or it'll fall out!"

"Lots of boys wear their hair long," I protested.

"Aye, and they do it up in a braid," Bessie agreed. "But we've not time."

I was out the door and moving quickly. I nodded to Jamie. "Which is next?"

"I've got the shoes heating," Jamie said, "take the mare."

I glowered at him but moved toward the indicated horse. She sniffed at the hand I raised to her and, satisfied, turned back to her master.

"You're lucky," the officer said, "she usually bites."

I said nothing, merely nodding and raising her near fore hoof to inspect it. The shoe was new and well-placed. I lowered the hoof and turned to catch Jamie's eyes. He nodded grimly — these horses didn't need shoeing.

The soldiers had walked off a bit, toward our walker, eyeing it carefully.

I moved away from the mare and back to Jamie to whisper, "What are they here for?"

Jamie shrugged.

"Tell them the horses don't need shoeing and send them on their way," I urged. Jamie looked alarmed.

"What sort of a thing is this?" the officer nearest our walker said, turning to Jamie.

"Ach, it's something my little sister thought of," Jamie said dismissively. "Merely a child's fancy, nothing more."

"Is she the lass that served us?"

"Nay, that was Bessie our maid," Jamie said easily.

"You must do well to have a maid and be able to make playthings for your sister," the officer observed.

I felt the hairs on my neck stand at his tone. I worried that these weren't any soldiers but tax collectors or such sort.

A raucous noise from the archway announced the arrival of our three shipwrights. They stopped talking the moment they spotted the three soldiers and moved forward more cautiously.

"Jamie!" Mr. Stoops called, "a good morning to you!"

"Your father's not about, I take it?" said Mr. MacArdle.

Mr. Henry grinned, "He was a wee bit free with the drink last night!"

The three sailors pretended to notice the soldiers for the first time.

"And who have we here?" Mr. MacArdle asked, moving quickly to the officer nearest our walker.

"Lieutenant Anderson," the young officer said, nodding curtly to the seamen. "And you are?"

"Ach, you're from down Prestonpans way, aren't you?" Mr. MacArdle said. "Your father's got a farm, there."

"Aye, and we were on our way there to meet the British," Mr. Anderson replied, relieved to learn that MacArdle was a local. He nodded toward the other two. "That's Lieutenant Cameron and Ensign Cameron, of the Lochiel regiment."

"A pleasure," Mr. MacArdle said, nodding toward the two men. "And you're off to fight the British? Prince's men?"

"King's men," Ensign Cameron corrected him. "We'll see King James restored to his throne."

"Is that why you want your horses re-shod?" I asked, unable to contain myself.

The two Camerons spun to face me, surprise on their face.

"You're no boy!" the lieutenant cried, moving to me and pulling off my hat.

I stepped away from him even as the three sailors shouted.

"Hey, leave off!" Mr. Stoops cried. "That's our Danni, and you're lucky to have her tend your horses."

"You?" Lieutenant Anderson said, moving from the walker to face me. His expression changed. "I've heard of you." He said to the others, "This is the one that works with the clockmaker, Mr. Pugh." He drew himself up and gave me a curt bow. "Miss Walker, I'd be honored if you'd do my horse's shoes."

"They really don't need them," I told him honestly. "Those shoes were well placed and they've miles of wear in them." I shook my head. "Honestly, ye'd be doing your mare a harm to have them replaced now." I gave him a probing look and added, "And a farmer's lad like you would have to know that."

The two Camerons looked surprised but Lieutenant Anderson merely laughed.

"Ach, ye've caught me out," he admitted. He waved to his friends. "We'd heard about this steam walker of yours and we wanted to see for ourselves."

"Well, if you're about tonight, come to the Grass Market and you'll see it racing against MacAllister's machine," Mr. MacArdle said, moving to stand protectively beside me. "But it would seem to me, that if your horses don't need shoeing, you should let the lad and the lass get back to their chores."

"We could pay you for your time," the older of the Camerons offered.

"We did nothing, there's no price," Jamie said. He glanced at the two. "Are you really Highlanders, then?"

"What, do ye not ken we are?"

"I've seen a few but never officers."

"Ach, well, ye'd best get used to seeing more," the younger one said with a laugh.

"And learn Gaelic, so's ye can speak properly," the older Cameron added with a grin.

"Or French, so's ye can speak to the Prince!" Lieutenant Anderson added with a strange, almost angry expression.

"I can speak French," I said. I nodded to Jamie, "So can he but his accent's atrocious."

"And how is it that you know that foreign tongue?" the elder of the Camerons demanded.

"Ach, well, we live in Edinburgh," Jamie said as if that explained it all.

"So, Anderson, you live near Edinburgh, how come you don't speak it?" the elder Cameron said.

Lieutenant Anderson flushed and said, "Well now, Allan, how do ye know I don't?"

The younger Cameron laughed at the expression of the older.

"Ensign," Lieutenant Anderson said to him, "it's not polite to laugh at your superiors."

"Sorry, sir," the ensign said.

The three retrieved their horses and made to mount them. Astride, Lieutenant Anderson turned to look at our walker.

"You know, I could ride underneath it and not touch my plume on the underside," he said thoughtfully. He turned to me. "And what's the view like from the top?"

I shrugged. "We haven't taken it all that far, only to MacAllister's and back."

"Well," Lieutenant Cameron said, "obviously you could see further from it than on a horse."

The three tipped their caps to me, nodded to the sailors and Jamie, and turned their horses toward the archway, walking slowly through it. A moment later, we could hear the horses break into a steady trot.

#

"That's all the better then," father said that night as we sat at dinner. "The soldiers will add to the betting, you can be certain."

I'd spent the rest of the day going over every inch of the boiler, engine, gears, and cables to make certain that everything would work. I was tired but excited and eager for the race.

"But, da, they know Danni's a girl!" Jamie said, casting a troubled look my way.

Father frowned. "So ye said," he replied, his eyes looking no less worried than Jamie's as he said to me, "Maybe it's best ye not come tonight."

"But father!"

He shook his head to stifle my protests but I wouldn't be silenced.

"There's no one who knows the engine and the boiler better than I," I reminded him. "If you want to win, you'll have me there."

Father sat back in his chair, stroking his chin in thought. He glanced at Jamie who shrugged in agreement. Finally, he sighed. "Very well, I suppose you're right."

Jamie shouted in delight and I wanted to join him but, knowing my father, I merely said, "Thank you, father."

"I'll steer, though," he said. "And if I tell you, you're to get down."

"Yes, father," I said demurely. A movement in the distance distracted me and I saw Bessie bobbing on her feet, her eyes imploring me. "I'll bring Bessie to stand in the crowd with my things, if needed."

The smile that blossomed on her face was payment enough for my effort.

We had just finished our tea when we heard the three sailors approaching.

Bessie answered the door but father told her to have them meet us in the courtyard and we went out through the kitchen, grabbing our gear.

"We saw MacAllister on our way over," Mr. Stoops said as we met him.

"Danni, Jamie, get up there and start the fires," father ordered when he heard this.

We needed no urging and soon had a good fire burning under the boiler while I switched the pressure plug for five atmospheres — I wanted to be sure we won.

#

In no time the boiler was making full steam. Father climbed up, looking about. He frowned.

"It will be dark by the time we get there," he said. He called down to Mr. MacArdle, "Would you hand us up some torches?"

"With pleasure, if we might keep one for ourselves," Mr. MacArdle replied.

"Please do."

As soon as the torches were secured, father turned to me and said, "Are we ready?"

"Yes, father."

"Then back us up slowly, and I'll turn us around," father said.

I gave the steam valve a quarter turn, saw the engine start to move, waited a moment and engaged the lever that connected the cables.

Slowly, our walker moved backwards, out into the courtyard, turning so that we were pointed toward the archway.

"Forward, now, Danni," father said, "same speed."

I disengaged the drive, and slid it into the forward. With a lurch and a creak, the walker stumbled forward.

"Aye, there's the lass!" Mr. Henry cried in joy as the walker started toward the archway.

When we were through, father turned us south, on the path toward the Grass Market.

We had not gone far when we saw a trail of steam coming toward us.

"It's Mr. MacAllister with his scuttler," Jamie called back from his position at the front, rather the 'bow' — as our shipwrights insisted — of our walker.

"Danni, more steam," father said. "Just a touch."

I donned my gloves and turned the steam valve open just a bit more.

Slowly our walker increased its pace. A breeze, like that on a horse at a good walk, wafted by. I was sorely tempted to open the valve full, imagining that we might go forward as fast as a horse at a trot.

The Scuttler hove into view. It was in front of us and merged onto the road.

"Slow her back down, Danni," father called. "We'll follow MacAllister's beastie."

Fair enough. I turned the valve back, still itching to see what we could do full out.

"Ho, Walker, you're slow!" Hamish bellowed from his steam platform.

"The race doesn't start until we're inside the market, Hamish," father called back.

"Well, don't make us wait too long," Hamish said, turning back to direct his machine.

"Danni, match his pace if you can," father called over his shoulder. With a grin, I turned up the valve a bit.

In a short while we were gaining on MacAllister and I backed off on the steam until we just matched its pace.

The Scuttler was every bit as ungainly as I'd thought it would be when I first designed it. One stiff leg would scuttle forward, then another, another, and the last. It looked like a four-legged spider scampering drunkenly. The platform lurched up and down with each leg and I was very glad I wasn't riding her, imagining how hard the motion would be on my stomach.

"Okay, now, Danni," father called, "slow us down as we're going through the arches."

I looked up and saw that we had already come upon the arches that opened into the Grass Market. My heart pounded faster and I was surprised to hear a huge crowd before us.

Time seemed to crawl as father navigated our way carefully through and under the arches. They were just a bit lower than the arches leading to our back yard but, fortunately, no narrower — not that we would get stuck; as I'd designed the walker to be just a bit wider than a regular cart, knowing full well how narrow were Edinburgh's streets.

And then we were through. Hamish's Scuttler was just in front of us and father turned our walker to come up beside it, telling me, "Get ready for full steam."

Jamie came back and stood by the power lever, ready to push it out to disengage the engine.

"Stop!" father called as we pulled even with Hamish's beastie and Jamie quickly kicked the power lever over, disengaging the engine while at the same time I turned the steam valve open.

"Hamish," father called loudly, "are ye ready?"

"Aye."

"To the far end and back, first one back wins," my father reminded him.

"To the end and back," Hamish agreed, smirking at us. "On my mark. Get set — go!"

Of course he had a faster start, being the one to call to his crew. I spotted Samuel who urged me to get moving. Without further urging, I turned the valve full open and shouted at Jamie, "Go!"

Jamie kicked in the engine and we lurched forward under full power for the first time.

"Whoa!" Jamie cried as he struggled to keep his balance. The walker bounded forward and caught up with the Scuttler. I could see Hamish shouting at Samuel and the others but in a few moments we were beyond them and the far end of the market was fast approaching.

"Slow us down!" Father shouted in my direction. "We'll want to slow down for our turn."

I turned the valve back down again and our walker settled back into a more sedate movement even as father started our turn. We had just finished when we heard a loud *crash* and our heads jerked behind us to see that the Scuttler had slammed into the house at the far end of the Grass Market.

"More steam!" father called, bringing me back to my business. I wrenched the valve full open and again we lurched forward, tearing off back the way we'd come.

"Slow down!" father called only a moment later. And then, "Stop!"

Jamie kicked over the power lever and we stopped. The roar of the crowd rose over the sound of the steam and I looked around to see the Scuttler barely a quarter of the way back.

We'd won.

"*Mon Dieu!*" a voice cried nearby. I turned and looked down to see an elegantly dressed, bewigged man staring up at us. But I had no more than a moment for my father's voice called out, "Hamish, I'd say ye lost the wager!"

From the Scuttler came a shout of anger and the sounds of MacAllister pounding on his apprentices. I was glad to see that Samuel was too close to the boiler to draw MacAllister's attention, leaving the other two apprentices to bear the bulk of MacAllister's wrath.

"It's not fair, Walker, we had an accident," Hamish called. "I'll have a rematch."

"And we'll be happy for it but the wager stands and you've lost," father called back. "If you want to try again another time, say for sixty guineas?"

Hamish's spluttered in fury.

I spotted the gallant Lieutenant Anderson near the bewigged gentleman and called out to him, "Lieutenant Anderson, could we trouble you to collect our winnings?"

"Ach, lass, it would be an honor!" the good lieutenant called, nodding to his superiors and striding over to the Scuttler. Hamish glared down at him but presently pulled a small bag from his pouch and handed it down. The lieutenant took it and brought it over to my father.

"Well done, sir," he said, handing up our winnings. In a voice for our ears alone, he added, "I'm glad I put my money with you and your lass."

Father took the purse and hefted it, checking its weight. He raised it toward Hamish, shouting, "So, Hamish, when do you want to try for sixty guineas?"

An unintelligible grumble came back in response.

"Well, let us know when and we'll see if we're able," father called. To me he said, "A quarter steam, Danni." I turned the valve as he said to Jamie, "Set us forward."

And slowly we made our way back under the archway, cheered by all Edinburgh.

Outside, I called to father, "Please can we go faster?"

Father shook his head. "No, Danni, we need to leave well enough alone."

And so we made our way slowly back home, under the arches and into the courtyard where we halted and I opened the relief valve to spill all our steam from the boiler.

I was itching to see how fast we could really go. I wanted to see what we could do and I had this notion that we could — like an oversized horse — try our hand at fences.

"See to the beastie," father said, "and then come in to bed."

"What?" Jamie and I cried in unison.

Father turned to us and smiled. "If ye think you've had excitement tonight, wait until the morning."

CHAPTER SIX

BUT THE MORNING BROUGHT RAIN, CLOUDS, AND COLD, DREARY WEATHER. IT WASN'T until midday that the rains broke and then it was still cold.

Bessie and father, however, were very busy throughout the day, answering the door and entertaining guests — most of whom shamefacedly deposited rather large bags of our winnings.

Jamie and I lounged around the forge. In truth, forced from the house to avoid the visitors, I longed for a chance to pour a decent cast and start work on a bigger, better engine. For, even with just the short run, I'd got some notions on how to make things better.

At lunchtime Mr. MacArdle, Mr. Henry, and Mr. Stoops appeared, escorted to the forge by father who nodded to me.

"I can see you're itching for work," he said to me and then nodded to the sailors. "They say they're ready for that engine we promised."

"Yes!" I cried. I turned to the shipwrights. "Have you got the copper, then?"

"It's on its way from the docks," Mr. Henry said. "But we wanted to talk with you about the engine."

I nodded. "You're thinking a sea engine?"

"Aye."

"So the biggest problem is keeping the fire from the decks," I said.

"We could use a furnace," Mr. Stoops said. "Like they use to heat shot."

Sometimes sailors in battle would heat up a cannon ball to fire it, flaming against the enemy in the hopes of setting the enemy ship alight. I'd learned that much in talking with the sailors.

"I was thinking of something like that," I agreed. "But I was also thinking of making the boiler better."

"It's just a boiler, what would you do?" Mr. MacArdle asked.

So I told them. I explained as how I'd noticed that if we could angle the boiler so that one part was closer to the flame, it would naturally set the water inside churning, heating it faster and more efficiently.

"I think it'd be better to go with what we know works," Mr. Henry said dubiously.

"You could," I agreed, thinking perhaps to give them the boiler from our walker and making the new one for ourselves.

"And so then the big problem is how to use the engine to move the ship," Mr. MacArdle said.

"Nay, it's still keeping the fire from setting the ship alight," Mr. Henry protested.

"We've got the same problem with the walker," I reminded them.

"No, not quite," Mr. Stoops objected. "You don't have to worry about a rough sea tilting the ship and the boiler."

I hadn't thought of that. I was itching for a stick of charcoal and paper, so I could draw out my ideas. Father must have noticed for he said to them, "I think we're going to have to leave Danni some time to think, gents. Perhaps you could come back in the morning?"

"You'll start on the new engine, though?" Mr. Henry asked hopefully.

"Let me think on that, too," I said to him. "After all, you're thinking of hooking it to a paddle, aren't you? Like a waterwheel?"

"Aye, that's the very thing!" Mr. Stoops agreed fervently.

I thought to mention my idea of using the Archimedes screw or something similar but decided against it — the shipwrights were a conservative lot, asking too much would probably scare them off altogether. But I'd no real idea of how to convert the back and forth motion of the steam engine into the circular motion of a waterwheel.

My musings were interrupted by the rush of horses charging under the archway. I recognized the three gallant officers I'd met the day before.

"The British have landed at Dunbar!" Lieutenant Anderson cried, jumping down from his horse. He swept off his hat and gave me a low bow. "We were hoping that you might sharpen our swords that they might fight for the King across the water."

Lieutenant Anderson and the two Cameron lads were quite dashing and I found myself blushing and nodding both.

Captain Cameron produced a gold guinea and pressed it into my hand.

"This won't cost that much, sir!" I cried in surprise, even as I turned to our sharpening stone.

"That's your part for introducing us to your marvelous machine," the captain replied, waving a hand in salutation to our rain-soaked walker. He grinned at me as he added, "We wagered quite heavily — and well."

"I'm flattered."

"You shouldn't be," Lieutenant Anderson said as he passed me his sword and I examined it, checking the structure of the blade, the cut of the edge. It was well-honed but could do with an extra edge. "Your work inspired us."

"And the Prince was most impressed," the other Cameron added, seeming upset that the others had dominated me in conversation.

"Gentlemen, if you'd prefer wait inside, I'm sure Bessie could make you a cup of tea."

"I'd prefer watch the master at work," Lieutenant Anderson said gallantly.

"Unless you'd like a cup yourself?" the younger Cameron suggested, looking around the gloomy yard. "Do ye?"

"Well," I said, trying to hide my blush, "I wouldn't say no."

And so the younger Cameron strode briskly across the yard to the kitchen while the other two gathered around the sharpening stone, watching intently as I spun it up faster and faster with my foot.

I laid a good fine edge on Lieutenant Anderson's sword and had started on Captain Cameron's when the younger Cameron returned with Bessie toting a tray alongside.

"Take a rest, you've earned it," lieutenant Cameron said but I shook my head, "I've just started on this blade, it'd be wrong to stop until it's finished."

They all gathered around while I finished up Captain Cameron's sword and then insisted that I take some tea, "While it's still warm."

I was happy to do so and thanked Bessie who looked askance at the three gallant highlanders. I could tell she was having a harder time following their speech than she did mine.

"You ought to say something to her in Gaelic," I said to the younger Cameron. "She's English born and doesn't know a word."

Well, if it was a cold day before, you'd swear it'd had started snowing for the reaction they gave that news.

"What?" I said, looking up at them. And then, from their expressions, I caught on. Haughtily, I told them, "Bessie's loyal to me and this house."

There was a silence in which I beckoned for the younger Cameron's sword. He blushed and passed it to me.

"We don't mean no harm by it, Miss," he said to me, glancing to Bessie. "It's just that — well, we're all a bit scared."

"Ye needn't be," I told him, as I finished putting a fine edge on his sword, "your blade will cut through anything."

I passed it back to him and nodded to the other two.

Lieutenant Anderson nodded in response and gestured toward the others. "We'd best be off," he said, turning to his horse only to stop in surprise as he realized it was gone. He turned back to me and I laughed at him, shaking my head, "Well, you don't think Jamie'd leave it in the rain when there are perfectly good stalls nearby!" I turned toward the stables and shouted, "Jamie, the horses if you would!"

In a moment Jamie came out, leading the three horses. Lieutenant Anderson rushed over to them, taking his and mounting quickly. The two Camerons were nearly as quick and, with one final dashing wave of their hats, burst forward into a trot.

"Long live the King!" they cried before they were out of earshot.

"Aye," said Bessie, "but which one?"

I hardly heard her for I was watching the sharpening stone spinning slowly to a stop, watching the rise and fall of the foot crank, my eyes unfocused. "That's it!"

#

"So our paddle wheel will be like your grinding stone," Mr. Stoops said after I'd finished my explanation to them, two days later.

"And the steam engine will be your foot, going up and down," Mr. MacArdle added, his head cocked to one side as if not certain of his words.

"Precisely," I said.

"Only instead of being up and down, it'll be forward and back," Mr. Henry added.

I nodded and smiled at them. The three looked at each other, then Mr. Henry said, "Aye lass, that could work."

"What do we need, then?" Mr. Stoops asked, looking at me and then the others. "A strong beam, a shaft, and the wheel itself?"

"No, you're going to need a smaller wheel on one end of the shaft that the engine will turn," I said. "The stroke of the engine's not enough to turn a large wheel, but it can turn the shaft the big wheel's on."

I pointed at my sketch and one by one, they nodded.

"When can you get started?" Mr. Henry asked.

"When can you get me the parts?"

"When can you get us a ship, Mr. Henry?" Mr. MacArdle added.

"Aye, there's the rub," Mr. MacArdle agreed with a shake of his head. He looked at me. "What you're describing, lass, it couldn't be easily undone if it doesn't work."

I shrugged. I'd never thought of undoing the work.

"That means that we'll need a ship we won't mind losing," Mr. MacArdle continued.

"That'd be the *Rosemary's Way*," Mr. Henry said. He turned to me, "Unless we could do this in something smaller?"

"You see how big the boiler is and we've got to add protection to keep it from setting the ship alight," Mr. Stoops said, shaking his head. "*Rosemary's Way* is about the smallest."

"Aye, but she's a witch," Mr. MacArdle said. He explained to me, "She's more of a wreck than a ship."

"She's the only thing we've got," Mr. Henry reminded him.

The two others exchanged glances and Mr. Stoops blew out a heavy sigh. "So be it."

"When can ye get started?" Mr. MacArdle said to me. "You've got the ship whenever you want."

"We'll pull her out of the water and I'll set a gang to re-caulking her beams," Mr. Henry said. He gave a small smile as he added, "The lads could use the work."

"Can you get me the plans for her?" I asked. They all looked at me, so I explained, "I need to know where we'll place the engine and the boiler. I assume will put the wheel amidships."

"I don't know if she *has* plans," Mr. MacArdle said.

"I'll get Morgan to draw us a set," Mr. Henry said. He winked at me. "We'll need 'em for the patents, won't we?"

I smiled at him. Patents for a steam-powered sea-going vessel would be worth quite a bit.

Mr. Stoops dipped his head as he said, "I'm sorry we can't put your name on them."

Women weren't allowed to do such things. If I were married, I could get my husband to file patents for me. Mr. Henry had told me so, adding a light-hearted offer of his own. Fortunately father had been out of the room, not that Jamie's reaction was much better. He'd nearly laughed himself sick even as I'd told Mr. Henry that I already had an understanding.

"An understanding?" Jamie had repeated later when the sailors had left. "With whom?" I looked at him and he froze. "Not Samuel Cattan?"

"He's a nice lad," I agreed.

"But he doesn't even own his clothes!" Jamie cried. "Do you think he'll ever be in a position to ask for your hand?"

"Jamie," I said, leaning close to him, "shut up."

Now, however, none of that mattered. I was going to make another boiler and a new engine. I was excited.

#

"Why are you always changing things?" Jamie complained as we contemplated the working before us. "Wasn't the last boiler good enough?"

"It was good, this is better," I told him.

"Aye, if it doesn't blow up," Jamie muttered.

Father had examined each step we'd taken and had grudgingly approved my suggestions. It was apparent that he was unhappy but it took me a while to realize why. Actually, it was Jamie who explained it to me, "You've gone beyond him."

"What?"

"What you're doing," Jamie said, waving at the giant castings we'd built, "it's beyond him, Danni."

"But —"

"And you're using steel, you figured out how to get our forge hot enough to melt it in bulk so we can make this casting —"

"Bronze isn't strong enough!"

"I know that, even father knows that," Jamie shot back just as hotly. "But you're doing stuff no one's done before, Danni, and it worries him."

I had no answer for that. I was always trying something new and father had been the first to encourage me. I couldn't grasp that I'd run beyond him.

"Well, the metal's hot enough, it's time to pour," I told him.

"Aye," Jamie said, moving with me to the forge and helping me pull on the ropes that moved the huge cauldron off the intense fires that were fanned by the sets of bellows we'd rigged just for that purpose.

We centered the cauldron over the mold and switched to the ropes used to tilt it. Slowly the red-hot molten steel poured into the mold. I checked all around to be certain that the mold was holding and breathed a sigh of relief when I saw not one drop below.

"Well, we'll let that set now," I said to Jamie, pulling off the thick gloves I'd donned for protection.

"So we'll have this new-fangled boiler of yours, then what?"

"Then we test it."

#

Between working on the new steel — something that we could get cheap enough because a fellow Scot, Mr. Neilson, had perfected an efficient way to fuel hot-blast furnaces — and making the molds, I'd spent a great deal of time with Mr. Pugh, talking about gears, wheels, and pressure valves. We'd decided that my original design was flawed and came up with a much better design, one where we could add weights to increase the pressure in the boiler while also adding a relief valve. Mr. Pugh had convinced me to add a whistle and the three shipwrights had heartily agreed to the addition, considering the idea much better than a ship's bell for warning of fog.

Of course, once the pour had cooled, the real work began. We had to break the mold open, gingerly move the cast steel out, refurbish the mold for the second pour — because the boiler was made of two halves — and, at the same time, get to work with metal files to smooth the various jaggies and other irregularities left over from the mold.

After that, we could start fitting in the pipework. That had to wait until we were finished with the second pour and had cleared that half of the boiler of jaggies. We cut out a nice felt gasket to make the seal between the two halves and carefully joined them, tightening the bolts around them in careful order so that we didn't buckle either half.

Finally, we had the basic boiler all put together and were ready to try some simple tests.

Temporarily, we had mounted the boiler on a separate stand which we'd cobbled together from bricks. Underneath we built a fire of coal and stoked it up, with the lowest pressure valve. It didn't take long for the valve to pop so we came back and added the next weight. When that popped, we repeated it for three, four, and five atmospheres.

The sailors were thrilled when we popped the valve at five atmospheres and insisted that we give the whistle a try before we tested up at eight atmospheres — the last level before a full ten atmosphere test which would be at twice the normal level.

We'd rigged the whistle so that we could pull a rope.

The seamen all had to have a go after I'd first tried it. They tooted and tooted on that whistle until we were low on steam.

"I think that's enough, lads," I told them. "We've got to let her cool off now."

What we didn't expect was a horseman galloping up. It was Lieutenant Anderson, looking all bothered.

"What was that infernal racket?"

"Just a whistle," I said. "It's not a bother, is it?"

"Bother?" Anderson cried, gesturing to the hilltop behind us. "You've got the whole garrison watching you!"

We all turned around as one and looked up the hilltop. As sure as day, there were hundreds of soldiers looking down from the ramparts in our direction.

Lieutenant Anderson. "His Highness thought that perhaps the gates of hell had opened and Cerberus was howling."

"It *is* a deep note," Mr. Henry said by way of agreement.

"I wouldn't have thought Cerberus, though," Mr. Stoops said. He turned to the lieutenant. "That's the three-headed beast that guards the gates to the underworld, isn't it?"

"The very same," Lieutenant Anderson agreed fervently. He looked to me and then to the boiler. "And how is it you make that noise?"

I explained and showed him the rope but told him that there wasn't enough pressure to make it whistle.

"Well enough, his Highness was most upset," Lieutenant Anderson. He glanced up at the ramparts where the troops were slowly dispersing, adding thoughtfully, "Though not as much as General Guest and his crew."

"Ye're not thinking of storming the Castle, are you sir?" Mr. Henry asked with wide eyes.

"Well, if we were, wouldn't it be good to have the Brits distracted?" the lieutenant replied. He glanced over at our first steam walker. "Could you put a whistle on that?"

"What and confuse the Brits into thinking we've got Cerberus on our side?" Mr. Stoops asked. "I don't think they're that stupid."

"You want to distract them," I said, "and then what? Where would you attack?"

"The gates are the only place," Mr. Stoops said.

"If you could plant a charge, you might breach them but you'd have to be certain they couldn't get to it before it went off," Mr. Henry allowed thoughtfully. Lieutenant Anderson gave him a piercing look and Mr. Henry explained, "I've been a gunner a time or two."

Lieutenant Anderson gestured to our steam walker. "Could you mount a cannon on that?"

"What?" I cried even as Mr. Henry's eyes grew thoughtful. "Why would you want to do that?"

"A three pounder, no more," Mr. Henry said a moment later.

"Some swivels?"

"Swivels, too, and some riflemen, perhaps," Mr. Stoops added.

"Could you carry the explosives under her belly?" Mr. MacArdle wondered, looking at me. "Put 'em on a sling and lower them when you get to the gates, then back off."

"Get MacAllister's thing to scuttle out on this back wall with a whistle to startle 'em," I said, drawn in against my will. Then I shook my head. "But ye'd never — I don't think she'd be up to all that weight."

"Won't know 'til you try, lass," Mr. Stoops said. He glanced at the thick legs. "Your walker seems sturdy enough, much better than MacAllister's."

All too true. Even though I knew the seaman was playing on my pride, I couldn't help nod in agreement.

"This must be brought to the attention of His Highness," Lieutenant Anderson said, climbing back into his saddle. He waved his hat at us and then clapped his heels to his horse's flank and they were off.

"Well, that was interesting," Mr. Stoops said as horse and rider disappeared. He gestured toward the cooling boiler. "I suppose now, Miss Walker, ye'll be starting on our engine?"

"We've already started," I said, pointing toward where Jamie and I had been working on the molds. "We'll pour the cylinder tomorrow and the piston the next day."

"And when will it be ready?" Mr. Henry asked.

"Ach, George! Leave off or ye'll reduce her to nothing but skin and bones —"

"She's that already," Mr. Henry protested.

"Excuse me!" I cried, going bright red in indignation.

"Ach, lass, ye ken they're just pulling your leg to see if it'll come off," Mr. MacArdle told me with a laugh. He gave me a scrutinizing look before adding, "Not that they're not right, ye ken. Ye could use some more feeding."

The three of them were so eager for their engine that they insisted on doing all they could to help. In short order I discovered that they all had some understanding of molds and pouring and so I had them help us, particularly in melting the steel for the pour.

By the next morning, we were two days ahead of schedule — and didn't know how lucky we were.

Father, Jamie, and I were just finishing breakfast in the kitchen when a loud clatter of hooves trotting alerted us to the approach of a platoon of horseman.

"It's the King!" Bessie yelped from the front room.

"It can't be the King, he's in France!" I cried, wondering what possessed the girl.

"It could be King George, ninny!" Jamie retorted, making a face at me.

"Whoever it is," my father replied, rising from the table, "we've guests and should behave accordingly." He turned to shout at Bessie, "Make us a fresh pot of tea and see what else you can set out, Bessie!" To us he said, "Come, let us greet our guests."

I spotted the heads of my new orphans disappearing into the stables as the group of horsemen emerged from under the arch into our courtyard.

I gasped in astonishment as I took in all the finery arrayed before me. Bessie was almost right — it wasn't the King but I was most certain that the figure in the finest clothes was Prince Charles Stuart.

"Close your mouth," Jamie hissed at me.

"Bow," Father said to him. "Curtsy," he told me.

That was easier said than done as I was in trousers, ratty ones at that, ready for the day's work.

Prince Charles caught sight of our steam walker and gabbled to the older gentleman next to him, "*C'est encroyable, n'est-ce pas?*"

I glowed with delight that the Prince would consider our walker incredible.

"*Certainement,*" the other replied in passable French. The scowl on his face was at odds with his words. His next words made his doubts clear. "*Ça marche?*"

"*Oui, monsieur generale, ça marche,*" I replied moving forward. "*Ça marche trés bien.*" It works very well!

"It won the race," Lieutenant Anderson added from his station two horses back. In poor French he added, for the benefit of the prince, "*Il a gagné la course.*"

"*Je me souviens,*" Prince Charles replied with a dismissive wave of his hand. Of course he'd remember, he was there! He turned toward the general, "*Va il suffit?*"

"If not, sir, we lose nothing but the attempt," Lieutenant Anderson put in urgently.

"And if it does, we secure our rear," another officer added.

"Excuse me," father said, stepping forward, "but what are you talking about?"

"And you are?" the older gentleman asked.

"Daniel Walker, I own this property," father said with a curt nod. "And that's my walker."

"We were thinking, sir," Lieutenant Anderson said hastily, "that perhaps we could commission it into service."

"Service?"

"This young lad has suggested that your 'walker' might be used to assault the castle," the older gentleman said, glowering at Lieutenant Anderson. He pursed his lips tightly then added, "I have my doubts, personally."

"We'd lose nothing, sir!" Lieutenant Anderson protested.

"I'd think that, first, you'd want to see if you could secure my permission for such a rash enterprise, gentlemen," father said acerbically.

"*Pour le roi?*" the Prince asked. For the King?

"And how would this aid the king?"

"It would remove the garrison as a thorn in the Prince's back while he fights to regain the throne for his father," the older gentleman said rather stiffly.

"Lord Murray is right, sir," Lieutenant Anderson said. "You'd be doing your monarch a great service." He paused. "One which doubtless would be remembered."

"Providing we win," father added caustically.

Lord Murray snorted in agreement. "Precisely, sir!" He glanced toward the steam walker. "Can your contraption do it?"

"It's not the contraption I'm worried about, it's the people," father said.

"We could man it with troopers," Lieutenant Anderson offered.

"Ye could not!" I cried. "Why the first one to lay hands on —"

"Danielle!" Father's tone was quelling. He never called me Danielle unless he was very angry. "Ye'll not talk that way to these gentlemen."

His eyes held a look of warning that I couldn't decipher. He turned to the Prince. "I am but a poor worker. The walker represents a significant investment on my part."

"Ye'll be paid, if that's what ye're asking," Lord Murray said.

"My daughter spoke rashly but she is not wrong: this contraption takes skill, patience and an engineer's training," father continued, unashamed.

"If the plan works, sir, we may want more of them," Lieutenant Anderson said. He glanced toward Lord Murray. "If for nothing more than to awe the enemy's cavalry."

Lord Murray's look grew less hostile and more thoughtful.

At this point Bessie staggered out of the kitchen bearing a full tray and a pot of tea.

"Help her, girl!" father hissed at me. I gave him an angry look — I'd taken on Bessie particularly to relieve me of such work — and trotted over. I relieved her of the pot and gave her a reassuring smile.

"It's all right, he won't eat you," I told her with a wink.

"Why not?" she cried in a small voice. "I'm English, aren't I?"

"You're in my care," I told her. "And he wants our walker; he wouldn't be foolish enough to upset us." All the same, I added, "Just keep your mouth shut."

Bessie whimpered quietly in response.

With her holding the tray, I served up tea in our best dishware, offering the first cup up to the Prince.

"Better let me try, first," Lieutenant Anderson said, motioning to me. With a wink, he added, "In case it's poisoned."

Having sipped the tea, he pronounced it pleasant and I brought the cup to the Prince who took it awkwardly, then passed it back to me. My eyebrows rose in confusion until he dismounted and came around his horse to me.

As he got down, so did the rest of the party, including the stuffy Lord Murray who stalked off over toward the steam walker, eyeing it dubiously.

I served him last, bringing the cup over to him.

"This will really move?" he asked me as he took the cup.

"Aye, sir, it will," I told him. I explained about the boiler and the engine and how the cables pulled on the legs.

"Just like a horse walking, then," he said as he looked at the huge wooden beams that were its legs. He turned back to me. "Can it trot?"

"Oh, I don't know sir," I told him honestly. "Aside from the one race, we've not done much with it."

"Hmm," he said thoughtfully. "I think it would be a very good idea to see how fast it can go, particularly compared to a horse."

"Well," I said dubiously, "we're working on the ship engine right now, so we're rather distracted."

"Ship engine?"

"Aye, sir, an engine adapted for ships."

"And how does that work?"

I told him and watched with a combination of increasing pride and fear as his eyebrows rose higher and higher on his forehead.

"And how fast would this vessel go?"

"We've no idea," I told him honestly. "We've yet to assemble the engine to see if it even works."

"And how is it that you, a mere strip of a girl, know such things?"

"My father had me helping out Mr. Pugh the watchmaker in return for lessons."

"Lessons?"

"Yes sir," I told him. "French, geography, mathematics, physics, Latin, whatever came up."

"You can read?"

"Can't everyone, sir?" I replied. "The Calvinists believe that everyone should be able to read."

"Not so much girls," Lord Murray said to himself. Of me, he asked, "Are you a Calvinist, then?"

"Not so much, sir," I replied. "They asked me to stop coming."

"Asked you to stop coming?"

"They said I asked too many questions, sir."

Lord Murray snorted. "Hoist by their own petard, I should say!" He glanced back at the steam walker and then to me. "If this works as you say it does, it could change the ways of war."

"Sir?"

"Cavalry would be no match for it, it could carry guns right up to the battlements of any castle."

"It wasn't built for that, sir."

"What do you mean?" He asked me suspiciously.

"I just mean, sir, that if you want to do a good job you should have the proper tools." I pointed at the steam walker. "That's not the right tool for what you're talking about."

"Yes," he agreed soberly. "I rather doubt it is."

A call from the others caused us to turn and we saw the Prince beckoning to Lord Murray.

"Excuse me," he said, pushing the cup back into my hands and marching back to the others.

I trailed behind him, placing the half-drunk cup on a stump near the stables — I knew one of the orphans would take it and I expected the cup to be returned.

#

Father gave me the job of attaching our new whistle to MacAllister's Scuttler while he and the seamen worked with our walker and the prince's soldiers for their assault on the castle.

MacAllister, either drunk or drunk with fear, proved no use and it was myself and Samuel who did the bulk of the work. MacAllister would mutter to himself and wave his arms importantly but that was the extent of it.

"We'll have to drill into the boiler," I said to Samuel, shaking my head.

"We've got a hand-drill, so that's no problem," Samuel said.

"You're not thinking!" I swore at him. "It'll weaken the boiler."

"Only a little," Samuel said.

"Tap in a screw thread and I'll put one on the whistle, so we'll be able to screw it in tight," I said, still feeling uneasy about the whole operation. That was my first boiler and I wasn't sure what sort of sound we'd get out of it with just the one atmosphere of pressure.

Samuel got his drill and began the difficult task of hand-drilling on a spherical boiler. I got the threading gear, put the whistle in a vice and started the slow project of whittling screw threads into the pipe.

"I'm working with a quarter inch bit," Samuel said, glancing over as I set the width of the thread-cutter.

"That's good," I replied. "It shows ye've got some sense."

Samuel reddened slightly and put his weight to his work but the drill bit slid around the corner.

"Put a notch in with an awl, first, ye ninny!" I told him as I worked hard to twist the thread-cutter around the pipe, grunting with the effort.

He glowered at me even as the other apprentices standing nearby all snickered at him. He turned to one of them and said, "You there, Jenkins, get a punch."

Jenkins looked toward MacAllister who was oblivious to the whole thing, then trotted over to the tools cabinet and back again with the appropriate punch and, unasked, a small hammer.

Samuel took them both with a scarce nod and proceeded to punch a small dent in the boiler's surface. He handed the two tools back to Jenkins and picked up his drill once more.

"Jenkins," I called, finally wondering why I was doing MacAllister's work for him when he had perfectly good apprentices to hand, "come here and take over."

Jenkins gave me a wide-eyed look but I nodded firmly to him and he scuttled over.

"I've never done this, miss," he told me in an undertone.

"Well, it's about time you learned," I said, wondering to what purpose MacAllister put his apprentices if not to cutting thread when needed. "And you're lucky I've got it started."

I guided his hands to the tool and showed him how to turn it.

"It's important that you keep straight and level or the threads will be crooked and it won't fit," I told him, showing him how.

Jenkins took a deep breath and took over from me. He made a mistake right off and shot me a terrified look but I told him, "Just back up a bit and start again."

Slowly but much more quickly than my tired muscles would have managed, the worried apprentice managed to turn out an inch's worth of screw thread.

"Well done," I told him. "Now back off just as straight and slowly as that'll put the final thread on it."

I turned to the other apprentice, wondering what required MacAllister to need three of them? Did the man do *no* work of his own? And, if so, why was it that one of his apprentices — no, two by the admiring look of the other — knew nothing of cutting screw threads?

"You, do you have any glue?"

"Glue?" the lad repeated, bug-eyed. He looked no more than eight and underfed at that.

"For the threads," I said, gesturing at the whistle. "With the glue, we'll be able to hold it in better."

"Ain't got no glue," MacAllister said. "Not a cabinet-maker, missy." He seemed to find that funny and chuckled darkly to himself.

"Tar, then," I said. "Surely you use it on your joining?"

"Ain't no cabinet-maker," MacAllister repeated dully. Drunk, for certain.

"Can I send your boy to our place to get some?"

"No need," MacAllister said. "Your whistle will work fine without it." In a lower tone, he mumbled, "Slip of a girl! Knows nothing of the craft!"

"Without the glue or tar at least, the chance of the whistle twisting free increases, Mr. MacAllister," I told him coldly. "Do you want it to blow off?"

"No glue," MacAllister grumbled, climbing down from his scuttler and trundling inside.

"Gone for more lubricant," Samuel said in a low voice to me. "Can you rig that thread-cutter for the bore?"

"Jenkins, have you got it off yet?" I asked.

"Just now, miss," Jenkins said, handing the tool to me. "I don't see how you can use it for the inside."

"Ach, it's easy," I said, turning the tool in my hand and going to the cabinet. "We swap out these outside teeth for these inside teeth."

It required concentration and the light was low but I managed it and passed it over to Samuel.

"Cut true, Samuel Cattan."

"Of course, Danni Walker," he said, raising the thread-cutter to his head and saluting me with it.

Ten minutes later, the work was done and we screwed the whistle into the threaded hole.

"Samuel, if you'd get some pliers to tighten it down," I said, standing back and inspecting the result with satisfaction. Samuel sent the second apprentice, Malcolm Reynolds, off to get the pliers and tightened the whistle in well. When he was done, I took them and tested the fit myself.

"Ye don't trust me?" Samuel asked, sounding hurt.

"Do you want to be baked in raw steam?" I asked. I shook my head at the whistle, adding, "I really wish we had proper glue."

"But if you glued it in, miss, how would you get it out?" young Reynolds asked after he finished clambering back up.

"Glue only helps a bit," I told him. "A good pair of pliers will still get out it again."

"I'd best let the master know we're done, then," Samuel said, wiping his hands on his trousers and preparing to clamber off the Scuttler.

"I've a better idea," I told him with a grin. He raised an eyebrow at me skeptically. The eyebrow rose even higher when I'd finished explaining. To convince him, I added, "It'd be a *proper* test."

"I'll get the coal!" Jenkins offered, running off to the coal shed.

Pretty soon we had a good head of steam in the boiler. I nodded to Samuel, "You've the first honors."

Samuel looked at me as I handed him the pull rope. He looked at the other apprentices and then, with a wince, pulled the rope, hard.

Scree! The sound rent the air and filled the stables, startling the horses and apprentices both.

The sound was nothing like the sound we got with the proper boiler but it was loud enough.

"What in the name of heaven?" MacAllister roared, staggering out of his house and looking around frantically. He spotted the glow of the fire and us atop the Scuttler.

"Just testing the whistle, Mr. MacAllister," I said, yanking the rope from Samuel's hands. MacAllister looked angry enough to whip whoever had woken him but I figured he'd think twice about putting a hand to me.

"Very clever, missy," MacAllister said, lumbering toward the Scuttler and slowly climbing aboard. "Show me."

"Don't we want to save it for later?" I said.

"You won't be here later," MacAllister said, "so show me."

I gave him the rope and told him, "Just pull."

MacAllister pulled sharply and just as quickly let go of the rope with a jerk as the whistle — and whatever he'd been drinking — nearly split his skull with its noise.

"Good," he said, glancing at his boys. "Get it out of the yard and on the road."

"Yes sir," Samuel said, with an obsequious nod. MacAllister gave me one last glower and then clambered down. On the ground, he called up to me, "Ye can run on home to your daddy, now girl."

I expected no words of thanks but his tone made it clear that he resented my presence.

"A good evening to you then, Mr. MacAllister," I said, climbing on down. On the ground, I glanced up at the apprentices. "And a good evening to you too, gentlemen."

"Gentlemen!" MacAllister scoffed. "I suppose they're gentlemen in your eyes."

His tone angered me and it must have shown in my eyes.

"Ye're getting old enough to be wed," MacAllister said, eyeing me appraisingly, "so ye should know now that none of them is gentleman enough for you, lassie."

His eyes continued to slither over me. I didn't like it. I turned and walked away quickly, aware that he was staring after me — and that he was aware that I knew it, too.

#

I was halfway down the road when I heard the Scuttler lumber out of MacAllister's and on to the dirt road that wound around below the far side of the Castle.

I had to jump off the road as a horse came galloping by but its rider reined it to a halt and looked down at me.

"Miss Walker?" Lieutenant Anderson asked, eyes wide. "Why are you alone at this hour?"

"Just going back home," I told him.

"I thought you were with Mr. MacAllister and the Scuttler," he said, looking down the road. He glanced back toward our house. "I've just come from your father's. They've already left. They're probably in the Hay Market or further by now." He seemed thoughtful, then bowed in his saddle. "If you wouldn't consider it an affront, I could offer you a ride to the Scuttler."

"I'd prefer go to my father," I told him, looking anxiously to the dimness of the Hay Market. It would take forever to get there on foot but minutes on horseback.

"I'm afraid I've been ordered to attend to the Scuttler," Lieutenant Anderson said. "And your father was quite specific that you were not to take part in the attack on the castle." He pursed his lips. "And I must say that I am in complete agreement."

I sniffed. It was my Walker!

"It would be a tragedy if any harm were to befall you," Lieutenant Anderson explained. He reached down a hand. "Come, I must insist. It's not right for you to wander the roads in the darkness."

I had no choice, really. I reached up an arm and jumped as he tugged on it. In one fluid moment, I was seated behind him on his horse. With a quick cry, he set the horse into motion.

Minutes later we'd caught up with the Scuttler. It was stopped and off the road. I heard MacAllister's bellowing before we'd halted.

"Mr. MacAllister," Lieutenant Anderson cried, "what seems to be amiss?"

"These buggers got us off the road!" MacAllister roared. I heard the sound of leather whistling and the piercing shriek of one of the apprentices as a whip hit him hard. "We can't move."

I jumped down before the Lieutenant could react and clambered up the side of the Scuttler.

"You!" MacAllister said, raising his whip arm in surprise.

"Let me see what can be done," I said, grabbing MacAllister's whip and deftly pulling it out of his hand. "You won't be needing that. You might get it caught in the cables."

I glanced around and looked over as I heard a noise coming from the side. It was Lieutenant Anderson. He arrived, wide-eyed.

"Is there anything I can do?" he offered.

"Which one of you rides?" I asked, looking at the apprentices. My eye settled on Mr. MacAllister. "Sir, if you would, Lieutenant Anderson's horse needs be led away."

"This is my —" MacAllister began hotly.

"Then, sir, select one of your apprentices," I told him, turning away from him and bending to look at the cabling. The Scuttler was less complicated than the Walker but that didn't mean that it couldn't be mired. In fact, it was more likely so. "Samuel," I called out decisively, "switch that cable there and then apply power."

"Missy, ye're not giving orders here!" MacAllister swore.

"Fine," I told him, getting ready to climb down. "If you think you can get this sorted yourself, I'll leave you to it."

"Ach, have it your way, then!" MacAllister swore, jumping off the platform and stumbling as he hit the ground. "I'll take the lieutenant's horse."

Slowly, steadily, we got the Scuttler back on the road.

"Do you know what to do now?" I said to Samuel.

"No," he said. "Mr. MacAllister insisted on steering it himself."

That explained how it got mired, I thought.

"Well, it's not hard," I said. "Get over there," I told him, pointing to the center of the controls. I pointed at the first one. "That controls the direction, left and right." I pointed at the steam valve. "And that controls the speed but don't go too fast."

With his lips pursed tightly, Samuel released the steam valve and took hold gingerly of the steering. "Like this?"

Slowly, the Scuttler lurched its way down the road, Samuel making corrections jerkily.

"That's it," I encouraged. "Just don't be afraid of it." I looked around for the other apprentices. "Jenkins, more coal. Reynolds, grab the whistle."

"Me, miss?" Reynolds asked in surprise.

"Or you, lieutenant," I offered.

"I think I'll just watch, miss," Lieutenant Anderson said. He glanced down at the ground below and then back to me. "Can it go faster?"

"The Scuttler?" I snorted, shaking my head. Then I thought better of it. "Maybe a little."

"It's time for the whistle," the lieutenant said, instead. "Make it a loud, long sound, if you can."

"Me?" Reynolds squeaked, looking white even in the darkening sky.

"Just pull and hold," I told him with a grin. "Jenkins, pile on the coal, we'll need it for the steam." I sidled over to Samuel. "Have we enough water in the boiler?"

"I filled it halfway," he replied, "just as you said."

"Good," I replied. I had no idea how long half a boiler of steam would last, particularly when using the whistle.

A loud, long, piercing cry split the evening sky and steam rose from the whistle.

"I need some torches," Lieutenant Anderson said. "We're to make noise and light, to distract the garrison."

"There, sir," said Reynolds, pointing to a sack at the prow of the Scuttler.

"Good," Anderson said. He glanced to me. "Perhaps you'd care to help."

I nodded and the two of us lit torches, placing some of them in the holders that had been nailed on earlier and holding others over our heads, waving them in the night darkening sky while Reynolds made the whistle hoot and roar.

"Samuel, turn around and let's go back the way we came," I said, as the Scuttler neared my home.

"Turn around?"

"Slow down, then pull all the way on one lever," I instructed.

We turned and, gaining confidence, Samuel increased our speed once more as we started back the way we'd come.

"I can see them," Anderson said, looking up at the parapets lining this side of the castle. "Can you count them?"

"In this light?" I complained. I squinted. "It looks like a lot."

"All the guard?" the lieutenant asked hopefully.

"Maybe."

"Good," he said. "The more of them looking at us, the less looking for the attack."

"And when will that be?"

"Mr. Reynolds, are you prepared to strike a blow for Bonnie Prince Charlie?"

"Sir?"

"Three hoots, quick hoots, on that whistle and you'll start the attack," Lieutenant Anderson told him.

"No, Reynolds, come here and take that torch from the lieutenant," I said. To the lieutenant, I said, "I think the honor is yours, sir."

The lieutenant beamed at me and moved back to the boiler, grabbing the whistle's rope. He looked back at me. "I just pull?"

"That's all," I assured him.

He pulled once, twice, three times in quick succession, holding the whistle open on the final pull till our ears seemed ready to bleed from the noise.

"More coal!" I shouted above the din to Jenkins. I moved to grab the second shovel and started throwing in more of the coal to feed the fire. I looked at the rapidly diminishing pile of coal with worry.

All too soon we were out and, slowly the whistle began to change its pitch and the Scuttler to lose its speed.

"Samuel!" I shouted. "Slow down!"

"Can ye see the flag?" the lieutenant bellowed. "Can ye see it?"

It was there a minute ago. I glanced back toward the flagpole. It was night, weren't they supposed to pull it down?

Suddenly a light shimmered and a shape appeared on the pole.

"There's a white flag!" I cried.

"That's it! That's it!" Lieutenant Anderson roared, letting go the whistle. "They won! The castle is ours!" He grabbed me into his arms and hugged me tightly. "We did it, lass, we did it!"

I allowed myself to be crushed against him. It felt good. A moment later, and I saw the look in Samuel's eyes and pushed back.

The lieutenant seemed to realize that he'd overreached himself and turned scarlet, pulling away and clearing his throat loudly. "Well done, miss, well done indeed!"

CHAPTER SEVEN

JAMIE TOLD ME ALL ABOUT IT LATER. AND WHAT HE MISSED, THE ORPHANS ADDED. WE were gathered near where father had parked the Walker after returning it triumphantly from the assault on Edinburgh Castle.

"I had to stay behind," Jamie said. "So when we reached the hill, I got off and Mr. Henry and Mr. Stoops and a squad of troopers climbed aboard.

"They'd placed a net full of gunpowder barrels below the walker so it was protected while they made their way up to the gate, moving as quick as any horse at a trot — you were right that it could go faster, Danni."

I was not relieved at this revelation, as you can imagine.

"The garrison was distracted and only started back when the Walker was already at the gate. By then, it was too late, the barrels were loaded, the fuses lit and the walker started moving backwards.

"The explosion deafened me and no one could see a thing but father rushed the walker forward through the smoke and dust. He was right to do so, the gates were down and the walker was through before the guards had a chance to react. The soldiers on the walker shot most of the survivors and then the rest of the prince's troops rushed in. It was over in minutes, the garrison surrendering pretty much as soon as they realized what had happened."

"So I could have been there," I said, glowering.

"No," he said. I glared at him. "We needed the distraction and ye've already told me that if you weren't there, the Scuttler would never have moved."

I wanted to argue that but couldn't.

"Let that be a lesson to you, Danni," my father's voice boomed from behind. Jamie and I both turned, startled, unaware that he'd been listening. The orphans vanished.

"Sir?"

"Ye don't have to be in the thick of things to make a difference," father told me. He reached over and ruffled my hair. "Jamie's right, if it weren't for the Scuttler, we couldna done it." He glanced toward the stables. "Am I to understand, then, that we've acquired some more livestock?"

"They've been helping, father," I told him. "And they'd freeze and starve without us."

"Well, as long as we've got enough to go around," my father said, "they're welcome to it." Then he looked stern. "But if ye're gonna take my hospitality, ye've got to introduce yourselves."

"Come on out," I called with an exaggerated sigh. "Father won't bite."

Slowly, Mapes, Meara, and Mary emerged.

"Where's Billy?"

"Dead, miss," Mapes said. "Died the other night. We took care of his body."

"Died?" my father said.

"He was cold in the morning," little Mary said. She pursed her lips and her face scrunched as she added, "he wouldn't move when I pushed against him."

"And where is he now?"

"We left him at the pauper's gate," Mapes said. He gave my father an apologetic look. "We borrowed one of your barrows, sir, begging your pardon."

My father looked long and hard at me, then said, "Ye'll get them blankets and feed them properly. And they're not to sleep in the stables any more."

"Sir?" Meara asked worriedly.

"There's enough death without adding to it," my father said in a tight voice. He jerked his head toward me. "They were in your charge, lass, the lad shouldna died."

"He was sickly, sir," Mapes said, standing straighter and moving to my defense. "And we didn't want to tell her for fear — "

"I know what ye feared," my father said. "But it was up to her to check on you, not to go off playing with boilers."

"Sir?" My voice was small and there were tears in my eyes. Little Billy had been such a sweet child.

"Ye want to be a grown up, lass," father said to me coldly, "ye've got to take responsibility."

"I'm sorry, sir," I said, lowering my head.

"You see to them before ye do your work," father said, turning away abruptly.

A while later, we could hear father working on the forge, hammering loudly.

"You're not to blame, miss," Mapes told me stubbornly. "It's me that's supposed to look after the little ones."

I looked up at him and then down to the earth once more, shaking my head. "Father's right."

"Well enough, then, Danni, enough of your moping," Jamie said suddenly. "Ye heard father, ye're supposed to look after this lot, so you'd better get to it before the sailors and the prince come along."

"Is he really a prince?" little Mary asked with big eyes. "He spoke funny."

"He spoke French," I told her. "He grew up across the water, in France." I shook myself. "Right, Jamie, go tell Bessie that we need breakfast for three." I looked over to Mapes. "Is there a place in the stables we can make up into a barracks for you?"

"There's a warm spot," Mapes offered reluctantly.

"Show me," I told him. I nodded to Meara and Mary. "Head over to the kitchen.

You're not to set inside until I tell you but Bessie can pass the food out to you."

They nodded and ambled after Jamie who stopped and beckoned to them to hurry up.

"Your father had no right — " Mapes began hotly.

"He had every right," I cut across him. "I'd allowed you to stay in his stables, I'd committed to caring for you."

"Don't need caring," Mapes said.

"And that's why you're still here?" I snapped back. He glowered at me. "The fire's warm, and ye get food for guarding. That makes you his charge. He never met little Billy." But father understood about responsibility. I hadn't really understood it until now. "Now that he's met you, you can be certain that my father will see you cared for as best he can — "

"I don't need — "

"It's not your need, it's his," I told him. He glanced at me questioningly. "Ye must know it, Mapes. Else why did ye look after wee Billy?"

"He was..." he broke off as understanding lit his eyes.

"As much as you wanted to do well by him, father wants to do well by you," I told him.

"I see."

"So we'll get you decent quarters and father will start working you as an apprentice," I told him.

"An apprentice?" Mapes' eyes went wide.

"Aye, and why not?" I said. "If he's to do well by you, why not teach you his trade?"

"What about Meara and Mary?"

"If they stay, they'll work."

"At the forge?"

I gave him a measuring look and then leaned in toward him, trying to ignore the smell of his unwashed self and clothing. "I was thinking that Bessie could use a hand and Mary would do well with her," I told him. "Meara doesn't seem that sort."

"No," Mapes agreed. "She's not like you, either."

"There's work a girl can do that'd suit her better," I said. "I imagine she'd have a fair hand at mending clothes and making them."

The sound of approaching horses thundering out from the city gave us plenty of warning. Mr. Henry and Mr. Stoops were both eagerly overseeing my assembly of the new engine, having told me, "If it works, lass, we won't be able to always come to you if we've troubles."

I rather suspected that they hoped to learn enough to make their own in the future. As I'd already come up with some ideas for improvements, I wasn't so wary of the notion as they might have believed.

The hardest part, of course, was fitting the piston into the cylinder and sealing it. The seals worried me most of all — if they burst, they'd release the steam under immense pressure and the burns could be fatal.

The Prince and his troops walked their horses slowly into our work yard, pulling up well away from our work. Lieutenant Anderson rode close to the side of General Murray. An aide dismounted and held the Prince's horse, General Murray and Lieutenant Anderson dismounted and moved beside him.

Father had come out of the house at the sound of their approach and gave the Prince a curt nod. The Prince nodded back and gestured toward General Murray.

"Mr. Walker," General Murray said, "the Prince and I were most impressed by the impact of your machines on the garrison of the Castle."

The Prince motioned for the General to continue.

"The Prince is of the opinion that your 'Walkers' could be useful to us in restoring His Royal Majesty, the Prince's father, to his rightful throne." From his tone, it was clear that General Murray still had his doubts. His expression grew more sour as he continued, "As we have now in our possession a modest force of cannon, His Highness wants to know if you could construct Walkers sturdy enough to convey them with our army." He paused for a moment then added, "Needless to say you would find yourself handsomely rewarded and His Highness is willing to confer upon you the title of Royal Artificer of Walkers with a monopoly."

"That's very gracious of His Highness," my father said slowly, bowing to the Prince who smiled and nodded back. Father moved to speak into the General's ear and I, used to his ways, sidled up beside him. "Does such a title not depend upon his father regaining the throne?"

"Of course," General Murray replied stiffly. He twisted his head toward our one Walker and asked, "Are you saying you've no faith in your own invention?"

The general's comment galled me. It was *my* invention and everyone knew it.

"It's not the invention alone that will be put to the test," father replied. He frowned as his gaze lighted upon our three sailors. "And I've obligations already which I cannot honorably neglect."

General Murray in his turn frowned at the sailors. "If I may be permitted to ask, what obligations have you made?"

"We're building a steam ship," I spoke up from father's side. I gestured toward the completed engine. "In fact, we're just about to start trials."

"How soon, sir, would it be before the engine is installed in a ship?" Lieutenant Anderson asked with a respectful nod toward the general. He saw the general's frown deepen and added, "I was thinking that a ship that worked against the wind would be as unstoppable on the sea as the Walkers on land."

General Murray's expression grew thoughtful and he turned back to the Prince for a hurried conversation in French. I did not catch enough of it to understand what was said. When the general turned back to us, he had a pained expression on his face. "I've been instructed by His Royal Highness to offer you the additional position of Royal Steam Ship Artificer with all the rights that would entail if you would consider employing the ship in our cause."

"It's not mine to give, sir," Father said stiffly, nodding toward the three seamen.

General Murray's brows rose and he turned to the seamen. "Gentlemen, history is beckoning. What say you?"

Mr. Stoops gestured to the other two and they leaned together in a hasty huddle. When they broke, Mr. Stoops turned to the General. "First, wouldn't it be wiser to see if it works?"

General Murray nodded and conversed with the Prince. Fortunately for our honor, while I'd been engrossed in hearing all I could of the conversation, Bessie had prepared tea and biscuits and now brought them out, offering first the Prince and then the General. Each took the offering with good grace, causing Bessie to go white with both fright and pride.

The general and the Prince finished and the general told the sailors, "How soon would it be before you'd know if the engine works?"

The three turned to me and General Murray's look turned to one of disapproval but there was no way out of it — I was the one who knew that engine and the new boiler.

"If all goes well, a week," I said slowly, adding two days to hedge against the unexpected.

"And how long would it take to build, say, six new Walkers?" Lieutenant Anderson asked.

"A dozen would be better," General Murray put in.

My eyes had gone as wide as saucers at the lieutenant's words only to stretch to the size of our dinner plates with the general's correction.

Before I could answer, my father spoke up, "We'd have to think on that before we could give you a decent answer."

"If it would be too much, we can ask Mr. MacAllister," General Murray said. "Indeed, we plan on paying him a visit regardless."

The general didn't know my father and so didn't understand his reaction but I did. Father was furious at such high-handedness.

"I'm sorry but we would really need to consider before we could give you a decent answer," father repeated.

"How soon could you give an answer, sir?" Lieutenant Anderson asked respectfully.

Father glanced my way and I very surreptitiously winked with one eye. Father's mood lightened at my secret communication.

"If you gentlemen would give us a day to ponder upon it," father replied, "we could give you a decent answer."

"Cumberland's troops are already forming," General Murray muttered, "we must

THE STEAM WALKER   83

not delay."

"But against the Walkers — " Lieutenant Anderson protested.

"They've not been tried in battle," General Murray interjected. He glanced toward me coldly. "They may turn out to be no more than a child's fancy."

"It was a child's fancy that took the Castle, general," Mr. Henry spoke up. Beside him, the other two sailors braced together in solidarity.

"With surprise," the general countered.

"Surprise which was generated by the other Walker, sir," Lieutenant Anderson said.

General Murray glowered at him for a heated moment. "It was still surprise."

The Prince, perhaps feeling left out of things, spoke again to the general who conferred briefly, then turned back to us.

"We shall return tomorrow," the general said, nodding toward the Prince's aid who brought up the royal charger. "Until then — " he glanced around "— gentlemen." He pointedly ignored me.

They mounted and trotted away, turning down the path to MacAllister's forge.

"A child's fancy!" I swore as they moved out of earshot. I'll show him! I turned toward our new engine. "Let's get this hooked up."

Mr. Henry glanced at me apprehensively, then to the other sailors.

"Aye, lass," Mr. Stoops said, glancing possessively at the engine and its boiler. "I can't wait to get it aboard and see how she deals with the waters."

"Jamie will take charge of that, Mr. Henry," father said, turning his gaze from the vanished horsemen back to us. He nodded toward me. "Danni I'll need for myself."

I raised my brows pleadingly but father was not moved. In a low voice to Jamie, I said, "Be careful."

"Always."

#

Once we were in the front room and Bessie had left the tea, father exploded. "Dammit, Danni, I wish we'd never thought of this thing!"

I involuntarily pushed back in my chair, ready to run from the angry ogre who had been my father.

He must have sensed my fear, for he blew out his breath in one great sigh and motioned for me to stay where I was, saying, "Sorry, Danni, but we're right in it make no mistake."

I didn't understand.

"Och, Danni, you're good with things but never so good with people."

"Sir?"

He gestured in the direction of the castle where the Prince and his soldiers had triumphantly installed themselves. "We're damned if we do and damned if we don't."

I thought on his words for a moment then nodded, thinking I understood. "If we don't build the walkers, then Hamish will."

My father dismissed this with an angry wave of one hand. "Och, no, lass, that's the least of it." He saw that I didn't understand and sighed. "You and I know we can build these things. Hamish might think he can but you and I know better."

I nodded; that much was obvious. Hamish might be able to make copies of the Scuttler but I was almost certain that even the engine of our Walker would confound him. Worse, he might build it only to have it explode owing to his usual shoddy work.

"So say we build these things," father said, waving out to our forge and making a bitter face. "Then what?"

"The Prince will pay us well, father," I said hesitantly. "We could build more and maybe even more ships."

My father smiled thinly and shook his head in sorrow. "Oh, lass, ye're still not seeing." He took pity on me. "Stop thinking of the machines for a moment; think about what they mean."

I looked at him wide-eyed.

"One of two things will happen if we build these machines the Prince wants," father said, lifting up his hands. He ticked off one finger on his right hand. "The Prince and his troops will defeat King George and put James back on the throne — " he ticked off another finger "— or they'll be defeated in battle even with our walkers."

I nodded. "But if they win, that will be good, right?"

"For the Prince, yes," he said. "For his father, certainly. For us?" he shook his head. "And it'd be worse if they lost."

"Why?"

"How happy do ye think the English will be with those that made war machines for the Prince?"

"Oh." I hadn't thought of it. Then, I said, "So we just make certain they win."

"And then what?" father asked. "What happens next?"

I gave him a confused look.

"Do we make more walkers for the army? Are we allowed our freedom?"

"Sir?" Why would we have to worry if they *won*?

"Right now, there's only two people in the whole world who really know how to make Walkers," father told me in a soft voice. "I'm one. I'm looking at the other."

I didn't follow him.

"What about the French?" father challenged me. "Or the Prussians? Or any other sovereign power? What wouldn't they do to learn how to make walkers of their own? If that thought hasn't occurred to the Prince, it will certainly occur to his generals — and his father."

"They would put us in prison?" I cried, looking around, wondering if soldiers weren't already on the way.

"Not so much," father said, waggling a hand from side to side. "A gilded cage, more likely. Plenty of work building better war walkers."

My face fell. Father was right: I *hadn't* thought things through.

"What if the Prince loses?"

"Then how happy will King George be with those who made his weapons, lassie?" father replied, shaking his head. "No gilded cage, that's what I'd imagine."

Prison. Cold, lightless, with nothing to do, slops to eat, scraps of clothes, no heat and a short life.

Father caught the bleak look on my face and smiled wanly. "It may not to come that, either way." His expression grew cunning. "For one thing, there's Hamish."

"Sir?" Why would Hamish MacAllister be anything but a further thorn in our side?

"Hamish, lass, is a crafty old thief who thinks he's smarter and better than everyone."

True. I couldn't see how that was helpful.

"So maybe we can use that to our advantage," father said, smiling. "Certainly we can make it so that we're not the only ones who know how to build walkers."

"Father!" I cried in outrage. Let Hamish know our secrets! Why?

He smiled at me. "Then we're not the only target." His eyes grew more canny. "Didn't you ever hear the riddle, 'How many people can keep a secret?'"

I shook my head.

"'Two: if one of them's dead'," father told me in a cold voice. "So we'd best make sure that the walkers don't stay secret."

"So that no one thinks of killing us," I said in a sad but wiser tone.

"Precisely." He pushed an empty cup toward me and pulled one toward himself. "Now pour us some tea and we'll start figurin' how to make all this work." He paused while I poured, before adding with a grin, "And not get us killed."

An hour later the tea was cold, despite Bessie's efforts to heat it up — twice — and father was shaking his head angrily.

"No, Danni, it wilna work," he said, "ye can't turn out enough engines and boilers with just the three of us — "

"Four, you're forgetting Mapes," I corrected.

"The *three* of us — I'm not counting yer brother," father countered.

I frowned at our sketches and our estimates. So close. We were so close. But father was right, without at least one more person well-versed in working metals —

"We'll get Sam!" I said, flushing in pride at finding the solution.

Father sat back and gave me an odd look. "Are you meaning, by any chance, young Samuel Cattan, Hamish's first apprentice?"

"He could do it," I said, waving a hand toward MacAllister's forge. "The rest are middling at best. They could handle the woodwork — "

Father interrupted me with a snort and I gave him a surprised look. "Ach, lass, that's about all they're good for, isn't it?"

I twitched my head in agreement. "Samuel — "

"Didn't you call him Sam?" father interrupted.

"I was in a hurry," I said, preparing to make my point —

"As in 'Oh, my sweet Sam!'" My father knitted his hands together, elbows on the table and sat his head in them, batting his eyelashes.

"Father!" I roared.

Father roared back with laughter. "Och, lass, ye should see yer face! You're as red as yer hair!"

I could feel it, too. So I took a deep breath and sat back in my chair, willing myself to relax until father was done with his jest.

"Hamish is going to want to know how we do it," I said when he was able to breathe once more. "And I think we can trust *Samuel* to keep our confidences."

"Oh, I'm certain you can think of something to ensure his loyalty," father said, lips creasing upwards once more. I glowered at him and he waved a hand dismissively. "Ah, lass, it's not like we can't all see the sparks between ye two!"

"I don't know if I'll ever marry, father," I said, my nose in the air. "A married woman has no rights."

"And an unmarried woman is a drain on her family," father shot back. He caught my look and waved my hurt away. "I dinna mean you, lass." He sat back in his chair, looking up at nothing, lost in thought. "You're right, Danni. Your Samuel could do the work, could keep Hamish happy, and maybe provide you with some protection — "

"I don't need protection!"

"If only from your mouth, if nothing more!" father roared back, leaned forward in his chair, his eyes flashing as hotly as mine. After a moment he shook his head. "Ye should have been born a man," he said softly, "or I should never have let you near a forge — "

"But — !"

"You're a natural, Danni," father said, acknowledging my heated protest. "It's in your blood, it's a calling and you can no more deny it than you can deny air to your lungs."

"Maybe I could learn something different," I allowed.

"Like a fish could learn to fly," father said, shaking his head. He gave me a level look. "I could have stopped you — " he raised a hand to forestall my quick retort "— I could have beat it out of you, for your own good — " his words stunned me to silence, not that he'd said them, but that he'd thought them and I knew that, if he'd really tried, he could have made my life so miserable that I would bolt in terror at the mere sight of a forge "— but I didn't."

He sighed. "I didn't because... because you were that good." His lips twitched ruefully. "I wanted to see what you could do."

"I can still *do*, father," I said, reaching across the table for his hand. "I'm glad you gave me the chance. I'll never let you down, sir."

Father covered my hand with his and sighed. "It's not that I fear, Danni," he said wearily. I quirked an eyebrow. "It's me letting *you* down that worries me."

He took his hand off mine and gestured toward our work. "All right, then, assume we can get our own pet spy — Mr. Cattan — then how do we proceed?"

I leaned forward, brows drawn together as I examined our calculations and tried to add in what I knew of Sam's abilities. Our previous conversation was over; we would not revisit it.

"Weellll... Sam's strong, so we should have him doing the harder work and heavier lifting," I said, half-expecting father to reply with a gibe about my own strength. It was true that I was stronger than most girls my age and had — to some — an unseemly amount of muscle on my shoulders but there was no denying that Samuel had more. Father settled for a quick grin before nodding.

"Right, so if we can get our materials in order — "

"I'll talk with the merchants — "

"No, let the Prince's men handle it," father said. He smiled up at me. "Perhaps your Lieutenant Anderson could be pressed into the role — "

"You know he wants to know how we make the walker almost more than Hamish," I cautioned him.

"So we'll oblige him," father said. He grinned at my look. "We'll make him an expert in the materials needed, running him ragged while we're constructing and then again when we get the first beasties finished — "

"How?"

"Put him in charge of training," father said quickly. "He'll know what's needed to build them, how to operate them but..." he smiled devilishly "... not *how* to build them."

"As soon as they're done, he'll figure that out," I warned.

"Nay, lassie, as soon as they're done, he's off to the war with them," father corrected me. "And the sooner, the better for all of us."

I wasn't listening to him, however, a sudden distant noise coming to my ears. Father caught my expression and turned his head toward the back door. As one, we rose and moved toward the kitchen.

"There!" I cried, catching the unmistakable sound of the whistle we'd built for the ship's engine.

"How many?" Father asked. It was important because we'd arranged that, if all was well, Jamie would give three long blasts on the whistle. Anything else and we'd come down to help.

"Two," I said, craning to hear.

There! Another long whistle.

"Three!" Father said, reaching for me and dragging me into a tight embrace. "Ye did it, lass, ye did it!"

I turned in his arms.

"I didn't expect it, to be honest," he confessed. He crushed me against him. "But 'third time's the charm!' Ah, Danni, ye did it!"

"Let's go see," I said.

"We'd never get there in time, Danni," he said, his expression falling.

"On foot," I said, pointing over to our Walker.

"Ach, Danni, it'd take half an hour just to get the fire going," father said.

"Not if we filch coals from the forge," I corrected. I turned toward the stables and shouted, "Mapes! Mapes, we need some help!"

"Even so, Danni, by the time we've enough steam — "

"Father, do you think the sailors will stop with just a blown whistle?" I said, racing toward the forge and pulling out a coal bucket.

Father was only a few steps behind.

It took all of the half hour father had guessed to get enough steam for the Walker to take her first step but after that she was quick and steady. Our longest time was navigating our way back under the archway and then we made good time, particularly as I'd managed to convince father to let me drive, with Mapes as stoker.

"Danni, she fairly flies!" Father called from his vantage point at the front.

I flashed him a smile, turning back to Mapes and checking on the gages. We were steady at just under five atmospheres and I was getting the feel for the timing. The Walker was moving as fast as she could without breaking into a trot — and I wasn't at all certain that the legs would handle such movements.

Near fore, far hind, near hind, far fore: one, two, three, four, they all moved like clockwork, clunking hard on the ground below as the Walker hustled forward.

We took the far approach to the docks and —

Toot! Toot! Toot!

"Danni look!" Father called, pointing to the sea.

There was the ship with Hoop and the others up in the rigging, waving and crying like madmen while Jamie was down at the boiler, shoveling in the coal for all he was worth.

"By God, she flies!" Father called. He cupped his hands around his mouth to boom out, "Ahoy the ship!"

Toot-toot! Jamie had certainly seen us.

There was something strange about the ship but I was so busy working the controls of the walker that I couldn't quite place it.

"Danni, she's going into the wind!" father shouted back to me. "She's sailing *against* the wind!"

Toot-toot! Jamie waved at us while in the rigging Mr. Hoop was madly waving his hat.

"They want to race us!"

"Father," I said, looking doubtfully at the roaring fire under the boiler, "I don't know if we can."

"Now's the time to find out, then!" he cried rushing back past me to the boiler, shoveling more coal on the fire.

"Father, are you sure?" I asked.

"Aye, Danni, it's time to give it a proper rip," he gestured behind us and I spotted a line of horsemen gamely charging toward us. "It's time to show His Highness and the Lords what she can do."

I looked ahead — a broad flat plain spread out before us; perfect ground for a run.

"Get the tongs and slip this on, then," I said, fishing out the six atmosphere plug. Father looked at it with a raised brow. "Are ye sure, Danni?"

I shrugged. "If ye want to go faster, that's the only way." I nodded toward the lanyard for the whistle. "You can always let off steam with the whistle."

"Very well, Danni," father said with a nod and a wink. "Six atmospheres it is." He took the tongs and carefully stacked the new weight on top of the other before shoveling more coal onto the fire. "Now, let her fly."

We flew. It took a few minutes for the boiler to build the extra pressure but once it did we could feel the difference. The gait seemed almost to change as the beat of the legs on the ground increased and the platform lurched for moments before steadying.

The engine was puffing and blowing so fast it made a steady chuff-chuff-chuff noise above which father could be barely heard when he shouted, "Look at 'em!"

He was pointing to the sea and I turned my head to see that we were outpacing the ship.

I risked a quick glance behind and saw that the horsemen had fallen behind — all except one who had urged his horse into a full-on gallop.

Chuff-chuff-chuff-chuff-chuff!

Woot-woot! Father pulled on the whistle and waved merrily at the approaching horseman. His horse swerved in fright at the sound and the poor rider was nearly unseated; only his skill kept him in the saddle.

A few more bone-jarring minutes later, father called to me, "We've made our point, let's slow down!"

"Turn the valve," I said, pointing to the valve that connected the boiler to the engine, "and then remove the six plug."

Father hastened to obey and we slowed considerably and then — *scree!* — I turned in time to see the five atmosphere plug go flying into the sky, fired off by a huge vent of steam.

"Get back!" I shouted. "Father, get away from the steam!"

My father went one better, racing toward me, grabbing me between his arms and diving over the side.

"Ugh!" The breath was knocked out of me as I hit the ground from a fall of eight feet. Fortunately, father had flung himself to one side so he landed beside, rather than on top of, me.

Above us, like a malevolent demon, the steam from the boiler hissed and spewed up into the clear sky as though the steam was racing to join the clouds above.

"Are ye alright, Danni," father asked as he rolled over and sat up.

"Yes sir," I told him as I looked myself over.

"Live steam like that is dangerous," father said in answer to my unspoken question. "Better to be far away than scalded."

I nodded; I'd enough burns from pouring molten metal to readily imagine the dangers of steam at such pressures.

The sound of hooves clattered on the damp soil alerted us to the approaching rider and father shot to his feet to wave and shout, "Stay clear!"

"Are you all right?" the rider called back. It was our Lieutenant Anderson.

"We're fine," father called back. "We lost our plug and decided to be safe." He glanced toward the walker. "Can you see if it's still steaming?"

Lieutenant Anderson, perched on his horse, craned his neck up to peer at the walker before nodding. "Not much."

"We need to dump the fire, father, we'll be out of steam and will have to fill the boiler before she can move again."

"Aye," father said. He winked at me. "Maybe we need to think over our procedures a bit more."

I nodded fervently. Already I realized that I wanted a way to dump the fire when needed as well as being sure to secure the pressure plugs so that they wouldn't fly away like our errant missile.

The sound of more horses galloping alerted us to the arrival of the Prince and Lord Murray.

"*Mon Dieu!*" The Prince exclaimed when he saw us. "Are you all right?"

"*Oui, mon* prince, just a little chagrined," I said, giving the Prince as proper a curtsy as I could in mere trousers.

"Was that the fastest your walker could go?" Lord Murray asked.

"Perhaps a bit too fast, m'lord," father replied. He reached for me and tussled my hair, adding, "We've a few improvements in mind."

"And the ship?" the Prince asked. "Is that yours?"

"Nay, Highness, that was built on commission to three sailors," father said.

"But they would be willing to help our cause," the Prince asserted. He turned to Lord Murray. "With this walker and that ship, the throne is ours."

"Aye, your Highness," Lord Murray agreed. He gave us a long look, his eyes seeming to rest mostly on me. "You are served by Providence in this matter."

"*Oui*," the Prince agreed with a firm nod of his head. "Monsieur Walker, when can we have more of these?"

CHAPTER EIGHT

"So ye'll get all the glory and what will I get?" Hamish MacAllister spat after father outlined the plan. He shook his thick neck, his face wrinkled in a frown. "Nae, I'll no do it, Daniel Walker, not even for the Prince."

"Ach, Hamish," father said, shaking his head slowly, "I'm sorry to hear that." He slapped his knees and rose from the table where they'd been seated, talking over the plans and moved back to join Jamie and me who stood by the door of the inn. "I'll have to ask Carter, then."

"Carter?" Hamish roared, leaping from his seat. "Ye'd take work from a fellow smith and give it to a cartwright?"

"Weel, ye said ye'd not do the job," father allowed. "And the Prince is adamant that we build six more of the walkers."

"I could build him some scuttlers."

"Aye, ye could," father agreed mildly, "but he doesna want them as you ken."

Hamish growled.

"Hamish, be fair, man, ye know that the Scuttler can't keep close to a Walker," father said, trying his best not to sound smug.

Hamish glowered but said nothing.

"The wagon, though, we could use that to build a Walker," father pressed on, still standing at the door.

"I'd be happy to sell it to you, for forty guineas," Hamish said.

"Ach, Hamish, don't jest!" Father replied. "Ye know the wood's worth only a pound or two. As for the rest, it'd be more of a problem to take apart than to have Carter build from scratch."

"What about the engine then?"

"Keep the engine, you can use it to make swords for the army," father said.

"But he wants Walkers, not swords!"

"So if you help us, put your lads to building the wagons and the legs, sort the rigging, ye'd get his thanks," father said.

"And his gold?"

"Well, he knows we can't work for free," father allowed.

Hamish gestured him back to the table. "So what are you thinking?"

Father sat back down and beckoned for Hamish to lean forward so that he could speak for his ears alone, conspiratorially. After a moment, he turned in his chair and said to us, "Ye two have more to be doing than holding up the wall! Go on, get to your chores!"

Hamish chuckled at the abrupt way father dismissed us, particularly when he heard my heavy sigh.

"I'll bet ye'll be glad to get that one off your hands, Daniel," Hamish chuckled as we headed out the door.

Outside, in the weather, I shivered.

"You shoulda worn a sweater, Danni," Jamie told me.

"It's not the cold," I growled at him, swinging on my heels and pointing back to the inn, "It's Hamish."

"What? Isn't your plan working?" Jamie asked. "He'll leave Samuel behind with the others and take our Walker off with the Army and that'll be the last we'll see of all of them."

That was the plan father and I had decided upon and it certainly did look like Hamish was going to fall for it. He always thought himself so smart and so quick to see his advantage that he was incapable of considering that others might plan on using his wit against him.

Hamish could take the first Walker triumphantly off to the wars while we worked to build the others and he'd consider himself the winner in the exchange, having a chance at loot and the Prince's ear. Father and I wanted neither.

With the success of the steam ship, he and I had already started to consider other ways we could harness the power of the steam engine and make a decent living, even though the three sailors — Mr. Stoops, Mr. Henry, and Mr. MacArdle — were planning on keeping the steam ship market to themselves. Already, they'd received three commissions to convert ships to steam power and that was only the start. Although, the fools, they'd been taken in by the Prince's suggestion that they use their steamship to aid him in restoring his father to the throne, promising them much influence in court and offering them the title of Royal Shipbuilders.

Father had been offered Royal Steam Artificer and even though I thought the title rather silly, I could see that it attracted him.

I hadn't ever quite imagined things would go this way; I'd only thought to teach Hamish MacAllister a lesson and build a pretty walking contraption. And now it was going off to war, the Prince was going to return his father to the throne and only the good Lord could tell how things were going to end.

I shuddered. Had I known what might come, would I have ever suggested building a steam walker? I couldn't say. Even now I was thinking of ways to improve the engine, ways to boil the steam more efficiently, ways the engine could be used, perhaps in mines and certainly in forges.

I could imagine a whole new world, a world where people didn't have to toil day long at back-breaking work, a world where people would be heated by generous steam which also relieved them of burdens. I could imagine ships crossing the seas under clouds of steam, people moving quicker than horses, carrying great loads and not worrying about the roads or the ground beneath them for the Walker could easily step over low fences and made nothing of hills.

This was the world that could come and I was both eager and fearful to see it.

Because the only way I could imagine it coming about would require the death of a King, a bloody war, and the restoration of the Stuarts to their rightful throne.

#

"Why the long face?" Mr. Pugh asked when he saw me next. I'd left Jamie to ready the castings and made my way to the Haymarket more for distraction than any real purpose, telling myself that perhaps Mr. Pugh might be needing my aid. He smiled at me. "I heard that your steamship has all the port talking and that the Prince has commissioned your father to make him a squadron of Walkers." His brushy eyebrows wagged in surprise. "I would have expected you to be over the Moon with joy."

"I suppose I should be," I admitted. "But... with the Walker and the steamships, will King George still fight?"

"Do you have a fondness for the German King, then?" Mr. Pugh asked.

I shook my head. Up until Prince Charles and his army arrived in Edinburgh, I'd never spent any time thinking about Kings. I might have just as easily imagined soaring with hawks and falcons.

"Well," Mr. Pugh continued, "I can't say whether your contraptions will turn the tide for the Prince and his men or not."

"That might be worse," I mumbled.

"Aye, I can't imagine King George being much taken with those who supplied such arms to his enemies," Mr. Pugh agreed. He tried to smile. "So we'll have to hope that your engines do the trick, won't we?"

I nodded glumly.

"And," Mr. Pugh continued, "I understand that some improvements could be made."

I looked up at him questioningly.

With a chuckle he said, "I'd heard something about a pressure plug flying off into the great beyond."

I must have made a face for his chuckle grew into a laugh.

"What, did ye did not imagine that every tongue from here to Prestonpans didn't wag about how your Walker beat the Prince's horse? Or how your steam ship sailed against the wind?"

I shook my head.

"Well they did," Mr. Pugh informed me. He gestured for me to follow him back into his workroom. "And while we're working on sorting that problem out, there are a few more that you might trouble that red head of yours to consider."

"About the steam or about the boiler?" I asked.

"Those, too," Mr. Pugh allowed. "Suppose we go back and work on some castings while we ponder on the best ways to ensure that neither King nor Prince take more of an interest in your pretty neck?"

"My neck?" I squeaked.

Mr. Pugh stopped abruptly and gave me a stern look. "Danielle Walker, like or not, ye've drawn the eyes of Kings and Princes and your life will never be the same."

#

When I returned to the forge, I was met by a furious brother. He was backed by Mapes whose look was a mixture of anger and fear.

"Where were you?" Jamie demanded. "We've got the cast ready for the pour and couldn't find you."

"I was with Mr. Pugh," I said.

"We went there!" Jamie cried, gesturing toward Mapes who nodded in agreement.

"We went to Mr. Gillie, we had to work on some things with the rigging," I explained, amazed at the fierceness of Jamie's assault.

"Don't you remember that father said you're not to go out alone?" Jamie demanded. "What would he have done if you'd gone missing?"

"I'm sorry," I told him contritely, "I should have thought."

"Och, ye should have *thought* years back!" Jamie said, shaking his head ruefully. "It's far too late to hope you'll start now." He savored my sorrowful look for a moment before chuckling and saying, "So, *now* are you ready to pour?"

Pour we did. I got Mapes to help, showed him how we wanted to do it, "So you'll be able to do it yourself next time."

"It doesn't seem hard," Mapes allowed.

"Och, it isn't if you do it right!" Jamie agreed.

"The trouble is when you do it wrong," I added.

"What happens then?"

"Well, if you're lucky, you melt it back down and do it again," I said. "But you'll have to make a whole new mold."

"And if you're not lucky?"

"Then you don't realize it until you use the piece," Jamie said, nodding my way.

"And then?" Mapes pressed.

"Then, if you're lucky, it only cracks and doesn't kill anyone," I told him.

Mapes' eyes went wide and he glanced to Jamie for confirmation. Jamie nodded solemnly, saying, "And *that's* why you're careful on the pour."

"And why we test when we're done." I added in agreement. "We'll have to be doubly careful with all the work we're going to be doing."

Mapes frowned in confusion.

"The faster you do something, the easier it is to make a mistake," Jamie explained.

"But if that's so, why are you making six engines when you only need five?" Mapes said, keeping his eyes on Jamie. Even now, he had a time bringing himself to admit that I was in charge. It bothered me but not so much that I'd take issue with him, particularly as Jamie merely turned to me with raised eyebrows.

"We make six so that we've got a spare, in case one of the castings goes bad," I explained.

It was a lot of work and our yard was crowded with molds ready to be poured. Jamie and I had spent two days just building the molds. We'd discovered that it was easier to make the same mold over and over — if a bit boring. Naturally, we'd kept the patterns from which we'd built our molds — I'd learned that early on from Mr. Pugh — so it was easy create the six new sets of molds that we needed to create the six new engines and boilers. I forced Mapes to make two — his first was useless but his second passable — and even managed to borrow Samuel Cattan for a day to make two molds of his own — both quite respectable.

"Ye know that Hamish only let me come so's he'd could steal the designs?" Samuel said to me in a low voice when he'd arrived.

I smiled at him and he cocked his head in surprise. "That's the idea, Samuel, that's just the idea."

"Does your father know?"

"Och aye," Jamie piped up, shaking his head dolefully. "The two daft berks are practically giving away all their work."

"It's that or lose our freedom," I reminded Jamie darkly. My brother flushed at those words.

"You can trust the Prince!"

"Perhaps," I said. "But what of his father? Or some Lord?" I shook my head. "What about the English and their German King? What if the Prince doesn't win?"

"He'll win," Jamie declared stoutly.

"Och, Jamie, with our Walkers, he'll win," I agreed. I turned back to Samuel. "And now, Mr. Cattan, if you'd be pleased to build your molds?"

Our biggest problem had been securing the steel and coal we'd needed for the melts. We probably never would have used steel if it hadn't been for the brilliant and cost-saving invention of the hot-blast process for blast furnaces which reduced the cost of steel considerably — even more than Mr. Darby's innovation of using coke over coal in the blast furnaces used to make steel.

Not long after we'd finished the last cast, we heard the sound of hooves clattering under the archway along with a different, louder noise that caused all of us to turn toward the sound.

Father came out of from the house to greet the newcomers just as I realized what the other sound was — the noise of a gun carriage in the archway.

"Mr. Walker," Lieutenant Anderson said, jumping down from his mount briskly and sketching a quick bow in his direction, "may I present the gunners of the first battery of His Majesty's Royal Walker Artillery?"

"Hmph," was all father could say. Three men accompanied the gun. He examined it carefully and Lieutenant Anderson followed his gaze, saying, "This is one of the three-pounder cannon captured with the castle."

"How much does it weigh?" Father asked, his eyes going to our Walker standing silent beside the stables.

Lieutenant Anderson turned questioningly to the three men.

"Ach, na more than three hundredweight by itself," the eldest allowed, turning to his mates for confirmation.

"What about the recoil?" Jamie asked, moving forward, his eyes lit with an excitement I'd never seen before.

"That depends upon the charge," the grizzled artilleryman allowed.

Jamie gestured toward the Walker. "If it goes too far back, it'll run straight into the running gear."

The older man gave him a look but Lieutenant Anderson spoke up, "Listen to him, Sergeant, he was the lad on the steam ship the other day."

"He was?" the sergeant said not quite hiding his surprise.

"He ran the ship," I piped up defensively.

"And ye'd know, missy," the sergeant allowed.

"Sergeant MacLeod, this is Danni Walker," Lieutenant Anderson said reprovingly.

"Daniel Walker's a man, I met him," the sergeant countered.

"Then ye'd ken the resemblance," the lieutenant replied, pointing to father, "As that's him there."

"Good day to you sir," Sergeant MacLeod said to father, his tone unruffled.

"And, now, if you don't mind, we're asking the help of his son and daughter in mounting our cannon."

"I've no interest in it," I said, allowing my displeasure with Sergeant MacLeod to color my voice.

"I could help," Jamie said. He turned pleadingly toward me and father. "You've got everything in hand here, haven't you?"

"Danni, can you manage without him?" Father said. "I'll leave you Mapes and Mr. Cattan is due presently, but I've got to go to town and arrange supplies."

"Aye, father, I can manage."

"A girl?" the sergeant's disdain was obviously.

"Think Boadicea and her chariots," Lieutenant Anderson ordered.

"Or Grace O'Malley and her pirates," father added for my ears alone, the tips of which promptly turned scarlet.

"What's your plan, Jamie?" I said to my brother.

Jamie's face brightened at the implied permission then went blank as he thought furiously.

"Lieutenant Anderson, could your men help me move the Walker?" Jamie said. "We'll need room and the noise would disturb the workings here at the forge — and it'll give your men a chance to get acquainted with our steam walker."

I noticed that he called it "our steam walker" rather than the more damning "Danni's infernal contraption" that he used in private.

"On the road, we could position your gun beside it and test fire it to compare its movement against the length of the walker," Jamie continued.

I moved over to father and said for his ears alone, "If you see any of our sailing friends, you might want to send one back here to help Jamie." Father quirked an eyebrow questioningly. "They're used to guns on ships and I can't help thinking that our walker is more like a ship than a field."

Father patted my shoulder in silent acknowledgement and, with a nod to Lieutenant Anderson and a call for Bessie, started his way under the arch and off to town.

"Right now, Mr. Mapes, we've a pour or two to start," I said, gesturing to the cauldron of liquid steel and the casts. "We start by aligning the mold carefully under the pouring spout..."

#

We'd not quite finished our pours when a loud, sharp report startled me. A few minutes later, just as I was inspecting the last pour and wondering what was delaying Samuel Cattan, there came another loud report. This time I could place its location — it was on the road outside our house.

"That'd be the gun, miss," Mapes allowed, cocking his head to sort out the sounds.

"Well, that's as may be," I said, keeping my surprise at the high pitch of the gun to myself. I'd always expected guns to have deep, loud *booms*, not high-pitched little *cracks!*

"I'd say your brother has them sorted, miss," Mapes assured me.

"Hmph!" I snorted. I glanced toward the archway which was annoyingly empty of one Mr. Cattan. "Well, if Samuel doesn't get here soon, we're going to lose a day."

"'Samuel'?" Mapes teased.

I growled at him. "Go make sure that the last of the steel's out of the cauldron or it will set."

Mapes nodded and moved off, leaving me alone with my thoughts. In no time I was standing with my eyes closed, wishing I had a sketchbook near to hand while imagining a totally new design of boiler, one with pipes sticking into a fire — one of the results of my lengthy conversation with Mr. Pugh. With the pipes in the fire, the heated water would rise and mix with the cold, bringing more water to the heat and — we thought — heating all that much quicker.

"I brought you some tea, miss," a voice piped up beside me.

I jumped and whirled. "Oh, Mary, I didn't hear you coming!"

"You seemed asleep, miss," little blond-haired Mary said. "Or maybe taken with a fit."

I realized that she was terrified.

"I was just thinking," I assured her. I looked around for a place for her to set her tray and couldn't find one. Instead, I poured a quick cup and took it, saying to her, "Thank you very much. Now, could you go to the living room and get my drawing things?"

"Miss?"

"Some paper and a charcoal stick," I told her. "No, make it the pen, I've got an idea I need to put to paper."

Mary nodded and trotted off back to the house, nearly tripping with the tray wobbling awkwardly in her hands.

A noise made me turn and belatedly, I realized that I'd had her leave before seeing to Mapes.

"Did you want some tea?" I said, moving toward him and proffering the cup. He seemed to recoil. "It's warm and it's wet."

"You'd let me drink from the same cup?"

"And why not?" I said. "It's not as if I'm all — " I broke off, turning red. I was about to say "all filthy" but Mapes had only recently been just that. He was wearing father's old things and we'd cut his hair short to rid him of nits — just as we'd done for Meara and Mary — but his hair was coming back in quickly and he was putting on enough weight that he no longer looked like a scarecrow.

"A girl's no dirtier than a boy," I finished lamely, raising the cup toward him. Then I saw the dirt and the dust on him, glanced down to see equal amounts on my clothes and added, "Actually we're both about the same."

Mapes shook his head. "A drink from the trough will be enough for me, miss," he said. "I know my place."

"There's some that *make* their place."

"Maybe," Mapes allowed, moving toward the horse trough. He cupped some water in his hand and drank from it before turning back to me. "But, miss, I don't think that's me."

"Do you not want to be a smith, then?"

"Oh, no!" Mapes said, moving back toward me and eyeing the forge fondly. "No, miss, I love the work and will never forget the kindness you and your father showed me." He pursed his lips. "But I canna think ever to rise higher than that."

"You, miss, you're always dreaming and looking for bigger things," he said wistfully. "It's like you were touched by the Fairies."

I sighed. Why is it that everyone wanted to call me 'touched'? Jamie by 'darker spirits' and now Mapes with 'the Fairies.' I suppose I ought to be glad that none called me a witch, particularly with my red hair.

"Well, Fairies or no, we've got work to do and if that Samuel Cattan — "

"Sorry I'm late!" a panting voice called from under the archway. It was Samuel. He was running as fast as he could, racing under the archway to arrive in front of me, gasping. He bent over to catch his breath and between gasps managed to say, "I stopped to help with the cannon."

"And is that your job?" I demanded sourly, still miffed by the whole 'Fairy' thing.

"They needed a hand getting it up on the walker," Samuel said. "The soldiers were no use and they nearly had Jamie do it all by himself — and him not into his full growth yet."

I made an angry noise at the thought of that old Sergeant MacLeod laying all the work on my poor brother.

"I set them straight," Samuel said, recovered enough to stand straight and meet my eyes. "That Lieutenant Anderson's all right when he remembers his rank. I had a quick word with Jamie and he took charge."

"Jamie took charge?" I said, surprised.

"I told him to act like you," Samuel said, his lips twitching. Beside him, Mapes chuckled.

"He had the soldiers sorted in next to no time," Samuel said in awe. "And that Sergeant was actually calling him sir by the time we had the gun mounted."

I was pleased for Jamie but some vague unease stirred my heart as I considered the sergeant's 'sir.' And, as for the way both Samuel and Mapes were looking, well...

"We've work to be doing," I said to them, nodding toward where the walker had been. "Samuel, do you see those timbers there?"

Samuel nodded.

"Well, you and Mapes have to take them down — carefully — and move them to MacAllister's forge."

"Move — ?"

"The timbers are the framework for the walker," I said, answering Samuel's half-spoken question. "When you get them set up, you'll raise your Scuttler up on them, remove the legs and we'll begin the conversion."

Samuel nodded in comprehension. He turned to Mapes. "Well, sir, it seems the good lady has given us our orders." He gestured toward the thick timbers. "Shall we?"

#

Hamish MacAllister, with all the thought typical of a man who only looked for gain, had dismantled the engine of his Scuttler before we'd arrived the next morning and was busily installing it in the rigging of the drop hammer which it had originally powered.

"We need the engine to move your Scuttler!" I cried when I saw the mess.

"Why not use your new engines?" Hamish demanded petulantly.

"Because they're not ready!" I cried.

"Hamish," father said consolingly, "don't ye remember the plans?"

"I've a commission for swords," Hamish said, waving at the drop hammer.

"You've a commission for the walkers, too," father reminded him.

"Och!" Hamish threw up his hands. "Do what ye will!" He glanced toward me, "Or what your ginger child tells you." His eyes rested on me uncomfortably. "I suppose you despair of ever getting her married."

"She's still young, Hamish," father allowed mildly, gesturing toward the walker. "And we've enough to be going about for a while."

"I'll want the engine set up when ye're done," Hamish said, moving toward his house and leaving us in the yard.

It took us an extra hour to get the Scuttler engine rigged once more and half an hour to get enough steam to move it over to the works. After that, we had to wait while the steam bled and the engine cooled before we could haul it back.

In the meantime, I had the others start undoing the rigging of the old Scuttler and preparing to remove its ungainly legs. They were shorter than the Walker's but not hinged, being one straight six foot length rather than the Walker's two four foot lengths.

I'd discussed with father the idea of building a walker with five foot lower legs and four foot uppers, allowing it to easily clear five foot fences but he was leery of the change. "It works well enough now, Danni."

I stayed on long enough to be certain that everyone knew what they were to do before father sent me back to our forge to check on Jamie and Mapes.

As I walked the two miles, I reflected that father had probably sent me as much to ensure the work was progressing as to get me away from Hamish MacAllister. With me gone, there was a chance father could needle the man into doing something approaching a decent day's work.

Jamie wasn't in the yard when I arrived.

"Jamie!" I cried to the house, wondering if he was answering a call of nature or having a snack.

"He's not here, lass," Mr. Stoops' deep voice answered unexpectedly from the forge.

"Mr. Stoops?" I said, hastening to him. "I would have thought you to be with the ship."

Mr. Stoops gave me a pained smile. "His Majesty has prevailed upon us to remain here and give you a hand."

"Prevailed?" I repeated blankly. Then, "Us?"

"Aye, lass, all three of us," Mr. Henry said, standing from where he'd been squatting beside a new cast. He glanced down at it. "I was just admiring your handiwork."

I snorted. Admiring! Stealing, more likely. His Majesty or no, I'd no doubt that the plans for the engine and boiler would soon be in foreign hands in exchange for large amounts of gold. I drew a breath to shout at them but let it out slowly — that was father's plan, wasn't it?

"I doubt the Prince would be happy if news of these walkers got into the hands of his enemies," I said slowly.

"Never fear of that, Miss," Thomas MacArdle assured me solemnly. Then his face split in a grin. "It would be no good for His Royal Steamship Artificers."

"Well, now you seem to be helping on the mounts of the Royal Steam Horse Artillery," I said. "And with your help, perhaps we can get caught up."

"You've promised three more in a fortnight," Mr. Stoops said. "That's a tall order."

"We've got MacAllister's lads building the carriage and the legs," I said. "We've got to get the engines and boilers built and tested."

"What of the rigging?" Mr. Henry said. All three were master riggers but he was the best.

"Father's getting the parts and we were thinking..." I broke off. "Mr. Henry, have you some new ideas?"

The old sailor grinned at me and nodded.

"He's some drawings if you'd like to see," Mr. Stoops said giving me an imploring look.

"I'd be honored," I said, dipping my head respectfully to the seaman.

Mr. Henry fairly beamed and then his face fell. "But lass, haven't ye got to start with the engines?"

"Indeed we do," I agreed. "But it'd go quicker with five." I gestured around to include myself, Mapes, and the three sailors.

They heartily agreed to that — helping to construct the boilers and engines would further increase their mastery — and we all fell in with a will.

It took us three hours but, when we were done, we had no fewer than five finished boilers to test at once. With a groan, I realized that we had no pressure plugs. I explained the problem to the concerned looks of the others and then said, "Mr. MacArdle, perhaps you'd escort Mr. Mapes and acquaint him with Mr. Pugh whom I'm sure will supply us."

"Certainly," Mr. MacArdle said after giving Mapes a measuring look. To him, he said, "Lad?"

"Sir," Mapes said, giving me a fearful look.

"It was Mr. Pugh who taught me casting," I said to him. "He took me on when I was ten. His eyes are not the best and you might mention that father has taken you on as an apprentice."

"Miss?"

I leaned close to him and said into his ear, "Father would never say no to having *two* trained casters."

Mapes' eyes rose as he took my meaning. "Are you certain?"

"I am," I assured him and patted his arm, waving him toward the archway, "now be off with you as we can do no more without the plugs." I turned to the two remaining sailors. "Now, Mr. Henry, I think perhaps we could adjourn to the kitchen to view your drawings."

#

Mr. Henry's drawings and the new rigging were inspired. I could see how much easier it would be to steer the walker with the rigging *and* I was certain that it'd be faster and more limber. Why, I might even figure out how to get a trot.

Our conversation widened and I mentioned my new boiler and some of the ideas that Mr. Pugh and I had tossed about. With Mary hovering nearby we were never short of tea; I apologized to the men that I was unable to offer them anything stronger — I knew enough about sailors to not be too distraught over that for even with enough beer the conversation would have grown unruly and not have been as insightful as it was.

We thought of this steam horse as a war horse and designed it with the notion that it would be attacked. We thought of adding sidewalls which we could position at an angle to make it harder for someone to climb up, we determined how to bury our cables so that they could not be severed and then — this was a combined machination — we came upon the idea of using the hot coals in the boiler as an emergency defense, dumping them atop of any would-be attackers.

That idea prompted me to recall Mr. da Vinci's famous steam cannon and to consider how to adapt it further.

"These are great ideas, gentlemen, but father has rightly pointed out that we are under contract to reproduce our proven walker and not some new experimental beast," I said when our conversation ebbed.

"Were ye not to build five more walkers?" Mr. Henry asked.

I nodded.

"But there are six full sets of engines and boilers out there."

"One's a spare in case of poor pouring," I said.

"But if they're all sound..."

"We've not the wood or the gears or the rigging," I protested. And how to keep it a secret from father?

"Did you not say you could get it to trot?" Mr. Henry asked temptingly.

"Perhaps," I allowed. I'd spent a lot of my spare time watching horses at the trot and realized that it was an entirely different step than their walk. Trying to build a steam horse to do the same was a daunting prospect.

"Six walkers will need a large number of trained men," Mr. Henry observed.

"I don't see how your father will fail to be drafted," Mr. Stoops said. "At which point, who will be left to mind the forge?"

Well, it was certain that I wouldn't be asked to crew one of the walkers, not that I objected — I'd no desire for such a frolic, particular with the notion of building a *trotter*.

"The Prince will want us here," Mr. Henry said. "So it'd be fair enough that we'd offer to keep an eye on you and your father's property."

Yes, it would at that. I got the uneasy feeling that father would not be too happy with me plotting behind his back like this. On the other hand, if I were safely here working on a new machine, he need hardly worry about me following him, would he?

Before I could respond, the sound of feet outside alerted us to the return of Mapes and Mr. MacArdle. Only there were *three* pairs of feet approaching.

Without speaking, we all rose and went out to the yard.

"Hello, Danielle!" Mr. Pugh called cheerfully to me. "I understand that you're about to test your latest batch of steam machines and I wonder if I could persuade you to let me watch?"

"Mr. Pugh, you'll be very welcome!"

CHAPTER NINE

"WELL THAT'S SIX," MR. MACARDLE SAID LATER THAT EVENING AS THE SUN WAS SETTING, eyeing me speculatively. Apparently he and Mr. Pugh had found much to talk about during the rest of the day, as had Mr. Henry and Mr. Stoops and now the watchmaker was fully aboard with the notion of building a 'trotter' after the Prince left for the war.

"If they needed, then we could sail it down and meet them," Mr. Henry said, clinching the argument.

The more I'd thought about my father — and probably one Mr. Cattan as well — off fighting in rebellion against one King for another, the more nervous I became.

"That's only the boilers," I replied, "we don't know about the engines and they're far trickier."

"At this rate, we'll know tomorrow," Mr. Henry replied. "And not long after that, you'll have nothing to do."

The others grinned at that and I stifled a protest for they knew me too well — I *hated* not having something to do.

Greatly daring, I'd invited all four men to dinner, sending Mary off to get more victuals while Bessie did her best to stretch out what was already in the pot.

I was surprised not much later to discover that father brought Samuel Cattan with him.

"Where's Jamie?" he asked, reflecting the question that had been on my mind for a good while.

Just then, a clatter of hooves rattled under our archway and two horses came trotting through — with me unable to prevent myself from carefully examining the movements of their legs.

Two men dismounted and tied up their horses to the post. I recognized one as Lieutenant Anderson but the other —

"Jamie!" I cried rushing toward him.

He braced to attention, clicking his shiny boots together and called out clearly, "Ensign James Walker of His Majesty's First Steam Artillery wishes to present his respects."

The speech completed, Jamie turned to me and gestured toward his uniform, "Doesn't it look great, Danni?"

#

"And I suppose, *Lieutenant*, that it didna occur to you that the lad is underage and required his father's permission to undertake such an oath?" Father demanded frostily when everyone had recovered and we'd all moved inside to the very overcrowded dining room.

Jamie was standing next to Lieutenant Anderson, both trying to become invisible and beseeching me silently with big eyes. Mr. Pugh was clearly as unsettled as father while the three sailors were all silent in support of Jamie.

I couldn't say exactly what I felt. I was a mixture of fury, pride, and worry — and all three emotions fought for possession of my tongue with none gaining a clear superiority.

"It wasn't I, Mr. Walker," Lieutenant Anderson replied. "Your son was honored by none other than His Royal Highness, Prince Charles."

"I've dealt with him," Mr. Henry offered, "and he's not one to easily turn down."

"He said he'd be offering you a commission as well, father," Jamie spoke up. "He talked of the honor, of the glory — "

"He didn't talk of the dying!" I spoke up, fear winning for a moment the battle for my tongue.

All eyes turned to me.

"Jamie, you could die!" I said, trying to get him to see reason.

"Sister, I *will* die someday," Jamie replied manfully. He turned his attention back to father. "The Prince said as much but he allowed that a *man* chooses his path, while destiny chooses his time of death."

Royalty or no, the Prince was very lucky he wasn't in the room at this moment. It would be hard to wager who would be fiercest with him — me or father. Perhaps, I thought, that was why the affable Lieutenant Anderson had been sent. He was a likeable person — handsome, too — and local. We couldn't quite bring ourselves to be as cross with him as we might have with the Prince or his generals.

Hmm.... "And what did Lord Murray say about this?"

"I'm assured that Lord Murray and all the generals are in favor of anything that will lead to the desired outcome," Mr. Henry spoke up, glancing toward Lieutenant Anderson for confirmation. The young man gave a jerky nod which seemed at odds with his expression — he seemed not quite as certain as Mr. Henry.

"It makes sense," Mr. MacArdle said, "that the Prince would seek to get those who've the most experience with the Walkers to go with them off to the war."

Father glared at the sailor but Mr. MacArdle continued unperturbed, "That's one — who'll captain the others?"

"I have the honor of one," Lieutenant Anderson allowed. He glanced at father. "I understand that Mr. MacAllister has accepted a commission to command another one."

"Lieutenant MacAllister?" Father choked out, growing red in the face. He gestured wildly toward Jamie. "And has he got a fine uniform like my son?"

"I suppose he shall," Lieutenant Anderson allowed.

"So when will the Prince ask Mr. Walker, here?" Mr. Stoops asked the lieutenant.

The lieutenant reddened in embarrassment and was a moment before answering in a low voice, "I think His Royal Highness thought your efforts best employed here, at your forge."

My father was out of his seat in an instant, throwing his napkin down at storming off. "We'll see about that!"

"Father?" I called after him, wondering, like everyone else at the table, whether we should accompany him or continue our meal.

"Stay here! I'll not be long."

Moments later a horse galloped under the archway and out toward town and Holyrood where the Prince was holding court.

Jamie and I exchanged glances, he looking uncomfortable and me looking angry. Nearby, Mr. MacArdle and Mr. Henry exchanged words too low for me to hear but their chuckling caught my attention.

"What is it?" I demanded.

At this point all three seamen became instantly silent and dropped their eyes guiltily.

It was Mr. Pugh who answered. "Unless I'm much mistaken, Miss Walker, I rather fancy that the Prince has outwitted your father and our sailor friends have apprehended that fact."

"Aye, Daniel Walker is a smart man with a forge and metal but Prince Charlie has been gathering loyalties since he could first talk," Mr. Stoops acknowledged. He glanced toward Lieutenant Anderson. "So, that's four now. You need two more, don't you?"

"Ye're not thinking of taking our Danni are you?" Mr. Henry demanded of the lieutenant.

"Of course not!" Lieutenant Anderson said promptly. "Women have no place in war."

"Behind it, perhaps," Mr. MacArdle allowed with snigger in a low voice. He was instantly reproached by Mr. Stoops and Mr. Henry. He turned to me, "Sorry, lass — an old sailor's talk, pay no attention."

Jamie spoke up. "I heard that it would be Samuel and — " he cut himself off with a nervous look my way.

"Not the Weasel!" I cried, sitting up in my chair.

"No, I think it was his apprentice, Adams," Lieutenant Anderson said, hoping to cheer me.

"Aye, Jock 'the Weasel' Adams," Mr. Henry agreed sourly, looking ready to spit. "His name's all about Edinburgh, it's a wonder he's not been put in the ground years back."

"But why?" Lieutenant Anderson asked.

"He has a way with the ladies that's not well-regarded by most," Mr. Stoops said, glancing toward me uneasily.

He was telling me nothing new. The Weasel mostly avoided me; Samuel saw to that. Hamish MacAllister was more of a worry, particularly if he was commissioned lieutenant to Jamie's ensign: I hated to guess how MacAllister would taunt my brother.

I was so lost in thought that it took me a moment to realize that everyone was staring at me expectantly. Someone had asked a question but I hadn't paid attention.

"I'm sorry, was someone talking to me?" I said, glancing at the perplexed faces.

"I said, Ms. Walker, had you ever encountered Mr. Finlayson?" Lieutenant Anderson repeated, clearly trying to divert the conversation from its earlier less salubrious course.

"The instrument maker?" I said, glancing toward Mr. Pugh. "Isn't he the one who wanted those brass knobs the other day?"

"The very man," Mr. Pugh agreed enthusiastically. He turned to the lieutenant. "He's quite gifted in his area of expertise, sir." He turned back to me. "Do you remember how he showed us his microscope when he'd finished it."

"Aye," I said. "Jamie, that's where I saw my hair looking as big as a log."

"Ach, Danni, I can see that with my own eyes," Jamie replied dryly, earning a harsh glower.

"No, truly," Mr. Pugh said, "that microscope was a wonder of invention." He turned to Lieutenant Anderson. "Why do you mention him, sir? Is he an acquaintance of yours?"

"He might be," Lieutenant Anderson replied brightly. "He was beseeching the Prince for a commission in the artillery."

"Well, if he's a mind for it, I'd say he'd be a great addition," Mr. Pugh responded enthusiastically. "Quite solid, quite solid."

A hiss from the kitchen distracted me and I turned to see Bessie beckoning to me urgently. I got up, saying, "Excuse me." As I left, I gave Jamie a meaningful nod.

I raced out of the dining room and nearly collided with Bessie. "What?"

"The food's ready, miss, what do I do? Your father raced off and he's not back yet."

"Where's Mary?" I asked, looking around.

"She's tending the pots," Bessie said. "We can't wait too much longer or things will burn."

"Have you a soup?"

"Of course, miss."

"Well serve that up, along with some wine," I said.

"Ah, but miss, that's the problem," Bessie wailed. I gave her a look which must have been quite frightening for she took a step back. "Your father keeps the key to the wine, you know that, miss."

"Oh!" I'd quite forgotten, wine never being something that attracted my attention.

"Well, start with water and the soup," I said. "Father should be back before long."

Bessie dipped her head in acknowledgement and trotted back to the kitchen.

I returned to the dining room, did a quick count of settings and realized we were two short. I rushed to Jamie and whispered in his ear, "You're not hungry."

He gave me a startled look and I added, "Nor am I." He glanced down the table, followed my logic and nodded glumly.

"Sirs," I said, nodding to all around the table, "my brother and I will wait our dinner for our father's return but we're certain he wouldn't want you to wait any longer." I gestured toward the kitchen. "We'll be serving soup for starters, please be seated."

There were hearty denials from all around until I said, "I'm certain that father would want it thus, gentlemen and, besides, the soup would get cold." I paused for a moment before adding, "And our Bessie did go to such efforts to get it just right."

"Well, then I suppose we can't say no," Lieutenant Anderson agreed gallantly. "And my compliments to your marvelous Bessie."

Once the soup had been served by Bessie and Mary, I realized that the issue of the wine would shortly become paramount. Usually, father and the others drank beer with dinner but that required a trip to the tavern. For special meals — and this surely was one — he had a reserve of table wine. I knew where he kept it in the cellar but I also knew that he kept it locked, probably more out of habit than for any particular fear. What I didn't know was where he kept the key.

There was a key chain in his office but I doubted the key would be there. Even so, I had little choice but to try. So, while the soup was served, I went to father's office, grabbed the keys and raced to the root cellar where the wine was stored in a cabinet. I tried key after key with no luck.

Desperately, I recalled a conversation I'd had with Mr. Pugh a year ago. He'd described how locks worked and had joked that a clockmaker like himself would find none to bar him. I'd thought nothing of it but now... I wondered if perhaps I might have the same level of skill.

"Mary, get me an awl," I called.

"An awl?" Mary said.

"Ask Bessie, she'll know," I called back. "And hurry, the wine will need to be served soon."

"Wine?" Mary repeated in confusion.

"Just do it!" I snapped. "And bring a light with you."

In the meantime, I examined the keys I had, looking at how they were made. It didn't take me long to realize that Mr. Pugh was correct — a clockmaker had much the same requirements as a locksmith. Each key had a raised tooth, each with different profiles. The tooth turned the lock. The only question was mimicking the right profile in such a way that I could turn the lock.

Mary returned with candle and awl.

"Great, now get back to Bessie," I told her, "I'll be up shortly."

"The wine, miss?" Mary asked, wondering how the tools she'd deliver could solve our problem.

"Just go!" I said. After I was sure she was gone — one lockpick was enough — I looked at the awl and the keys. It took a moment to bend the awl to have a hook at the end and then more time while I struggled to find the right approach but in a few minutes I was rewarded with a *click!* — and the lock opened.

I felt both very pleased and very fearful at the same time. I was now a full-fledged thief, stealing wine from my father's cabinet. I searched for what I hoped was a decent bottle and pulled it out, figuring that I'd leave the locking to father when he returned.

I raced back up to the kitchen, passed the bottle to a surprised Mary and returned to the dining room just as the others finished the last of their soup.

"Miss!" Bessie hissed at me urgently. "We've a roast and your father always carves."

Just as I was about to say — against all my better judgement — that Jamie could do it, a loud clatter of hooves raced to the front of the house and stopped abruptly. Two pairs of boots clattered up the front steps.

"I'm sure there'll be plenty, not to worry," I heard my father's voice say assuringly and then the front door opened.

"Father!" I cried just as Mary rushed by with the wine. "Mary! Go back and get two more glasses."

Wide-eyed, Mary whirled in her tracks and raced back to the kitchen.

"Captain Finlayson, permit me to introduce you to my daughter, Danielle Walker," father said, waving a hand graciously toward me.

I was making a curtsy just as father added, "And I'm sure she's got an amusing explanation as to how my special wine was spirited from a locked cabinet."

"Captain Finlayson," I said as I rose from my curtsy. "Are you by chance related to the John Finlayson I've just heard our Mr. Pugh praise so highly?"

"I am indeed," he replied, bowing to me, "being the one and the same." He rose and gestured to father. "Your father and I petitioned the Prince for commissions in his forces. I have studied artillery and fortifications while your father has provided His Royal Highness with a most marvelous and amazing creation."

"Come, John, you must be parched," father said, gesturing for the other to precede him into the drawing room. He turned back to me, saying, "I think another bottle will be in order shortly."

I nodded and scampered off, pleased to leave the introductions to father and also to have some time to consider Captain Finlayson's words.

Back in the cellar, it took only a moment to acquire another bottle of the same vintage — a robust red from France — but as I turned to retrace my steps, a thought brought me to a halt. Father had accepted a commission?

I wondered if that hadn't been the Prince's intention from the beginning. As an officer, father would be not only allied to but also in allegiance.

I could understand his desire to protect Jamie from the machinations of Hamish MacAllister and also how his skill with the Walkers would be invaluable to Prince's forces but my heart sank as I recalled what I'd heard about the 1715 uprising and how brutally it had been repressed afterwards.

Father, Jamie, and — to hear tell — Samuel would all be going off to the war. And where would that leave me?

"Miss!" Bessie's cry from the kitchen shocked me out of my reverie. "Miss, please hurry!"

#

"Oh, Danni, don't be so jealous!" Jamie said as he crawled in to bed late that evening. "Girls don't fight, you should be glad."

"Glad!" I snorted, causing Bessie to flinch in her sleep. The bed was too small for Mary who insisted on sleeping in the rude quarters we'd built in the stables. "Glad that you and father are *both* going into harm's way!"

"Nothing will happen," Jamie assured me glibly.

"Nothing will happen!" I snarled. "Bullets will be flying, Jamie, or did you forget?"

"We'll be too high for the bullets," Jamie assured me with a yawn. "And the Walker's will move too fast for anyone to aim properly."

"Unless the boiler blows up!" I said. "What then, Jamie? What will you do all covered in steam and the Walker stopped dead in its tracks?"

"The boiler won't blow up," Jamie replied through a yawn. "We tested them, remember."

"Tested once isn't the same as tested every day," I muttered but, like Jamie, fatigue was taking the heat from my words. "Oh, go to sleep, Jamie! Your brain's gone already."

Jamie's soft snores were his only reply.

#

Father was fitted out for his uniform the next day. The Prince himself had suggested a tailor and, despite my horror at the price, father had commissioned two sets of garb. He'd been made Captain, just like Mr. Finlayson.

While he was getting fitted, it was left to Jamie and myself — more myself than him — to press on with the work and the pace was even more frenetic than it had been.

I found myself having to walk over to MacAllister's to check on their progress and was pleasantly surprised to discover Samuel Cattan — newly made ensign himself — supervising the finishing touches on the first of the new Walkers, the one rebuilt from the old Scuttler. Legs, cables, and the chassis for the second Walker were waiting nearby while the Weasel — who had only been made corporal rather than commissioned as an officer to his disgust and everyone else's delight — oversaw the work on the timbers for the third.

"We'll have all four by the end of the week," Samuel told me, "provided you've managed to assemble all the boilers and engines."

I had, of course. In fact, we were going to be done testing all the engines by the end of the day and I'd come to discuss their transportation to MacAllister's yard.

"When you've got the Scuttler done, bring it over to our yard to pick up the finished equipment."

Samuel's eyebrows rose. "That's quick work!"

"Well, you know how we managed," I reminded him. He'd seen how we'd poured multiple castings from the same mold and how making the same parts had allowed us to speed up all the work overall.

"So what will you do when we're all done?" Samuel asked, his expression troubled.

"I'm to be left behind, as you no doubt know, and set to keeping the yard and the running of the house," I said, my voice coloring with indignation.

"Well, women don't go to war," Samuel reminded me.

"What of Boadicea and her chariot?"

"So you like it to be Danni and her chariot?" Samuel countered, shaking his head. "What about the words you had with Jamie?"

I knew the words he meant and I wasn't surprised that Jamie had repeated them. They were the same I'd said in the night after the supper, the same words I tried again on father the next morning and the same words I'd used on Samuel himself — all to no affect, of course.

Of the three, father and I had had the most honest discussion while Jamie had been completely unwilling to listen to reason and Samuel — Ensign Cattan — had been very much the middle of the three.

"Danni," father had said when I'd approached him the next morning, "we've discussed this."

"You never said anything about going off to fight."

"That was before the Prince commissioned my son," father replied hotly.

"He expected you to demand a commission of your own," I said. "The Prince played you for a fool."

"Not a fool, Danni," father replied softly. "A parent." He gave me a sad look. "Would you really want me to let Hamish order Jamie about?"

I made a face and shook my head. "No, no I wouldn't want that," I admitted. And then I blurted, "But you might get killed!"

Father gave me a sad smile. "As my son said so poignantly, no man can escape death."

Chapter Ten

"Miss, miss!" Bessie's voice came urgently in my ears. I opened my eyes and groaned. Bessie was fully clothed and bore a tray with a slice of buttered bread and a cup of hot tea. "It's time Miss."

I sat up, reached for the tea, took a small sip — it was piping hot — and spurred myself out of bed.

"The boilers?"

"Mapes took care of them, Miss," Bessie said. Her voice sounded a bit odd when she said 'Mapes' and I wondered if perhaps she was getting a bit of a crush. If so, I realized that I'd best warn her about Meara — it wasn't at all clear where *that* one's heart stood but if she wanted Mapes, his only hope would be to give in gracefully.

Ach aye, I know, what's Danni Walker doing taking about affairs of the heart? Steel and steam, Danni, that's your forté. Even so, some things are just obvious.

So the boilers were lit and soon the four finished Walkers would be ready to march off to war for King James and the Prince his son.

Going with them would be my father, my brother, and all that I held dear.

We'd promised the Prince six Walkers in four weeks, we had four ready in three weeks and his generals had decided that the last two could follow on.

They'd be ready by the end of the week anyway, even with just myself, Mapes and the idlers from MacAllister's yard left to do the assembly.

It wasn't really that bad, as we also had the three seamen helping us — "As we've no work of our own at the moment." — said Mr. Henry with a wink.

The truth was that they were probably just as eager as I to see the others leave and the last two Walkers following on. For, though all of us had worked so hard that we fell asleep wherever we could and whenever we could, the seamen and I were fired by the notion of a *trotting* steam horse.

Mr. Henry had struck up an acquaintance with Mr. Gillie, the puppeteer, to work out the rigging for such a motion. He'd come back elated one evening and showed us Mr. Gillie's drawings. When he rolled them out in front of me, I had to put my knuckles to my mouth to keep from squealing with delight. I know, not terribly lady-like and certainly not in keeping with propriety but you had to *see* those drawings!

"The biggest problem is balance," I said, pointing to the drawings, "as two feet are off the ground at all times."

"Aye, lass," Mr. Henry agreed, cocking an eye at me, "and how are you going to handle it?"

"I imagine you and Mr. Gillie already have an answer," I replied primly, "and you're just testing me."

"Perhaps," Mr. Henry allowed. "Or perhaps we were wondering if you could devise a better solution?"

"Let me think on it, after we've got the fifth Walker finished," I'd said, rising from the table and the papers and making my way to the front door, it being on the shortest route to MacAllister's forge.

"We'll be along in a bit!" Mr. Stoops had promised, leaning over the drawings to trace parts with a finger.

But now it was time to say goodbye to father, Jamie, Samuel, and all those who were following the Prince to war.

"We are going to Carlisle first," father had told me one night. "Colonel Grant believes that our Walkers will prove decisive."

"Are they planning the same ruse used on the Castle?" I asked, pointing in the direction of Edinburgh Castle. Our captured 3 pounders had come from there but only two of the Walkers carried them, the remaining four were to be equipped with the lighter 1 1/2 pound cannon.

"Something like that," father said, touching the side of his nose to indicate that it was a secret.

"Why Carlisle?" I asked. "Why not Newcastle? You're going clear to the other side of the coast."

"I understand that General Wade is organizing in strength at Newcastle," father told me. "So the Prince and his generals decided it would be wiser to be where the General Wade is not."

"Won't you have to fight him sometime?"

Father shook his head. "If we do it right lass, we'll inflame all of England to the cause and Wade's troops will vanish."

And now they were going. The cavalry went first, then the troops and finally the four Walkers, steaming and hissing as they plodded steadily, resolutely, without pause, in the rear of the small army.

Father's Walker, named *Defiance* was in the van, followed by MacAllister's *Destroyer* which was really nothing more than his rebuilt Scuttler — and privately called "Old Dodderer" by the rest of us for, try as we might, we could never quite get the cables and rigging right and the poor thing looked like it would fall over with every step.

Jamie came next with *Dominion* and the first of the smaller 1 1/2 pound cannon. He waved his hat at us — me, Meara, Bessie, and Mary — as his Walker rumbled by and then it was the turn of the Weasel — Corporal Jock Adams — looking thoroughly displeased as he brought up the rear and dealt with all the dirt raised by the passing army as he fought with the controls of his *Kingdom*. For all his desires, the Weasel wasn't comfortable with steam nor with coal nor with anything that interrupted his routine of being as lazy as possible. He'd only volunteered, so Samuel had told me, because Hamish had expected him — and because the Weasel decided there were riches to be had with the victorious army.

Knowing the Weasel as I did, I knew that he'd arrange to be on the winning side even if it wasn't the side he'd started on.

"I'll bet he packed a second coat," I'd said to Samuel when he first spoke of it.

"All he has to do is drive his Walker to the enemy camp and he'll get all the riches he wants," Samuel said. "Which is why he's going with the first group."

Samuel and Lieutenant Anderson remained behind, ready to bring on the two final Walkers when they were completed.

In fact, just after the army had passed, I found them buried in the guts of rigging the fifth Walker over at MacAllister's. Wordlessly I pitched in to help, joined not long after by Mapes and the three seamen who explained, "We've nothing better to do until November."

November? I quirked an eyebrow at Mr. Henry but he put a finger to his nose in much the same way as father had earlier.

Once father had explained that the Prince was intent on Carlisle, the reason for not using the steamship had become clear to me. But I sensed that something more than mere proximity would keep the three seamen from not using their new ship to the best of advantage. It seemed to me that what was really keeping them in port was some financial incentive on the part of the Prince.

It wasn't that Mr. Henry, Mr. Stoops, and Mr. MacArdle weren't "loyal to the cause" — although I suspected they were loyal only as long as they were in earshot of those whose tongues might wag — but they were seamen first, businessmen second, and crown subjects last.

What occurred to me was that a ship like our steamship would be very useful in moving items that other ships might find more difficult or might not be able to handle in the winds that prevailed.

Coupled with their interest in "The Trotter" and the way they were unconcerned about what armament we might put on it and I gathered that some time in November the problem of armaments would be resolved.

None of which had anything to do with the moment, particularly as Lieutenant Anderson was almost petulantly insistent of completing the assembly of his *Prestonpans* at the earliest possible moment.

"I'd petitioned the Prince himself for the name," the lieutenant had explained on the first day he arrived to look at the construction of his Walker.

Samuel had selected the less pre-possessing name *Edinburgh* but had been so enamored with his steed that he'd painted her name on the bow of the platform.

We had been convinced to use nautical terms for our land Walkers by the three seamen who decided the matter by repeated usage. Besides, while it did not necessarily made sense to refer to port and starboard on a platform that was nearly four feet wide, it was quite sensible to use 'bow' and 'stern' to refer to the business end and the steam end of the Walkers.

Also, as Mr. Henry had sagely observed, "Half your cannoneers are going to be sailors and there's no point in confusing them more than necessary."

Both Walkers were to have the smaller 1 1/2 pound cannons which was fine with me as I was still nervous about putting the heavy 3 pound cannons in the Walkers. Despite all the assurances of both Colonel Grant and Captain Finlayson, I was concerned that the recoil of the larger gun would do damage to the delicate cabling of the Walkers or that one of the cannon's own ropes would give and the thing would recoil right into the gear housing, even going so far as to pin the pilot between it and the boiler.

I noticed that neither Colonel Grant nor Captain Finlayson had requested command of a Walker for themselves, preferring to go with the remaining wheel-mounted artillery.

I thought that after the siege of Carlisle they might change their opinion and, if so, I fervently hoped that one would displace the Weasel of his command.

"Danni!" a voice pulled me out of my reverie and I realized that it had called at least once before. It was Samuel. "Pass up that cable, please."

"Sorry," I said, seeking out the cable he was pointing to from among the many other cables and grabbing the head of it to hand up to him.

"If you can keep from dreaming, we'll have this one finished by the evening," Samuel told me.

I made a face but bobbed my head. The sooner he and the Lieutenant were away, the safer father and Jamie would be.

No one knew how the Walkers would fare in battle. Sure, our first Walker and the Scuttler had done well enough in the assault on the Castle but that had been a special case, the first time the Walkers were ever used in war. How much news of their actions had reached Carlisle was anyone's guess but news always traveled faster when it was novel and the British were certain to pay dear for any news explaining the Castle's loss.

We worked until it was too dark for even torches to let us see and then called it a night. Samuel, for all his urgency was wrong: his Walker wasn't yet finished.

Early the next morning, however, he and his crew ran it through its paces. Samuel, who'd worked the Scuttler, was well-pleased with his mount and grinned from ear to ear as he raced it across the fields.

"It flies, Danni, it flies!" he shouted as he raced past me, leaving a trail of steam and smoke as the loud, steady, thump-thump-thump-thump of the Walker made a dance on the ground.

He turned it around gamely — better than I'd managed, I regret to say — and raced it back to the forge, ready to mount the guns.

"The guns wait until we've finished the second Walker, ensign," Lieutenant Anderson reminded him, gesturing toward his still-unfinished *Prestonpans*.

"Aye, sir!" Samuel said, saluting and blowing off the steam of the boiler. He grinned at me and called, "Danni, get a barrow and we'll see how your latest invention works!"

Rather than racing myself, I nodded toward Mapes who gave me a look but dutifully trotted off to get the wheelbarrow. It was one of MacAllister's so I cared not the least whether it survived.

"That's right!" I called to Mapes as he positioned it under the Walker. "Now get away!" As soon as he was clear, I waved at Samuel and said, "Any time now!"

With a whoop of joy, Samuel pulled a special lever that had only been installed on these last two Walkers and, in one loud roar, the entire load of fire and flaming coals that had been feeding the boiler were dumped out of their grate into the waiting barrow below.

There was a smoldering and then a loud *whoosh!* as the dry timbers of the barrow caught fire and just as quickly turned to ash.

"We'll tell Hamish it was an accident," Samuel called down from the Walker where he'd craned his neck over the side to get a view.

"I'd hate to be anyone below when that was done," Mapes said, echoing my own sentiments.

"It would certainly cool their ardor," Lieutenant Anderson agreed, eyeing the burnt barrow warily. "Mapes, get a bucket and put that fire out, if you please."

Mapes nodded and rushed off, grabbing one of MacAllister's remaining apprentices on the way. It was going to take more than one bucket.

"It'd be better if we could arrange to dump only part of the fire," I said, looking at the Walker looming overhead. "That way the Walker could move on and not be immobilized."

"Aye," Lieutenant Anderson agreed. He eyed me speculatively, "And how long would that take, Miss Steam?"

I shook my head. "Let me think on it," I told him. With my eyes closed, I imagined the changes that might be made. When I opened my eyes again, Samuel was standing in front of me.

"Don't set your hair on fire, Danni," he said to me affectionately. "I'm sure the Lieutenant will give you a day before you deliver your next miracle."

#

But the solution was easy, as I explained the next day, "See, all we do is split the grate into two halves, so we can dump each half separately." I showed the quick sketch I'd made that morning to Samuel and Lieutenant Anderson.

"That's brilliant, Danni," Samuel agreed. "But we've no time to do it with these two; it would require whole new castings."

"It would only take a couple of more days."

"We need to be off as quickly as possible," Lieutenant Anderson said solemnly. "I appreciate the thought, Miss Walker, but time is of the essence."

"Why?" I asked peevishly. "They're still on the march and won't reach Carlisle for days yet."

"Could your invention save us two days?" Lieutenant Anderson asked skeptically. He saw the look on my face and continued, "Then we'll have to do without."

I lowered my head, frowning and then looked back up again. "We could send the castings to you."

"Ach, Danni, and how would we fit them?" Samuel asked. He reached forward to pat my shoulder. "We'd need a fitted yard and several days for all the work."

"Let's talk of this later," Lieutenant Anderson said, waving toward his still unfinished Walker. "Our duty is clear."

Samuel nodded and the two of them returned to their efforts to assemble the final Walker.

A moment later, my heart heavy for reasons I couldn't explain, I moved to help them.

#

We finished *Prestonpans* early the next morning and Lieutenant Anderson and his crew eagerly took it out for a trial walk. I stayed behind as Samuel and his crew stoked up the fires on their *Edinburgh* and then made to give chase.

As *Edinburgh* reached the gates of MacAllister's yard, Samuel called back to me, "Aren't ye coming along, Danni?"

I shook my head. "I'd best be getting back to my yard."

He waved in reply, turning his attention to his tiller and gears as the Walker clonked away.

Bessie was waiting for me at the archway when I arrived.

"Are they done?" she asked. I nodded. "And they'll be leaving tomorrow?"

"Yes, I imagine so."

"Is Mapes going with them?" Bessie asked. I nodded glumly. "Will he come back?"

"Bessie," I said, grabbing her by the shoulders and pulling her close, "I don't know if *any* of them will come back."

Bessie sobbed against my chest. My tears dripped onto her blond hair.

"Miss!" Meara' voice interrupted us. I turned to look at her and Mary, coming from their room in the stables. Meara had a very determined look on her face, one that brooked no challenge — the sort of look I got from time to time. "You can't let him go!" she said to me. "He's English, if they capture him, they'll hang him."

It took me only a moment to realize that she was referring to Mapes. I shook my head. "I can't stop him, Meara."

"Then I'm going with him," Meara declared stoutly.

"They're not having any women with them," I told her. "Even wives are staying behind." Mostly. I knew of a few who refused and were following on, officially not part of the Prince's army but there all the same — and, I suspect — quite welcome.

Meara cupped her chest. "I'm not all that big, with trousers and a shirt, I could pass for a lad."

I didn't argue — it was true enough. Meara was just about as large in the bosom as I was which was nothing much at all. I didn't mind; large breasts would have interfered with my work.

"You'd go as a boy?" Bessie squeaked. She turned to me. "And you'd help her?"

"I've got nothing better to do," I said, smiling at Meara. To Bessie, I said, "Get the sewing kit and meet us in the dining room, bring the white and the black cloth."

We'd kept bolts of both so that we could make rough clothes easily enough as forge-work always ate clothing. I was quite a hand at sewing, even if I didn't like it nearly as much as working metal. For me, cloth was far less demanding than molten metal and so something of a relaxation.

"Meara, get Mary and we'll have a sewing party!" I said.

"She's not to come," Meara declared.

"Ach, no, but she can help with the sewing," I said waving aside her objection. "If she doesn't know how, there's no better time than now to learn."

Meara was off in a flash back to the stables while I followed Bessie into the house.

We worked until it was dark and then Bessie made us a quick, simple meal of bread and butter but by then we'd two well-made if rough sets of clothing that fit Meara quite well. We'd also made Mary a new set of house clothes, long black skirt and white apron.

"Now all we need are shoes for you and boots for Meara," I declared.

"I could go barefooted," Meara offered.

"Not on a Walker," I told her, shaking my head firmly. "Too many hot things that could burn."

"Mapes is going with Mr. Cattan, isn't he?" Mary asked. She didn't wait for a answer before plunging on, "Won't he recognize Meara?"

"If he does, he'll say nothing," I told her, reminding myself to have words with him.

"But haven't they got their men already?" Mary persisted.

"We'll take care of that," I said, nodding to Meara who had given me a panicked look.

"What are they going to call you?" Mary ploughed on. "You can't say your name is Meara, 'cuz that's only a girl's name."

I looked to Meara, my brows raised questioningly.

"I'll be Billy," she said after a moment, her lips dropping at the memory of the young orphan who'd died. "Billy Walker," she glanced at me for permission, "if that's all right with you, Miss."

"A relative from Leith," I suggested. "I'd heard about you and you came recommended for apprentice."

"That would be marvelous," Meara said, a huge grin spreading across her face.

"But what about Mr. Walker?" Mary asked, glancing my way.

"There are a lot of Walkers around here," I told her. "Not even father knows all of them."

Mary seemed satisfied with that and turned her attention to her dinner.

She was *not* pleased when I had her and Bessie boil enough water for the four of us to take baths.

"It'll be the last time for a while before Meara gets to see a tub again," I'd said, putting an end to any argument. "Besides, Mary, you're to sleep with us tonight."

"Here?" Mary asked, all big-eyed. She glanced toward Meara. "What about the stables?"

"Meara won't be there," I told her. Meara gave me an odd look. "She's going to be with Mapes at MacAllister's."

"I am?"

"Yes," I said. "We'll be going there after we're finished getting you all clean." I nodded toward the now-empty tub and gestured for Mary to get in. Being littlest, she was last. Bessie finished toweling herself off and got dressed while I poured the soapy water over Mary's very dirty self.

Meara, in the meantime, had put on her new clothes but came back with a terrible downcast look. "My hair's too long!"

I nodded. I'd already thought of that. "Sit yourself over there and we'll take care of that," I told her. "Bessie, you're dressed, finish washing Mary."

Bessie sighed resignedly but took my place, made a face at Mary, causing the younger girl to laugh.

"After I'm done, I'll want you to cut my hair, too," I told Meara. She gave me an odd look but said nothing as I'd picked up the scissors and started on her bangs. "Some of the Highlanders wear their hair long, even in a braid," I said as I snipped. "But a proper Edinburgh lad wouldn't have his so long."

"Just as long as I don't look like a girl," Meara said determinedly.

She made a face when I was finished and dusted off the remaining bits of hair as she stood up from the chair but said nothing as she waved me to the chair.

"How short?"

"Like yours," I told her. In a low voice that didn't carry far, I added, "I don't want to get any nits from Mary."

"She doesn't have any," Meara swore but began cutting anyway. She wasn't very skilled and I feared it would be a while before I could pass a mirror without shuddering but the deed was soon done and I thanked her.

"So now we go?" she said as I stood up and dusted the last red strands from my body.

"Not yet," I told her. "We've got to check on the other two."

Meara snorted in agreement. While Mary and Bessie were both diligent, they were still young enough to find excuses for shirking their chores.

"Also, I want to raid father's closet," I told her. She gave me a worried look. "It's getting cold, if there's an old jacket or a sweater, you're welcome to them."

Meara nodded a silent thanks and we went upstairs. Father had left his door unlocked and in his closet we found an old long jacket and a sweater that wasn't too shabby.

"Can't have you dying of the cold, can I?" I said as I passed the things to her.

"Thank you, miss," Meara said, her tone reminding me that, in spite of our best efforts, we'd let just that happen to little Billy, her namesake.

Back downstairs, I made certain that Bessie and Mary could manage dragging the tub to the back yard — "And then straight to bed with you! I'll want it properly warmed by the time I return."

The two girls giggled at the notion.

#

Meara — Billy — and I walked the way to MacAllister's in silence. It was dark out and the night was none too warm but we knew the way so we had no trouble following the path.

We made good time and I wasn't surprised to see torches burning as the crews of the Walkers finished their preparations.

"Who's there?" a young, nervous lad challenged.

Instead of answering, I nudged Meara and pulled my collar up so that I would be hard to recognize.

"My name's William Walker and I was sent by Miss Walker," Meara said in a husky voice. "She told me they were looking for apprentices."

"Go away, she told you wrong!" the voice replied.

Meara gave me an imploring look but I nudged her forward.

"She said to speak to Mr. Cattan," I said in my own gruff voice.

"Ensign Cattan is too busy," the voice replied.

"Too busy for what?" Samuel Cattan's voice called out from the night. "For what, private Stibbens?"

"Sir, there's a lad here says he was sent by Miss Walker," the young private reported stiffly.

"Perhaps I should talk with him then," Samuel said. "Come here."

This time I didn't have to nudge Meara into motion but I could hear her ragged breath and realized that she'd never been this scared in her life.

Samuel's eyes creased as he tried to make out Meara' — Billy's — face in the dusk.

"Did you speak with Danni, then?" Samuel asked and the longing in his voice made my heart skip a beat and I could hear my blood pounding in my ears.

"I did," Meara said, pitching her voice low. "She's a bonnie lass and a distant relative."

"A relative?" Samuel asked.

"Aye, but we're from Leith so we didn't see them much," 'Billy' replied. "But when I heard about the Prince and the Walkers... well, I made my way to her."

"So you wish to serve the King over the water?" Samuel said.

"Aye," Meara said simply.

"I'm afraid to inform you, then, that our crews are full," Samuel said.

Beseechingly, Meara turned toward me.

"Billy here is a good friend of Mr. Mapes," I said, trying to keep from being too loud. "You'd get a great crew with the two of the."

"I would, would I?" Samuel said. "But Mr. Mapes is serving with Lieutenant Anderson on *Prestonpans*." He pursed his lips in thought. "Let us ask him."

Reluctantly we followed him to the second Walker where Lieutenant Anderson was desperately trying to get his men to finish re-rigging some cables.

"Show him what you know," I urged Meara. She shot me a nervous look but took a deep breath and moved forward to join the work. In a moment, Lieutenant Anderson's voice could be heard asking in amazement, "And you want to fight with us?"

"Aye, sir," Meara said gruffly enough. "There's no work at the docks and these are rare beasts, they are."

"It'll be crowded and cramped," Lieutenant Anderson warned.

"I'll manage, sir," 'Billy' said, bringing up his right hand in a simple salute.

"Very well, report to Sergeant Mapes and then right back here," Lieutenant Anderson said cheerfully, "I'll want to see how you are with the rest of this rigging."

Mapes was nearly our undoing. He took one look at Meara and squawked but she made a quick motion and said, "Sergeant Mapes. I've heard about you from Miss Walker."

"Miss Walker?" Mapes repeated. "And you are?"

"William Walker, a distant relative," Meara told him quickly.

"Oh! Oh, pleased to meet you, Mr. Walker," Mapes said, catching on and stretching out a hand. "If you're recommended by Miss Walker, I'm sure you'll work out just fine."

His eyes sought me out and he gave me a poorly disguised wink. I coughed and hastily backed away, preparing to make a retreat only to find myself bumping up against someone. Samuel.

"I'm sorry," I said gruffly.

"Did you come from Walker's forge?" Samuel asked, giving me a hopeful look.

"Aye." I was a bit worried about the growing intensity of his gaze.

"How do you know it?" Samuel asked, his eyes narrowing.

"I'm a friend of Mr. Pugh's, he sent me," I told him.

"You're a friend of — " and then he recognized me. Before he could say anything more, I nudged him in the ribs and dragged him off into the darkness.

"Danni," he said in a hoarse whisper, "what are you doing?" His head turned back towards Meara. "And who was— not *Meara?*"

"Don't you tell anyone, Samuel Cattan," I ordered, nudging him once more in the ribs. "She's in love with him and won't stay behind."

"And she's good at the job," Samuel agreed reluctantly.

"She *is* good," I agreed, surprised at her competence. She must have been watching our work with the Walkers more carefully than I'd realized at the time. "And Mapes won't tell."

"They could both get killed, you know."

"As could you," I reminded him. I regretted my words instantly. "Samuel, I — "

He reached forward, leaned down and kissed me. At first I struggled, surprised and frightened but then... I moved closer to him, felt his arms wrap around me and I didn't want the moment to end.

"Ensign!" a voice called from the work area.

Samuel stood back. "One moment!" He smiled down at me and leaned forward, resting his head against mine before straightening once more.

"Come back to me," I said, my heart racing and my palms sweaty. "Promise you'll come back."

Samuel shook his head, his expression downfallen. "I canna make that promise, Danni, and you know it."

"*Try, then!*" I swore at him.

He smiled. "Aye, Danni, I'll try to come back to you." He turned and waved over his shoulder as he raced back to his duty. He turned back to me once more. "That much I can promise, that I'll try."

And then he was gone and I was left to walk back the long way home.

#

"It'll be all right, Miss, don't worry," Bessie told me anxiously as we joined the throngs that had gathered to watch the last of the Walkers head off to the war. "Don't cry so, please."

I wiped my eyes and nodded at her young wisdom.

The two machines passed us at a fast walking pace. I'd impressed upon Lieutenant Anderson the need to conserve coal and suggested that it would be wise not to stress the engines too much in the first day. He had been mulish but Samuel had backed me up in my opinion.

"It would not be in our interests to have one explode before we joined battle," Samuel had observed.

And so the Walkers moved slowly out of sight, finally disappearing around a bend, saluted by a single gun fired from the captured Castle.

CHAPTER ELEVEN

"Stand still, Mary, or I'll prick you with the needle again!" I warned as I lightly swatted the little girl on the shoulder to add emphasis to my words. "I know you're excited, we're all excited but if you don't stand still we can't finish your outfit and until we do that, we can't go Guising!"

They tell me that in the Colonies they've some strange celebration around Hallowe'en where children dress up and go to doors looking for sweets but I can't imagine that it's anything nearly as good as Guising.

Mary stood still and I went back to work watched by a worried Bessie.

"Oh, come on, Bessie, everyone will be doing it!" I said in answer to her expression.

"But not dressed as a *boy!*" Bessie complained.

"That's only me," I reminded her. "You're dressed as the noble lady of the house."

Bessie bit her lip to keep from speaking which is probably just as well or I would have hit her.

We *needed* to go Guising. Needed it more than I'd let on. I'm pretty sure that Bessie, who was in charge of our larder, had a suspicion of my sudden cheer over the traditional holiday where children prance about Edinburgh reciting verse or performing skits for the delight of households in return for sweets, apples, and other rewards.

Every little bit would help and — besides, it'd give me a chance to test my disguise. I was pretty sure that Bessie had tumbled to my plan but she'd have to go along with it, particularly if no one recognized me when we went Guising tonight. If they did, then I'd have to try something else.

"Now remember, for tonight I'm Samuel Clarke just up from the next smithy."

"Yes, Mr. Clarke," Mary chirped dutifully, perhaps wary of my hand with the sewing needle. She glanced down at her finery and her eyes widened.

Sewing wasn't my first love but I took pride in anything I put my hand to and this particular creation was coming along nicely. When I was done, little Mary would look every inch the princess while Bessie was already primped up to be a queen.

And I? I was dressed as a prince, naturally.

Our skit would be a play on courtly manners, neither obsequious nor insolent.

Good manners were prized in Edinburgh town where all too often it was all we had and courtly manners had come back into vogue with the arrival of Prince Charles.

One final stitch of frill onto Mary's cuffs and...

"Done!" I said. "Go look in the mirror."

"I never thought she'd look so pretty," Bessie admitted as we followed little Mary to the mirror and watched as she preened and pranced in delight.

"I'm a princess! I'm a princess!" Mary squealed happily.

"A little less prancing, princess, or your costume will come undone," I warned her. Instantly she stopped, scrutinizing her garment with wide eyes.

"Are we ready?" I asked, looking to Bessie but it was Mary who turned and pointed to me in alarm.

"Your hat!" She said.

"Yes, quite," I agreed, turning back and grabbing the hat that, until early this morning had been nothing but a lump of wool in the style that many of the Highlanders wore. Now it had a jaunty long feather sticking out of the back, said feather belonging to that useless cock of ours that had finally found its way into the cooking pot.

I put the hat on and then dropped low in a courtly bow, "Princess and Princess, our night calls."

#

We had a marvelous night and everyone cheered and praised the outfits of the princesses. They eyed the taller 'prince' with slightly less favor but never in the whole night — even when we went to Mr. Pugh's — did anyone take me for other than a lad with a poor costume.

I was elated and our sack was full of the sort of things that would keep our bellies from grumbling for the next several days which was the true purpose of our outing.

I think that Bessie enjoyed herself; I know Mary did for she was babbling about it all the way home and into bed, dropping off mid-word as she slipped into a sound sleep. I smiled at her little snores and glanced at Bessie who put her clothes away carefully and slowly.

"How bad is it, Miss?" she asked as we crawled in on either side of the sleeping Mary.

"What?"

"You were more worried about the treats than the performance," Bessie said in a low voice so as not to disturb Mary. "You wouldn't do that unless you were worried. So how bad is it?"

"We'll do fine," I assured her. She gave me a doubtful look. "I've a plan."

"Oh, I was afraid you'd say that," Bessie replied. "Your plans frighten me so."

"But they work," I said in protest.

"That's what frightens me," Bessie agreed. But she slipped an arm over Mary to grab my shoulder and stroke my cheek before pulling it back to wrap around Mary's waist and closed her eyes.

#

"This will never work!" Bessie protested the next morning when I had her dress. "I look nothing like you!"

"That won't matter because those who see you won't know," I assured her. "Mary will keep an eye out and when someone comes whom we know, I'll take off the cap and fluff my hair. Otherwise I'll be Mr. Clarke, apprentice come to help with work here at Walker's while Mr. Walker is away."

"And you expect people to believe that?" Bessie said, eyebrows raised as high as they would go.

"Of course, why wouldn't they?"

"That Mr. Clarke and Miss Walker are never in the same place?"

"Well, that's not true, you'll be Miss Walker when strangers come calling," I assured her.

"People talk, Miss," Bessie reminded me. "What happens when they talk about Miss Walker looking like me to those who know you and your red hair?"

"Do you have a better plan?" I said, fuming. She was right but I was hoping that it would work anyway. We needed the money. No one would be willing to let a girl shoe their horses or mend their metalwork but they'd think nothing of giving the same jobs to a gangly lad. "Anyway, as soon as word gets about, people would come looking for Mr. Clarke and that's when we'll have to be careful."

"If the Deacon learns about this, what will happen to you?" Bessie persisted. "Please, Miss, there's got to be another way."

"Tweet! Tweet!" Mary's cry came from the front of the house. Someone was coming who she didn't know.

I put on my hat and pushed my hair up under it.

"How do I look?"

Bessie was too frightened to answer and then it was too late as a horse clattered through the arches.

"I've post for a Miss Walker," the man said. "And my horse needs shoeing if there's any can do it."

I nodded firmly to Bessie while saying in a gruff voice, "I can do it."

The man looked at me critically.

"I'm apprenticed," I assured him. "I was sent up to help out while Mr. Walker's away."

"Then you must be his Danielle," the man said, smiling to Bessie and reaching inside his tunic to pull out his letter. He frowned at her. "You look a bit shorter than I'd imagined." He handed her the letter. "This is for you."

"May we offer you something to drink? Tea?" I said, turning toward his horse and reaching to hold the reins while he dismounted.

"I'd appreciate it," he said. "I'm parched. I'd even drink water if it was offered." He jumped down and nodded at me, relinquishing his mount.

I walked the mare over to the post and tied her reins to it. A moment later, I'd inspected all four hooves and had set shoes in the fire. The old shoes were well worn, one was even cracked from hard riding.

"Where did you come from, if I may ask?" I said, while removing the nails from the old shoes and throwing the useless remnants toward our pile of scrap.

"Near Carlisle," the man replied. "I brought dispatches from the Prince and Mr. Walker asked me to bring a letter to his daughter."

"Are they well then?" I asked, my heart skipping a beat. "And the Walkers, how are they?"

"Those infernal machines!" the man swore. "Frightened my horse so badly the first time we laid eyes on them that she bolted. That's half the wear to those shoes, right there!"

"Two others left a few days back," I observed.

"Aye, and they frightened her again while we weren't halfway here," the man growled. "They must not have stopped once, they moved so fast."

"What of Carlisle and the Prince?" I asked, pulling the first shoe from the fire and beating it into shape. I nodded toward the horse. "Will she take a hot shoe?"

"Hot shoe?"

"Aye, a hot shoe molds better to the foot, fits tighter," I told him.

He shook his head. "No, she'll not take one of those. Next you'll be wanting to fit her with one of those infernal steam engines."

I smiled and shook my head. "I'm sure she's fine the way she is."

"Raised her from a foal," the man said. He turned to me and nodded. "My name's Williams, Sean Williams."

"Samuel Clarke," I said, nodding in kind before returning to my work.

Fortunately Mary and Bessie returned at that moment with a pot of tea.

"Mr. Williams here was just telling me of the steam horses," I said to Bessie. "He's not so sure he likes your invention, Miss Walker."

"You invented them?" Mr. Williams said, eyebrows rising. "A girl?"

"Ach, Mr. Williams, ye're not to go believing all that ye're told, you know," Bessie said in a terrible imitation of a Scottish accent. I couldn't understand how she could get it so wrong; she'd grown up here most of her life and she knew our soft Edinburgh accent. She was trying too hard and I made a face at her from behind Mr. Williams.

"I wasn't here so I only got to hear about them, not see them," I said to Mr. Williams. "What are they like?"

I turned back to my shoeing while he took his tea and put together his answer.

"Well, the basis of them all is a cart body," he said after a moment. "But it's raised on four wooden legs eight feet off the ground and on top of that there's a steam contraption, ropes as thick as a man's wrist and cannon at the front."

"How do they sound?"

"Hissing and clumping, they sound like the Devil's steed," Mr. Williams replied. Then his expression changed. "And they're fast, fast as a horse can walk, sometimes faster."

"Faster?" I repeated, surprised. Father and I had discussed the need to hide the Walkers' true speed, to keep some in reserve for when it was really needed. "How much?"

"Ach, I couldna keep up with one at a trot the other day," Mr. Williams said, taking another sip of tea. He gave me a look and I realized that I'd been talking too much and working too little. I turned back to the shoeing but nodded meaningfully to Bessie.

Good girl that she was, she picked up my meaning.

"And the British, what do they think of them?"

"I don't think they've yet seen them," Mr. Williams replied. "I've heard rumors along the way and they're more terrible than the steaming beasties themselves."

The steaming beasties. The words caught my ear and I decided that I liked them.

The mare was good or too tired to protest but either way I had her shod fresh in less than a quarter of an hour. He haggled a bit over the price but I was adamant and he settled quickly enough.

"Will there be time for the Miss to read her letter and write a reply?" I asked him, wondering how I could absent myself long enough to do that without raising his curiosity.

"No," Mr. Williams replied, patting his satchel, "I've dispatches for His Majesty the Prince." He nodded toward Bessie and then gave me a more curt look before climbing back into his saddle.

"Give my kindest regards to my father!" Bessie called after him. He acknowledged her with a wave of his hand and then was gone through the archway, trotting steadily down the southern road on the way to Carlisle.

No sooner than he was out of sight, I grabbed the letter from Bessie, tore it open and read it hungrily.

#

27 October 1745
En route to Carlisle

My dearest daughter,

This is a quick note to let you know that I and your brother are doing as well as can be expected.

Your Walkers are more than keeping pace with the speed of the infantry. Hamish and his idiot apprentice have already had a trotting race with some of the cavalry and were thrilled — and somewhat enriched — by their victory. I warned them both to keep their speed in reserve and to be careful to keep their engines properly oiled. I fear that Ensign Adams — yes, he is now Ensign, for Hamish talked the Prince into his commission — and his crew will be derelict in this duty but, as he is assigned directly under Lieutenant MacAllister, I am limited in the amount of attention I can apply to him.

Colonel Grant — an excellent fellow in all regards — and Captain Finlayson have joined with me in discussing our best option for the forthcoming siege of Carlisle. We all agree that a ruse or a show of force to gain the city without bloodshed would be the best. Captain Finlayson and I have devised a plan which we will present tonight to Lord Murray, the Prince, *and his advisers. Hopefully, it will turn out well.*

> *Please keep us in your thoughts as we keep you in ours.*
> *Your loving father,*
> *Daniel*

#

"That idiot Weasel!" I swore as I wiped the tears that were running down my cheeks.

"Miss?" Bessie said. I passed her the letter. She gave me a woeful look; she was not much practiced at reading.

"Take it inside and read it to Mary," I told her. Bessie's eyes widened but I had no pity. "She's got to learn to read herself, so you can teach her at the same time."

Bessie's look brightened at the notion and I guessed that she'd use her 'teaching' as an excuse to do the reading at the slow pace she usually employed.

"Go on, now!" I told her, making a shooing motion with my hands. "I've work to do."

Bessie looked around the empty and clean yard. "What work?"

"Never you mind, I'll think of something," I told her. "And while I am, you and Mary should start thinking about this evening's meal."

Bessie nodded and walked toward the kitchen, glancing now and then at the letter in her hand.

I'd warned the Weasel. If he wasn't careful with the oiling of the engine, he might find it breaking when he least needed it. Worse, if he was neglecting something that simple, what else would he do?

How, I wondered, did he and MacAllister win their race? I regretted showing them the other steam plugs and feared that they'd set their boilers at a higher pressure. I recalled how Hamish looked oddly at me when I'd explained that I'd tested the new boiler to ten atmospheres.

"Why not run them that high, then?" he'd asked at the time.

"Because we don't know how they'd handle the extra strain," I'd told him tetchily. He'd snorted. "That's easy enough," he'd said, "just try them."

"Ach, but at that pressure if the boiler were to give, it'd produce such a cloud of steam — "

"Ach, lass, ye worry too much!" Hamish had interjected. "I've had a bit of steam on me and it's only left a wee burn, nothing more."

Try as I did, I couldn't get him to understand that steam at higher pressures was also at a higher temperature as well.

"Steam's steam," he'd said dismissively.

In a few more minutes, I'd been reduced to angry splutters and he'd stomped off, feeling that he'd triumphed over a 'silly girl' — as he'd muttered, thinking my ears weren't able to hear him.

My reverie was interrupted by a set of loud voices suddenly booming in the archway to the courtyard. I pulled over my cap, recognizing them as belonging to our three seamen.

"Aye, Danni, are ye ready for some real work?" Mr. Stoops called as he caught sight of me.

"What are you thinking?" I asked, hoping he was referring to the trotter.

"We've a cartload of timber and steel just behind us and we thought you might be able to put them all to some use," Mr. Henry said to me with a broad smile.

"And ye'll have three bored seamen ready to hand," Mr. MacArdle added with a nod and a wink.

"Is there any way you can think to use all that?" Mr. Henry finished as the sound of a heavily laden cart rattled through the archway.

I grinned back at them, infected by their enthusiasm. "I suppose there might be something we could do with all that, provided you've coal enough for the forge."

"Coal and coke," Mr. Stoops agreed. "That's in the next cart."

And where, I wondered to myself, did three poor seamen manage to find such treasure as to afford all this? I wondered if perhaps they'd already sold plans to agents in Leith port. Even now, plans for the Walkers might be making their way to the palace at Versailles.

Ah, Danni, I thought to myself, but a Trotter!

"Then perhaps two of you would be so kind as to unload and start the construction of the platform while the third helps me in setting up the molds."

"Molds?" Mr. Henry asked, eyebrows quirking upwards. He gestured toward our already completed engine. "Why do we need molds?"

"I was thinking, Mr. Henry, that such a special beastie might be best powered by *two* engines and two boilers."

All three seamen stopped and turned to stare at me, gawping in surprise.

It was Mr. Stoops who found his voice first. "Why not cast two more and we'll put one our ship?"

I smiled at him and nodded. "I think that would be a marvelous idea."

"An engine for port and another for starboard," Mr. Stoops said to the others. Their expressions changed from the quizzical to the delighted.

And so we were committed to building two more engines and making a super Trotter as well as a super steamship.

#

I missed Jamie. He was always the one that would ask the questions I hadn't considered. That night I was in the study making new drawings for the double engines. With two engines, I could rig one for each pair of legs. As I started the new drawing, I could hear Jamie say, "But, Danni, how will you keep the engines running together?"

Don't be silly, I thought to myself, I'll just —

But how would I? I suddenly wondered. I could just control them both, firing first one and then the other as needed but that would mean doing twice as much work and that would mean twice as many chances of getting the plug timing wrong.

"And what if all the legs moved at once?" I could hear Jamie ask.

Well, either the Walker would start a gallop or it'd come crashing down to the ground and we'd have the devil's work getting it sorted. Worse, live coal and hot steam would be splashing about the platform.

"You're taking on more than you can handle all at once," I could imagine Jamie saying. "You're trying to gallop when you can't trot."

I sighed. Even though he wasn't here, he was right. I missed having him close by to explain to, to have him raise an eyebrow or to splutter at my latest schemes. At least I had his memory to set me straight.

But we were committed to two engines. What would I tell the three seamen?

#

"How about we build two Trotters?" I said to the seamen the next day.

"Two?" Mr. Henry said, raising a hand to scratch his balding pate. "Why two, Danni?"

"Two would be good," Mr. Stoops said even before I could answer. "The platforms aren't all that hard."

"Who will crew them?" Mr. MacArdle asked the others.

"And can you be done in three weeks?" Mr. Henry asked, glancing at the other two with a knowing look.

"Three weeks for two Walkers?" I chided them. "And didn't we build six in six weeks?"

"There's that," Mr. Stoops said to the other two.

"But there was more help," Mr. Henry reminded him.

"And isn't the rigging going to be different?" Mr. MacArdle asked.

"We could get Mr. Gillie and Mr. Pugh to help," I said, feeling inspired.

"I don't know," Mr. Henry said, shaking his head. "Mr. Pugh is not a young man — "

"And not Scottish," Mr. Stoops added.

"Neither are you," Mr. MacArdle told him.

"Mr. Gillie, though, would he be interested?" Mr. Henry asked.

"He'd want paying, naturally," I told them. "But he's the one for rigging."

The three sailors looked affronted. When he recovered, Mr. Henry said, "Ah, lass! Don't ye think we might know a bit about that?"

"It was Mr. Gillie who designed the original rigging," I reminded them. "And he's helped with the trotter rigging, too."

"So he might like to see it for real," Mr. Stoops said approvingly.

"And he'd keep mum," Mr. Henry said conspiratorially to the others.

"And where would you be going on the twenty-first of this month?" I asked the three sailors in sudden exasperation. "And how were you hoping to keep it a secret from me?"

Mr. Henry glanced to the others who nodded for him to speak on their behalf. "We were going to tell you when the time was right, lass."

"Ach, George, you're not fooling anyone, it was you who said we should see what the lass can ken on her own," Mr. MacArdle chided him.

"I ken that you're going to take your steamship and any others that you've commissioned — " I saw them exchange looks and smiled at learning that I'd guessed right on that score "— for some mission for the Prince." Mr. Henry started to reply but I raised a hand. "And that got me to wondering what would cause seamen with a mind for profit to wait so long in using their very special vessel, a ship that can sail as easily with as against the wind.

"Such a ship could easily evade any sailship, including any warship," I continued. "And so, it seems that whatever enticed you three would involve weapons and that only means artillery, heavy artillery and, given that you've admitted to building more steamships, it means a fair bit of artillery."

The three exchanged startled looks. Clearly, my guess was spot on.

"Add to that your desire to help me build the trotters and I have to imagine that you're hoping to mount some of that artillery on our trotters — and that speed will be of the essence."

"Right in all particulars, lass," Mr. Henry conceded with an approving gleam in his eyes. "And now that you know, I'll have your word that you won't tell anyone else."

"Not even your father," Mr. Stoops added.

"Nor your Mr. Cattan, either," Mr. MacArdle warned.

"I'll have to tell the girls," I said. "They'll need to keep the secret when I'm gone."

"Gone?"

"Two trotters?" I said. "And only I know how their built?"

"Well," Mr. Henry admitted, "we'll know."

"And the crew?" I asked. "You've crew enough for your steamship and two trotters?"

Mr. Henry glanced to the others who both spread their hands in defeat.

"What sort of guns?" I asked before they could think of further objections. "I presume two of you plan to be the gunners."

"We hadn't thought of two guns until just now," Mr. Henry admitted. "And the Prince didn't know for certain but there's hope for a brace of eighteen pounders."

"Eighteen pounders?" I cried in amazement. "And how much do they weigh?"

"About three tons," Mr. Stoops said, glancing to the others for agreement.

"And do you suppose, with all the weight of our boiler and engine, that we'll be able to *trot* with three tons of cannon?" I demanded. I shook my head at them. "You're mad, you are."

Mr. Henry grinned at me. "Aye lass, we know that," he said. "We figured you were just as mad as we are, thinking to go off to the war with us!"

Well, he had me there. But I'd been thinking and thinking and I just couldn't see staying here at home while the war went south. I'd had two days of it so far and I just knew that I'd never manage more than a fortnight without grabbing a horse and charging after.

What the sailors were offering was much better.

"And where would we going, then?"

"Up north to get the artillery and then south," Mr. Henry replied evasively.

"Aberdeen, then," I guessed by their shocked looks that I was way off, so I continued, "okay, so not Aberdeen but then — London? That'd be where siege artillery would be needed most." I pursed my lips. "But you'd either have to meet the Prince there or bring at least another regiment of troops to guard the trotters."

"Cavalry would be better," Mr. Stoops said.

I shook my head. "Then you'd need horses and fodder when you already need coal." I raised a hand as they started to reply. "If you had any Scottish troops they'd have no trouble keeping up with us."

"It all depends upon the Prince," Mr. Henry said. "We'll have to see how he does."

"Not if you're going to sail north and then south to meet him, even in a steam ship, that'll take time."

"Less than a fortnight," Mr. Stoops corrected me.

"How were you planning on mounting this great gun of yours?" I asked. "The recoil would go through the boiler and engine both, wouldn't it?"

Mr. Henry and Mr. Stoops exchanged looks. Mr. MacArdle whistled in appreciation, saying, "We hadn't thought of that, lass."

"Have you an idea?" Mr. Stoops asked hopefully. The other two nodded, eyeing me expectantly.

"No, none at all," I told them with an irritated shake of my head. "But give me some time to think on it."

"We've not got much time lass," Mr. Henry reminded me.

"Which is why we need to get those castings started and need to start construction," I told them. I frowned for a moment then said, "We should build to the same length and width as before." I pursed my lips and glanced at them again. "Three tons, you say?"

They all nodded sheepishly.

"Well, soonest started is soonest finished," I said, moving to the forge. "Someone heap on the coke and we'll get a melt going."

#

Mr. Gillie was glad to oblige and proved a deft hand with the rigging, having surprised the three sailors by confessing that he'd been a sailor before becoming a puppeteer.

"More money in sailing, less danger in puppets," he'd explained when asked.

Mr. Pugh declined to have a direct hand in our efforts but was willing to cast small pieces and build as many plugs as we needed.

"No one knows how things will go," he confessed to me. "I was born in England and I'm hoping that either way I'll be still able to go there someday."

The three sailors were surprisingly sympathetic.

So we set him to small castings and intricate work. He had several suggestions from our earlier talks and his experience with the Walkers all of which proved invaluable.

Bessie and Mary were sworn to secrecy but they were obviously both terrified of the thought of me leaving them until I managed to get Mr. Pugh to keep an eye on them and join in on the pretense that Bessie was "Miss Walker."

"She needs to let Mary do all the errands," Mr. Pugh warned. "Otherwise too many in the town will compare stories."

Mr. Clarke became much talked about, particularly after I let the three sailors in on my deception.

"Aye, that'll work," Mr. MacArdle said. "You'll ship out with us as Mr. Samuel Clarke and no one will know otherwise."

#

"But what about the letters?" Bessie had asked when I'd told her my plan.

"Letters?"

"Your father will be expecting you to write back and he'll be sending his letters here," Bessie had said. She was right; I hadn't thought of that.

"Well, you'll write back, then," I told her. She looked appalled. "We'll try it with this letter now." I nodded at her. "What do you think I'd say in reply?"

"Well... you'd thank him for his letter and tell him to be careful and that you love him," Bessie said, starting slowly and gathering speed with each of my reassuring nods.

"And remind him to tell the Weasel to oil his engine," I added sharply.

"Of course," Bessie agreed, her tone making it plain that she couldn't understand my obsession with metal at all. Well, it's probably like Jamie said: I'd been touched by the metal fae as a child.

"So just write that," I told her.

"But, Miss, he'll know your writing and mine doesn't look like it at all!"

I pursed my lips. "You're right," I agreed. "Say that I'm writing with my other hand because I smashed my thumb." I nodded firmly, pleased with my solution.

"Ach, he'll have no trouble believing that!" Bessie agreed.

I glared at her but she was unrepentant.

#

2 November 1745

Dearest Father,

I was delighted to get your letter the other day and have read and re-read it many times, it warms my heart so.

Please forgive my poor writing but I bashed my thumb the other day — nothing too serious, you know how distracted I can be — so I am forced to write you with my other hand.

I am worried about the Weasel and his Walker. Please impress upon everyone the urgency of oiling and maintaining the machinery. Also, you should warn everyone that the extra plugs are not meant for general use. There's every reason to hope that at five atmospheres the boilers and engines will work perfectly — and no reason to assume that they'll not blow up at higher pressures.

Please take care of yourself and write again when you're able.

Your loving daughter,

Danielle

P.S.: You'll be pleased to know that we're getting help from an apprentice lad sent up from the south, a Mr. Samuel Clarke.

P.P.S.: Don't tell Samuel! Or if you do, don't let him get jealous.

#

"Well, it's not quite what I would have written," I said as I read through Bessie's effort. Her face fell and I added hurriedly, "But it's fine all the same." She brightened once more. "Now all we need is our Mr. Williams or some other courier and we'll send it off."

"The sailors are waving at you, Miss," Bessie said. My back was to the yard as she'd just come to me with the letter. She lowered her voice as she added, "Are ye certain you're not working yourself too hard?"

"Ach, Bessie, what makes you say that?"

"Well, you're out like a light when it's dark, Miss," Bessie said. And then, gathering her courage she added, "And you snore, Miss."

"I don't snore!" Jamie used to tease that I did and I was certain that I *didn't*.

"Ah, Miss, maybe it's Mary but the noise only comes when you're in the bed," Bessie said diplomatically.

"I've got to get back to work," I said, turning away from her. Over my shoulder, I reminded her, "We've got *two* Walkers to build, you know!"

"Aye, I know," Bessie said in a soft, worried voice. I heard the door clatter and knew she was back in the kitchen.

"Are ye right, lass?" Mr. MacArdle called as I walked back to the forge. "Only we've got these castings waiting for ye, like."

I nodded slowly, stifling a tell-tale yawn. "Aye," I said, forcing my lips upwards, "I was just reading the letter Bessie wrote."

"I still don't ken why you did that," Mr. Henry said. "Your father won't be able to tell anything just from your writing, will he?"

"He might at that," I said. "But I was thinking more for when... the trotters are finished."

"Still planning on coming along?"

"And who would ye get to drive them?" I asked. "How much time do we have to test before you've got to go on your secret journey?"

"Hush, lass, hush!" Mr. Stoops hissed at me, eyes wide. "There are ears all over and ye never know who's bought them."

"Mr. Stoops," I said slowly, "those ears can't do much without arms to back them. And if they had them, we would have seen them before now."

"Don't be giving anyone ideas, lass," Mr. Henry warned me. I nodded, recalling father's words to me: I was good with steam and steel but people were another matter.

"Let's get these molds poured," I said, gesturing to the castings that lay waiting for their molten steel.

It was careful work but we got all four boiler halves poured in two hours. Mr. Henry tamped the sides of the molds gently while we were pouring to remove any bubbles or air pockets.

We took a break when we were done, waiting for more steel to melt and then we poured pistons, cylinders, and sundries.

We were done before the sun set.

"Would it be all right if we ate out here?" Mr. Henry asked, surprising me. I'd seen him talking with the other two when I'd come back from a trip to the little house. They stopped when they saw me and pretended to be working.

"Outside?"

"It's those ears," Mr. Stoops said. "We think it'd be best if the yard was guarded."

"And after?" I asked. "When it's dark?"

"If you don't mind, we'll keep sentry," Mr. MacArdle said. He flushed a bit. "I've already sent on to the Missus and she's sending our tents."

Tents? I knew that they would need something to sleep in when in the field but I hadn't thought of tents. I know, silly Danni, all steam and steel!

"There's the stables and we've a room — "

"Aye, lass, but a tent's more obvious," Mr. Henry interjected smoothly. He gestured toward the house. "Perhaps we'd best discuss this inside?" he asked, glancing around the yard meaningfully.

I nodded, still nervous at their sudden fears but led the way back into the kitchen.

Bessie and Mary looked startled when we came in but Mr. Henry waved them back to their work. "We're just coming in for a palaver."

"Worried about others hearing, are you?" Bessie guessed, glancing to Mary who snickered.

"Did you hear everything we said?" I demanded.

"Not everything," Mary said quickly.

"And?" I prompted because it was certain that the two of them — even little Mary! — had thoughts on the issue.

"With all respect, Miss," Mary said, doing a quick but poor curtsy, "I'd say the gentlemen have a point."

"And what would you know?"

"It was a way we used to get money, Miss," Mary told me. "Beggars and orphans will get money any way they can and it's a quick way, for certain."

"Would you know who's getting your money now?" I asked, glancing at Mr. Henry to see if he was following my reasoning.

"No, Miss," Mary said, shaking her head. "It'd've been Mapes or Meara who did the snitching. Billy and I were too little, you see."

"Mary," Mr. Henry said, "would you be able to find out who is selling information now?"

Mary's eyes went wide with fright and she shook her head nervously, her eyes going to me. "Don't set me back on the street, Miss, please don't! I'll be good, I swear."

"Ach, Mary," I said, moving to grab her shoulders and give her a hug, "I don't think that's what Mr. Henry meant at all." I hugged her tightly. "And as long as I've breath, you'll have a place with us."

It was the best I could do but in Edinburgh in 1745, in the midst of a war, it wasn't really all that much. No one could say if I might catch a chill and die in the night, nor could they say whether or not some spy might come and drag me away to torture me for what I knew of the Walkers or use my body to torment my father and brother into treachery. But it was all that I could honestly tell her and it seemed enough for she relaxed and said, "Thank you, Miss."

"What I meant, Mary," Mr. Henry said, "was to wonder if you could find out who was snitching and maybe offer information."

"Lie to them?" I asked, shaking my head. "I don't want Mary to lie to them. If they found out..."

"Aye," Mr. Henry said ruefully. He ran a hand through his thinning hair and shook his head. "But if it were for Miss Walker — "

"Anything sir," Mary said. She turned her head up to meet my eyes. "I'd do anything for you."

"It'd be better if it was me," Bessie said.

"No, you're supposed to be me," I reminded her. "If too many saw you, it'd get confusing."

"So have Mary say she's me," Bessie said. We all looked at her. "That way, if they come for someone, it'll be me and not her."

"Brave words, lass!" Mr. Henry said approvingly. "Brave words!"

#

The tents arrived and we set one up visibly in the front of the courtyard, not too far from the archway that led to the road.

We had dinner in shifts — well, the sailors did, the rest of us ate together while we planned Mary's snitching.

"It can't be too obvious and it can't be wrong," Mr. Stoops said in between bites of his stew.

"Aye, we figured that already, Hector," Mr. MacArdle told him. "We figure first to have Mary tell everyone that all she knows is that we're building special Walkers."

Mr. Stoops nodded. "And after?"

"That we're planning on joining the rest of the Prince's Army," I said. "That we're hoping our faster Walker will have no trouble catching up with them."

"Ach, that would work!"

"And it's no lie, either," Mr. Henry allowed. He winked at Bessie and Mary, adding, "But it's best if that weren't known by all."

"But if we say we're going after the Army, we're going to have to start South," I warned the others.

"Aye, I've thought of that," Mr. MacArdle said. "We figure we can double back around toward Dunbar where the British off-loaded before Prestonpans."

"Word would get out," Mr. Stoops warned.

"Aye but it will do no good," Mr. MacArdle said. "We'll be long gone by then."

"How are we going to load the trotters?" I asked.

"Ach, there's the trick!" Mr. MacArdle said, rubbing his hands in glee. Mr. Stoops joined him with a chuckle.

"We'll use hoists and just lift them aboard amidships on our two steamers," Mr. Stoops explained. "And the same when we get off again."

"We'll need to lash 'em tight in case of rough weather," Mr. MacArdle warned.

"And next ye'll be teaching me how to candle eggs, Thomas!" Mr. Stoops replied.

"I could teach you, if you want," Mary put in shyly, being too young to see the joke. We'd replaced our useless rooster and the hens were laying again — it was her job to collect the ones we could eat, so she'd just recently learned how to candle the eggs, a chore she seemed to enjoy greatly.

"Ach, lass, I ken already," Mr. Stoops told her kindly. "It's another way of saying so."

Mary looked no more enlightened but slumped when she realized that she wouldn't be asked to do her bit of teaching.

"One thing, lass," Mr. Stoops now said to me, "why the funny pipes on the new boilers?"

"They'll heat faster, I hope," I said. I explained how the four pipes would be heated by the flame while the rest of the boiler wouldn't; how I expected the heated water in the pipes to mix more quickly with the cold water above, allowing us to get steam that much quicker.

"And that'll work?" Mr. MacArdle said.

"If not, we'll have to do another casting," I told him in all seriousness. He and Mr. Stoops exchanged worried looks and I laughed, waving a hand at the pair of them. "I've already tried it with some old pipes."

"And it worked?"

"Of course," I said. "But nothing's ever certain, particularly with steam."

"And steel," Mr. MacArdle agreed, fingering a recent burn tenderly.

"Anyway, heating faster will not only give us steam sooner but it'll mean we'll burn less coal for the same result," I said, unable to stop myself from preening.

"Efficient," Mr. Stoops said, nodding approvingly.

"That's me," I said, "Efficiency Walker."

"A good Scottish lass who knows how to do," Mr. MacArdle agreed, slapping me affectionately on the knee.

I yawned and the two sailors exchanged glances.

"We'd best be off and leave you to your rest," Mr. Stoops said, slapping his knees and rising from the table. He nodded to Mary and Bessie. "Ladies, I thank you for a marvelous meal."

Mary and Bessie both glowed with the praise.

"Aye, lasses, it was good plain fair, nothing could be better," Mr. MacArdle agreed. Then he added with a wink, "But don't say that to me Missus, she'd not take it kindly."

The two girls giggled and rose to gather up the dishes.

#

The next morning started with the cock crowing and a loud sound from just outside the front of the house.

"I've got him! I've got him!" Mr. MacArdle yelled and I could hear the sounds of fists striking a body and a small voice crying out in fear and pain.

I rushed down, still in my nightdress ready to lend aid as needed. At the door I grabbed a walking stick, figuring it a suitable weapon and rushed out the door.

As soon as I was through the door, I shouted to Mr. MacArdle, "No, no, let him go, let him go!"

Mr. MacArdle did not let him go but grabbed him by the scuff of the neck and swung him toward me.

"And why," he asked, gasping for breath, "should I let him go, Miss?"

"That's Malcolm Reynolds," I said, "he's one of MacAllister's apprentices. He's only eight or so."

"He was spying, Miss, and you know what that means," Mr. MacArdle said, not releasing the lad.

"Bring him inside," I said, suddenly realizing how cold I was in just my nightdress.

"Miss, miss!" Bessie came charging down the stairs with a robe. "You'll catch your death Miss, and then what will we do?"

"It's all right, Bessie, we're going back inside." I took the robe from her anyway and put it on gladly.

"I'll get the fire going," Bessie said, rushing toward the kitchen.

We all moved to the kitchen where Bessie poked the fire into life while Mr. MacArdle dragged Reynolds in by his ear and forced him into a chair.

"So, you useless piece of trash, what have you said and to whom?" Mr. MacArdle demanded. Seeing Bessie with the fire he said, "Yes, Bessie, get the poker white hot and we'll soon have some answers from this trash!"

Poor Malcolm squealed in terror. Bessie gave me a horrified look but I gave her a huge wink in reply. Her eyes went wide for a moment and then she turned back to the fire, putting the poker into the hottest spot.

"I'll get more coal, shall I?" I said heading to the back door. "There are probably live embers still in the forge."

"No!" Reynolds wailed, squirming to get out of his chair but failing, still pinned by Mr. MacArdle's grip on his ear. "No, I didn't do anything wrong."

Mr. MacArdle nodded for me to continue saying to Reynolds, "We'll be the judge of that." He smiled grimly at the lad. "Are you familiar with the Prophet Isaiah?"

"N-n-no," Reynolds replied.

"Ach, a heathen who doesn't know his Bible," Mr. MacArdle spat. I heard no more, pushing the door closed behind me — I knew all too well about Isaiah kissing a hot coal to seal his lips in the presence of the Lord.

Malcolm's screams and cries followed me into the yard as I found a metal bucket and filled it with coals. I didn't expect to use them on the boy but the kitchen fire was pretty cold and this would heat us all rather quickly.

The screams grew louder as I started back and suddenly ceased. Alarmed, I trotted to the kitchen, slamming open the door and dropping the bucket by the hearth, ready to battle with Mr. MacArdle if he'd done MacAllister's lad serious harm.

"And that's all?" Mr. MacArdle said in a low voice to the lad as I approached.

"I swear on my life, sir, I've told no one!" Reynolds turned toward me and added, "I only kept an eye on her like Mr. MacAllister ordered."

My ears burned and my face flamed at the notion of Hamish MacAllister setting this one to spy on me. My temper snapped and I raced over the lad, slapping him viciously. "What did you tell him? What did you say to MacAllister, you little worm?" I shouted as I rained down blows on either side of his face while he cowered, hands raised uselessly to protect himself.

"Miss, miss!" Bessie wailed from behind me but I didn't really hear her.

"There's a poker here if you want to hit him properly," Thomas MacArdle spoke up from my side, gesturing with a white-hot poker tip. "You could put your mark on him for all to see."

My fury ceased, dowsed by his words and I pulled back in horror, looking at the pitiful wretch crying wordlessly to himself.

May the Lord forgive me, I'd never done such a thing before and I pray that I never will again. Is this how people learned to kill? Did they let their fears overwhelm them and give them free reign? Did they let their lust for violence overcome their better nature?

Could I become just like them? Sitting in my own kitchen before me was solid evidence that I could.

It's a lie when they say that women are the weaker sex or that we are innocent and know nothing of violence.

Mr. MacArdle passed the poker back to Bessie. "I don't think she wants it."

I went white with fright at the beast I'd seen within myself and then green as my stomach churned at the thought of purposely tormenting any man with a flaming poker. I'd too many accidental burns to be ignorant of the full agony that would entail.

"Did he tell us the truth?" I asked Mr. MacArdle when I found my voice.

"I swear, Miss, I swear!" Reynolds burbled through his tears. "It was only on the orders of my master!"

My fury returned but I knew it now and refused to let it rule me again. I knelt down before him and grabbed his chin tightly in my hand, forcing his eyes to meet mine.

"What did you tell him?" I asked, the cold fury in my voice causing him to flinch as if struck.

"Nothing yet, Miss, nothing!" Reynolds swore.

"And what were you going to tell him?"

The young lad's eyes drifted from mine, so I tightened my grip on his chin.

"I'll have that poker," I said to Mr. MacArdle in a tight, deadly voice.

"You'd never, Miss," Reynolds said to me with a newly defiant look in his eyes.

"I wouldn't bet on that, lad," Mr. MacArdle warned him. I could feel his gaze shift toward me. "I've seen others do it."

"It's not a question of whether I'll do it, Reynolds, it's a question of whether you'll tell me now or after," I said to him. I didn't realize until now how much I hated and feared Hamish MacAllister. I knew the man had designs on me, could recall all the veiled looks he'd sent my way, had heard my father remark on Hamish's hints that I was 'ripe for marrying' and I knew that if ever there was a person I should fear, it was MacAllister. For he'd mount me like a horse and ride me until I was broken and then demand that I work until I collapsed from exhaustion. An evil man, a man never to be trusted. If he knew what I was planning, there's no telling the trouble — or the blackmail — he could cause.

Reynolds saw all that in my eyes. Saw a part of my fears and all of my resolution. He started sobbing.

"Nothing, Miss! I told him nothing!" he said through his tears. "Mr. Cattan made me promise." He glanced up again as he said, "I saw you two kissing. I'd never peach on you, miss, never!"

"You saw us kissing?" I exclaimed even as I heard Bessie's squeak of surprise and Mr. MacArdle's soft chuckle. Damn! I'd wanted to keep that secret.

"I didn't tell," Reynolds swore. "I didn't tell a soul."

"Until now," I growled, glancing at the other two in the room and then back to him. He paled at my words.

"Sorry, Miss," Reynolds said. "I was scared."

Mr. MacArdle gently pushed me aside and knelt in my place. "And you'll swear that we're the only ones to know?"

Reynolds nodded firmly.

"So, Mr. Reynolds, what do you know about this yard and what's being done in it?" Mr. MacArdle asked him in a kindly voice.

"Bessie," I said, standing and turning to her, "get some eggs and start some pancakes, enough for all of us."

Bessie nodded and started reluctantly for the door, her eyes trailing back to the pitiful Reynolds.

"Go on," I said to her, shooing her out the door. "He'll be alive when you get back, I promise."

"Yes, Miss," Bessie said, going through the door at last. Outside, she raced to the coop, hoping to grab eggs and run.

Slowly, with steady encouragement from Mr. MacArdle, Malcolm Reynolds divulged all that he knew.

Bessie came back, raced upstairs to wake Mary and get her started on chores, raced back down and started on the pancakes, made the first stack and laid them on the table before Reynolds was finished.

"I'll bet you're hungry," Mr. MacArdle said to the boy, reaching for the plate and wafting it toward him enticingly.

I could see Reynolds start to drool and I didn't blame him, the recipe was one of the few of my mothers' that survived her and it was very good. I'd taught it to Bessie and she'd taken it as her own, finding joy in cooking a 'proper' breakfast.

"When you've answered all the questions to Mr. MacArdle's satisfaction, you'll get one," I said, moving to the table and gleefully helping myself to two pancakes. I slathered fresh butter on them and sliced them up with large motions, being certain to 'ooh!' and 'aah!' with every motion.

"Ah, these are *so* good, Bessie!"

Bessie looked at me disapprovingly. "Grace, Miss."

I looked properly mortified, hastily dropped my fork and my head and said, "Lord, we thank thee for the bounty thou hast provided us. Amen."

I heard the others echo 'Amen' and I started eating once more, still feeling the blush on my cheeks.

"Join me, Bessie, before the pancakes get cold," I said, glancing toward Reynolds to be sure my words had the desired effect.

He glanced from me back to Mr. MacArdle. "What else can I tell you, sir?"

"How long have you been spying on us?" I asked, swallowing my bite hurriedly.

"Only since they left, Miss."

"And what do ye ken we're doing here?"

"Building two more walkers to join the Army," the lad said immediately.

"How are we going to find them?" Mr. MacArdle asked, gesturing for me to return to my meal.

"I don't know, sir," Reynolds said. "I suppose you'll follow them."

"How will we catch up, they're down in Carlisle now as you no doubt know."

"Go faster?" Reynolds suggested hopefully.

"And how would we go faster?"

"Use more coal, miss," the lad said. "And put on one them heavier plugs like Jock said he would."

"Jock Adams is an ass," I said, making a face. "And he'll get himself killed if he uses a heavier plug."

"No loss there," Mr. MacArdle said with a snort. He gestured to the table. "Sit yourself at the far end there, lad, where we can keep an eye on you."

Reynolds sat where indicated and Mr. MacArdle sat near to him. With me on the other side, Reynolds was trapped.

I passed the platter of pancakes toward Mr. MacArdle who took one with a polite nod and then passed the platter to Reynolds.

The lad looked longingly at the pancakes left but took only one.

I rose, took the platter in my hand and tipped the last pancake on to his plate, turning toward the stove.

"Bessie, when you're done, you can start some tea," I said, turning to the skillet and starting a fresh stack of pancakes.

Mary arrived and took my place, then Bessie finished and I took her place at the table, along with another pancake and some piping hot tea.

About that time, Mr. Stoops and Mr. Henry arrived. They were surprised to see Reynolds and then furious, causing the poor boy to cower once more, particularly when Mr. Henry demanded angrily, "So what are we going to do with him?"

"We'll keep him," I said. The others looked at me and I shrugged. "Well, it's either that or turn him over to the fort."

"As a traitor," Mr. Stoops growled.

"They'd hang him for certain," Mr. Henry agreed.

I knew that neither of them were joking, not in the slightest. Some people think that life is sacred, a gift of God, but that doesn't mean that traitors aren't hanged, nor blasphemers sent to the Gallows.

Reynolds whimpered with fear.

"We could manacle him to the forge," Mr. Henry said.

"We'll do no such thing!" I shouted, surprising myself with my ardor. "This my father's forge and we'll have no slaves working here!"

The three sailors exchanged surprised looks.

"It'll go ill for you, Miss, if he escapes," Mr. Henry warned me. "Ill for us all but worse for you."

"MacAllister would use what he learned to force you to him," Mr. MacArdle said to me.

"That will never happen while my father's still alive."

"Aye, Miss, but he's off to the war," Mr. Henry told me solemnly. "Ye can't guarantee that he'll come back."

My face fell at his words but I could say nothing in return: he only said what we all knew.

Finally, I said, "We keep him." I turned to him. "Mr. Reynolds, will you swear an oath to us, unencumbered that you'll stay with us no matter what?"

"Where are you planning on going, Miss?" little Mal asked. He was only eight but he'd been around MacAllister long enough to get older than his age.

"We're going to war, lad, we're fighting for the bonnie Prince to restore his father, the King across the Water," Mr. MacArdle told him.

Reynolds took a breath and nodded. "I, Malcolm Alistair Reynolds, do swear upon my immortal soul to follow you, Danielle Marie Walker, wherever you shall go and to serve you as you wish and give my life to protect yours."

How did he know my middle name?

"Well said, lad, well said!" the three sailors cheered.

And so now we had another mouth to feed.

#

On the other hand, as I soon realized, we not only had another mouth, but another pair of hands. He was no Jamie, not even a Samuel but he was an excellent and quick "go for" person and soon we had him tending the fires, running for cables, sawing wood and working without complaint until he fell into a straw bed in the barn — one of the ones we'd made for the orphans — late evening each night for the next fortnight and more.

He was up with the cock crow, firing the forge, bringing live coals for the kitchen fires, helping Bessie with the eggs and the breakfast. In fact, I noticed that he was helping Bessie a lot. Oh, they were just kids but it was clear that there was some feeling between them. Even Mr. Stoops remarked on it.

"I've seen it be that sometimes two people get together and just stick," he said when I mentioned it. His eyes danced as he added, "I think we all saw that with you and your

Mr. Cattan."

I blushed but couldn't say anything.

With Mal — as he was soon called — helping, it was easier to keep a watch at night.

I was exempted no matter how hard I tried to take a place as were Mary and Bessie. When I complained loudly to Mr. Henry, he said, "Miss Walker, who do you think they'd like to get their hands on the most? And what would they do with a pretty young thing like yourself?"

"But they're supposed to think that I'm Samuel Clarke," I protested.

"Aye, and if they did, they'd have no problem busting your head wide open if they had to," Mr. Henry had replied, shaking his own head firmly. "No, I couldn't answer to your father if that happened."

And so I stayed indoors at night and slept with the girls.

The two trotters grew more real day by day. By the end of the fortnight the engines and boilers were completed and tested. In fact, I tested them at ten atmospheres and full load for over three hours — with both boilers and engines.

"Why, lass?" Mr. Stoops had demanded when I'd first insisted on the more stringent tests.

"Because then we'll have a chance of knowing that they won't blow at eight atmospheres and they *certainly* won't fail at five!"

None of the seamen argued with that although Mal shook his head in wonder at my obstinacy, having never heard of such things in his work at MacAllister's.

"And that, Mal, is why Hamish's stuff is such tripe!" Mr. Henry had said when the boy had approached him on the subject. He shook his head and nodded approvingly toward me. "At sea we learn never to trust a knot we haven't tied ourselves, never to short a rope or let a worn sail be set. Too many a seaman has tried to do it the easy way and is at the bottom of the sea for it."

So we did it my way, even though it took special precautions to keep us clear in the off chance that one of the boilers might blow. It was also hard to figure out a way to stress the engines sufficiently but we finally came upon the simple expedient of having them pump water up to the rooftop. I timed our coal in the boilers to last a full three hours and we waited an extra half an hour to be certain and then, when we were done with all the tests, I insisted on tearing one of the boilers and engines completely apart to see how they'd worn internally.

The three seamen *did* grumble at that but they subsided when I pointed out the various signs of wear that we wouldn't have seen unless we'd done so. At the end of that, we reassembled engine and boiler with better gaskets and ran the test a second time. *That* engine and boiler were the ones we put into *my* platform.

"We've two days of testing before we have to put to sea," Mr. Henry told me that evening.

I nodded. "That will work just fine."

Both trotters were built and rigged, we'd tested the movements of each leg and all their joints. We'd tested the fire dumps each of which would dump half the fire grate and could dump either forward or backwards. I'd insisted that we put a special man-sized hatch in the middle of the walkers so that we could climb down or up via a rope or a rope ladder.

"And why would anyone want to do that, lass, when they can just as easily climb the legs?" Mr. MacArdle had demanded when I'd first suggested it.

"Those eighteen pounders of yours..." I said, cocking an eye at him. He gestured impatiently for me to go on. "Could we rig them *under* the walkers? Build their mounts on the underside?"

"And how would you load them?"

I smiled at him and tapped my nose.

"Don't keep it a secret from me lass, I need to know what you plan."

I told him. At first he roared with disbelief and then he grew silent and thoughtful, particularly when I pulled out the drawings I'd done. He poured over them and then had called Mr. Henry and Mr. Stoops over to look.

While they were looking, I'd snagged Mary and sent her off after Malcolm.

"And why do you want the lad?"

"He's another pair of eyes trained to see," I said with a shrug. As I'd said, he was not as good as Jamie but he was learning and learning quickly.

"So you're planning on letting the legs take the recoil, then lowered the front legs so that the swabbers on the ground can swab out, then raising the front legs, lowering the rear, so the rammers can ram in charge and shot," Mr. Stoops followed each drawing with his finger. "And then — someone primes the gun and fires from your trap door?"

"That was my thinking," I said. "Obviously we won't be firing these guns that often. Leaving them below allows us room for two swivel guns — one pounders with grape shot — to keep us safe."

"Hmmm..." Mr. MacArdle looked to the other two and then moved aside as I waved Malcolm in and set him to work looking at the drawings. "... with a trained crew it could be done."

"An eighteen pounder, that takes a crew of five, doesn't it?" Mr. Henry said.

"On a warship," Mr. Stoops agreed. "But the way Danni's thought it out, you could do with three, two in a pinch."

"One, if you loaded everything before you met the enemy," I said to them. "That'd leave two each for the swivels and any muskets we might get as well as room enough for a stoker and a pilot."

"A crew of six if you make the gunner one of the swivel gunners as well," Mr. MacArdle suggested. As I'd thought that as the best arrangement, I merely nodded.

"You'll still need enough coal and decent water — not muck or the boiler and the engine will choke — to get where you're going."

"Or places to stop for fuel and water," Mr. Henry corrected. I nodded.

Mr. Stoops broke into a smile. "We could do it, by Jove, we could do it!"

"What?" I cried, "did you doubt me?"

"Not you lass," Mr. Henry said, "just how to get the crew for two of these beasties."

"We still have to see if they'll move the way we hope," I reminded them all.

"Even if they only walk, they'll do well enough," Mr. MacArdle had said. "The Prince had — "

I coughed and nodded significantly toward Malcolm.

"He'll have to know sometime," Mr. MacArdle told me softly.

"Later rather than sooner?" I pleaded.

He shook his head. "Now, lass, is as late as we can allow."

"And why's that?"

Mr. MacArdle nodded to the other two men. "Is it time?"

Mr. Stoops grinned and nodded fiercely, Mr. Henry merely grinned.

Mr. MacArdle pulled open his satchel and drew two rolls out of it.

"These are blank commissions in His Majesty's Royal Steam Artillery," Mr. MacArdle said, laying them on the table on top of my drawings. "Prince Charles left them with us for whomever we might find."

He slid one toward me. "You'd be sworn in as Ensign Clarke, of course."

Before I could say anything, he slid the other toward Malcolm. The boy's eyes nearly popped out of his head. "You're young for this lad and you'd only get it if our 'Mister' Clarke here agrees but we think, with enough help, you could manage yourself as an officer in charge of a trotter."

"His Highness does not play by halves," I breathed as I took the parchment nearest me and unfurled it, reading the gleaming commission and the brilliant gilt seal upon it. The commission was dated and signed but the name was still blank as was the rank. I slid the parchment back. "I cannot do it."

"Why?" Mr. MacArdle asked glancing to the other seamen in surprise. Mr. Henry grinned at him and held out his hand, saying, "Pay up."

Mr. MacArdle held up a restraining hand toward him and looked back at me.

"Sign this and you get to go be with your father, your brother and your Mr. Cattan," he told me.

I shook my head.

"But why not, lass?" he asked. "You've already shown you're able for it and you're no stranger to men's clothes or even our rough ways." He nodded to the others. "And we'd be there to protect you from any prying eyes or hands."

"I know."

"Then why?"

"I cannot swear an oath on a false name," I said, naming my first concern.

"You've already done that, lass," Mr. Stoops told me. "You've done that on the smithy work you've done for that Mr. Williams and any of the others who've come looking for the apprentice-lad working here."

"That was different."

"Not in kind," Mr. Stoops persisted.

"Hector," Mr. MacArdle said softly, "there's more to it than that." He glanced my way. "Drop the other shoe."

"I'd not sign my name falsely for such a low reward," I said. I know that I shouldn't have let my pride get in my way but I was also thinking practically: if I were subordinate to Hamish MacAllister, it could cause me no end of trouble.

"Low reward?" Mr. Stoops repeated in amazement.

Mr. MacArdle snorted with laughter, pointing a finger at him and saying to me, "Then out with it lass, what rank must we give you?"

"I'd settle for nothing less than lieutenant," I told him. "Our Samuel Clarke will be Lieutenant Clarke with the same rank as Hamish MacAllister."

"Ach, good one, lass!" Mr. Henry roared approvingly. "And she's got a point, a good point."

"So, *Mister* Clarke, would you settle for a lieutenancy then?" Mr. Stoops asked.

"And the girls would have to be seen to, I can't leave them and they're not going."

"If you'd like, I can ask Mrs. MacArdle to take them under her wing."

"They'd have to stay here to keep up the appearance that I haven't left," I said.

"Perhaps your Mr. Pugh would oblige," Mr. Stoops said.

"That won't work, Hector, as he knows our Danni too well," Mr. MacArdle reminded him. "And Mr. Gillie has signed with us."

"Why not set him as an Ensign?" I asked.

Mr. Henry made a face and Mr. Stoops tapped the side of his nose knowingly. "Mr. Gillie will be helping the cause in other ways, lass."

Other ways? How could a puppeteer help in a war? And then I realized — a puppeteer would never be suspected of anything. I had a feeling that Mr. Gillie would be headed London-way shortly.

I looked to Malcolm. "If we do this, you have to be *my* ensign. You take orders from me, not Hamish MacAllister." I frowned. "In fact, you need to keep away from him altogether."

"That won't be hard, lass," Mr. Stoops assured me.

"We'll be in the same battle, Mr. Stoops, how can that be so?"

The three seamen smiled at me but said nothing. Mr. MacArdle carefully took back the parchment commissions and placed them in his satchel. He rose as he did so, yawning widely.

"You've the night to think on it, tomorrow we'll see how your beasties do, Lieutenant," Mr. MacArdle said with a nod toward me.

Lieutenant. And off to war.

For all that I was exhausted, it was very hard to sleep that night.

Chapter Twelve

Bessie met the courier at the front of the house, to keep him from seeing the two trotters in the rear yard.

"I can't stay," he said, thrusting the letter down toward her. "I'm expected back immediately."

Bessie gave him a polite curtsy. "Thank for your kindness."

The courier touched his hat and trotted on off down the road south to the Prince's army.

He had scarcely gone out of sight before I rushed out the front door and grabbed the letter from her hands. She gave me a grimace but said nothing as she followed me inside. I sat at the kitchen table and gestured for her to sit so she could read beside me.

#

10 November 1745

My dearest daughter,

The letter began. The letter was four days old.

It is with a heavy heart that I tell you that Carlisle has surrendered to us but not without loss.

Beside me, Bessie gasped in horror. I read faster.

Neither Jamie nor I are injured and I believe you will be also relieved to learn that Mr. Cattan is quite safe.

I let out a breath, not realizing that I'd been holding it.

I cannot say the same for Jock Adams and the rest of his crew on the Dominion *which itself is no more. I am afraid that you were quite correct in your fears on Mr. Adams' maintenance and the dangers involved.*

As near as we can tell, the boiler was plugged to eight atmospheres pressure — the consequences of which I am sure you can all too well imagine.

The back door clattered open and the three sailors bustled in, looking around expectantly. When they saw her, Mr. Henry said, "Lass, why are you— " he stopped when he spotted the letter. "Oh, a letter. Is it from your father?"

"Jock Adams is dead," I told them. The sailors exchanged looks.

"How?" Mr. Stoops asked.

I briefly recounted what father had said, then continued reading aloud:

He and Hamish volunteered to head to the south of the castle and make noise while the rest of us attacked from the north. The hope was that the defenders would find themselves surrounded and surrender all the quicker.

Although he denies it, I believe that Hamish egged Mr. Adams on in a race. They were just coming up to their position when the Dominion's *boiler blew. Even from where we were, we could hear the screams as the steam boiled the four men alive.*

Apparently, it was their horrid screams that convinced the defenders that we must be in league with the Devil and impelled their surrender.

Hamish at first tried to blame the design for the fault until Captain Finlayson recovered the heavy plug. A surreptitious inspection of Hamish's Destroyer *revealed that it, too, had an eight atmosphere plug in place.*

Needless to say, the rest of the walkers were kept to the proper five atmospheres and, after this sad event, we had no trouble in ensuring that all the walkers were oiled and inspected daily.

We now march south, with five walkers, two in the van and the other three interspersed throughout the column. The other soldiers are wary of them and some would prefer them all off on their own but no one can deny their affect on the enemy.

I have heard that an apprentice has been sent to aid you and am very glad of the news. I hope that you are treating him —

I broke off here but Bessie, the traitor, continued:

— treating him with a proper amount of respect and deference. Not everyone finds your ways easy or normal in a girl.

I snorted in annoyance. The three men exchanged glances but said nothing.

I think of you always,
Your loving father,
Daniel

"Nicely read, lass," Mr. Henry said when she was done. Bessie beamed at the praise but glanced to me for confirmation. I gave her a nod of assurance but I was much affected by the terrible news.

Jock "The Weasel" Adams was never much of a person but no one deserved such a death. And I had a hand in it.

Mr. MacArdle saw my look and said, "Lass, ye warned them all — it's all ye could do under the circumstances."

Mr. Henry and Mr. Stoops rumbled in agreement.

I nodded jerkily, still shocked at the news.

Mr. MacArdle looked over to Mr. Henry. "The letter says they took Carlisle."

"They'll probably move straight on down to Manchester," Mr. Henry said by way of agreement.

"They're moving fast," Mr. Stoops said.

Thomas MacArdle grinned at him, "Of course, Henry, they're Scots."

Mr. Stoops looked to me. "The next letter will take longer to get here, lass."

I nodded. The further south they went, the longer it would take for the couriers to get back to Edinburgh. At some point, the army might stop sending couriers to Edinburgh because there'd be no need. Except — I glanced sharply at Mr. Henry. "The couriers are coming for you, aren't they?"

Mr. Henry looked at the other two sailors who spread their hands proclaiming their innocence and gave me a pleased look. "Clever, lass."

"I told you no cobwebs grow on her, George," Mr. MacArdle said, smiling at me. He glanced meaningfully at Bessie.

"She'll know soon enough," I reminded them.

"Aye," Mr. MacArdle agreed, "she will."

"I'd prefer later than sooner," Mr. Henry said.

Bessie rose from beside me. "I've ears, you know," she said, glaring at the sailors before saying to me, "if you don't mind, Miss, I've work to do."

"Don't be mad, Bessie," I begged her, resting a hand on her arm.

Bessie shook her head and removed her arm. "I'm not mad, Miss," she said, glancing back toward the sailors, "I know about secrets and all."

"We'll tell you when it makes sense, lass," Mr. Henry promised.

"What you don't know can't be beaten out of you," Mr. Stoops reminded her.

"Won't stop some sorts from beating me anyway," Bessie reminded him before moving out of the kitchen and stomping upstairs.

Once she was out of earshot, I turned to the three men. "When do we have to leave?"

Mr. Henry glanced at the others before answering me in a voice pitched low so it wouldn't carry, "A day or two, no more."

"And we'll need our lieutenant and our ensign to be ready," Mr. MacArdle added. "You'll need to sign for some things for the Prince."

"*I* will?" I said, suddenly alarmed. I was silent for a moment, thinking quickly and then I glared at them. "Is that why none of you wanted this honor?"

Mr. Stoops glanced at the other two but none of them would meet my eyes, their heads hanging innocently.

"It's more that you speak French," Mr. Henry said as the silence dragged on.

It took me only a moment to catch on: whoever we were meeting included Frenchmen and I was to be the go-between.

"Two days," I repeated, glancing at them to be certain of the time. They nodded dourly. I slapped my hands on the table rose, turning toward the back door. "Then we'd best get to it, hadn't we?"

"To what, lass?" Mr. Henry asked.

"The trotters are ready for testing," I said. I saw the way they looked at each other.

"Lass..." Mr. Henry said slowly, "are you sure you want to?"

I nodded firmly, pushing open the back door. "Of course."

\#

I was ready but it turned out that *they* weren't. Or, at the least, they were quite reluctant to be the first to test our new trotters.

"If worse comes to worst, lass, we've still got to be able to do our part," Mr. MacArdle said, glancing to the other two sailors for agreement. They, the miserable pair, nodded fervently.

"Fine," I said, moving toward my trotter, which I'd decided to name *Lightning* in anticipation of its speed. I called up to Malcolm who had already started stoking the fires, "Are we ready?"

"Almost, Miss," Mal called back.

"Throw me down a rope," I called back. We'd decided to have knotted ropes that could be thrown over the sides of the walkers that we could climb and draw up after us. A rope came falling toward me and I caught it, pulling it tight before climbing up it, glad that today I was dressed as Mr. Clarke, with proper trousers. I would never have attempted the climb in a dress!

Up on top, I looked down at the three sailors who'd drawn themselves away, toward the forge. The look I gave them must have been sulfurous for they backed up further.

I could not call them cowards, much that it would have given me pleasure, because they were correct in their thinking. If something happened to me, they would still have to do whatever they'd promised the Prince; I hoped it was enough to ensure a victory for King James over the water. Not, to be honest, because I had any particular interest in who was king but because the lives of my father and brother, not to mention a certain Mr. Cattan, were tied to the Prince's success.

"They aren't coming?" Malcolm asked as he paused in his shoveling to glance up at the plug and feel the heat coming off the boiler — careful enough to place his hand at a distance.

"We've got the honor," I told him with a small smile. Honor, risk — two sides of the same coin. I pointed to the two grates. "You know what they're for?"

Mal started to nod but I raised an eyebrow and honestly overcame him. "Not a clue, Miss."

"It's Mr. Clarke to you, Mr. Reynolds," I said severely. "And don't forget it."

"Uh, of course!" he replied reluctantly.

"No one will listen to a girl, Mr. Reynolds," I reminded him. "As far as anyone is concerned, I'm Mr. Clarke the apprentice."

"And lieutenant," Mal added hopefully.

I nodded toward the boiler. "That depends."

"Sir?" he asked. He was getting the hang of things.

"On whether this works or not," I explained.

"Of course it'll work!" he declared loyally.

"That remains to be seen," I told him. As if in answer, the four atmosphere plug juddered and a wisp of steam escaped. We were ready — the steam in the boiler would all too soon be at the full five atmospheres we needed — if the boiler didn't explode the way the Weasel's had.

"Keep an eye on the plug," I said to Mal, turning back to my controls. Over my shoulder I added, "And pray."

"I've been praying all morning, Miss — sir."

Good.

One of the changes we'd made between the old walkers and our new trotters was to set up a stand for the pilot and run the controls directly to it. The sailors liked it because it reminded them of the helm on a ship although it looked nothing more like a box open at the rear. The controls were set standing in the floor of the box — actually on the bare platform floor which was the same — levers that I could pull to control the motion of the legs, as well as the flow of steam to the engine. With our new controls, a pilot cold steer without having to turn around, keeping his eyes forward at all times, except when reversing.

"We're going to walk out to the road," I called to the sailors. Mr. Henry waved his arm in acknowledgement.

I engaged the levers and slowly the steam filled the engine. The left foreleg lifted and moved forward, then the right rear, right fore, left rear.

Slowly, steadily, with little steam, we moved towards the archway. I was particularly careful to be sure to be straight when going through — the archway was so narrow that at any angle we might get stuck.

For a moment we were in shadow as we passed under the archway and then we were once again in the morning light. I increased our speed a bit as we neared the road proper and then turned to the left, heading south.

"I'm going to speed up," I called for Mal's ears. I opened the lever controlling the steam and felt as the walk speeded up. I pulled the lever for full steam and suddenly the wind was in my face.

"Are we trotting?" Mal called from behind me, his voice warbling with fear.

I waited for the left foreleg to lift and switched the levers. "We are now!"

Left fore, right hind were both in the air and we wobbled for a moment but they were back down again and then the right fore and left hind were up and we wobbled again but only for a moment as they reached the ground.

The wind seemed to roar at us — we were trotting.

"The road!" Mal called warningly. We were nearing the end of the straight and I was not ready to try cornering at the trot. I waved to Mal behind me and switched back, closing the steam to the engine at the same time. We were walking and slowing at the same time. I cried out with sheer delight. It worked!

I turned us around and sped us up again, hitting the trot as soon as I felt we could. We raced past the house and I had just time to wave at the three sailors before they were behind us, dwindling rapidly.

I slowed us before we were too far up the road and turned us around, taking a slower walk on the way back.

"Why are we going slow?" Mal asked in elation.

"Too many eyes might see," I said, pointing off toward the castle walls above us.

"But they would have seen already, Mi — sir," Mal called back, even as he shoveled more coal under the boiler.

"Aye but if we're lucky they didn't believe their eyes and only saw us ambling when they took a second look," I told him, feeling irritated with myself for not having considered all the implications before we'd passed the house.

"Maybe," Mal agreed dubiously.

"We can hope."

At our leisurely pace we returned to the front of the house.

"What happened?" Mr. MacArdle asked, eyeing *Lightning* carefully.

"What went wrong?"

I pointed to the castle walls. "I thought it wise that not too many see everything."

"Oh," Mr. Henry said, "clever of you."

"I should remember to tell father," I said. The sailors looked confused. "It's always a good idea to keep some margin for error."

I turned to Mal, "This is a good place to test dumping the fire." To the sailors below I called the warning, "We're going to dump some of our fire."

Mr. Stoops rushed back through the archway calling, "Wait until I'm back."

In a few moments he was back, bearing two buckets full of water.

"Okay, Mal." He'd already placed one of the release levers in its slot and now he gently pulled it forward, tipping half of the grate backwards.

"Coming down now!" I called to those below.

"Aye, lad!" Mr. Henry called back, remembering that I was supposed to be Mr. Clarke. "We see it."

"All done, Mis — ter Clarke," Mal said, correctly himself at the last moment.

"Very well, let's back up and see what it's like," I said, pulling on the reversing lever and calling down to the sailors, "I'm going to back us up!"

Slowly we moved backwards until I could see the small pile of coals myself. I realized as I did that it would probably be a good idea to have someone at the very front — the bow, as the sailors wanted me to say — of the walker to spot and give the pilot close-up directions: my position at the pilot-stand was a good fourteen feet back.

Mr. Stoops handed off one of the buckets to Mr. Henry and the two moved forward, dowsing the coals that had fallen to the side of the road. When they were done, they poured the rest of their water over the large pile which obligingly produced large quantities of steam and smoke.

Certain that our pressure had fallen in the boiler, I said to Mal, "We'll bring her back under the archway and then dump the last."

"As you say, Mr. Clarke," Mal returned promptly, bringing a knuckled hand up to his forehead in a sketchy salute. I couldn't help but grin back before calling down to the sailors, "We'll bring her back inside now."

"It seemed quite a short time," Mal said with a hint of sadness.

"I don't know what you're gloomy for," I told him, checking over my shoulder as I started us in a careful backwards turn, "It'll be your turn with *Thunder* when we get back."

Mal emitted something very much like a mouse's squeak and I smiled at his expression.

"It's all right," I assured him, "I'll be there to guide you."

#

But, in the end, I had to retract those words.

"No, lass," Mr. Henry said solemnly when we were back, safe in the confines of our back yard, "we need you to stay behind."

"Why?"

"For the same reason that none of us went with you, Miss," Mr. MacArdle said.

"But I told Mal — "

"Not to worry, Miss, Mr. Henry and I will be with him," Mr. MacArdle assured me. "We'll trade off, too, so that we've all got a bit of a feel for these new beasties."

"But you don't know about the trot!" I cried.

"We watched you and we listened when you spoke of it," Mr. Stoops said. "I'm sure we'll get the hang of it."

I was silent then, staring from one to the next and the other. They were *jealous!* I couldn't believe it. *Men!* Even these men who should have known better were still chagrined that a red-haired girl could do something that they hadn't.

"Just be sure to time it right or she'll stumble and crash to the ground," I warned.

"Like a horse uneasy on its feet," Mr. Henry said, nodding to himself.

"We'll be careful," Mr. MacArdle promised.

#

It took a bit for the pressure in *Thunder*'s boiler to rise and then, with Mr. Henry at the controls, they slowly made their way under the arches.

"It's okay, Miss," Bessie said to me as I wondered whether to stay in the yard or watch what I feared would be a terrible disaster, "I'll take your part, you stay here."

I could tell that the little brat was enjoying my worry but instead of admitting it to her, I said, "You do that and report back to me when they've let Mal have a go." Before she was out of earshot, I added, "And be sure that they don't trot near the castle!"

Bessie waved and scooted under the archway.

I stood in the yard for a moment feeling useless and then marched into the kitchen, determined to check up on Mary.

Instead, I found the house abandoned. Mary was on the stairs out front, straining her eyes south after the nearly invisible walker in the distance.

With a sigh, I went into the study and sat down, determined that no one would learn of my unease. After a moment, a thought struck me and I pulled out paper and a charcoal stick, making a quick set of sketches.

I heard a loud cry from outside and the squealing of Mary's voice but realized that it was a sound of delight and encouragement not of fear and death. I forced myself back to my work, pulling out another sheet of paper and drawing yet another sketch.

Steel. With a steel frame the whole machine would be stronger. And it could flex like a spring or the back of a horse. In a gallop.

I worked on in silence, becoming lost in the drawing and the visions in my head. What would it be like if we used steel in the legs? I mulled on that and shook my head as I finished guessing on the resulting weight: too heavy. Wood for legs, a short steel frame, carriage springs to cushion against shock, a wooden platform not quite so thick and — maybe — two engines and two boilers.

Yes, that could work. I carefully lettered: *Galloper.*

"Miss, Miss!" Bessie's voice came through the front door. "Mr. Reynolds is trotting!" Beside her, I could hear little Mary's squeal of delight.

Okay, enough work. I jumped to my feet and raced to the door just in time to see a grinning Mal pass by in on *Thunder* deftly bringing her from a trot back to a fast walk.

I shouted in joy and waved at his back. One trotter was luck; two were science. We'd done it.

Thunder roared south and back again several more times before Mr. MacArdle brought it to a halt in front of us, a grin just as broad as Malcolm Reynolds on his face.

"*Thunder* is a beautiful piece of work."

I could say nothing in reply, my thoughts so recently full of the drawings for the galloper.

"The question is," Mr. Henry said, moving up beside me, "whether the two of them will do what we need them to do."

"Ach, George, don't fash yourself so," Mr. Stoops said to him. "If they can't handle the big ones, they'll do well enough with the others."

Henry turned to me. "You were thinking of slinging them underneath, weren't you?"

I nodded. "I've an idea."

"You do?"

"But I think first we should practice moving the two of them together," I said, gesturing to Mr. Henry. "Are you ready to pilot or will you stoke?"

Mr. Henry was silent for a moment and then jerked his head toward the house and the yard beyond. "I'll stoke first."

"It'll take twenty minutes to get steam!" Mal reminded me.

"Fifteen," I replied, shaking my head. "I've had a few thoughts on that, too."

The three on *Thunder* all started at me, then Mr. MacArdle said, "Well, Hector you and the young one can catch us up, we'll be down the road a piece."

Mr. Stoops waved acknowledgment even as he opened the front door and gestured for me to precede him.

In the back yard, he turned to me, "What's your plan then, lass?"

"I banked the coals on the forge," I said to him. "We'll hoist up enough to lay in a good fire."

"That'll work," Mr. Stoops agreed.

I took us a bit more than ten minutes to get the fire laid but the water in the boiler was still warm so it wasn't too long after that before we had enough steam to start moving, if only at a steady walk.

"Did you want to take her under the archway?" I offered. He hesitated until I added, "We can't say what sort of tight spots we might find ourselves in so I think it's best to practice soonest."

I moved back to the coal and the boiler, picking up the shovel and eyeing the heat of the flames, making a note to equip each of our trotters with a set of hand bellows which would make getting a decent fire going that much easier.

Mr. Stoops moved *Lightning* forward slowly and set her up to move straight through the archways, pausing to ask me to check his positioning.

I grinned at him. "You're doing fine, Mr. Stoops."

We moved under the archway at a slow clip but soon we were out and turning on to the road.

I checked the pressure plug, noting how it was moving on its slide and guessed that we were at about four atmospheres. I piled on some more coal to the fire knowing that it would take time for the heat to build.

The pipes that protruded from the bottom of the boiler were doing their job brilliantly and I was convinced that the new design cut the time to get steam by a quarter or more.

"We've not quite got enough pressure for a proper trot, Mr. Stoops," I called over the hiss of the steam, the noise of the engine and the steady *thump* of the legs on the ground. "But we'll be there soon enough."

Mr. Stoops waved in acknowledgment and thus encouraged, opened more steam to the engine.

Our pace increased and I could tell from his movements that he was getting into the gait of the steam walker.

That was why I was quite surprised a moment later when he brought us to a halt.

"Do you think we could lower the platform?" Mr. Stoops said, turning to me so that his words carried clearly.

"Lower?"

"Kneel, say, like a person or maybe even squat."

My eyebrows shot up. "I don't know."

"Let's see then," he said and, before I could respond, he'd worked on all four legs, pulling them all up as if to move them. *Lightning* groaned in protest but obediently sank, as if to her knees but remained mostly level.

Mr. Stoops paused to grin at me. "How's that, then?"

"Why?" I cried. "And what if we can't get her back up?"

In answer to the second question, Mr. Stoops reversed what he'd done and *Lightning* slowly rose like a sleeping behemoth back to her full height. With a grin, Mr. Stoops played on the controls once more and I heard a *stomp, stomp!* as he made one of *Lightning's* forelegs paw the ground like some giant steam horse, eager for a run.

"Hold on!" he called before turning back to work the levers some more. The platform tilted and suddenly *Lightning* was nearly sitting on her hind legs like a dog. A moment later, he'd reversed things and I had to grab on to keep from falling forward to the ground. "What do you think?"

"You're treating her like a dog!" I cried, not certain whether to laugh, cry, or scream in pure frustration.

"No, like a gun platform," he said, moving levers again so that *Lightning* crouched low the ground, her hind legs tipping us just slightly forward. "Swab," he said, then worked the levers and leveled us up, "load," and then we were fully up once more until he played with the levers and called, "aim."

"We must write father!" I cried. "They don't know how to do it."

"But can they, with the walkers?" Mr. Stoops asked, returning us to level once more.

I thought on that for a moment. We'd all spent some time planning on this better design for the controls; I was certain that our first walkers were in no way as sophisticated but whether —

"No," I said as another realization came to me. "If we tell father, then I'll have to admit that we've made more walkers."

"Perhaps," Mr. Stoops agreed.

The pressure plug rattled at the top of its holder. We had full pressure.

"Mr. Stoops," I said, pointing to the plug, "we've enough pressure for you to see if you can trot as well as you can cavort."

Mr. Stoops grinned at my teasing and then threw a quick wave before turning back to the controls. "Then hold on, lass, and we'll show the others the sort of tricks you get when you can tame *Lightning*."

I thought he was joking for only a moment. And then Mr. Stoops took us from a walk to a trot in no time at all and we were flying. I'd thought that I'd been speedy but Mr. Stoops taught me that there were still many things about the trotters that even I didn't know.

In a moment we were moving in a side-to-side motion that was only unsettling because of the speed at which we were going. As I looked to the side, the ground and buildings were all a blur. We were travelling far faster than a horse's trot, nearly up to a full gallop and yet still *Lightning's* legs were only moving on diagonals; left fore, right hind; right fore, left hind.

I couldn't help myself, I shouted in pure delight at the movement, at the proof that our new design was all that I'd hoped for, that *Lightning* lived up to her name.

In no time we'd caught up with and then — to my horror and astonishment — had turned *around Thunder* at the trot!

"How did you do that?" I shouted at Mr. Stoops over the roaring of the steam, the legs and the creaking of the platform.

"Ah, lass, it's just like steering a ship through a gale!" Mr. Stoops called back, laughing out loud.

The others in *Thunder* followed us with their heads, jaws wide open at our antics and then Mr. Henry took the controls and, with a roar, charged after us.

"Race me, will you?" Mr. Stoops called back. To me he said, "Keep an eye on them and let me know if they get close."

"I've got to pour on more coal," I protested.

"Aye, get it done and we'll have a race back to the house, and then we'll show the others our new paces."

Never in the history of the world, in all the ages, had there been a race like the one we had in the next five minutes. The wind was roaring past us, the ground thrumming with the beat of two sets of legs in full trot, and it seemed like the whole world held its breath as it watched us in awe.

And then it was over. Mr. Stoops pulled us to a walk, turned us deftly and moved off the road to avoid being struck by *Thunder* as it roared past, unable to move as gracefully as Mr. Stoops steered our beautiful steam beastie.

We laughed and waved as the others steamed past and then jeered as they slowed, turned and made their way, almost repentantly back toward us.

Mr. Stoops waited until they were halted beside us and then, with a wicked grin, he made *Lightning* bow to them. As they all stood in shock, he sidled our steam horse close to theirs and calling over his shoulder, "Take over, Mr. Clarke!" he lithely stepped from our platform to theirs.

"Hector, you mad Dutchman, show us how you did that," Mr. MacArdle said to him, moving forward to clap him on the shoulder.

"That was brilliant," Mr. Henry agreed. Behind him, Malcolm could only nod, wide-eyed and slack-jawed in amazement.

"Ach, George, you've just got to treat her right and she'll be eating out of your hand," Mr. Stoops replied with a dismissive shrug. "There's nothing to it at all."

We all snorted in derision. Mr. Henry insisted that Mr. Stoops teach us all his tricks, being particularly thrilled with Mr. Stoops' gun handling movements.

"You'd have to jump down for the swabbing and the ramming," Mr. Henry allowed, "but aside from that you've got it all right."

"Don't listen to him, it's brilliant," Mr. MacArdle said as he sidled *Thunder* away from *Lightning* and carefully tried the movements himself.

We practiced for what seemed hours and then had another race with Mal steering *Thunder* and me handling *Lightning*. Malcolm won, much to my annoyance.

"Didn't your brother say steel and steam for you, Danni," Mr. MacArdle said as he caught my expression. "You're not so good with horses, even steam ones."

"Don't listen to that old one," Mr. Stoops told me. "You'll get it sorted in time."

I nodded. I would. It would never do to have one of Hamish's apprentices best me... at least, more than the once.

"And," Mr. Stoops added for my ears alone, "think of how it helps Mr. Reynolds. Now he's got something that he can best you at."

"Tomorrow morning we'll practice some more," Mr. Henry called.

"And then, George?" Mr. Stoops asked.

"In the afternoon we'll need to get ready for the ships."

"So soon?" I asked.

"Not soon enough, perhaps," Mr. Henry replied solemnly. He nodded down at the trotter. "Your father's walkers will help the Prince but these trotters — they'll win the throne."

The other sailors all chorused agreement.

#

Bessie was always a special one; I'd known that when I first connived to bring her on as a maid. She was English and she'd never say how she came to be in Edinburgh but we'd all seen — Jamie, father, and myself — the terrible bruises on her body, so we knew that at least part of her story had to do with abuse.

It had taken a lot of effort on my part to convince her that we weren't going to betray her, weren't going to sell her off, or do something equally horrible. In the years since I'd first brought her in, we'd come to be more like sisters — even though we were nothing alike in temperament.

So it was that I could tell from the moment I returned to the kitchen that evening that she was in a foul mood; angry and scared both at the same time. Mary, beside her, was little better.

"It's going to be all right — " I began only to be cut off.

"Miss, how can it be?" Bessie asked, her hands tightly clenching the cloth of her apron as though to hold them from lashing out at me or being thrown toward the Heavens in imprecation. "You're going, your father's gone, your brother's gone, and we know that you could all die in this war." She gestured toward Mary. "And then what becomes of her?"

"I can make arrangements with Mr. Pugh — " I said only to be cut off once more.

"Mr. Pugh is a marvelous old man, Miss but he *is* an old man and not making out too well in these times, saving what you've managed to bring in for him," Bessie said. Her tone changed as she spoke, as if to break the news to me gently. I thought about it and realized that Bessie, with her errands and all, would have a better ear for the gossip of the town than I ever would. She was more intrigued by such things; I was more intrigued by machines.

"I've put some money by — "

"Did you see the prices at the market?" Bessie asked. I shook my head. "They're going up, people are afraid and the merchants are charging what they can."

"Bessie," I said to her, taking a breath and speaking calmly, "I have to go."

"Why?" Mary asked, moving to huddle closer to Bessie in a way that nearly broke my heart.

I looked down and met her eyes. "Because, sweeting, if we don't help the Prince win, father and Jamie — at least — will both be for the hangman. Or worse."

I could see that they were worried but that neither of them quite understood.

"The walkers and the trotters are such that every King and every army will have to have them once they see them," I told them.

"But doesn't that mean you and your family will be safe then, Miss?" Bessie asked. "Won't they need you to build more?"

"Or they could kill us to keep us from doing the same," I told her. "Or lock us in their dungeon and force us to do their bidding."

"You should never have made them, Miss," Bessie told me sternly. "I tried to warn you what happens when a girl gets notions."

"It's too late for 'ifs and ands'," I said. "They're built now, they're going off to war, and the only choice we've got is whether to help the Prince win or to lose alongside him and the army." I sighed. "If they lose, it won't be long before the English will be up here looking for those who built them."

"And they'll get me, acting as you," Bessie said, wide-eyed with fright.

"No, don't fash yourself so, Bessie," I said shaking my head and speaking soothingly. "As soon as we're gone, you can go back to being just Bessie. Answer any letters father sends."

"And if someone comes asking for you?"

"Tell them I'm busy or sick or gone visiting," I told her. "But if anyone comes you can be just Bessie because Mr. Clarke — " I pointed at myself "— will have gone off to the war."

"But how will we eat?" Bessie asked, returning to the original topic.

"I've laid enough money by to keep you and Mary going until the New Year," I told her. "That's the best I can do and far longer than I expect you'll need." I gave her a stern look as I added, "I expect a full accounting of every farthing." I nodded toward Mary.

"And you're to teach Mary her numbers and reading while I'm gone."

Mary made a small sound and I looked at her sharply. "If you can read and write, you'll find it easier to gain employment, if need be." I turned to Bessie. "And teaching her will stand you in good stead if you need to become a nanny or teacher."

"I thought you said we would be okay, Miss," Bessie said.

"I did," I replied, "but it never hurts to have more than one plan."

Bessie was silent for a moment and I decided that rather than give her more time to think, I should distract her.

"Now, I'm hungry and we will all need a good night's sleep. What's for dinner?"

"Only gruel, Miss," Bessie told me, "but it's got fresh peas."

Gruel was oats with anything else and what most regular people ate. Meat was what we entertained with, just as we drank water with our meals when we had no company, rather than wine.

Bessie had learned her cooking first from me but had become adventuresome and had learned of different herbs from the housewives at the market. She'd acquired a smattering of them that she kept close to her person.

Of course, dinner was not our big meal of the day, that was reserved for breakfast and so a small bowl of gruel — particularly with Bessie's strange spices — was enough to warm our stomachs and get us drowsy for our bed.

#

"I need you to cut my hair," I said to Bessie in the morning. It had grown some — not much — since the last cutting a fortnight before but I wanted it as short as I could get it when I started off. Besides, I had a plan.

"Miss?" We were in the kitchen and I was dressed in a rough tunic and trousers.

"Let's do it upstairs," I said, nodding toward the stairs. "I'll want you to collect it all and keep it."

"Keep it?"

"Find an old cap and some glue," I said, as we started up the steps. "If you do it right it can look like you've got strands of red hair sticking down."

A girl never went out without her head covered. Most of us wore a cap or a simple bit of cloth tied under the chin. If Bessie were to wear the cap with my red hair sticking out in places, it would be easy enough for most to be convinced that she was me — especially at a distance. Up close the difference in our height and even in our bust — though mine was only modest it was more than Bessie had at twelve years — would not fool anyone who knew me well.

"Cut it short like a man's," I said, as I sat on the stool.

Bessie gave me a look but said nothing, pulling a lock of my hair and eyeing its length consideringly.

"I could crop it to your head like a baby's," Bessie suggested with a sly smile and snipped quickly with the scissors. I gasped before I realized that she'd done no such thing which was fortunate for most men wore their hair shoulder length or a bit more.

Bessie was quick and her cuts even. Afterwards I looked in the glass and saw that she'd done a creditable job. She looked down at the red hair held in her other hand, her lips pursed tight.

"You look just like a boy," Bessie said sadly.

"Good."

"But you're not, Danielle, you're not!" Bessie told me with unexpected fervor. "You should never forget it, never."

"If I want to be safe, I'd best keep it well hidden," I reminded her. "Women who follow armies have bad reputations."

"Then maybe you should stay here, Miss," Bessie suggested.

I shook my head. "We've been over that." I stood from the stool and ran my fingers through my hair, mussing it the way I'd seen Jamie muss his hair and then shook it out.

"I could tie it in the back, like the sailors," Bessie suggested. She found a bit of black ribbon in a drawer and made quick work of the job.

"There, just like a taller version of your brother," Bessie said, "except that he's no ginger."

"There are red-headed men in the Prince's army," I reminded her.

"So there are," Bessie agreed half-heartedly, "and now there's to be one more."

"Lieutenant Samuel Clarke, at your service," I said, bringing my feet together and sketching her a bow.

#

The sailors arrived not long after the sun rose and we were ready for them. Malcolm and I had refilled the boilers with water and laid fires under both, so it took only a few puffs of the bellows to get us enough steam to start our way out of the yard and under the archway.

We turned south, moving no faster than the walkers could move, and continued on for such a long way that I wondered where we were heading.

"We're going to Prestonpans, where the Prince fought the English back in September," Mr. Henry told me when I asked. "Mr. Stoop wants to give us a feel for a longer march and a chance to practice far from prying eyes."

Well that was fine with me.

"Are we going to meet our crews there, then?"

Mr. Henry shook his head. "I wish I could say you would but none of us have a thought of how we'll find them."

"Malcolm and I can't pilot, stoke, and man the guns by ourselves," I muttered, wondering what the point of all this work if there was no way to use the trotters.

"Aye, we know it well, lass — lad," Mr. Henry said, correcting himself when I glared at him. It wouldn't do for them to be confused in the heat of the moment or for my secret to come out to the wrong people. "But today we'll be your crew and then tonight we'll guide you to the docks."

"I can't help but think that traipsing down to Leith won't attract attention."

"Aye, that's why we're not going down to Leith," Mr. Henry said with a wink.

"Where then?"

"We're taking a note from the English," he told me with a smile, "and we'll be using Dunbar, far from most eyes."

"So that's why we're here," I said, waving my arm at the fields and works in front of us. I'd been curious to see more of the battlefield since I'd first heard of it from Lieutenant Anderson — God preserve him — and here we were. I squinted at something in the distance. "What are those lines?"

"Rail line from the mine," Mr. Henry explained. "Some of the English tripped over them in the fight and that helped our side."

"Well, I don't think *we'll* trip over them."

"Let's see, shall we?" Mr. Henry said. "Do you think you can get your *Lightning* to trot over them?"

In response, I opened the steam and, following my memory of Mr. Stoops movements, broke us into a good steady trot. A shout from behind me showed that we'd caught the others unawares but then Mr. Henry shouted, "Ah, good lad!" Adding, "Young Malcolm's no slouch, he's gaining on you."

"We'll see about that!" I said. "Shovel more coal into the fire, if you please."

"Aye, sir."

There was no way Malcolm Reynolds was going to beat me twice. At least, not today.

Gauging the interval on the rail lines was tricky but, determined to keep my lead, I only changed the angle we made with them, twisting slightly so that our legs would fall on either side. We traipsed across them easily but a shout from the rear and a series of cries told me that Malcolm had not been so lucky.

"Ach, you should have seen it!" Mr. Henry shouted to me from behind. "Your Mr. Reynolds nearly ploughed *Thunder* into the ground but he managed to catch her just before she struck and nearly jumped her back onto her feet. Ach, that lad was wasted with MacAllister!"

We continued on for a good three more minutes before Mr. Henry shouted to me, "Mr. Clarke, sir, Mr. MacArdle seems to be imploring us to stop."

I worked the levers, pulled us neatly back to the walk and then slowed us all the way to a halt, turning beforehand to face Mal's oncoming beastie.

As they drew up in front of us, I smiled and worked the levers, neatly backing and sidestepping so as to place us beside them, platform to platform.

"Well done, well done indeed!" Mr. Stoops said, waving to us.

"What now?"

"Now, I think we get Mr. Stoops to instruct us again on the antics he performed yesterday," Mr. Henry said.

It didn't take me long to figure out Mr. Stoops' maneuvers, partly because I'd seen something of them yesterday — or at least felt them well enough — and I'd had the night to ponder on them.

Mal was no slow study, either, mastering the moves nearly as quickly as myself which, I think, cheered him greatly after his poor showing in our race.

At my insistence both Mr. MacArdle and Mr. Henry learned as well — "Just in case."

And then it was time to drill. First we drilled marching together, then side by side, then in a pirouette where each moved slightly in front of the other and then — when we'd exhausted those moves — we combined them with the gun-drill we'd practiced earlier.

At the end of it all, I suggested that we have a race through all the drills. Mal looked nervous but I assured him, "It's not so much who wins, Mr. Reynolds, as how we take the challenge."

In the end it was too close to call which made all five of us very cheery.

It was Mr. Henry, gauging the time, who said, "We'd best head back now."

"And later?"

"We'll have about two hours to get ready and then we'll march out," Mr. MacArdle replied.

As we walked our steam beasties back to the forge, I realized that tonight I would not be sleeping in my own bed. In fact, I would be sleeping further from home than I'd ever been in my life — and it would only be the first of many nights further and further away from home.

"Why the long face?" Mr. Henry asked, catching my look when I glanced back to see how *Thunder* was keeping up with us.

"Nothing."

"Nothing, did you say?" Mr. Henry said, shaking his head. "It didn't look like nothing."

I turned back to face forward, waving aside his words.

#

I'd left Mary and Bessie to sew me two sets of knee-length trousers, two tunics and whatever they could provide for a decent-looking military jacket and hat.

They were eager, as soon as we'd leapt off the steamers, to have me try them on.

As we three girls left the gentlemen downstairs, Mary said to Malcolm, "You come up for yours when we call."

What I didn't expect was the quality. Even the cloth was fine.

"Mr. Pugh felt you might want the better fabric," Bessie said when I gasped in surprise as I pulled on the tunic.

"And we had enough of the coarse fabric to make you and Mal a full set of those, too," Mary chimed in.

The trousers were fine and there were nice knee socks to go with them.

"You'll look like a proper gentlemen," Bessie said even as she helped me into the jacket. They tried to put the hat on me — and it was fine but I stopped them, saying, "A gentleman doffs his hat indoors."

"Doffs?" Mary repeated, having not heard the word before.

"It's rich talk for 'takes off'," Bessie explained knowingly.

"Doffs," Mary said again, trying to fit the word in her brain. On the way down the stairs, carrying the hat, she kept bringing it up toward her head and lowering it again, each time saying, "Doffs."

We found the others outside and I properly doffed my hat, turned to Mary and Bessie and touched it in salute as I'd seen Mr. Anderson and the other officers do to the ladies. The two looked at me and giggled.

"Well, gentlemen, will it do?" I asked, pulling myself up to my full height and dropping my voice as much as I could.

"Sir, you have the advantage of us," Mr. Henry said, bowing lowly. "We are only lowly sailors but you, sir, are clearly an officer of the King."

Well, at least *one* of them, I thought to myself.

Mary and Bessie snatched Mal and dragged him into the house for his fitting.

"Doesn't it seem like he's protesting rather feebly?" Mr. Henry said to me with a broad wink.

"Well, I'm sure he's in more trouble than he imagines," I replied, "for I'm pretty certain that he's pining for Bessie while Mary's pining for *him*."

The three men all guffawed.

I looked at my clean uniform and turned back to the house. "I think it best if I save this marvelous clothing for more formal occasions."

"We'll be getting the walkers on the ship and that'll doubtless be dirty work," Mr. MacArdle said in agreement.

"Go, go!" Mr. Henry added, making a shooing motion with his hands.

I shooed.

#

Upstairs I found a blushing Malcolm who refused to divest himself of anything more than his jacket. That wouldn't do at all and I told him so, quite brusquely.

"You and I are going to be seeing enough of each other on the march that we've no time to be prudish now," I growled. "And we've no time to waste, so get on with it."

To show him that I meant business, I quickly disrobed, and threw on my travelling clothes all the while staring at him challengingly.

"Come on, Malcolm, there's a dear," Mary said encouragingly.

"When we're in company, you're going to have to help me keep my gender secret," I reminded him as I buttoned up my shirt.

The notion seemed to steady him. He was only a boy, not much older than Mary, so he didn't really have any cause to be shy.

I was downstairs again, ready to lend a hand to the seamen who were stowing our extra gear when we heard a loud cough from behind us.

"Make way for his Majesty's ensign!" Mary called in a squeaky girl voice.

We all turned and there, on the steps, stood a sight. Dressed and cleaned, Malcolm Reynolds looked a good year or two older than he really was and stood with two girls on either arm.

"Marvelous!" "Smashing!" "Let's hear it for the ensign!"

"Ensign Reynolds," I called to him, "you may return and change into your travelling gear." I nodded to him solemnly as I added, "I find that you do properly pass muster, sir."

I wasn't at all sure that they were the right words but they sounded like something that Lieutenant Anderson — goodness, I had the same rank! — or one of the generals would be expected to say.

I must have not been too wrong for Mal saluted and turned smartly while behind me the three sailors murmured, "Well said!"

#

All too soon, Mal was back with us, the gear was stowed and we were down to parting farewells.

"Hear, miss," Mr. Henry said, pressing a small purse in my hand, "for the girls."

I turned and hugged him tightly. "Thank you." I called to Bessie and pressed the purse into her hands.

"We've enough to get by," Bessie protested, more — I think — out of loyalty to me than any real conviction.

"Then keep it and remit it when they come back," I said to her because it was obvious that all three men had chipped in and, for all that I was heartstruck at the gesture, the weight and feel of the coins in the bag did not promise much wealth.

Bessie grabbed Mary and gestured her to follow her curtsy. "Thank you kindly, sirs."

Mal looked abashed and I raised an eyebrow. He moved close enough to say into my ear, "I've nothing to give."

"Then give them hugs," I said, moving forward to do the same. "You two take care of each other."

I found tears springing from my eyes and running down my cheeks and berated myself for behaving in such an unmanly manner until I saw that the three sailors were all crying, too.

Malcolm hugged Bessie and then Mary and then Bessie again. Mary, not to be outdone, hugged him a second time.

And then I cleared my throat and nodded to Malcolm. "Mr. Reynolds, to your mount."

I hugged the two one more time and said into their ears, "I'm counting on you."

"We won't fail you." Bessie swore.

I broke away from them and turned to my *Lightning*, not trusting myself to look back until I was in position and the steam gently wafting through the boiler to the engine.

And then, before we went under the arch, I turned and gave them the best salute I could.

CHAPTER THIRTEEN

MR. HENRY TOLD ME LATER THAT BESSIE AND MARY FOLLOWED US OUT TO THE STREET and kept waving until they were out of sight.

Our morning excursion set the pretense that we were just going out for more of the same. We would not be missed by any spies until the next morning and by then we would be well away.

The steering and the stoking were such that neither Mr. Henry nor I felt much need to talk and, even as the afternoon grew cooler and we endured a short shower, we were warm enough from our exertions that we felt no discomfort.

We passed through Prestonpans and waved at the few who came out to see us pass by; then we were on to Dunbar and parts beyond my ken.

It took us about another three hours to bring Dunbar's harbor into sight. We'd had to stop once to take on more water for the boilers. Mr. MacArdle had us pull up beside a barn and went forward on foot.

While he was gone, we tended our beasties. He was back in less than twenty minutes with four other men who he identified as fellow sailors.

"How many ships are there?" I asked, suddenly curious.

"Three," Mr. Henry told me with no small amount of pride. "All steamers."

Mr. MacArdle conversed with the four new men who looked up at our beasties reservedly but I was Scots, I could tell that they were surprised and nervous, however much they tried to hide it.

"Mr. Clarke," Mr. MacArdle called up from the ground, "If you'd be so good as to take Seaman Fletcher and Seaman Morrissey aboard, I'd be much obliged."

"Certainly," I called back gruffly, aware that this was the first time I would appear as Lieutenant Clarke among strangers. Danni Walker would be mentioned no more. I kicked over our knotted rope and called down, "Climb aboard, men!"

Two men climbed up. Neither was taller than I which made them rather short for men but they looked healthy, appearing to be in their late teens or early twenties. I glanced over to Mal who was receiving Mr. MacArdle and the other two seaman. He caught my look and I raised a hand to my hat. He returned the salute readily then turned his attention back to Mr. MacArdle.

"Where away, lads?" I said to our newcomers. They traded glances, then one spoke, "If you continue down the road, sir, you'll see our ships."

I got the notion that Mr. MacArdle might be trying out candidates for our crew, so I turned to Mr. Henry, saying, "Pass your shovel to one of these lads and let them have a turn, Mr. Henry."

"Aye, sir," Mr. Henry replied, knuckling his forehead in salute. He thrust a shovel at one and showed him what to do. I turned to our remaining sailor and said, "Move to the bow and keep a look out."

"Aye, sir," he said, moving forward slowly, not certain what to expect.

"We can step over anything as high as four feet but we don't want to get caught in a rut or slip on a patch of frost or mud," I shouted up toward him. He turned back to me, his brows furrowed and I gestured at him in irritation, "Your eyes on the path, not on me!"

We moved slowly through the narrow streets and I had Mr. Henry tell our new stoker to slacken off somewhat as we didn't need much more steam.

We stopped at the docks beside one ship which I saw, much to my surprise, had been named *Danielle*. I caught Mr. Henry's eye and glanced toward the name and he shrugged, nodding over to Mr. Stoops as if to say it was his idea.

It turned out that the *Danielle* was the name given our first steamer which, until then, had been the *Rosemary's Way* — the one I'd helped construct and had raced against when Jamie was at its controls. It seemed a very long time ago.

"Mr. Henry, how do we propose to board?" I said, trying to sound nautical.

"Ach," Mr. Henry replied quickly, "as an artilleryman you wouldn't know all that much about hoists and the like."

I bit back a hot response: I knew quite well about such things but I realized that he was speaking for our new seaman and covering my gaffe.

"I could imagine that might work," I said after a moment, "but I wonder if it's not a bad idea to leave the hot coals in the grates of our boilers."

Mr. Henry just grinned at me. "Mr. MacArdle's got that all thought out, sir."

I nodded and said nothing. Presently Mr. MacArdle approached and passed the sailors stout lines which were formed into loops and tied far above us. They formed a cradle on which to lift our platform.

"When you're high enough, sir," Mr. MacArdle said with a slight emphasis on my "title", "just pull the legs up like we've practiced and then dump the grates."

"On to the ship?" I protested.

"Nah, into the water!" Mr. MacArdle said.

Shortly I was left as the only person aboard *Lightning* and the creak of hoists and the puff of the *Danielle's* steam engine showed that slack was being taken in. A moment later there was a jerk and I squeaked in surprise as I felt *Lightning* leave the earth.

"The legs, Mr. Clarke, sir," Mr. MacArdle called up to me as I stood swaying a good twenty feet in the air. Obligingly, I performed the maneuver that collapsed the legs. Then I locked them into place and moved — gingerly — back to the boiler and the fire grates below.

"Ready when you are, Mr. MacArdle," I called, waving from my high perch.

"Now!" Mr. MacArdle called back.

I pulled on the forward grate and heard it tilt, the coals hissing and crackling as they fell through the air and then hissing more loudly as they were drenched by the sea below. I removed the lever from its slot and put it in the slot for the rear grate, repeating the maneuver just as quickly. Again the sea below boiled with the sound of hot coals extinguished.

And then, feeling so much lighter, I pulled on the whistle of the boiler, intent of relieving the last of the pressure.

The loud *wheet* tore through the evening sky even as it warbled further and further into bass ranges.

"By all that's Holy!" I heard someone cry from below me.

"Mr. Clarke," Mr. MacArdle called up to me.

I peered over the side down to him. "Yes?"

"What was that?"

"I was letting the last of the steam off."

"Perhaps not so wise, sir, as I'm afraid you've put the fear of God into anyone in the next twenty miles."

Oh! I hadn't thought of that. I glanced toward Mal and the waiting *Thunder* below.

"Mr. Reynolds!" I called. He waved up at me. "I suggest that you don't repeat that."

"Aye, sir," Mal said. I could tell that the cheeky bugger had all he could do to keep from bursting into peals of laughter. Rather than being angry, I was rather relieved for I had an inkling of the sort of treatment that he'd had at the hands of Hamish MacAllister and the evil Jock Adams.

When we'd learned of Adam's death, Mal's hands had gone protectively to his throat. He'd snatched them back down before anyone noticed — save me — and had merely said, "Good."

"Good," I said, glad that he had recovered enough from his abuse to try to be cheeky with his elders — even if I was a girl.

"Steady on, steady all!" a call from below me pulled me back to the present and I saw that I was descending slowly onto the deck of the *Danielle*, just aft of her own engines. I wondered idly if there were a way we could rig *Lightning*'s engine to add to *Danielle*'s but then I heard, "All hands stand by!"

Followed shortly by the sound of Mr. MacArdle rushing up the gangplank.

"Ready on the steam!" Mr. MacArdle called as soon as he was visible. I turned to see that the steam engine on the *Danielle* was already manned and that the fires were burning brightly. "Single up all lines!"

I climbed down from *Lightning* and looked about. Aside from Mr. MacArdle there were four other men visible: one at the engine, one at the rear on the tiller, and another by the boiler with a shovel ready to stoke in more coal.

"Ready on the anchor line," Mr. MacArdle called, moving toward the engine.

"Anchor line on the capstan," the engine man replied. I realized that the seamen had made some changes in the rigging since I'd last seen it and moved cautiously toward it.

"Lieutenant, stand clear, if you would!" Mr. MacArdle growled at me, hand upraised. "It wouldn't do for you to pull another whistle at this time, sir."

I moved back, red-faced and annoyed. I glowered at him but he paid me no mind, intent on the task of getting ready for sea. Even so, I realized that he'd ordered me back less for fear of me doing something untoward than for fear of me seeing what changes they'd made to the engine rigging.

Well, I thought, let them have their secrets. I turned to the shore. "What about the others?"

"They'll follow along," Mr. MacArdle said. "But we're running late and we must be off."

I nodded and moved to the stern of the ship, where I could watch the shore as it started to recede and wave to Malcolm and the others in encouragement.

We were only just free of the land when another steamer pulled up to the dock and it was Mal's turn to perform the strange set of maneuvers that would get his *Thunder* safely aboard the *Majestic*. I learned the name of the steamer when Mr. MacArdle, satisfied with our course and speed came back to stand with me and examine their work through his telescope.

"If all goes well, we'll be in port again before dawn," Mr. MacArdle said, as he collapsed his telescope and placed it back into his pocket.

"Montrose, then," I said, recalling a map I'd seen at the University not too long ago. "And we're making more than ten miles an hour."

"We're making about eight knots," Mr. MacArdle corrected. "Here on the sea we measure in knots, not miles."

"Strange."

"And here, Lieutenant, in my ship, I'm Captain MacArdle," he said, pulling back and catching my eyes with his. "You know about sea captains, don't you?"

I did and suddenly chided myself for not having thought of it earlier. Clearly simple seamen, even frugal seamen, would not have the means to pay for the construction of a steam engine nor have spare ships to alter at their whim. I knew that the three sailors had money but I had not bothered to think how *much* they had.

"Captain MacArdle," I said. "I do indeed understand that the captain is sole master of his ship."

Mr. MacArdle nodded solemnly, then broke into a smile. "It's my *first* ship, lass, to be honest. Before, I was a master and a mate on several rewarding voyages."

Pirate? Privateer? Perhaps both, I thought to myself.

"We are going to Montrose," I said, trying to sound knowledgeable.

"We are," Captain MacArdle agreed. He turned back to his sailors and then back to the shore. "Those men, will they do?"

"They were too frightened to say more than a word and I know not which is Morrissey and which is Fletcher," I replied. My brows went up as I continued, "Why, you aren't proposing them for my crew?"

"I am," he said. "They're new, they're young, and — "

"They're all you could find," I broke in, sensing his embarrassment.

He opened his mouth to gainsay me, closed it again quickly and nodded. "Aye," he agreed. "Sailors are creatures of habit. More so than I'd realized. It took weeks to get these men to trust the steamer."

"Didn't they all bolt when they heard about the Weasel?"

"Ah... they haven't heard about that yet, Mr. Clarke," Captain MacArdle said slowly, lowering his voice, "and, for the moment, I think it's best it stay that way."

"It'll stay that way as long as you let me inspect your engines — all three of them," I said, nodding toward the distant shore behind us.

Captain MacArdle hissed in anger but I continued, "I need to know that they're not being too stressed and show your men how best to care for them."

The captain gave me a doubtful look but I held up a hand, anticipating him. "Remember, I'm the apprentice sent up to work with Mr. Walker and I helped work on these trotters, too."

"Aye," he said to himself, "then we wouldn't have to talk about the lass — " meaning me "— nor worry about your authority."

"As for your improvements, Mister — er, Captain MacArdle," I went on, "they matter not to me at all."

"They matter much to me, George and Hector," he returned sharply.

"I understand," I told him. "If I can profit from them then, on my honor, I shall share the profits appropriately."

Captain MacArdle considered this for a moment, then struck out his hand. "Welcome aboard, Lieutenant Clarke."

I took it and we shook solemnly, each thinking we were getting the better of the other.

Once Captain MacArdle was satisfied with the running of the ship, he brought me forward — "amidships" as he called it — to the steam engine, boiler, and gear.

The first thing I inspected was the plug to be certain that they hadn't been foolish like Jock Adams. The plug, I was relieved to note, was the regular five atmosphere plug. The engine and gears were well-oiled, the boiler well-maintained. The rigging was strange and it took me some time to sort it all out.

"That one goes over there to the tall drum with holes — "

"The capstan," Captain MacArdle corrected. "The holes are where we insert bars so that the men can push on it. The capstan is built with a ratchet so that the men can rest and not have whatever they're pulling on fall back down."

"But you've hooked it up to the engine," I said, following another line.

"Aye, it saves the crew the effort of hauling the anchor," Captain MacArdle said. "I figure with some work, we could rig it to help set and trim sails as well."

I nodded appreciatively. I could see how that would all work and save immense effort but — "There's no emergency release."

"Well, it's just new, lass — sir," Captain MacArdle said, hastily correcting his slip but then making things worse by looking around to see if anyone had noticed.

"What if something goes wrong?" I demanded. "How would you handle it?"

"I suppose we could cut the line, if need be," the captain replied, nodding toward an axe stowed against one of the masts. "But, honestly, lass, this is a well-crewed ship, what could go wrong?"

"Accidents, Captain, always seek the unprepared," I said, sounding as if I were quoting old knowledge rather than in

venting the saying up on the spot.

"Well, you've about six hours, sir, to think of a better solution," Captain MacArdle allowed. He turned back toward the rear of the ship. "Now, if you'll excuse me, sir, I think I'd best be about my duties."

"Of course," I said. I looked around, wondering what I was to do.

"There's a cabin below, you can rest until we come to port," Captain MacArdle allowed.

I nodded and looked around, trying to find some way down. The captain gave me an amused look and then relented, reaching toward me. "Come along, lieutenant, I think I can see you to your cabin before I'm needed at the helm."

There was a wooden ladder that went down and then we were engulfed in gloom which seemed not to bother Captain MacArdle a bit. He deftly led me toward a lightening and then pushed open a door to the side. I could barely make out, in the dimness, a bunk built onto the ship's side.

"In you go," he told me cheerfully. "No one should bother you here."

I took his words to mean more than intended and nodded gratefully before realizing that he probably couldn't see the motion and saying, "Thank you kindly, Captain."

"Think nothing of it, Lieutenant." I heard the door close and found myself in the darkness.

I decided that I could climb into the bunk and, perching carefully, could remove my boots, jacket and loosen my shirt before lying on top of the coarse blanket. I was not at all sure of the prior occupants and whether they had lice or fleas for company. As the hour passed, I realized that I was too cold and tired to care and so pulled the blanket over me.

After that, darkness engulfed me and I slept dreamlessly.

#

I was awakened by a rapping on my door.

"Yes?" I called, not recalling my bearings. "What is it?"

There was a long moment's silence outside my door before I heard a man's voice say, "Captain's compliments and land is in sight, sir."

I realized that I hadn't pitched my voice low at first and so I coughed deeply, then responded in a lower voice, "I'll be right up."

Apparently the deeper voice was enough, for I heard the man move away.

I buttoned my shirt, put on my boots and jacket, pushed my hair back, and made my way out into the dark corridor.

It was dark no more. Light filled it, not quite blindingly but certainly with fullness. I retraced my steps and found the wooden ladder, climbed it and looked about for Captain MacArdle.

"Stand clear, lieutenant!" his voice came down from above me. I stepped aside and looked up. He and his crew were busy with the sails.

"How can I help?" I called up to him. I heard some sniggers from the crew but Captain MacArdle called back down, "Best you can do, sir, is go to the helm and pitch in if they need it."

I nodded and moved aft. The helmsman nodded at me but seemed in no need of aid, keeping the wheel competently on course. I looked down the length of the ship and noticed that the engine and boiler were covered with a tarpaulin. Ahead I could see a dark smudge of shoreline.

"Why are we sailing in?" I wondered aloud.

"Don't want anyone to know we're a steamer, I imagine," the helmsman replied with a shrug.

"Ah, yes, indeed," I said, trying to sound as though it were completely expected. For good measure I threw in a yawn.

The helmsman gave me a look which I interpreted to be disgust that I would still be sleepy. I said nothing, deciding that lieutenants were above noticing such things.

A moment later, the helmsman appeared to change his mind, for he said, "I hear there's coffee below, in the galley."

"Would you like a cup?" I asked. "Is it all right to bring a mug on deck here?"

"I'd relish one, thankee, sir."

Mission in hand, I steeled myself to go down into the darkness and was surprised to find that it was not so bad as it had been at night. Firmly on deck — or as firmly as one can be on a rolling ship — I wondered how to find the galley. A smell, not quite appealing, assaulted my nose and I realized that I had only to follow it.

Sure enough, I found myself in a warm room where a man was busy with what seemed to be a pot of gruel.

"Can I get some coffee for the helmsman?" I asked as I stepped into the galley. I knew enough to know that was what sailors called their kitchen — having overheard my three sailors use the term often enough.

"Aye," the cook said, glancing at me in curiosity. "You're the officer that came with that steam beastie, aren't you?"

I nodded, not quite certain where the cook was leading. He poured two mugs and pushed them over to me.

"Is it true that a red-haired devil girl built them after making a pact with the Devil?"

"Pardon?"

"I heard she even lay with him for the knowledge," the cook said. He gave me a wink and a leer, "Hear he scarred her for life where a woman shouldn't be touched, if you know what I mean."

Some people! That sounds like something the Deacon's wife would say about me, the old biddy.

"I know nothing of the kind," I said stiffly, having no trouble remembering to pitch my voice low. "Some people make rumors just to see how swiftly they'll fly."

"That so, sir?" the cook replied, unconvinced. "And did you ever see this hell-fire lass set foot in a Church?"

"I know she's a god-fearing creature," I said coldly.

"God-*fearing* I'd doubt, what with ol' Nick driving her," the cook returned. "They say that one of those steam beasties blew up and killed all around it down Carlisle way."

"That I have heard," feeling somewhat relieved that the conversation seemed to be moving toward truth and away from superstition.

"The Devil's way of paying off those who would spurn him," the cook continued. He waved his ladle at me. "If I was you, lieutenant, I'd think twice about riding a devil spawn like that." His lips cracked in a gap-toothed smile. "Lest St. Nick himself take an interest in you."

"Thank you for that advice," I replied, barely able to keep my voice steady. "I'll bear it in mind."

"Or at least make your peace with your Maker."

I beat a hasty retreat and was glad to get back on deck, passing the helmsman his mug.

"You spoke with the cook?" the helmsman asked after downing a large gulp of the hot liquid.

I nodded. He laughed. "Ah, did Cookee tell you about the Devil and the Lord?"

"He had words to that effect," I agreed.

"You should have heard him with the Captain!" the helmsman said. He glanced over at me. "Did you see that red-haired slip they were talking about?"

I nodded.

"Was she as plain as they say?" the helmsman asked. He glanced toward the Captain up in the rigging. "The Captain's married, so he might not look too carefully, if you know what I mean."

"I don't know about plain," I said, feeling miserable. *Plain! Really?* "It was mostly the eyes that I noticed."

"What, did you not bother to look at the rest of her?"

"Oh, I did," I assured him. "But it was her eyes — "

"Devil's eyes?"

"No more than some," I said. "I liked her eyes."

Fortunately, Captain MacArdle swung back down to the deck at that moment.

"Is that for me, lieutenant?" he asked, gesturing at the undrunk cup in my hand.

"Certainly, sir," I said, passing it over to him while wondering whether I would dare return to the cook's lair.

"You've met our cook, then," he said, taking a gulp of his drink, his eyes dancing.

"He asked about the steam walkers and their inventor."

"No doubt regaling you with all the tales of demonic possession he could load upon your ears."

I blushed bright red.

"I thought, captain, that the lass was no more in league with dark forces than a seamstress or milkmaid," I replied. "It seemed that she was born with a God-given gift and had only the sense and support to use it for the good it could produce."

"Aye," Captain MacArdle said, his eyes dancing in delight at my discomfort, "that was my opinion also."

"Well, we shan't see her again, having left her safely in Edinburgh."

"No, we shan't," Captain MacArdle agreed strongly. "Although I will say that I never had a dull moment in her company."

"And if she'd been your own daughter, would you have let her create such things?"

"I imagine if she were mine, she'd be a rigging monkey and just as in love with the sea as I am," Captain MacArdle replied. "And I'd no more try to dissuade her from it than her father has done with her passion for steam and steel. Such gifts are to be treasured."

Thank you, I thought silently.

"Well, sir, while I agree with you about the gifts, it will remain up to us to ensure that they turn into the treasure we all hope."

"Aye," Captain MacArdle agreed, pausing to take another sip of his coffee. He turned to the helmsman, checked his heading, then called forward in a bellowing voice, "Hands below to breakfast!"

In an aside to the helmsman but also meant for my ears, "We can handle it for the moment."

The helmsman said nothing, merely changing his grip on the wheel.

Captain MacArdle drained his mug and passed it to me. "Perhaps, Lieutenant Clarke, you should get some food before the cook dowses the fire."

I nodded, taking his meaning and his cup. Below, with the rest of the crew, I was unlikely to have my ears turned by more of the cook's jabber.

The rest of the crew, such as there was, was more in favor of the steam power than against. They noted how much faster they could go, how easier it was — except for the stokers — and rubbed their hands gleefully when they considered how the *Danielle* would

fare sailing against the wind. Blockade running was a particular source of conversation —
at first hushed and then, later, louder as they decided that I would not gab, being both in
league with the Captain and Prince Charles.

I only nibbled at the food; it's not so much that the sea doesn't agree with me as the
fare that was on offer. I ate enough to keep body and soul together, hoping that I'd have a
chance to eat better — and more — later in the day.

Captain MacArdle noted my return with a quirk of his eyebrow and then moved
across the quarterdeck to me to say, "I'd prefer, lieutenant, if you'd remain below until
we're certain we're safe."

"And how long will that be?"

"I imagine we'll be in harbor in another hour or two," he replied. I nodded, gave
him a half-salute and turned about.

#

Fortunately, Montrose was in the hands of the Prince's supporters. We docked
readily but warily; Captain MacArdle made it a point to have the ship warped to anchor
out of the harbor and, under the guise of the cook's fires, kept a ready supply of hot coal
even.

"Aye," he'd said, "but it's the best we can do." He thrust his jaw forward,
challengingly, "Unless *you* can think of something better, lieutenant."

"I'll put my mind to it," I said.

"Not now," he told me, pointing toward the plank that was being set between ship
and quay as a gangway. "Now you'll be needed for your French and your guile, if I'm not
mistaken."

I gulped, for I was not certain I had much of either at the moment.

"Have you your commission?" he asked me now. I nodded, patting the inside
pocket of my dress jacket. I'd changed into it just as Captain MacArdle sent below for me.

"Very well, then, Lieutenant Clarke, leave us see about putting some teeth in your
Lightning." He turned to his first mate and said, "We're going to be getting more gear,
some of it heavy, so ready the hoists."

"Aye, sir."

We left even as the two other ships were still drawing into the harbor.

We did not have to go far before we were met by a small group of men on horse.

"Are you from the ship?" the leader, a young officer by his looks, demanded of us.

"We are," Captain MacArdle replied.

The officer turned to me. "And you?"

I nodded. He was a handsome lad, maybe in his early twenties, maybe a bit less.
Dark hair, piercing blue eyes and a measure of self-assurance that seemed almost arrogant.
But — *oh!* was he handsome! His accent was tinged with French but not so much that I
couldn't understand him.

"*Est-ce que vous servez le roi?*" I said, figuring that would be the quickest way to finish our introductions.

"What did you say to him?" Captain MacArdle muttered.

"Do you serve the King?" I translated.

"Oh," the captain replied. He made a gesture with his hand, like he was moving a mug away from and back toward him — the traditional motion for those who toasted "the King across the water."

The lieutenant smiled and made a half-bow in his saddle. "*Oui, je sers le roi.*"

"Then please take us to your commander," I said, not before getting an elbow in the ribs from Captain MacArdle — the young Frenchman was *quite* handsome.

Behind the officer, some of the others snickered and one muttered, "*He* is the commander, lad."

I took a deep breath. I expected someone much older, more mature. I gestured toward the captain. "This is Captain MacArdle and I am Lieutenant Clarke."

"I am Captain Jean-Michel O'Hara," the officer replied, performing another of his intricate half-bows.

"A pleasure, captain," I said, trying to recall the good manners of Lieutenant Anderson.

"We were told there would be artillery here," Captain MacArdle said, glancing around at the other horsemen. "And troops."

"There is some militia," Captain O'Hara said with an audible sniff. "They are supposed to provide us with security for our — " he broke off, suddenly, looking at us suspiciously. "Forgive me but these are trying times — how do I know you are who you say you are?"

With me, that was a *really* good question because, of course, I wasn't. But I'd been prepared, so I reached into my jacket and pulled my commission from the inside pocket.

"Here is my commission," I said with a tone that implied that should be sufficient. I wondered once again how a lad so young got a commission so high. Or, I suppose, so low if he bought it. Were his parents very poor or was he very talented?

I stepped forward and to his left side to pass it up to him. He took it and examined it for a moment before passing it back to me. "It seems rather... new."

"May I see your commission?" I asked. He reddened.

"My commission is from King Louis the fifteenth of France," he replied solemnly. "It is held by my relatives in Paris."

"May we see the artillery?" Captain MacArdle said, adding in an undertone to me, "That'll be better than seeing a commission."

"Certainly," he said. He glanced at us and back to the pier. "You have no horses, you shall have to ride behind us."

Oh, no! I wasn't sure I wanted to ride behind this man. Apparently, I didn't have a choice because he said, "You're the lighter, you'll ride with me."

I glanced to Captain MacArdle who merely gestured for me to mount up, while moving toward the next horse and rider.

Captain O'Hara lowered his hand and I clasped it, kicking off with my near leg to jump into the air and be propelled — neatly — onto the back of his horse.

"I had hoped you were light," the Frenchman said as I settled in behind him. "These Scottish mares aren't up to much weight."

The Captain led his troop off at a quiet walk but I sensed this was more out of concern for the horses than for any laziness on his part.

As we rode, I became uncomfortably aware of his body, particularly after a rut in the road caused me to be flung against his back. He muttered an imprecation and then settled, calling over his shoulder, "Sorry, I realize it is difficult for some to remain mounted without the benefit of stirrups."

It *almost* sounded like an apology but I could hear the sneer beneath. I held my tongue, thinking that I would have my revenge when I showed him *Lightning* in full trot.

In a quarter of an hour we arrived at an encampment just on the outskirts of the town. I could see some guards — none looking too happy — and a vast horde of canvas-covered stacks: artillery, weapons, ammunition.

From behind me, I heard Captain MacArdle gasp in delight. For myself, I tried to imagine how all of it would fit into our three ships.

Captain O'Hara reined his horse to a halt and extended a hand to help me down. I jumped off easily and waited for him to dismount. On the ground, he handed his horse off to an urchin who had apparently been drafted as orderly.

"See that she gets water and a rub down," he told the lad as he passed the reins over. The youngster, looking hungrier than the horse, nodded mutely.

"It is hard to get good help here," the Frenchman told me. I said nothing. Captain O'Hara waited for Captain MacArdle to join us, then gestured toward a tent.

Inside we found a field table and some chairs all set on rough ground.

Captain O'Hara gestured for us to sit then left for a moment to confer with his soldiers. When he came back, he seemed in better spirits.

I took the moment to examine his features more carefully. His jaw was strong, his hair long and tied in a queue in the back. He still seemed terribly young for his position. I wondered if he was scared and immediately saw the signs in the corners of his eyes.

"Assuming you are who you say, what do you want from me?" he asked as he sat in the chair at the head of the table.

"We've been ordered by the Prince to bring your artillery down to London," Captain MacArdle told him.

"Your ships could carry it but, once you get there, what then?" the Frenchman replied, spreading his hands open helplessly. "I've got gunners enough for four, perhaps five, guns but we'd need horses and escorts — "

"Did you not say there was militia?" I asked.

Captain O'Hara nodded. "They say there are over three hundred present." He made a face. "They took that many of our muskets."

"How many have you left?" I asked, curious.

"*Vingt et deux cents*," he replied, then translated, "Two thousand, two hundred."

Captain MacArdle whistled in surprise.

"And your guns?" I pressed, deciding that I had to seem more forceful than I felt.

"We have six field pieces ranging in size from three pounders to eighteen pounders," the Captain replied. "I have eleven men under me, having been left in command by Colonel Grant."

"Oh, Colonel Grant!" I exclaimed. "I've met him!"

"Is he well?" Captain O'Hara demanded eagerly. He shook his head. "I have heard nothing."

"The Prince captured Carlisle, and has moved south," I told him. "We had rumours that perhaps he'd also captured Manchester by ruse and he continues south."

"Which is why we must get these guns to London," Captain MacArdle said.

Captain O'Hara pursed his lips and threw open his right hand in despair. "Without troops to guard them, the enemy will soon have our guns."

"We'll take the militia," I said. He looked over to me in surprise. "They'll do their part."

"And we'll have a surprise when we land," Captain MacArdle said, winking at me.

"I have heard rumours of a secret weapon, some infernal thing of steam," Captain O'Hara said, glancing at the two of us. "Where did you say you came from?"

"Edinburgh," Captain MacArdle replied.

"I know something of the sea," Captain O'Hara said, his eyes glinting with suspicion, "you made good time."

"Yes," Captain MacArdle agreed. "Time is of the essence."

"And when we get there — to London — how will we meet up with the Prince's forces?"

"The Prince has employed several volunteers to maintain contact with us," Captain MacArdle replied cautiously. "We expect to meet one where we land."

"And if not?"

"If not, we'll advance on our own."

"You propose to take London with six light guns and three hundred militia?" Captain O'Hara said in surprise.

"We'll have a bit more than that," Captain MacArdle said.

"More troops? More guns?" Captain O'Hara asked. "And where will they come from?"

"We'll have surprise on our side," Captain MacArdle replied.

"It would have to be a great surprise," the Frenchman said, sounding dubious. He turned to me. "You've been quiet, lieutenant. What do you say?"

"Our surprise took Carlisle," I told him. "Only we've got better than that."

"And with your guns, we'll have better yet," Captain MacArdle added. He made an irritated gesture. "But we don't have time to waste."

"I was instructed to keep these guns and weapons safe for use by Colonel Grant," Captain O'Hara said, standing. "I'm not convinced that I should release them to you gentlemen."

"And if you don't what do you propose to do with them?" I demanded, suddenly annoyed with this fool. "Leave them here to rot? Or wait until the enemy captures them from you?"

"And would that not happen all the sooner if we take them to London?" Captain O'Hara demanded.

"No," I told him. "If we bring them to London, we'll take London."

"I have no reason to believe that."

"And we have no time to educate you, sir," I said. "But we've been sent by Prince Charles to get these weapons and bring them to London. How will you answer for your failure to follow orders?"

"I have been given no orders."

"You have now."

"By a Lieutenant?"

"By Captain MacArdle, then," I said, jerking my head toward the seaman. "Or Colonel Grant and the Prince by delegation."

"Without orders, I can do nothing," he said, spreading his hands in resignation.

"Orders!" I cried. And then a thought struck me. I patted my pockets and searched through them. There was nothing in them, of course, but I had learned a bit of acting from all my Guising. "Captain MacArdle, did I pass the orders to you, sir?"

Captain MacArdle's eyes widened and he drew a breath but, before he replied, I jerked my head toward the French captain and he caught on. "No, lieutenant."

"Oh, *mon Dieu*, I left them on the ship!" I cried. I stood up theatrically and gestured toward the French captain. "Sir, I must beg a horse so that I can return to our ship and bring you the orders." I bowed at him. "I deeply apologize for my error."

"It would be quicker, perhaps, if we were to prepare now, knowing that we could show you the orders when we get to the ship, Captain," Captain MacArdle added.

"You have seen these orders?" Captain O'Hara asked the seaman.

"Of course," Captain MacArdle lied smoothly. He glared at me. "I am surprised, Lieutenant, that you did not think to bring them along with your commission."

"Sorry, sir," I said, blushing and sounding quite contrite, "I thought that the commission would be proof enough of my sincerity."

Captain O'Hara sat back down at the table and spread a hand toward me. "Let me see that commission again, Lieutenant."

I passed the paper over once more and he spread them out on his table, peering at them closely. After a moment, he folded the paper up again and passed it back to me.

"You are right, that is proof enough," the Captain said finally. He glanced at us with something like hope in his eyes, adding, "And you say that there is a secret weapon that will aid us?"

"We can show you on the ship, sir," I told him.

"But time is of the essence," Captain MacArdle said. "We've still got to convince your militia to accompany us and we want to get underway before we run into any further entanglements."

"Like an enemy squadron?" Captain O'Hara asked.

"Exactly," I agreed with a fervent nod.

"We've seen signs of other ships in the past fortnight," Captain O'Hara told us. "I was worried that perhaps you were sent by King George."

"But, of course, we are not," I assured him.

"Can you lead us to the commander of the militia?" Captain MacArdle asked. "And can you have your men prepare to decamp?"

"They will not appreciate a return to the sea," Captain O'Hara said, seeming to go a bit green himself.

"We can promise them swift passage," I told him with a nod toward Captain MacArdle.

"No one can command the wind," Captain O'Hara protested.

"Oh, the wind won't be a problem, no matter which way it's blowing," I assured him, getting an agreeing snort from Captain MacArdle.

"A ship that sails into the wind has never been built!"

"Ach, no, lad, there ye're wrong," Captain MacArdle replied. "We've three of them now and more to come."

"I shall be most intrigued to see this," Captain O'Hara replied, rising again from his chair and calling for his orderly. He relayed his orders to his sergeant, having a private bring three horses.

I was relieved to be riding on my own this time. The trouble was that I was given a fairly randy stallion who was most amused to have a woman on his back and proved quite a handful. Captain O'Hara laughed at my discomfort, saying, "He's usually a perfect gentleman. It's only the ladies who get this sort of treatment — that's how we got him — he proved no mount for the local smith's girl."

Well, now, apparently he was proving a difficult mount for another smith's girl.

Captain MacArdle looked at me with an expression that was part amusement and part alarm.

"There's no horse I can't get under my control," I swore, pitching my voice low. "He's just showing his spirits."

He continued to show his spirits all the way to the militia camp. The camp was larger and better-housed than the artillery camp but not quite so well organized.

The men in the camp were Scottish Highlanders and not at all happy with being forced to idleness.

"So, Ensign, come to harass us once more with yer Froggie speech?" a man called out as he approached. He was dressed somewhat better than the others and carried himself like a leader.

"I'm here with Captain MacArdle and Lieutenant Clarke, they have orders from the Prince," O'Hara returned stiffly. "And it's *Captain* O'Hara, sir."

"Only because you begged your Colonel to promote you," the other man returned promptly. He turned to us. "And who are you gentlemen?"

"We've been sent to transport your troops and the Captain's artillery," I said quickly.

"Anywhere but here would be better," the man muttered to himself. He glanced back at his camp and then moved closer to us, pitching his voice lower, "But I'd not be telling ye the truth if I didn't say that the men could do with another month of training."

"That's always the case, sir," I said, glancing toward Captain MacArdle who nodded quickly in agreement. "But time is pressing, how soon can they be ready to move?"

"I don't believe we've been properly introduced," the man said, drawing himself up with pride. "I'm Colonel Lord John Drummond of the Royal Scots regiment."

"Lieutenant Samuel Clarke of His Majesty's Steam Horse," I said, bowing from my saddle in the same way I'd seen Captain O'Hara bow before. I gestured to Captain MacArdle. "This is Captain MacArdle of the ship *Danielle.*"

How I managed to avoid blushing when I named the ship, I'll never know.

"The Prince has ordered us to collect the artillery and your troops and depart immediately," Captain MacArdle added with an urgent tone. "How soon can you be ready?"

"Ready?" the Colonel's eyes flared. "We've been ready since before we landed, Captain. How soon can we leave?"

"As soon as we've got artillery and troops boarded, my lord," Captain MacArdle replied. "We've three ships at the wharf."

"And where are we headed?"

"London," I replied, "to join the prince."

"Very well," Lord Drummond replied, rubbing his hands briskly, "I'd feared we'd be stuck here forever guarding the ensign's guns."

"*Captain*, my lord!" Captain O'Hara protested.

"Your commission's only signed by Colonel Grant, lad," Lord Drummond replied, his eyes twinkling. "Before you were just an ensign."

"He carries himself like a captain, my lord," I said to my surprise.

"And who gave you your commission, lieutenant?"

"My commission is signed by the Prince himself, my lord," I said, being careful with my choice of words. "But it would appear to me, my lord, that it is the thought, not the deed which should count."

"A captain of twelve men is not much of a captain," Lord Drummond replied. He shook himself and raised an arm beckoningly.

"My lord?" a young soldier cried as he approached.

"Spread the word, Liam, we move out immediately."

"Aye, my lord."

"How many men do you have, my lord?" Captain MacArdle asked.

"Including your Captain O'Hara and his eleven, we have a bit over four hundred," Lord Drummond replied. "Plus arms and horses — "

"We've no room for horses, my lord," Captain MacArdle broke in, shaking his head.

"And how are we going to move the guns?"

"The steam horses will carry two of them and their crews," I said.

"But we've a dozen guns!" Captain O'Hara protested.

"I have been told, sir, that I may commission some of them for my ships," Captain O'Hara said.

"Two guns?" Lord Drummond repeated, pursing his lips doubtfully. He glanced to me. "And when are we to join up with the Prince's forces, lieutenant?"

I glanced at Captain MacArdle.

"I've been told that we'll get further instructions when we arrive, my lord," Captain MacArdle replied.

Lord Drummond looked thoughtful for a moment then flicked a hand in a dismissive fashion. "Clearly we are to be met by one of the Prince's 'scouts'."

Lord Drummond turned to O'Hara. "Do you vouch for these people?"

O'Hara shrugged. "They say they've orders aboard their ship."

Lord Drummond turned to Captain MacArdle. "I should very much like to see those orders."

"Lieutenant Clarke, run back and fetch the orders, please," Captain MacArdle said to me.

"I'd be quicker on a horse," I said, not relishing a solo ride with my rude stallion.

"By all means," Captain O'Hara said with a dismissive wave. "Just don't take too long, lieutenant."

I nodded, then drew myself up and saluted, turning back to the stallion and jumping up into the saddle before he could complain. I converted his skittishness into a trot with a dig from my heels and then, when the way was clear, into a steady gallop.

Even so it took a good quarter of an hour to return to the *Danielle*, throw the reins to a surprised seaman, sprint up the gangplank and rush back down to my cabin where I rooted out some paper and a pen, uncapping the ink bottle and stabbing the nib into it hastily.

I paused then, fortunately, to retrieve my commission and carefully scrutinize the writing. It was clear that the orders were scribed by another hand and only signed by the

Prince himself.

I had no time but this had to be perfect. Sweat beaded on my forehead as I placed the paper on the table and carefully started the first words:

To All Whom Read this: Greetings

By Order of His Royal Highness, Charles Edward Stuart, true Prince of the realms of Scotland, England, Wales, and Ireland, I urge, instruct, and order all who read these orders to obey their holder be it either Captain Thomas MacArdle or Lieutenant Samuel Clarke or their appointed representatives.

Fail not at your peril.

Signed,

Charles Edward Stuart

Forging the signature was easy by the time I got to it. I glanced over the letter, nodded, raised it up and waved it to dry, lowered it again to blot it. Rising from my seat, I picked up my commission and rushed out of the room and up to the deck. There, I carefully folded it and placed it in my pocket along with my commission.

And then it was down the plank, back onto the benighted horse and off again at the gallop to Lord Drummond.

Clearly, Captain MacArdle had been persuasive because the camp was already in the disarray of being struck, tents lowered, folded and packed onto carts. My heart sank as I saw that because they'd want to put their tents on our Walkers and I didn't think that would work at all well with the cannon. My heart lifted as I approached and heard Lord Drummond say, "We'll set out foraging parties when we land to acquire sufficient horses for the officers and carts."

Well, that made sense.

"We'll have room enough for your carts and gear, my Lord," Captain MacArdle assured him. "We'll put most of them on our third ship — "

"I am very interested in seeing these ships," Captain O'Hara interjected. When Lord Drummond gave him a reproachful look, the young officer explained, "Apparently they can sail *against* the wind."

"Not sail, sir," I corrected, "they *steam* against the wind."

"I shall be most interested in seeing that also," Lord Drummond said. He glanced at me and extended his hand.

I drew the hastily written orders and the commission from my jacket and passed them over to him. Once he took them in his hands, my eyes slid over to Captain MacArdle. The old seaman moved closer to me, perhaps prepared to start a defense if we were found out.

Lord Drummond perused both the orders and the commission for a long while and then made to hand them back but Captain O'Hara extended a hand toward him. "If I may, my Lord?"

Lord Drummond's eyes twinkled but he passed the papers over without a word.

'Captain' O'Hara examined them silently for a long moment and then frowned. "They're not in French," he said, glancing accusingly at me.

"His Scottish officers don't all read French," Captain MacArdle reminded him.

Captain O'Hara considered this for a long moment, then nodded his head and passed the papers back to me.

"If all meets your approval, 'Captain', perhaps we can proceed?" Lord Drummond said tauntingly.

"My men have already struck camp," Captain O'Hara replied, "all we need are beasts to draw our wagons."

"You can have that one," I said, glancing with no liking at my loaned stallion.

"Time is of the essence?" Lord Drummond said, glancing back and forth between Captain MacArdle and myself.

"Yes, my Lord," I said. "We don't know how soon the Prince will need us, or the large guns."

"It's the small guns he'll need most," Captain O'Hara said.

"*If* they work," Lord Drummond corrected.

"They'll work, my Lord," Captain O'Hara returned hotly. "I'll stake my life on it."

"Certainly," Lord Drummond agreed. "It's the other lives that worry me."

"Small guns, sir?" I said, turning to Captain O'Hara for explanation.

"Captain O'Hara's contribution to the war," Lord Drummond said drolly.

"Puckle guns were invented in England, my Lord," Captain O'Hara reminded him. "I merely made them practical."

"Puckle guns?" Captain MacArdle repeated, shaking his head. "I've not heard of them sir, my lord."

"They fire several rounds a minute," Lord Drummond said. "Rather like a squad of muskets all at once."

"And how many rounds?" I asked. Suddenly, I had several other questions. "And how many rounds do you have? How do you reload?"

"This can wait until we are aboard and moving," Lord Drummond said. Captain O'Hara agreed.

Puckle guns. Hmm. It seemed to me that Prince Charles was a collector of novel ideas. My thoughts were interrupted as Captain MacArdle said, "I'd best get back to my ships and get them ready for your arrival."

"Indeed, Captain, that seems an excellent suggestion," Lord Drummond agreed. "And your Lieutenant?"

Captain MacArdle glanced my way. "Lieutenant?"

"I could help you at the ship, sir," I said.

"Why don't the two of you take this excellent stallion back then?" Lord Drummond suggested. "That will doubtless save time and beasts all around."

And so we did, with Captain MacArdle discovering the damned stallion just as much a handful as I had.

\#

We were back in a good quarter of an hour, giving us time which Captain MacArdle used well, striking hatches and rigging tackle, before the first of the soldiers and artillery arrived.

Then we were all working for endless hours hoisting, stowing, cursing, grunting as we took aboard heavy eighteen pound cannon and lighter burdens wrapped in canvas — the Puckle guns, I guessed.

Finally, as the sun was setting, we were ready and the steam was raised. We made our way west into the large bay, turned east and made our way out to sea, our passage marked by the huffing and puffing of three steam engines.

Lord Drummond had elected to stay on the rear ship with the bulk of his troops while Captain O'Hara had decided to stay aboard the *Danielle* with me and Captain MacArdle. Ensign Reynolds had been happy enough to remain on the second ship away from all the high-ranking attention.

Captain O'Hara found me leaning on the taffrail watching the shoreline disappear from view. Soon, we would face the English and I would be a fool not to be scared.

"How much coal do you have and how much does your engine burn each hour?" Captain O'Hara asked suddenly, turning forward to watch the steady plume of smoke and steam rise up from the engine.

A good question, I thought. I moved forward to Captain MacArdle and started to repeat the question but he turned back to us. "I heard," he said tersely. "We'll stop in at Hull and refuel."

"And we'll get enough for the Walkers?" I asked, remembering to pitch my voice low. I mustn't have been very good at it this time for Captain O'Hara gave me an odd look.

Captain MacArdle noticed it too. "You need to save your voice for shouting orders, lieutenant," he said. "You're not that so old that your voice still doesn't break on occasion."

Behind me, O'Hara snorted. I reddened but nodded, as though properly scolded.

"To answer your question, though, lieutenant, we'll get enough for the Walkers, too," Captain MacArdle replied. "We've still room in the holds for tons of coal and even your beasties won't need that much."

I turned back to Captain O'Hara and raised an eyebrow to ask if the answer satisfied him.

"I shall be interested to see if they are all you claim them to be," he said to me.

"The Prince thinks so," Captain MacArdle said in a tone that brooked no argument.

"The Prince has always been a man of vision," O'Hara replied. His tone sounded evasive.

"And how came you to his attention, sir, if I may be so bold?" I asked, curious to know more about these guns of his.

"The Puckle gun was invented in England," Captain O'Hara replied. "His Most Catholic Majesty, Louis XV heard of it and desired to have some for himself." He nodded his head modesty as he added, "He commissioned me to make the attempt."

"You?" I said, unable to hide my surprise. He was so young!

He blushed angrily. "What, you do not think this is possible?"

I shook my head quickly. "No, of course not. I was merely surprised, sir!"

My words calmed him a bit but I could tell that the issue irked him. It reminded me a *lot* of how I felt when people expressed surprise at both my age — and my sex!

"You must be quite accomplished to have made something so difficult," I said, continuing to soothe him. "Could you explain to me how it works? And how we can use it with the steam walkers?"

"I heard tell that the person who invented the steam horse was a girl," he said, not quite answering my question. I nodded. "A young girl, *une jeune fille*."

"Yes, that's so," I agreed, careful to keep my voice deep, for he was eyeing me intently now.

"And did you greet her invention with scorn?"

"No," I said, trying to imagine how Lieutenant Clarke would have first viewed the walker. "In fact, and I hope you won't repeat this, but it scared me out of my wits when I first saw it."

"How so?"

"You have only seen them folded up at rest, here on the deck," I said. "When I saw the first one, it came steaming and clopping, towering above horse and rider, moving relentlessly, remorselessly, like some unstoppable creation of steel and steam."

"Hmm," Captain O'Hara murmured, trying to picture it. "So it is not just a steam horse then but more like a wagon?"

"Indeed, it is a wagon with legs instead of wheels," I said. "The legs go high enough that it has no difficulty going over small fences and fording streams."

"But they are dangerous, too," he muttered to himself. "Did one not blow up at Carlisle?"

"It was poorly maintained and over-pressured," I said, my anger rising. "Good men died because their leader was careless."

"The Puckle gun is like that also," he said. "If not managed carefully it could blow up."

"So could any gun, Captain," I reminded him. He accepted this correction with a nod.

He turned toward the covered form of my *Lightning* and then back to me. "How much weight can your steam horse carry?"

"As much as a wagon," I replied.

"How do you know?" A good question; we'd never actually tested.

"Well," I said, "that's what I was told."

"An eighteen pound cannon weighs three tons," he reminded me.

"I think it could handle that," I told him.

"You think?" His tone was scathing.

"Sir, one cannot be certain until one tries."

"It would be better to know beforehand," he said. He gestured for me to follow him. "Shall we go look?"

"Sir, it's rather late, perhaps we should wait until morning when the light is better?"

He pondered on that before finally nodding. "I see you are too tired to continue this evening," he said. "You are dismissed, lieutenant."

I considered arguing but decided it was not worth pitting my tired wits against his Gallic pig-headedness. So I merely gave him a sketchy salute and turned to go below.

"Ah, lieutenant!" he called after me. I turned back to him. "Would you happen to know where I am to be quartered?"

"We're pretty full, sir," Captain MacArdle called from his position near the helm. "You can sleep with your men, if you'd like."

"Is there not an officer's quarters?" he asked, gesturing toward me. "Where is the lieutenant staying?"

Oh, damn! What would I do if he stayed with me? If Captain MacArdle said that all the bunks were full, wouldn't O'Hara have the right to turf me out? And then I'd have to sleep either with his soldiers or with the sailors.

"There's only the one bunk in my cabin," I said desperately.

He shrugged. "I don't mind sharing; I've done it before."

I turned to Captain MacArdle but it was clear that he could think of no way out of the dilemma either.

"It's a small cabin, sir," I said. "Let me lead you down so that you might know where it is and then I'll rejoin the captain here while you prepare your bed."

"Lieutenant, you may do whatever you like, as long as I may get a decent night's sleep," Captain O'Hara told me, gesturing for me to lead the way.

I led him forward where he picked up his gear and then down the passageway and back to the cabins, showing him my — our — cabin before returning to the deck.

Captain MacArdle noticed my return and sidled over to me, leading me aft to the taffrail where we were out of earshot. "What are you going to do, Danni?"

"I'm going to wait up here until I think he's asleep, change quickly and get up before he does," I said.

"I'll have the messenger wake you," he said. "I go off watch in a few minutes myself or I'd let you have the use of my cabin."

I nodded but my thoughts were elsewhere: plotting how I'd change in the dark, crawl into bed so that we were top to tail. I wondered if I might spend some time binding up my midriff but decided that it wouldn't be necessary, being still rather boyish in that area.

I waited until Captain MacArdle was relieved by his mate and followed him below, stopping at my cabin and listening for a moment. Captain O'Hara was definitely asleep — he snored.

I grimaced and quietly made my way into the cabin, pulled off my jacket, pulled on my nightshirt and disrobed under it, being careful to place my clothes atop my bag so I could find them quickly again come morning. Then I crawled into bed, careful not to bash the captain with my feet.

His feet smelt. In fact, the young captain was a good many days away from a bath and was more ripe than I'd imagined. I was a few days closer to a bath and not as pungent — or so I imagined. Certainly my feet weren't so... fragrant.

I forced my eyes closed and made my breath slow down. The rock of the ship, the soreness of my muscles slowly won out over my worry and the smell and I drifted into a sleep troubled by images and nightmares I could not remember in the morning.

CHAPTER FOURTEEN

SOMEONE WAS TICKLING MY FEET!

"Stop!" I cried muzzily. The tickling stopped abruptly to be replaced by a thoughtful silence. The pitch of the ship reminded me where I was — aboard the *Danielle* in a bed with a French captain of artillery. A captain who thought me just as male as he. Had I spoken too much in my normal voice?

I slid out of the bed.

"Good," Captain O'Hara's voice came from behind me, "I need to relieve myself." He thudded to the deck behind me. "You have the daintiest feet for a man, did anyone ever tell you?"

I huffed at the insult. In truth, I had rather large, manly feet for a girl so I was miffed at his observation.

I pulled the door open and gestured him toward it. "Go, sir, and do your duty."

Captain O'Hara laughed at my choice of words but, clearly, his bladder had him in thrall and he was through the door in short order. While he was gone, I hastily dressed, pulling on tunic and jacket. There was no glass in the cabin so I couldn't say much about my appearance but I was reasonably certain that I looked as much as man this morning as I had the day before, so I took myself off to the galley for whatever food and drink I could find.

Captain O'Hara joined me not long after, sounding put off that I hadn't waited for him. "I suppose that's to be expected," he allowed, "you're certainly not much more than skin and bones. Doubtless you've got worms, too."

Worms! It was all I could do to bite back a hot retort. He grinned when he saw my reaction; clearly he'd been hoping to goad me so.

I finished before he did, turned my dishes back to the cook and made my way to the head, waiting until it was vacant before relieving my straining bladder. It is amazing how such simple things can get so complicated when trying to maintain a façade. I wasn't sure how this would bode for when we landed and I was placed in charge of my *Lightning* and a group of men. I would have to be doubly careful: for one thing was certain, no group of men would willingly let themselves be led into battle by a "mere girl."

As I was pulling up my trousers, something demanded my attention. Our steam engine had stopped. I heard urgent calls on the deck above and the sound of seamen climbing into the rigging.

I hurried myself back up on deck, glancing around and seeing the seamen setting sail.

"Is there a problem?" I asked Captain MacArdle.

"No," he said, shaking his head and pointing forward, "we're coming up on land."

Oh! And we didn't want people there to know that we had steam ships.

"Lord Drummond and Captain Stoops will be putting in first with *Anabelle*," he told me, referring to Captain Stoops' ship. "That way, if there's trouble, we'll have troops on hand."

I nodded.

"We should reach shore in an hour and, with luck, we'll be gone again before nightfall," Captain MacArdle said, crossing himself in the way of Catholics. I hadn't realized he was a Catholic and he caught my look and smiled at me. "It doesn't bother you, does it?"

"Not me, sir," I told him sincerely.

"There's some in Edinburgh who think differently."

"People have been hung for their religion," I said by way of agreement. In a lower voice, I added, "And some of those who did the hanging would just as easily hang me for a witch."

"A witch of steam and steel," Captain MacArdle said in agreement. He touched my shoulder. "Not to worry, lieutenant, you're more likely to die in the heat of battle."

Comforting thought! He caught my look and snorted. "Trust me, there are worse ways to go."

I took no more comfort in that than in his earlier pronouncement. I wanted to be home, safe in my bed and not for the last time did I repent of my foolish dreams of making steam walkers.

Something in my mood must have caused him anguish, for he said, "Don't worry, Danni, we'll see you safely through this."

#

An hour later a signal was raised from the top of Captain Stoops' ship and Captain MacArdle ordered us to make sail for the docks of Hull.

The sun was falling as we tied up but we found carts waiting and seaman and soldiers fell in to pull off cargo hatches and haul sacks of coal aboard, piled by the canvas we'd put over our engine and below in the holds with the guns. It was hot work. Because I was seen as a man and an officer, I felt it my duty to work alongside all the others — much to Captain O'Hara's surprise. After watching in amazement, he joined me.

He stopped for a moment to wipe the sweat off his brow and glanced at his men and the sailors. "They're working harder," he said in surprise.

"We're setting the example, sir," I reminded him. He gave me a curious look but bent back to work with a will.

We were soon loaded and it was with mixed emotions that I watched the lights on the shore twinkle and disappear as we made our way back out to sea. An hour later, we started our steam engines again and Captain MacArdle had the seamen furl the sails.

"I really should have them struck off the masts," he said thoughtfully. "It's doubtful we'll need them any more."

"But why go to all the extra work, sir?" I asked.

"If I could, I'd strike the sails, the yards, and the fore masts all," Captain MacArdle replied. When I still looked confused, he explained, "That'd leave less for the enemy to see... and less to hit with shot if they fire on us."

"Surely, they'd have to catch us first, wouldn't they?"

"Unless we run into them," Captain MacArdle replied. "And, while your steam engines are powerful, we're not as fast as a well-found frigate."

"But we can sail against the wind, surely that would save us!"

"Only if our destination is against the wind, lieutenant, only then."

Oh. I hadn't considered that.

#

19 December 1745
His Royal Majesty,
James III & VII,
King of England and Scotland
Sire,
I write to you with great news!

Today we met the English south of Derby and I am pleased to report that we have routed them, captured their artillery as well as nearly two thousand of their foot and sent the rest packing — minus the much-vaunted former Duke of Cumberland. I regret to say that he met his end on the battlefield. We buried him with honors consonant with his rank, as we did with all others.

Our victory was solely due to the bravery of our steam horse artillery, particularly to Major Walker, Lieutenant Cattan, and Ensign Mapes. Those three, in charge of three walkers, circled the enemy's rear, assaulted the baggage and camp, destroyed the artillery trains and set upon the enemy's rear to bring about their utter defeat and ruin.

I regret to report that in the course of this gallant action, one of our Walkers was lost, leaving us with only four.

Your loyal subject, obedient servant, and respectful son,
Charles Edward Stuart

#

19 December 1745
His Royal Majesty
King George II
Somewhere south of Derby
Your Majesty,
I wish I could give you better greetings, sire, but this message bears to you the gravest of

news.

The enemy has defeated us, routed our infantry, broke our artillery and overwhelmed our horse. What is left to us is less than a thousand foot fit for the field and scarce four hundred horse. We have no artillery.

They fell upon our rear with some weapon designed by the Devil himself as far as can be ascertained. It is a demon of steam and fire on which the enemy have mounted light artillery and sharpshooters. These steam walkers can move as quickly as a horse at a good walk or half-trot but they are tireless and stand eight feet high — taller than the heads of our horsemen. They overwhelmed our rear, and encircled our troops, causing great loss and our rout.

We are falling back in what order can be maintained.

I regret to inform your Majesty that the last time he was seen, His Grace, the Duke of Cumberland was stretched out upon the ground with grievous wounds. I do not know if he lived and is captive or he fell on the field of battle.

If you have any additional troops, please send them to join us with the greatest urgency lest the way to London be open to the Pretender Prince.

Your obedient servant,

John Ligonier, General of Horse, 1st Earl Ligonier

#

19 December 1745

Lieutenant Samuel Cattan

South of Derby

Danni,

I hope that this letter finds you in good health.

I am afraid that I am not good at writing letters, as you may have noticed, and worse at writing these kinds of letters.

As soon as you get this, Danni, make all arrangements to flee. Your life is in peril. Hamish MacAllister has been cozying up to the Prince and is trying to get rewarded your hand in marriage. The Prince is considering this proposal favorably, particularly in light of our last engagement.

We beat the British, Danni, we beat the best they had and sent them packing. It was your walkers that did it. Your father led us on a night march to the enemy's rear and we fell upon them when they were all unsuspecting and ready to engage our troops to the north. We tore through their camp, destroyed their baggage, sent their followers fleeing — and then we fell upon their artillery. What we didn't destroy we captured. And what we captured, we turned on the enemy's rear. It was a slaughter.

Sadly, it was not all one-sided. My injuries were slight but some brave cavalier gave his life to throw a torch on your father's walker and the fire caught, igniting the powder that was for the guns.

I regret to say that there were no survivors. As of this moment, you are an orphan and

Hamish MacAllister is seeking your hand in marriage.

Flee, Danni, flee for your life! Wherever you go, rest assured that I will follow you and find you if I may.

I remain,

Your loyal and devoted servant,

Samuel D. Cattan

#

"I am *not* sleeping this way again!" Captain O'Hara bellowed at me the next morning. "Your feet are noxious!"

I had arranged, just as the night before, to come down after he was asleep and slip in head to tails against him. I hadn't considered what a day in boots would do to the odor from my feet and socks and I'd been too tired to care.

But, to judge by the young captain's swearing, the smell was not pleasant. His feet weren't too sweet, either, but I'd dealt with smelly boys before — I recalled many hours spent fighting to get Jamie to take a bath — so I'd had acquired some ability to handle such smells. Not to mention that I worked with horses and knew Hamish McAllister.

As I had the whole day to consider the problem, I decided not to argue with him at that particular moment, choosing instead to visit the head and get dressed there, which was not as noxious a choice as it may seem. On ships, they place the 'necessary' at the head of the ship so that the winds blow the smell away (as winds are usually driving sails from behind) and as the head consists of nothing more than suitably bored holes in a wooden seat, it was not the smelly place one could easily imagine. I drove out the sailors and soldiers who were loitering there by right of my rank, did the necessary and dressed quickly, returning to my shared cabin in time to find Jean-Michel O'Hara half-in, half-out of his trousers. I chuckled at him and closed the door, not at all interested in seeing more of him — handsome though he was.

In the galley, I got a quick bite to eat and then made my way up on deck where I found Captain MacArdle already stationed by the helm, eyeing the clouds above us anxiously.

"The weather's closing in," he told me. "We might be in for a blow."

I'd endured plenty of wet and cold weather growing up in Edinburgh but it had always been on solid — if sometimes quite soggy — land. I wasn't quite sure that I liked the idea of handling the same on a wind-tossed ship.

"Have you ever steamed through one before?" I asked.

The Captain pursed his lips and shook his head slowly. He glanced toward the steam engine and the boiler. "How well will they handle a tossing?"

We'd discussed this when we'd first designed the naval version of my steam engines. On a ship it was quite possible that it would rock and roll in excess of thirty degrees from side to side, up and down, so we designed the fire box to be fully enclosed and sealable with air only entering through the bottom at the grate. I was pretty sure that would hold, although I wasn't sure how the boiler would handle being sloshed about. The engine itself was probably in no danger but the same couldn't be said for the pair of paddle wheels which descended amidships into the sea. Nor, come to think of it, had we considered what might happen if one of the paddles were completely immersed in water — they depended upon being partly out of water at the top to work.

"Maybe we should have put the engine in the mid-deck," I said after a long moment. It had been my original suggestion but all three sailors had rejected it, fearing the increased risk of fire and also citing the extra work required to set in the paddle wheels. Now, though, the danger that the boiler or the engine might be swamped made my original suggestion to place it under cover far more cogent.

"We could stop the wheels and pull them up," Captain MacArdle said thoughtfully, peering forward as if imagining the work.

"That would be difficult."

"And more of a problem if something broke," he agreed.

I nodded to show that I'd heard. After another moment I said, "I think it might be best to keep the engines running."

Captain MacArdle made a face but nodded. He glanced up to the masts. "I'll have some sail ready in case we need it."

Just then, the lookout cried, "Sail, ho! Fair off the starboard bow!"

"Can she see us?" Captain MacArdle shouted through his speaking trumpet.

"Perhaps."

"Port twenty degrees," Captain MacArdle snapped to the helmsman. To his mate he said, "Signal the others to follow us."

To me he said, "That could be a picket sent to search for us."

As we settled on our new heading, I said to Captain MacArdle, "There are dark clouds ahead."

"Aye," he said sourly. "Can't be helped." A moment later, he said, "you'll want to get below shortly, it's going to be rough."

"What about the coal?" I said, glancing toward my walker.

"What about it?"

"You can't light wet coal," I reminded him. I pointed over his shoulder to our rear. "And we might need it if that ship stays with us."

"I've not enough time for that," Captain MacArdle said, bending around me to bellow, "All hands aloft! Prepare to set the weather sails!"

His mate came up to him and they spoke quietly but urgently together. I realized that I was dismissed from his attention and sped off, down to my cabin where I found, as expected, Captain O'Hara.

"How many of your men have you got with you, Captain?" I asked as I entered the cabin.

He rolled over in the bunk and opened one eye at me. "What?"

"Where are your men?"

He looked very green and I could tell that the increased swell had affected his digestion.

"I've two squads below," he managed to reply.

"With your permission, I have a use for them."

"Would you please stop shouting," he cried, bringing one hand up warily to his head. I wasn't shouting; he was just that ill.

"Let me use your men."

"If that stops you from talking, then by all means, take them," he said, waving his hand wearily and turning back once again to the far side of the bunk.

I rushed off and found the artillery men cowering below, all looking rather green.

"Sergeant," I called out without bothering to identify any one in particular, "get your men and come on deck, Captain O'Hara's given them a mission."

"Sir?"

"Get up on deck, we've got to move the coal," I told him. "We're to bring it below, out of the weather."

"You heard the lieutenant, men, getting moving!" the sergeant bellowed, rousing himself from his torpor. As the men headed out, he came over to me and said, "How is the Captain, sir?"

"Not well," I confessed. "And I'm afraid the seas are going to get worse before they get better."

The sergeant nodded. "Never did have much of a stomach," he muttered to himself. He nodded to me, "Glad to see that's not so with you, sir. But tell me, if you would, why are we moving the coal?"

"We may have need of dry coal before too long," I told him. He considered that for a moment then nodded, gesturing for me to lead the way.

On board deck, the weather was worse. I had the lads gather up sacks of coal, and cart them down to the hold which Captain MacArdle reluctantly assigned.

"You can't get enough to give us steam when the storm's over," he said, "so why are you taking it?"

"I can save enough that we could fire up the boiler in *Lightning*."

"And what good would that do?"

I shrugged. "At the least, we'll have hot coals with which to heat the wet."

He frowned but waved me away as another of his sailors approached with a question.

The artillerymen made slow work of getting the coal moved — at least until they started to warm up from the effort and then things moved more quickly.

Not as quickly as the storm. When we came up for the final load, a sailor rushed to us and shouted over the winds, "Captain says to stay below, sir!"

I looked to the stern and saw that there were three men on the wheel, Captain MacArdle being one of them. I nodded to the seaman and hustled the soldiers back below.

"What now, sir?" the sergeant, whose name I had discovered was Donelly — Matthew Donelly — asked.

"Go back to your quarters and wait," I told him.

The sergeant looked unhappy with that news but nodded, hustling his troops away. And I?

I had no choice but to return to my cabin.

I was greeted at the door by the stench of vomit and moans from Captain O'Hara. The poor soul had taken the new heavier waves very badly and his stomach had rebelled, covering him, the sheets, and our bunk in its contents.

I took one look and headed to the galley. Not because I meant to abandon the room but because I needed supplies, particularly a bucket or maybe even two.

The cook grumbled when I made my request and I snarled in return, gaining the reluctant ownership of two buckets and some old rags. I also got sea water for one of the buckets, courtesy of the cook ordering a wandering seaman to do the task.

"The Captain said he'd kill me if anything happens to you," the cook grumbled when I pressed him for an explanation. I was certain that he gave me this news reluctantly, and expressed my gratitude as best I could when the grumbling seaman returned.

Possessed of two buckets, one with seawater and the other empty, as well as several rags of dubious quality, I returned to my cabin and the ailing captain.

It took far longer than I imagined to get everything cleaned up, particularly without getting anything too wet from my efforts. In the end, however, I'd managed to get the worst of the spew sopped up and the room smelled slightly better for it.

I was not at all happy at the notion, however, of climbing into the bunk with the captain. I could not say how long we'd be confined by the storm, nor what revelations would occur — and that worried me mightily. So mightily, in fact, that I considered using captain MacArdles'cabin instead.

I stood for a long moment considering that but decided in the end that while Captain MacArdle might rarely see his bed during this blow, when he did he would have full need of it.

I stripped off my jacket and my shoes but, given the state of the bedclothes, I decided to remove no more, clambering in to lie with my back to the miserable captain.

I did not expect that we would remain in such close quarters for the next four days. If I had, I surely would have taken myself to the captain's quarters.

If I had, I would have spared myself the worst of what was to come.

#

The storm grew stronger. As the ship lurched and rolled, I was thrown alternately backwards against Captain O'Hara and he, alternately, forward against me. When he rolled against me, he moaned in pain.

I tried to settle him but to no avail. Finally the storm grew so fierce that my stomach, assailed by the scents born in the air to my nostrils, rebelled and it was all I could do to crawl out of the bunk long enough to use the cleaner of the two buckets.

Behind me, I heard O'Hara retch once more as though in sympathy and this set my stomach to even greater efforts. Only when I was thoroughly befouled and too weak to do anything about it, did I manage to stumble back into the bunk. This time I was so wretched that I cared not how I lay.

When next I had coherent thought, I found myself face to face with Captain O'Hara. Fortunately his eyes were closed. I tried to turn away but he tightened his arms around me and muttered something in his sleep. I was too exhausted to fight him, so I closed my eyes and hoped that the worst of the blow was over.

I was wrong. The winds picked up again and we were tossed about like a seed in the wind.

#

Silence startled me to wakefulness. It was the silence of a calm sea, of a motionless ship, of an intense gave. I opened my eyes and found O'Hara's eyes focused on me.

I desperately searched for something to say, moving my eyes from his. "The storm's over."

As I tried to get out of the bed, I struggled against the sheets, my clothes — and his arms.

I was still struggling when a fist pounded on our door and Captain MacArdle stormed in. "Danni, we need you on deck." His eyes looked past me to Captain O'Hara, consideringly. "You too, Captain."

"What is it?" Captain O'Hara asked.

"Ships," the captain said. "Frigates. And they're flying the British flag."

I twisted around and slid to the deck, pulling on shoes and my jacket, leaving Captain O'Hara fumbling in my wake.

On deck, I could see the worry on the faces of the seamen who lined the side, peering off into the distance.

"How's our coal?" I asked, glancing toward the ship's engine.

"Wet," Captain MacArdle said sourly. "Soaked, in fact."

I grunted in response and jabbed a finger at one of the sailors. "You! Go below and get the artillerymen up here. And tell the cook to light his fires."

The seaman looked past me to Captain MacArdle who merely bellowed, "Run!"

As the seaman scuttled below, Captain MacArdle said to me, "What's your plan, Danni?"

Plan? I didn't have one. I was only certain of one thing — that if those ships caught up with us, we would destroy both Walkers and the ships' engines rather than let them be taken.

Even as I struggled to answer the question, another thought came to me. "We'll fight."

"Lass," Captain MacArdle said slowly, "there are two British frigates bearing down on us. We've no steam, our sails are in tatters and we've no way to defend ourselves." He had known me long enough to see the stubborn look in my eyes. "If there was only one, we might escape but they can split up and run us down."

"I had the lads store some coal," I told him. "We've enough to fire up a boiler."

"How much?" Captain MacArdle asked, turning to the distant smudge of sail on the horizon.

"Not enough to steam away," I told him grimly and waved to our sister ships. "And we'd have to leave them, unless they thought like I did."

Captain MacArdle's expression was answer enough.

"So we fight," I told him.

"How?"

"With the Walkers," I told him as the first of the soldiers and the bags of coal streamed onto the deck.

Captain O'Hara staggered up at that moment, spotted the ships and turned grimly to us. "I told you this was a bad idea."

"How quickly can you mount one of your guns on my *Lightning*?"

"What?"

I turned to the nearest soldier and told him, "Go below and get some tea for the Captain." Then I turned to Captain MacArdle, "Get your carpenter."

MacArdle looked at me for a moment and then bellowed out a name. A wiry seaman came rushing forward.

"I need you to follow the Captain O'Hara's orders," I said to the carpenter. To Captain MacArdle, I said, "We'll arm *Lightning* and fight."

"What good will that do?" Captain MacArdle demanded. "They can attack from any quarter!"

"So can we," I told him, pointing to my walker. "*Lightning* can turn to bear wherever we need."

"What sort of gun are you considering?" Captain O'Hara asked, eyeing the lumpy canvas covering the walker dubiously.

"We'll need all the range we can get," Captain MacArdle told him.

"Then you'll want either a long nine or the eighteen pounder."

"Take the eighteen pounder," I said.

"That gun will be too heavy."

"We'll see," I said, turning my back on him and moving toward *Lightning*. I ordered the soldiers to help me pull off the canvas.

"Wait!" Captain MacArdle said. I paused and looked back at him as he ordered two sailors to grab rope. "Let's keep our surprise from the enemy until we're ready."

"Good idea!" Captain O'Hara agreed emphatically. "At the very least," he said to me in an undertone, "we can keep the British from seeing the walker before we send it overboard."

I growled at him and he glared back. "Get with the carpenter," I told him. He took a breath and turned away, struggling to bring his feelings under control.

The next hour was a feverish blur of activity, frustration, exhilaration and worry.

It took longer to lift *Lightning* up with cables and winches than I'd feared and, once up, I had the devil of a time getting the fires to start. I had the cook bring up boiling tubs of fresh water and poured them into the boiler to speed things up. In the meantime, below me, Captain O'Hara, the carpenter, and two sailors hammered and sawed to build the mount for the eighteen pounder.

"It's ready," O'Hara called moments before I had enough steam, "now what?"

"We mount the gun, of course," I said, startled at his tone.

"How?" he asked.

"What?" I cried and, in frustration, jumped down from the top of the walker to the deck. I looked up at the mount and then at our location.

"We can do it," Captain MacArdle said, glancing around with a thoughtful frown. He jabbed a finger at a number of sailors and issued orders so quickly that I couldn't follow them. Hatches were opened, cables re-rigged and in short moments the huge snout of an eighteen pound cannon peered out from the shadows of the main hold.

"Captain, the frigates have split up!" A call from the mainmast came down to us.

"How far away?"

"Maybe three leagues," the lookout replied. A moment later, he added, "They're working over on the *Majestic*, looks like they've seen what we're doing."

Captain MacArdle moved to the stern and snapped open his telescope, studying the ship that lay a good mile to our stern.

"Ah, good lad, Mr. Reynolds!" Captain MacArdle shouted and raced back to me. "It seems your Ensign is following your lead, Danni."

I glanced nervously toward Captain O'Hara and Captain MacArdle's face fell as he realized his mistake. That was twice now he'd used that name.

"Look lively on that line!" Captain O'Hara bellowed at one of the seaman. I could see nothing wrong with the line. He turned back and took two quick steps toward me, grabbing my shoulders in his hands. "Well met, Danielle Walker, well met."

I gasped and then saw the smile on his lips. "How?"

"I had a chance to examine you in your sleep," Captain O'Hara replied. "I knew this morning that you were no man. What I didn't know was whether you were a spy or — something else."

"There's no time for this now," Captain MacArdle said.

"Indeed not," the blue-eyed captain replied, clicking his heels together as he came to attention and gave me a stiff bow. "So, *Lieutenant*, how do we proceed?"

I turned with him to examine the gun and the mount below *Lightning*.

"Give me your sergeant," I told him, racing to one of the walker's legs and scrambling up. At the top, I peered down, "We'll rig a tackle and use the engine to haul the gun in place."

"Very well," Captain O'Hara said. "Sergeant Donelly, up you get!"

Sergeant Donelly eyed the ascent dubiously but tackled it well enough.

"Welcome aboard *Lightning*," I said as the sergeant stood up gingerly. "Come on, we've no time to lose."

With Sergeant Donelly, I managed to tie on a new line and rig it to the engine.

We just had enough steam, so I called down, "Ready?"

"Ready, aye!"

"Shovel more coal into the fire, Sergeant, we're going to need it," I said to him as I engaged the clutch to the drive. Slowly, and steadily but gaining speed, the engine drew the line up.

"Belay, belay!" A voice called and I pulled the clutch.

A clatter from the fore leg startled me and I looked up in time to see Captain O'Hara clamber aboard and reach back down. He pulled some strange contraptions up after him. As he put them down, he looked back toward me and smiled, "I imagine we can find a use for these if things go bad."

"What are they?"

"O'Hara Repeaters," Captain O'Hara said. "Modelled on the Puckle guns of the British."

I could see that they were some sort of gun but it wasn't until a series of planks were thrown on the deck that I realized that Captain O'Hara intended to mount them on the fore corners of *Lightning*.

In short order there were four more soldiers on top, all hammering and nailing away.

"How were you planning to load?" Captain O'Hara asked gesturing to below to our cannon. I explained that and he nodded. "But how are you going to fire it, then?"

I pointed to the opening I'd had built into the two trotters. "If we center your gun under that, can you prime and load her?"

"Yes, that will work," Captain O'Hara said. "But how do we load the gun again?"

"I'll show you when we need to," I said. I gestured to the gun below us. "Are you ready?"

As if in answer, he called down, "Captain MacArdle, where are the ships?"

"The nearest is a bit more than a half mile away and bearing off our bow," Captain MacArdle called back.

"I'd say we have to be ready," O'Hara told me with a grim smile.

"More coal, Sergeant," I called to Sergeant Donelly. That worthy grumbled under his breath but bent to shovel more coal into the boiler.

"If I may, Lieutenant, I'd prefer put Sergeant Donelly on the job of aiming our gun," Captain O'Hara observed drolly. I gave him an apologetic look and he smiled in return. "Dawson, please relieve the Sergeant."

A strong, beefy private stopped what he was doing by the smaller gun and rushed back to relieve the sergeant.

Sergeant Donelly came forward, held a hasty conference with his officer and then the two of them turned to me and Captain O'Hara said, "Sergeant Donelly was wondering if you'd considered how we were to aim the gun?"

Oh, damn!

"Well, it's in line with the center of our deck," I said after a moment.

Enlightenment dawned on the captain's face. "Very good!" he gestured for the sergeant to follow him and pulled forth a knife which he buried in the center of the forward edge of the walker. "That will be our aiming stake, Sergeant."

"Is the gun loaded, sir?"

"No," Captain O'Hara said, turning to me.

"Everyone hold on," I cautioned the five others on the deck with me before I craned my head over the side and called, "Captain MacArdle, are we ready to load?"

"Ready sir," a voice I couldn't place called in response.

"Stand back," I shouted and turned back to my platform. With some trepidation I engaged the controls and waited nervously as *Lightning* began to bend at her knees. Slowly we lowered towards the deck.

"Set!" A voice shouted from below and I engaged the clutch, freeing the controls from the power of our steam engine.

At the front of the deck, Captain O'Hara peered over at the goings-on below. A moment later, jaw agape, Sergeant Donelly joined him.

Minutes later, Captain O'Hara turned back to me and shouted, "All done!"

"Very well," I said, engaging the engine once more and raising us to our normal position. "Captain O'Hara, please tell Captain MacArdle that we are ready to engage the enemy."

The words had scarcely left my lips before thunder and lightning roared toward us. The enemy had opened fire.

CHAPTER FIFTEEN

"FIRE AT WILL!" CAPTAIN O'HARA SHOUTED TO DONELLY.

"Wait!" I cried as loud as I could. There was little mistaking the tone and timbre of my voice under such circumstances. No matter, I had their attention. "Shouldn't we aim, first?"

"Excellent point, miss — er, lieutenant," Sergeant Donelly responded.

"Lower the canvas," I cried to Captain MacArdle, "let the enemy see us!"

Another boom and flash distracted me and I realized that we had not been hit by the enemy's first broadside.

Majestic had. Her sails lay in tatters and it seemed like her helm was not under control. The second broadside smashed into her with little apparent affect but I could see the ship lurch as the metal struck home.

"Need to come to the left a bit," Sergeant Donelly called to me. I engaged the clutch and started a slow pivot. "That's it! Ready — " I had just that much warning to slip the clutch and engage the safety tackle before *boom!* the whole world lurched and I feared that *Lightning* and every one of us would be pitched into the sea. With a haste and a knowledge I couldn't fathom, I engaged the clutch, set the engine against the recoil that had us doddering and fought *Lightning* back to her feet.

"A hit!" Captain MacArdle yelled from the deck. "You hit them!"

"Reload!" Captain O'Hara called from the front of my walker, even as he was scrambling back up to his feet. "Lieutenant, position us to reload!"

A moment later we heard an answering boom and all ducked, unable to note the origin.

"*Majestic! Majestic hit her!*" Captain MacArdle cackled gleefully.

"Steady men!" Captain O'Hara called. "We must reload."

"The second frigate is coming up on *Majestic*," Captain MacArdle warned even as I lowered *Lightning* back down to the deck to be reloaded.

"I see her," Captain O'Hara called from the front of my walker. He turned to his sergeant. "What do you think, Donelly?"

"Iffy, sir, a bit iffy," the sergeant said as he glanced toward the oncoming enemy. "Might hit our own ship."

"We'll concentrate on the first," Captain O'Hara declared. He stood up and waved a hand at me. "Raise the platform, lieutenant."

His condescending tone grated on me until I realized that he was putting on an act for his men — and himself, too?

"Aye, sir!" I called in response, nodding to the soldier assigned me to shovel in more coal while I coaxed *Lightning* back up on her feet and roughly in the direction of the twice-hit frigate.

"We've the height advantage, sergeant," Captain O'Hara said in an almost conversational tone, "I suggest we consider plunging fire."

"Plunging fire, sir?" Sergeant Donelly repeated in surprise. After a moment he nodded in agreement. "Never had a chance at that."

"Ready on the controls, there, lieutenant?" Captain O'Hara called back to me. I waved in acknowledgement.

"A little to the left," Sergeant Donnelly called. "And can you lower the hindquarters, sir?"

I considered this and let my hands fly over the controls. "How's that?"

"Excellent, sir," Sergeant Donelly replied. "Steady, steady, now!"

Boom! It was even harder this time to recover from the recoil of the gun, particularly as poor *Lightning's* arse end was nearly touching the deck. Even so, I managed to ride it out — more through God's good grace than any skill of my own, I assure you.

Even before I heard anything or my eyes stopped ringing with the noise of the eighteen pounder, I was bringing *Lightning* back into position to reload.

"Huzzah! Huzzah, men!" Captain O'Hara cried jumping and cavorting perilously close to the edge of the eight foot drop from *Lightning* to the deck below. "She's turning away!"

His cries were drowned out by the rest of the crew and then another boom from *Majestic* slapped into the other frigate.

"Captain, *Majestic's* signaling!" A sailor called from aloft. "She requests assistance."

"We're on the way!" Captain MacArdle said. "Stand by to come about!"

Sailors rushed aloft even as the gunners continued in their drill of swabbing and reloading the great eighteen pounder strapped below my *Lightning*.

Minutes later, Captain MacArdle's *Danielle* had reversed course and was charging back in aid of the imperiled *Majestic*. The british ship was still closing on our stricken sister ship.

"Aim for the bows!" Captain MacArdle called up to us from the deck, pointing to the british frigate. "Take out her bows!"

"Sergeant?" Captain O'Hara said, asking for that worthy's opinion.

"Tricky, sir," the sergeant said. He looked back over his shoulder to me and called, "A bit to the right, lieutenant. Keep her moving and I'll tell you when to stop."

I didn't try to explain how hard it was to make *Lightning* or any walker pirouette in place, I merely waved an acknowledgement and began gentling the controls for the movement he wanted. Slowly but with a grace that was all her own, *Lightning* was convinced to turn on one leg.

"That's it! No, back a bit, to the left!"

I followed the orders and stopped.

"Perfect!" Sergeant Donelly shouted. I could see him move back to the touch hole for the gun but that was all the warning I had with which to brace *Lightning* — and this time it was too late.

Boom! The great gun roared and *Lightning* skidded backwards, nearly going end over end. To my dying day, I'll never quite know what I did to save us but somehow we ended up with *Lightning's* four wooden legs splayed at all angles like a young colt on an icy day.

I was the only one still standing and I glared at Captain O'Hara even as I bellowed at Sergeant Donelly, "Next time give better warning, you Irish twit!"

Sergeant Donelly went bright red and turned beseechingly toward his commander but Captain O'Hara found it all he could do to contain his mirth. Unable to speak, he merely shook his head, pointing between his sergeant and myself.

"Prepare to reload!" I bellowed, ignoring both of them and moving *Lightning* back to her starting point.

"Belay that!" Captain MacArdle shouted. "Belay that and prepare to render aid."

What? I was startled by his words and then I looked beyond my walker to the outside world. The English frigate was dead in the water, her bow smashed. She was going down slowly at the front even as we watched. Far off, her consort prowled about, clearly more interested in helping her mate than in continuing the assault.

"We did it, we beat them off!" I cried in joy, running forward to hug both the sergeant and the captain in a great hug. "We did it!"

"Best not celebrate too early, lieutenant," Captain MacArdle called up from the deck. "*Majestic's* taken it hard."

I glanced toward our fellow ship and saw the truth in his words. The masts were both gone and while I could see troops laboring to cut them away, I could also see large splotches of blood and gashes which showed the destruction that had been rained upon her.

"Captain, we'd best see to starting your engine," I called from above. "We can use some coals from *Lightning* to feed your boiler."

"Can you see to it yourself, lass? We're a bit busy with the sails," Captain MacArdle called back up in a voice heavy with sorrow.

"Aye, sir," I called back down.

"Gun crew, secure from stations," Captain O'Hara called to his men. He turned back to me, "When they're done, we'll help you."

I nodded even as I turned back to my controls, preparing to vent the steam from the boiler and wondering why I hadn't considered some method of transferring steam from one boiler to another, and locked *Lightning's* legs back in place.

#

It took us the better part of an hour to get *Danielle's* boiler heated and provide power to the paddlewheels. In the meantime we'd cut in half the distance between us and *Majestic* and, with every yard gained, the sight only got worse.

Majestic had taken at least two broadsides from the frigates before they'd veered off and it showed: in the red splotches on her deck, in the bright gashes in her hull, in the lethargy of her crew.

Captain MacArdle kept me too busy to look often at the sight — not just to spare my feelings but because he needed all my expertise in coaxing the best out of the engine and the paddles. When he finally called for me to idle the engine, I went forward to the starboard side to prepare to board with the others.

"You should stay here..." the captain began, breaking off when he glanced to *Majestic.* "It's going to be bad."

"They might need me," I reminded him. "Especially with the engine."

"And we've our duty to the Prince," Captain MacArdle said half to himself. He gestured to the railings. "Have a care, then."

I scrambled over the railings and onto the splinters and wreckage that was *Majestic.* I wondered idly if the Lord had found the name too proud and therefore had decided to have the frigates make a lesson to us all.

"Danni?" Hector Stoops called as he saw me. His face broke into a grin for a moment and then went coldly grim. "You're just in time, he's been calling for you."

"Mal?" I cried, looking around and realizing that my impulsive ensign was nowhere in sight. "Where is he?"

"We brought him below," Captain Stoops said, gesturing toward the walker. "The last shot caught him square, he would have gone overboard but for the rigging."

I'd stopped hearing as soon as he'd said 'below' and started racing to the stairs and into the dark bowels of the ship.

"He's up here, lieutenant," a seaman said on catching sight of me, my red hair fanning out behind me — my hat being lost somewhere on the deck.

"Lieutenant!" the seaman called as I passed him. I turned an eye on him and he gulped. "It won't be a pretty sight, miss."

Did *everyone* know I was a girl? I wondered as I raced past.

Ruthlessly, I drove the question from my mind.

The smell guided me through the canvas door and into a scene from Hell.

"What — ?" the surgeon began but stopped as he recognized me. "He's over there, lieutenant."

I nodded and moved toward where he pointed.

I knelt down beside Mal and reached for his hand. His skin was whiter than snow, it practically shone in the dim room.

"I'm here, Mal, I'm here," I said, suddenly finding my eyes filled with tears.

"He was only holding on for you," the surgeon said from behind me. I kept my eyes on Mal's face; I didn't need the surgeon to tell me that there was nothing left of the boy below the waist.

"Miss?" Mal said in a small voice. His eyes opened.

"Here, Mal," I told him.

"Red hair," he murmured to himself. "Thought you were the devil for a moment."

"No," I said, finding my temper roused at the notion.

"The English?"

"They're gone, we drove them off," I told him.

"We did? I was afraid we'd missed," Mal said. "I had the devil's own time — " and the little imp's lips twisted upwards at the phrase "— convincing the others to mount the cannon."

"But you did," I assured him. "And the English never knew what hit them."

"They fired at us," Mal said. He coughed and I saw blood come up. Idly he raised a hand to wipe away his mouth and pulled it back in surprise as he saw the blood on it. He dropped his hand as though it were inconsequential, then looked back at me. "We fired back, the gunner was good but he was killed and I had to aim the last shot myself."

"You did great, Mal, just great!" I told him even as my heart shrank in my body. He was only a boy, only a little boy.

"And then I was flying, miss!" Mal said. "I was all like an angel and flying through the air! I never felt the like — "

His head fell back and his eyes dimmed and Mal Reynolds spoke no more.

"He was just waiting for you," the surgeon said, moving around me and pulling the canvas that had been draped over his lower half fully over the corpse.

"Wait!" I cried, throwing up an arm. I leaned forward, ignoring the surgeon's surprised remark, ignoring the dirt, the blood, the smell — I leaned forward and brushed my lips on Malcolm Reynolds cheek.

"You did well," I whispered into his now-deaf ear. "You did just fine."

After that, I moved aside and let the surgeon complete his work. I stayed in the cabin while he worked and looked in the gloomy light at the others. Fortunately, they were very few.

"Are there any others from the walker?"

"No," the surgeon said. "Most are falls from the top." From his tone, I could tell that he expected to be covering them soon. "Your young ensign was the worst, though."

I nodded shakily and turned to leave. I turned back again and met the surgeon's eyes. "Is there anything I can do to help?"

The surgeon looked surprised at the question. "No, I've done all I can, I don't need any help."

I took in a breath and the smells undid me. Jerkily, I pulled myself out of the cabin and back onto the deck, to the far railing where I heaved my guts until all I could do was wrack my stomach for bitter saliva.

I felt a hand on my shoulder and then another stroking the small of my back.

"It's never easy," Captain O'Hara's voice came from behind me.

"What?" I mumbled, wishing I felt better and wishing that his hand would never stop rubbing the small of my back for it was easing my stomach and all the muscles in my body that were suddenly all too weary to describe.

"It's never easy to lose a man," he repeated.

I turned then, away from the railing to look up at him. There wasn't that much difference in our height: I was a tall girl and he was a half-starved Irish lad.

"You've lost some?" I said, my words almost taunting.

"Many," he told me. I could see the truth in his eyes but he added, "I've been at war since I was ten."

Oh! Oh, I hadn't realized. That explained so much of what I couldn't understand about him. I wondered who had been his first: had it been a friend, a strange, or parents — even, perhaps, his own father.

"Your ensign?" he asked now.

"Dead," I told him. "He was cut in half."

"My men told me," he replied. "They say he was very brave and that he fired well."

I moved around him, toward the walker. "I have to see to the walker."

"I've got my men working on it," he said, making no move to restrain me. "Tell them what you want."

I waved a hand behind me in acknowledgement but I was moving away from him, moving away from the railing, moving away from the sick bay. I clambered up the foreleg of *Thunder* and pulled myself on to the deck. I moved to the control station and checked the controls, turned once to look over my shoulder at the pressure gage and then bellowed, "Ware!" before I deftly brought her back up into her steady position. Mal — or someone — had lowered her again for reloading.

"Danni!" Captain MacArdle's voice carried up from the deck. I lashed the controls and moved to the side. "We need coal for the boilers and I need you to check the engine."

"And the frigates?" I asked. I wanted them to come back. I wanted to beat them, to smash them the way they'd smashed Mal. I knew we could do it and I wanted it. I wanted them to *hurt*. I wanted them to scream in agony, to writhe with pain.

To feel the way they'd made Mal feel.

"They're gone, lass," Captain MacArdle replied in a steady tone. "They've got their tails between their legs and they're heading back to London to warn their king."

Fire burned in my eyes and I jumped down from *Thunder* to the deck of *Majestic*.

"They've not got our engines."

"And the wind's against them," Captain MacArdle agreed with a vicious grin.

#

It took us hours to get *Majestic* restored enough that she could steam with us. We steamed through the night.

Near dawn, Captain MacArdle ordered me below. I must have looked mulish for he repeated himself, adding, "I'm the captain of this ship, lass."

I thought about arguing but couldn't find the energy.

He smiled at me and patted me on the shoulder. "Good! You're going to need your strength soon enough."

I stumbled down into the cabin. Captain O'Hara was there already. He woke when I entered and made to leave the bed.

"I should get on deck," he said, gesturing toward the light that was starting to come through the prisms. I pushed him back on the bed, threw off my jacket, sat on the bunk and pulled off my boots. Then I turned and lay full length beside him.

"Just hold me," I said to him. "No words."

Arms wrapped around me and before I could muster a smile at his trepidation my eyelids drooped closed and I remembered no more.

#

I awoke to the smell of something savory and warm.

"The cook's made rolls," Captain O'Hara said as he pushed the cabin door behind him. "It's past noon and the lookout's sighted land."

I didn't even try to imagine how the captain had clambered over my slumbering body. Instead, I rolled myself out of the bunk and reached for a roll.

"I've tea, too," he said. I could have kissed him. It must have shown in my expression for he gave me a very pleased look.

"I've something to show you," he said after I'd finished my roll. "Your Ensign — "

"Mal," I corrected him.

"Pardon?"

"His name was Mal," I repeated. "Malcolm Reynolds, he was MacAllister's apprentice."

I felt a pang of worry as my mind strayed to Samuel Cattan. Where was he now? Was he, too, dead? Another cold body on some distant battlefield?

"It is not wise to dwell on their names," Captain O'Hara told me in a voice that was both cold and sad. I shot him a look. "The dead we can't help; it's important to look after the living."

He moved to the bunk and reached under it, pulling out some papers.

I raised an eyebrow questioningly.

"Besides artillery, I am an inventor," he said, as he held the papers in his arms. "I'm sure you'll recall that I mentioned devising a new Puckle gun for His Most Catholic Majesty, Louis XV."

I nodded.

"These are the plans," he said. He smiled at me. It was the smile of one inventor to another, and also the smile of a man to woman. In that moment he reminded me heartbreakingly of my Samuel.

"I had hoped to share them with someone who would appreciate them," he continued. "Perhaps even someone who could carry on my work, should anything happen to me."

Oh! So I wasn't the only one hurting from Mal's death. Of Captain O'Hara's men, only one had been wounded and he was well enough to continue in his duties — the wooden splinter had been dangerous but *Majestic*'s surgeon was well-acquainted with such injuries.

"I *had* hoped to perhaps share them with the remarkable Miss Danielle Walker — " his eyes twinkled mischievously "— whom I've learned was the true inventor of those remarkable walking machines but I have resigned myself to notion that I shall only be able to show them to her *lieutenant*, as it were." He smiled at me as he unrolled the first drawing and spread it on the table. "Can I trust you, lieutenant, to share them with her, should you happen to meet her before me?"

I smiled back and picked up the first drawing. "You may." I examined the drawing, traced the lines and compared them against what I'd seen of the real guns, then added, "And, if you wish, I will — on her behalf, naturally! — undertake to educate you on the workings of her walkers."

"I'm sure you will be a most enlightened teacher," he replied.

"I am pleased to admit that Miss Walker deigned to take me into her confidence."

"Lucky, very lucky," he said. He leaned forward and pointed to the lines of the drawing. "Here, in case you are not familiar with weapons, is what I call the receiver."

And so began my education in the newest weapons of war. Captain O'Hara was an excellent instructor. He was thrilled to have me as a pupil and, later, when we were done, I insisted on taking him through everything about the walkers.

This ended, naturally, with us at the controls of my dormant *Lightning*, explaining the workings of the engine, the boiler, the control levers and the notion of trotting.

"Trotting?" he repeated. "I thought they were called walkers."

I explained that those were the name given to the first ones built but that these last two were purpose built to trot.

"With the guns?"

I shrugged. "We haven't tried but I rather doubt it."

His gaze grew distant as he started imagining and I was amazed to see a kindred spirit at work. I'd never met anyone who could see what wasn't and imagine how to make it be in the way that I could — Jean-Michel was such a person and I reveled in it.

Oh, my brother Jamie could look at my drawings and spot errors or make suggestions and so, to a lesser extent, could Samuel Cattan. But neither had the look that

I saw on Captain O'Hara's face — the look of a dreamer.

"Sergeant!" he called when he came out of his reverie. "Get the carpenter and some rope, we've work to do." He turned to me and smiled at my surprised expression. "I think we can come up with an easy method of disengaging our cannon if we've need."

I raised an eyebrow challengingly and he smiled at me, raising a finger to demand that I wait.

Thirty minutes later, I had my answer.

"That will do," I agreed. "Although if we need the cannon again — "

"We will cross that stream when we reach it," he told me.

We were under *Lightning*, looking up at the changes he'd ordered made to the gun cradle. They'd arranged leather bindings in front of the gun which could easily be cut if needed. After that, all that would be required was a 'shrug' from *Lightning* and the cannon would lurch out of its mount and fall to the ground.

"And then, lieutenant, your trotters will be able to live up to their name!"

"We'll still have to do it for *Thunder*," I reminded him.

"I know," he replied. "And you'll need someone to command her."

I nodded.

He sketched a quick bow, saying, "Lieutenant Clarke, if I may be of service, I'd be honored!"

Captain MacArdle agreed almost before Captain O'Hara could finish his sentence.

"We can send a boat over now," he said. He glanced up at the sky above. "And it'd best be soon, if you're going to do it."

I was reluctant to see him go.

"I'm leaving Sergeant Donelly and Private Dawson under your command, lieutenant," he said formerly as the *Danielle's* only undamaged boat was lowered over the side.

"I'll take good care of them, sir," I promised.

"We'll meet up when we get ashore," he told me, stiffening to attention and snapping off a salute. "Until then, lieutenant."

I came to attention and returned his salute, for whose benefit — his, his men, or my own foolish pride, I cannot honesty say. "Until then, sir."

It was a wonder my voice didn't break when I spoke.

"We'll treat the lieutenant like she was our own daughter, sir," Sergeant Donelly promised, backed up by a reassuring grunt from Private Dawson.

"You'll treat me like a *lieutenant*, Sergeant, or you'll regret it!" I barked, my eyes flaring at him. The sergeant and private both visibly wilted.

Captain O'Hara worked hard to keep from smiling, adding under his breath, "I see you'll have no problems, lieutenant."

And then he was gone.

I dismissed my small crew and moved to the railings, following the little skiff with my eyes until it discharged its short Irish passenger onto *Majestic*. He clambered up, turned and snapped a salute in our direction.

Not to be outdone, I returned it just as jauntily.

CHAPTER SIXTEEN

"LIEUTENANT," A VOICE STARTLED ME INTO WAKEFULNESS THE NEXT MORNING. "CAPTAIN'S compliments and we're closing with the shore."

It was time. I noticed that my heart was beating loudly in my chest.

"I'll be up presently," I called back to the messenger. The door closed even as I stirred in the bunk. Once again, I'd slept in my clothes, discarding only my hat, jacket, and boots before sleep overcame me.

It was nothing to find them and put them on once more. My hat was worse for the wear, having been retrieved from the deck of *Majestic* when I'd lost it in my race to Mal in the sickbay. My jacket was as good as it was going to get, having been cleaned as best as possible of all vomit and blood from the past several days aboard ship. My boots were still comfortable and, if not as shiny as I might have wished were I to see the Prince, they were still quite serviceable.

As I reached the deck, I found Sergeant Donelly and Private Dawson arrayed as if on parade.

"Sergeant!" I called. "My compliments to the captain and we'll need coal thirty minutes prior to moving."

"Sir!" Sergeant Donelly said, snapping to attention and turning to Private Dawson. "Private! Inform the captain that the lieutenant will need coal for the trotter thirty minutes prior to moving."

"Yes, Sergeant!" Private Dawson shouted back, snapping to attention and moving off at the march toward Captain MacArdle who was waiting, his lips twitching, for the Private to repeat what had been twice-bellowed for all to hear already.

I wondered if the two Irishmen were 'taking the Mickey' out of me but decided to ignore it, moving instead to clamber aboard *Lightning*. At the top, I looked down to Sergeant Donelly.

"Sergeant, I recommend we load the guns as soon as we've got steam, how does that sound?"

Sergeant Donelly snapped again to attention. "Sir!"

Given that he didn't argue, I took that for agreement.

From my height, I had no problem spying the activity on *Majestic* as it steamed beside us. I waved over toward *Thunder* and was pleased beyond all reason when I saw an answering wave. The motion brought a spark to my heart followed an instant later by an impish grin.

"Sergeant!" I bellowed down. "I would be most unhappy if we were not to find ourselves ready before *Thunder*."

"Sir!" Sergeant Donelly bellowed in automatic response and then, an instant later, added, "Yes sir!"

For the next twenty minutes we were nothing but scuttling backs and arms, moving and twisting to fire up the boiler, get steam, load the guns.

"Ready, sir!" Sergeant Donelly called from the deck.

"Not until you're aboard, Sergeant!" I called back. The grizzled sergeant dutifully climbed aboard. I nodded in satisfaction. "Now, men, off hats!"

The two soldiers, with a look of surprise, doffed their hats. I pulled mine off my hat.

"And a cheer for *Thunder*!" I cried. Together the three of us bellowed and waved our hats, decorously declaring our victory in an unannounced race.

From *Thunder*, I saw Captain O'Hara remove his hat and bow low to us. Sergeant Donelly and Private Dawson both let out loud guffaws of laughter as they saw their captain admit his defeat. I felt that there would be no difficulty in working with these two.

"Left rudder!" Captain MacArdle called just as we finished our victory salute. "Stand by in the Walker!"

"Aye, sir!" I called back.

"Signal the others to follow us in," Captain MacArdle ordered his signalman.

"Aye, cap'n."

I peered at the approaching shore. We were coming up to a dock that appeared deserted.

"Private Dawson, man the Puckle gun!" I ordered, worried that all might not be as deserted as it appeared.

"Sergeant, as soon as we're able, I'm going to walk us off the ship," I warned Sergeant Donelly. The sergeant's eyes widened but he merely nodded and turned back to the approaching shore.

"Stand by!" Captain MacArdle called.

"Standing by!" I shouted back.

"All back on the engine!" Captain MacArdle shouted to his engineer.

"Aye sir, all back!"

The paddles reversed and we slowed. In a moment we were stopped.

I swallowed hard and engaged the clutch. *Lightning* lurched forward.

I got one leg on the dock and the motion pushed the ship away. I had a moment's panic before I managed to compensate with the hind legs and then put the next foreleg on land, then the first hind leg and then — we were on land.

"Forward engine, port rudder!" Captain MacArdle bellowed.

"Keep a sharp lookout forward, both of you on the Puckle guns," I said to my two artillerymen.

"Sir!" Sergeant Donelly barked in response.

I moved us forward, away from the sea and into the town proper but not too far.

With the bulk of the huge gun slung under her, *Lightning* moved ponderously and it took me a moment to get a proper sense of her. I imagine she looked rather like a sailor new to land — sloppy on his feet and floundering without the familiar roll of the sea — but we recovered quickly; even though my stomach was clenched tight with a combination of unease and disorder.

"Stand by!" I hear Captain Stoops yell and realized he was calling out to Captain O'Hara and those on *Thunder*.

"We'll scout to the left," I told my men as I set *Lightning* in motion once more. I forced myself to look anywhere but behind me as I heard the loud *clop!* Of the first wooden leg onto the dock. I couldn't stop myself from counting as the second, third, and — finally! — fourth leg clattered onto shore. *Thunder* was behind me.

"Full steam ahead!" Captain Stoops shouted in the distance as he moved from the dock to make way for the troops with Colonel Drummond on Captain Henry's *Anabelle*.

I had just finished scouting the southern part of the village when a figure emerged from the shadows of a nearby stable.

He raised a clenched fist up toward us and said, "It's a long way from Edinburgh, is it not?"

"Mr. Gillie?" I cried in surprise. I quickly brought *Lightning* to a halt and leaned over with a hand to lift him on board.

With my hat on and my hand tucked up under it and no doubt my fierce expression, he didn't recognize me.

"You have me at advantage, sir," Mr. Gillie said, doffing his hat. "You know my name but I have not the pleasure of yours."

I bit off my first quick response and said, instead, "We have friends in common, sir. I believe you know Daniel Walker and his children?"

He nodded reluctantly.

"I am Samuel Clarke, formerly apprentice at the Walker forge and now lieutenant by the commission of Prince Charles," I told him.

Behind me, *Thunder* clattered to a halt and Captain O'Hara called out, "Danni, we've searched the town and — "

"Danni?" Mr. Gillie repeated, his eyes going wide with surprise. His expression changed into a huge grin as he finally recognized me and then his face grew stern again. "What are you doing here?"

"Who is this man, Danni?" Captain O'Hara called, jumping the gap between his walker and mine.

"Captain O'Hara, I'd like to introduce you to Mr. Gillie, the puppeteer — " I said, waving a hand, before adding, "— and spy."

Mr. Gillie chuckled and ducked his head in acknowledgment. "Well met, Danielle, well met!"

"Spy?" Captain O'Hara repeated, his brows furrowing.

I reached a hand behind me to grab his. "For us, sir, he is for us."

"Indeed, Captain, the young 'lieutenant' has the right of it," Mr. Gillie said.

"He helped in the design of these walkers," I added.

"With *these?*" our artillery captain demanded.

The clatter of a small group of soldiers interrupted us and we turned to see a young messenger pause, catch his breath and salute Captain O'Hara. "Sir, the Colonel requires you to find twelve mounts immediately!"

"Mounts?" Captain O'Hara repeated. I turned to see him redden, ready to blast the young man for the message.

"Aye, and twelve carts with horses, if it please you, sir," the messenger added between gasps for breath.

"We've brought Lord Drummond and three hundred men," I explained to Mr. Gillie.

"You did? I thought they were in Montrose."

"They were," I agreed, gesturing to the harbor. "Captain MacArdle and the others fetched them."

"Ah!" Mr. Gillie said in understanding. "Three hundred may be too few." He glanced at our two walkers. "But two more walkers will be a great boon."

"They're not walkers, Mr. Gillie," Captain O'Hara corrected with a clipped voice and forced grin.

"No?"

"Miss Walker called them trotters."

Mr. Gillie looked at me with raised eyebrows. I smiled and nodded.

"I thought you might need mounts," Mr. Gillie said now. "The countryside is mostly bare, everyone having gone to London — "

"Why?" Captain O'Hara demanded.

"Because of the Prince, sir," Mr. Gillie replied. "They say the Prince will lay siege."

#

"Lay siege?" Colonel Drummond repeated when we met up with him thirty minutes later and filled him in on Mr. Gillie's news. He snorted. "He'd be a damned fool to try!"

"Without our guns, I'd say yes, sir," Captain O'Hara agreed. "But with them..."

"Where are your horses, Captain?" Colonel Drummond demanded. "Your guns may as well stay in the ships without horses to pull them."

"Begging your pardon, sir, but we've two of the best mounted on the trotters," I piped up.

Colonel Drummond beetled his eyebrows out me and snorted once more. "You'd probably think you could lay waste to London with a mere two guns, wouldn't you, 'lieutenant'?"

From his tone I could tell that my secret had leaked to him as well.

"Milord, there *might* be a way," Mr. Gillie spoke up, glancing nervously at the noble man.

"And a pupeteer would know it?"

"Milord, a direct assault against the main gates would be difficult— "

"Suicidal!"

"— but there is another way," Mr. Gillie concluded in spite of the Lord's objection.

Colonel Drummond frowned and seemed ready to rain more derision on Mr. Gillie but I stepped forward with a hand outstretched beseechingly. "Please, milord, Mr. Gillie was sent here by the Prince, shouldn't we listen to him?"

Lord Drummond glowered at me and he was quite good at it but I recalled poor Mal dying in the sickbay and glared back, giving as good as I got. Mal was going to be avenged and to do that, I needed Lord Drummond. Or at least his men. Before I could follow that thought further, Lord Drummond relented.

"Very well, lieutenant firebrand," he said, "let us hear what the Prince's acquaintance has to tell us." He wagged a finger at me, adding, "And you'd best hope it is good, for lieutenants are not above a good bare-hided whipping, particularly if they're guilty of insolence."

As Mr. Gillie began outlining his plan, I could see Lord Drummond's expression slowly change and his jaw unclench. When Mr. Gillie was done, Lord Drummond looked to me. "If your friend is right 'lieutenant', then I expect to brevet you to captain before the day is out."

I nodded in thanks — and shock — even as I felt Captain O'Hara stiffen beside me and I recalled how he had been breveted by Colonel Grant, much to Lord Drummond's disgust. It seemed that Jean-Michel O'Hara found the thought of us being equal in rank somewhat unappealing.

"In the meantime," Colonel Drummond said, raising his voice so that it could carry, "we have work to do and a kingdom to recover."

#

It took us a hard hour to get on the march and then only because Lord Drummond was as harsh with his own men as he was with his officers.

His Royal Scots were crack troops and thought nothing of moving out at the trot, not that they put *Lightning* or *Thunder* to any effort — being merely men and not horses.

We marched from noon to dusk, never stopping. Men who fainted along the way were lifted onto our walkers or into the few carts we'd managed to scrounge.

Colonel Drummond rode with me a while but I noticed that the motion of the walker was difficult for him and, as he turned a rather startling green, he decided that he'd best make room for his men instead. I nodded solemnly at this declaration deciding that, sick or not, his temper would not fail him. Besides, I recall being sick aboard *Danielle* and felt no reason to gloat.

Mr. Gillie rode with me on a fine horse which I'd never seen about him when he was up in Edinburgh. As I would have been the mostly like choice to shoe any of his steeds up there, I rather doubted it had started the journey with him.

When I mentioned it, he snorted and smiled at me. "In fact, it's my third horse so far," he admitted. I gave him a questioning look but he did not expand on his answer.

"Have you seen my father?" I asked a while later.

"Once," he replied, sounding weary.

"And?"

"He was in good form when I saw him."

I did not like the way he chose his words.

"And Jamie?"

"I'm surprised you're not asking about Samuel Cattan, lass."

"I was getting to him," I said crossly. "And Mapes and Meara, too."

"You heard about Jock Adams?"

I nodded and glanced down at my *Lightning*. "There's many things that can go wrong with the boilers and the engines; more if they're not properly tended."

"I can imagine," Mr. Gillie agreed.

I realized that he had not yet answered my questions but at that moment he begged to be put with Lord Drummond, saying that he'd remembered some important information.

Mr. Gillie was a kindly soul but I was not fooled. I found a moment to watch him with the Colonel and saw how the two looked in my direction, how Colonel Drummond was silent in thought and then finally gave Mr. Gillie some pronounced wisdom. Mr. Gillie looked relieved at the decision.

The news was bad. Was it father? Jamie? Samuel? All three?

A thud from a misplaced foreleg distracted me and I returned my attention to the way before us.

"Sergeant, the boiler needs more coal, see to it, please!" I shouted, partly to disguise my error but mostly because I realized that the pressure was getting lower.

Jock Adams had died because he hadn't paid enough attention to his walker; I had no right to do the same simply because I feared for my family. Perhaps Lord Drummond had thought the same and instructed Mr. Gillie to wait with whatever bad news he had — I could see the sense in that now.

Tonight we would be outside London. By morning — evening next at the latest — we would either have victory or ignoble death.

#

"Very well, we are here," Lord Drummond pronounced peevishly as dusk outlined the walls of the City of London. "Now, how, pray tell, will get in?"

He was looking at Captain O'Hara which wasn't fair: it was Mr. Gillie's plan. On the other hand, Mr. Gillie wasn't present at the moment having gone ahead — "scouting" as he said. He impressed upon the Colonel for a ready infusion of cash, in the form of several sovereigns, so I was reasonably certain he was lavishing bribes for information — or possibly he was thirsty and wanted a decent pint. Either way, he was gone at the moment.

We had arrived with the setting sun and had little time to set up camp before we were engulfed in the evening gloom. Gloom was the right word for it, too: the English lit their town so brightly I could almost read from the light that shone. I wondered what this meant for the Prince and his forces on the other side of the town. Were they not here? Had they already been defeated? Were we too early or too late?

"I'm sure Mr. Gillie will have a plan, milord," I said as the silence grew oppressive.

"Well that's *so* much comfort, lieutenant," Colonel Drummond retorted scathingly. "As it happens, however, I am in command of this detachment, so my opinion weighs rather more heavily than a mere 'lieutenant', wouldn't you say?"

"Sir," Captain O'Hara objected forcefully. The Colonel turned to stare at him in surprise. Jean-Michel licked his lips before continuing, "It is true that we are all risking much in this endeavor and that our lives may well be forfeit if we fail."

Colonel Drummond gave him a sour look but, after a moment, nodded. "Quite right." He glanced over to me. "My apologies, lieutenant, my nerves are rather frayed at the moment."

"Perhaps, sir, we should climb up on *Lightning* and see what a long glass brings," I suggested, gesturing up at the eight foot tall platform.

"I suppose we should at that," Colonel Drummond found himself agreeing.

I was first up, alerting my artillerymen and the resting infantry before Captain O'Hara scrambled up and then lent down to help the Colonel climb aboard.

It was dark but the Colonel brought out his glass and trained it on the city. I waited silently, scanning with my bare eyes.

Wait!

"There's something going on!" Colonel Drummond called excitedly. "I can see flashes at the far side of the city." He turned to Captain O'Hara and passed him the glass. "You've younger eyes, Captain, tell me what you see."

Jean-Michel took the glass and trained it toward where the Colonel pointed. "I see nothing — no, wait! — yes, there is a brightness — gunfire?"

"Where is that dratted man?" Colonel Drummond muttered, looking around as if expecting Mr. Gillie to materialize on demand. "There's a battle going on and we're sitting here doing nothing."

"The men are tired, sir," I reminded him.

He barked a laugh. "Lieutenant, the men are *always* tired. Wars are never won by well-rested men."

"We could try to rush the gate," Captain O'Hara suggested, lowering his glass.

"I don't see how we could prevail," Colonel Drummond replied. "Unless the gates are still open and I find that difficult to consider given the advanced hour and the disturbance on the other end of the city."

"Unless..." I began, turning back to the gates. "My lord! The gates are opening!"

"What?" Lord Drummond cried, snatching his glass from Captain O'Hara. "So they are! I wonder if we've Mr. Gillie to thank for that?"

A moment later he added, "Ah, yes, apparently so! There are people leaving by the gates, with carts and such-like."

He lowered his glass and stuck it back in his greatcoat with relish. "Rats abandoning the ship!"

He turned to us, "We've got to rush that gate!"

"Sergeant, place the fires!" I shouted down over the side of my platform.

"Yes, sir!" Sergeant Donelly called. "You heard the lieutenant, get a move on there!"

"What?" The colonel demanded of me.

"I can get us moving in five minutes, sir," I told him.

"*We* can have the walkers at those gates in ten," Captain O'Hara added, correcting me.

"Private Dawson!" I shouted over my shoulder.

"Sir?"

"Mount the Puckle guns!"

"Sir!"

I turned to Jean-Michel. "*Lightning* has the guns and the eighteen pounder, she should lead."

"With your permission, milord?" Captain O'Hara said, glancing to our mutual superior.

Colonel Drummond pursed his lips, glancing at me thoughtfully. "Don't think for one moment, 'lieutenant', that I don't full well know *exactly* who you are."

"Then, milord, you must know that I am perfectly trained for this action," I replied. My father, my brother, Samuel, Meara, Mapes — all were at the far end of this city, fighting for their lives. Fighting because one foolish red-headed girl thought it would be fun to build a walking machine.

"Very well, lieutenant Boadicea, you may lead," Colonel Drummond said, moving to the side and clambering back down to the ground, his voice rising into a bellow as he called, "Sergeant Major MacGregor! Rouse the troops, prepare for battle!"

"Sir!" A voice boomed back in the darkness.

Steel buckets came up the side and hot coals from the campfires were placed under *Lightning's* boiler. The water in the boiler was still warm — I'd taken care to ensure that, ordering blankets be placed around the bare metal, much to the sniggering of the men. Now my precaution would pay off.

"All troops, man your positions!" I bellowed as I heard the first chug of steam hit the engine. In addition to my two doughty artillerymen, I'd acquired a small squad of the Colonel's Royal Scots — mostly the ones who were suited the walker's pace and smart enough to prefer riding to walking.

"MacDonald, George, you're on the guns!" I called, moving forward to them. Two privates moved to the Puckle guns and gazed at them in perplexity.

"Sergeant Donelly, show them what to do," I called, turning back to my pilot-stand and then back to the boiler and the toiling Private Dawson who'd insisted upon stoking the boiler himself.

"Captain O'Hara, we're ready to move out, sir," I called as I engaged the clutch and began slowly walking *Lightning* forward.

"Remember, lieutenant, you're to take the gates and hold them for my troops!" Colonel Drummond called as I moved off.

"Yes, milord!" I called back. In a lower voice, I told the men on *Lightning*, "Hold on, lads, we're going to see how fast we can go!"

With that, I opened up the throttles full, found the road and bore down upon it.

On the regular road, I had no worries about unseen potholes even though it was dark. We had torches rigged around the top of *Lightning* — though that was dangerous for two reasons: it announced our presence; and it was a fire hazard. There was no choice in the matter although in future I resolved to get sea lamps which were enclosed and offered greater protection.

I turned to glance behind me and saw *Thunder's* lights further in the distance.

Ahead of me, at least a league away, maybe even two, were the open gates of the city of London.

How long they would remain open, I could not say. I called over my shoulder, "More coal!"

With that, I opened the throttle full and let *Lightning* pick up her pace. She was slow to get moving but game enough even with the infantry and the huge eighteen pounder slung on her underside. I could feel how heavily her feet hit the ground with each stride and I worried about the damage they were taking under such a load, determining to examine them carefully when there was time, and increased the pace once again.

"Mind the torches!" Sergeant Donelly called and I looked up to see that the flames on the torches were curled back, streaming against the wind, their tendrils threatening to reach outward.

We were too far. It was taking too long. Another hour, at the least. I couldn't imagine Mr. Gillie keeping the gates open for that length, no matter what.

"Prepare for the trot!" I cried over the wind. "Brace yourselves!"

I slipped the gears, found the right moment and changed the step. For a moment,

I felt *Lightning* shudder as if in complaint or ready to miss her pace but then the foreleg struck ground and then the next and the next and — we were trotting.

"Lieutenant!" one of the privates called from in front. "There are horsemen approaching!"

"What colors?" I cried. "What standard do they fly?"

"None, sir," the private called back.

I swallowed hard. I would hate to fire on our own people — they were so few — but if these were King George's men, then we had to deal with them as quickly as we could.

A shot rang out in the night. It came from in front of us.

"Hold your fire!" I cried. "Sergeant Donelly!"

"Sir?"

"Man the gun!"

"Yes, sir!" Sergeant Donelly called back. I could almost feel his worry and confusion — the eighteen was best assaulting thick walls or wooden ships, it was not as good when engaged mere horsemen.

"MacGregor, George!" I called out.

"Sir?" they called back in chorus.

"Fire only when you have a good shot," I ordered. "Musketeers, you may fire when you have a good target."

"Sir!" Came a small chorus of acknowledging cries.

We would be upon them shortly. Should I reduce speed or should I charge through?

"We're going to charge through them!" I called. I hoped that they would scatter.

The distant figures became more and more distinct. I could hear their shouting and saw a group break from the road. I saw another group at the rear — was that a gun? — and then we were upon them.

There was no more time for orders. The cartridges for the Puckle guns were stacked close to hand, the infantry had their powder and balls.

Ahead of us loomed cavalry: arranged in two columns, barreling down the road.

A moment later, the first musket fired from my *Lightning*. I saw a trooper in the lead stagger and fall out of his saddle and then I was too close to see more.

One Puckle gun opened fire and the clatter of five bullets flying through the air in less than a minute ripped through the night. The cavalry stalled, appalled at the destruction that rained down upon them. Even as they were recovering, the second gun fired.

We had fifty magazines with five rounds each. The cavalry came on and the Puckle guns cut them down.

Lightning pushed aside the dead, the injured, and the wounded as she charged on down the road.

Suddenly the cavalry turned, no longer interested in attacking us — fleeing for their lives. A cheer roared up from *Lightning* as we realized what we'd done — we'd sent the King's cavalry packing!

I looked ahead — the Gates! They were so close!

A sound startled me and I was suddenly on my back. I scrambled up again and grabbed the controls, ensuring that *Lightning* did not alter in her course or speed.

"Are you alright, lieutenant?" Private Dawson called from his position at the boiler.

"Just shaken," I told him.

"Lucky to be alive," Dawson muttered and I gave him a startled look. He saw me, grinned and turned back to his work.

The cavalry hadn't panicked, I realized — they'd drawn off and were regrouping around some wagons.

Boom! The sound of a cannon burst the night air. *Crash!* The ball hit the ground not far from us.

"Infantry, aim at the cannon!" I shouted. I doubted we were close enough to hit them but I wanted them distracted. The gates were very close now but I had a dilemma — should I take them and leave the cavalry in our rear?

The cavalry and the cannon would tear up Colonel Drummond's short battalion with ease. It would do no good to capture the gates unless there was someone to use them.

I decided, veering *Lightning* toward the cannon that was firing at us.

"Sergeant Donelly!" I called. "Your target is the cannon!"

"Sir!" Sergeant Donelly called back in acknowledgement.

"MacGregor, George! As soon as you're in range, engage the cannon. Before that, destroy the cavalry!"

"Sir!" A cry from Private Dawson startled me. "They're coming — " A shout rang out and I heard him fall and the shovel clatter to the ground below.

"Musketeers, to the rear!" I cried, realizing that some of the cavalry had swung around behind us — and had discovered our weakness. If they knew enough to shoot at the boiler — if they punctured it — we'd all die, burnt in a ball of superheated steam.

A pair of musketeers moved to the rear and took station. They added the sounds of their muskets intermittently but I worried that it was not enough to dissuade the cavalrymen who seemed quite desperate to destroy us.

I didn't understand — before we came they were fleeing London, running away. Why were they now fighting so valiantly? What were they guarding?

Even as I thought that, I knew the answer.

"Sergeant Donelly!"

"Sir?"

"New target!"

"Sir?" He repeated, surprised. I twitched the controls on *Lightning* and we veered back onto the road.

"Your target is the largest wagon on the road, the one surrounded by the most guards," I called out to him.

"Sir!" Sergeant Donelly replied. I could tell from his tone that he was confused by the change in plan and resolved to talk with me about it later, when there was time.

A cry from behind me and the sound a soldier falling onto the ground below alerted me that one of my rear guard had fallen. There was nothing for it now, we had a bigger target.

"Muskets! Target the troops!" I cried. I heard a grunt of acknowledgement and a moment later, the bulk of the fire was directed toward the large wagon we were fast approaching.

"MacGregor!" I cried to the gunner on my left. "Keep firing at that cannon. George, fire ahead as you can!"

"Sir!" the two privates called back.

A strange noise startled me and then it came again. It took me a moment to realize that it was the sound of bullets passing by my ears.

I heard another cry from behind me and the second musketeer pitched off the deck of *Lightning*. We were now unprotected to the rear. There were only four musketeers left. I decided to leave them in front and trust to our speed — and perhaps the approach of *Thunder*.

"They won't fire, sir!" Sergeant Donelly called back toward me.

"What?"

"If you're hoping for help from Captain O'Hara, they won't fire, sir," he told me.

"Why?"

"They might hit us," the sergeant said simply.

Oh! I hadn't thought of that. We were in trouble. I thought furiously. "How soon until you fire?"

"Can you stop us a moment, sir?" he replied.

"Not bloody likely," I called back, thinking of the cavalry to my rear and the pure impossibility of hauling *Lightning* back from a trot.

The Puckle gun on my left roared and roared again shortly thereafter, peppering the gunners on the ridge above us and sending them fleeing.

A moment later, the other Puckle gun fired to front.

"Stand by!" Sergeant Donelly cried. "We're on target!" And then he pitched forward.

For a moment I stared at him stupidly until I realized that there was a hole in the back of his head. My stomach clenched but I ignored it, rushing around my controls and grabbing the burning match from his hand. I leaned down and touched it to the gunpowder that he'd drizzled down into the touch-hole of the eighteen pounder. And then —

BOOM! Lightning shook and faltered. I heard cables snapping and the engine labored — seemed to halt for a moment — and then we lurched forward again into the smoke and dust that the cannon had bellowed in front of us.

I stumbled back to the controls, steadied *Lightning*, put her back on her pace and looked forward as we cleared the last of the smoke left by our cannon — the wagon was still there.

I felt my heart flutter. We'd missed. Sergeant Donelly, the others — they'd all died for nothing. In fact, even as I watched, the wagon was circling, preparing to flee before us. If it got back through the gates, and the gates were closed —

"I need a man to shovel more coal!" I cried. A private looked up, scuttled back and looked around for the shovel. The shovel. It had gone over with Private Dawson. "Use your hands!"

Numbly, the private obeyed, careful not to burn himself as he threw coals onto the flames below the boiler. How much steam had we left? How long had we been trotting? I didn't know and couldn't care. We had to get that wagon, I was certain.

I rushed passed the dead Sergeant Donelly, leaned down the hole to the cannon below and looked at it. Captain O'Hara had rigged it so that we could drop the gun. It sat in its mount but it was held in at the front only by a leather strap. I pulled out Sergeant Donelly's long bayonet and began sawing away before I realized that I had other things to do.

"George!" I called, rising from the hole. The private rushed back. "I need you to cut the canvas strap on the front of the cannon." I handed him the knife. "Be quick, let me know when you're done, and get back to your gun."

"Sir!"

Back at the controls, I reviewed the motions required to do what I'd planned. If I were right, *Lightning* would soon be flying. In the meantime, however, I had to slow her down. I slipped us from the trot to the walk. In front of me I heard cries of surprise; I couldn't tell if they were from my men or the enemy — perhaps both.

"Done, sir!" Private George called as he headed back to his gun. If only he'd waited a moment longer, I thought as I heard a *thud!* and saw him pitched forward to the deck, unmoving.

"Ready, lads!" I cried and threw *Lightning* from a walk to a sudden stop. She lurched in protest and I feared she was going to fall to her knees — but somehow I managed to keep her up.

Clang! The noise from below came just as I felt the difference in *Lightning*. Freed from the three tons weight of the eighteen pounder, she felt like a bird ready to fly.

"All right men — CHARGE!" I shouted, pushing *Lightning* straight into a trot.

And she flew. She flew straight toward the carriage that was so desperately fleeing from us.

MacGregor fired his Puckle gun again and again, whittling away the cavalry that so valiantly charged at us. A *boom!* From nearby showed that the enemy was back at his cannon but he had just as good a chance at hitting the carriage as he did us.

"Brace yourselves!" I cried as we crossed the last few yards. "Down on the deck!"

The remaining soldiers plunged to the deck even as *Lightning* crashed through the last few horsemen who were either too brave or too slow to get away and then —

Crash! We were through the carriage. *Lightning* stumbled, went down on one leg and then, with a shudder, spilled over onto her side.

"Off!" I cried even as she slipped from my control. I jumped from the high side and rolled with my fall.

I crawled away, got to my feet and started running, crying, "Run!"

I don't know if anyone heard me. I doubt it. They were probably all too stunned from the turn of events and I'd never had a chance to warn the musketeers of the dangers of the boiler — a strange *Whoosh!* came from behind me and suddenly the air was hotter.

I threw myself to the ground in desperation, wondering if my next breath would be filled with burning air, steam at high pressure that would burn everything inside and outside of me and —

Nothing. I got up slowly, turned around and surveyed a scene from Hell.

The wagon, *Lightning,* and all around were lifeless, dead, burning feebly. As I watched, the small flames disappeared, drowned in the expanding mist that was the steam from *Lightning's* boiler — the steam that had killed all who had breathed it.

I turned around again, facing back the way we'd come and saw that we'd left a swath of destruction in our wake.

There was no sign of Captain O'Hara and *Thunder,* nor of Colonel Drummond and the rest of his troops.

I turned again as if some sixth sense had warned me and found myself looking over the distance into the mouth of the cannon on the hill. I saw it belch forth fire and saw the ball come racing toward me — and I knew I was dead.

CHAPTER SEVENTEEN

I KNEW I WAS DEAD. THE BALL SNAKED UNERRINGLY TOWARD ME AS IF, IN ONE FINAL pointless blow, the enemy hoped to wipe me from the earth.

I was too tired to run, too drained from the battle, from the wreckage, from the blood that was draining from my wound, from the sheer horror of what I'd unleashed.

I could only stand and watch as the ball grew larger and larger in my eyes and I wondered if the artillery men had actually aimed just at me or had fired by accident. I was going to die, that much was certain.

And then, as I resigned myself to my fate, sent one desperate thought toward Samuel, Jamie, and my father — a miracle occurred.

Out of the night, screaming with the strain, raced <u>Thunder</u>. She raced straight into the path of the ball.

In my amazement, I saw Jean-Michel O'Hara, saw him raise his hat to me and turn *Thunder* just in time to take the ball herself.

I had just enough time to duck before the world once again was boiled by burst steam and *Thunder* fell to the ground, a lifeless ruin bearing only lifeless bodies. As I fell, I heard a roar, a cheer in the night and wondered who it was for and why. Then I heard no more.

#

His Most Catholic Majesty, James III and VII
Written in the House of Parliament
On this the twenty-fourth day of December, 1745

Sire,

It gives me great pleasure to report that you are restored to your throne. London is ours, King George II is no more and Parliament and the City have voted to receive you with all honors.

While your loyal and bonnie troops from the north took the city from the west, a detachment of Colonel Lord Drummond's assaulted the city from the east and, in the ensuing melee, engaged King George's retinue as they sought to the flee the city. In the battle that resulted, I regret to inform you that King George was mortally wounded, along with his wife and others of his House. I must commend most highly Colonel Drummond for his gallantry and dedication. I regret to inform you that the gallant Captain O'Hara of the artillery as well as a Lieutenant Clarke of the Royal Steam Walkers, gave their lives to this victory. Their steam walkers were also, sadly, lost in the battle. I have, with your approval, appointed Hamish MacAllister as Master and Artificer of the Royal Steam Walkers, he being the only officer remaining of this gallant group of men.

On a separate matter, I have acceded to Major MacAllister's request for the hand in marriage of one Danielle Walker, daughter of one of his fellow officers. Given that the poor child has lost all her relatives in the pursuit of our victory, I believe that it is only charitable to assure her the comfort of the last remaining steam smith.

Your obedient servant and devoted son,
Charles

#

"Danni, Danni!" someone roared as they shook me. I opened my eyes. I was on the ground, my head cradled in a lap. A face peered down at me and beamed.

"Samuel?" I cried, twisting to sit up. A strong arm held me down.

"Don't move!" Samuel said urgently. "You're out of sight for the moment."

Out of sight?

"What is it Samuel?" I said, realizing that something was wrong. He was dirty, wet, and bloody. "Did we win?"

"Ach, lass, did we win?" Samuel said, his face splitting into a strained smile. And then his lips pursed into a thin line. "I've bad news."

"What?" I said, my stomach clenching in dread. I remembered Mr. Gillie talking with Colonel Drummond. I thought of all who had died here.

"Captain O'Hara?"

"Who?"

"The other walker," I mumbled.

"No one survived," he told me.

"Father?" Even as I said it, I could see the answer in his eyes.

"Didn't you get my letters?"

"No."

"Your father and now..."

My heart lurched. "Jamie?"

Samuel closed his eyes. Tears dripped from them. He could not speak but merely nodded.

We were silent. And then Samuel Cattan spoke again. "You must flee, Danni."

"What? Why?"

"You must flee, you must go now before the others notice," he said, moving back and dropping my head to the ground. He moved around me and lowered a hand to help me up. "Hamish has petitioned the Prince for your hand."

"My hand?"

"In marriage," Samuel said. "He means to force you to build more walkers for him." Samuel glanced around at the two hulks nearby. "If he sees these — "

I was up and on my feet. My head cleared as I considered Hamish MacAllister as my husband. My stomach lurched.

"You need to destroy them," I said, glancing at the walkers. "Burn them, douse them in oil and set them alight."

"Aye," Samuel agreed. "Sergeant! We're going to destroy these wrecks to ensure that no one can use them again!"

"Sir!" a voice called back.

"Where's Colonel Drummond?"

"In the City celebrating," Samuel told me. I looked askance at that and he explained, "Did you know that King George was in that carriage?"

"I guessed," I told him.

"Did you know that you killed him?"

I shook my head. "I'd hoped to capture him."

"His body was too important to leave here," Samuel said. "Colonel Drummond knew that showing his corpse would finish the enemy, so he brought it through the gates just as we were coming to you."

He paused for a moment but I could fill in the silence: Colonel Drummond had told him that everyone was dead but Samuel had come to see himself, wondering about this strange Lieutenant Clarke. And he'd found me.

"Danni, do you want to marry MacAllister?" Samuel asked me now. I shook my head. He nodded but did not seem relieved. "As far as they know, you're dead. You've got to run, to hide because if MacAllister finds out — or anyone else — your life will be forfeit."

My eyes flashed as I thought to argue but he stopped me with a raised hand and shook his head.

"I can't come with you or Hamish will wonder," Samuel told me.

"Bessie? Mary?" I asked, thinking of the only two other people left now in my world.

"Where are they?"

"Back home," I said. "Bessie's pretending to be me — "

"So she's been getting my letters," Samuel said with a groan.

"— and Mary's pretending to be her," I told him.

Samuel pursed his lips then nodded. "I'll see to them as best I can."

I moved forward then and kissed him on his cheek. He held me for a moment and then pushed me away.

"Leave your jacket and hat here," he told me.

"If I leave my hat, people will know I'm a girl," I told him.

He smiled. "Good thing, too, easier to get away."

I frowned. "Colonel Drummond knows — "

"He only knows that you're dead, he's alive — and enjoying the Prince's favor."

I glanced to the fallen men all about me. Then I looked back to Samuel. "Will you give them a proper burial?"

"With all honors," Samuel promised. He handed me a backpack, it was heavy. "Take this — it will help you on your way."

"Samuel — " I began.

He gestured me away. "You must go now, before people begin to notice."

I nodded. At the moment, Samuel could explain me away as some looter on the battlefield. Too much longer and there'd be questions.

"Shout me off, Samuel," I told him, my heart straining in my chest. "Shout me off like you'd shout a looter!"

Samuel gave me one long look and then raised his voice. "Leave these men, you! Leave them in their honor!"

As quick as my tired body could manage, I raced away, into the distance, to the open gates of London — and a world that I had changed.

~FIN~

ABOUT THE AUTHOR

TODD J. MCCAFFREY IS A U.S. ARMY VETERAN, A CROSS-CONTINENT PILOT, A COMPUTER geek, and a *New York Times* bestselling author.

He feeds his weirdness with books, large bowls of popcorn, and frequent forays to science fiction conventions. He is the middle son of the late Anne McCaffrey and is proud to list among his credits eight books written on Pern—including five collaborations.

His website is: http://www.toddmccaffrey.org

To learn more, scan the QR code.

CPSIA information can be obtained
at www.ICGtesting.com
Printed in the USA
LVHW011646120922
728178LV00002B/380